WHERE MY SUNFLOWER WISHES TO GO

Sam Red

WIND PUBLISHING
ST. JOHNSBURY

Library of Congress Cataloging-in-Publication Data
Red, Sam

ISBN 9781936711406

1. Fiction
Cover Art – Wiliam Blake
Jacket design by Sharon Kenney Biddle

First Edition 2014

Published in the United States by
Wind Publishing
394 Railroad Street, Suite 2
St. Johnsbury, Vermont 05819

Where My Sunflower Wishes to Go

Being a Romance of the Apocalypse, in which Many
Wondrous Prophesies of Old
Are Fulfilled in these Our Present Times

Epigraph and Synopsis

Ah Sun-flower! weary of time,
Who countest the steps of the Sun:
Seeking after that sweet golden clime
Where the travelers journey is done.

Where the Youth pined away with desire,
And the pale Virgin shrouded in snow:
Arise from their graves and aspire,
Where my Sun-flower wishes to go.
–Wm. Blake

[Editor's note concerning the words "the travelers (sic)
journey" in the above Epigraph. The Editor has allowed this
egregiously dis-apostrophed neologism to stand, out of
deference to the many generations of anthologists who have
chosen to shame Mr. Blake by repeating it without correction.
What Mr. Blake did to these people the present Editor does
not care to know, but it must have been terrible indeed.]

Also by Sam Red

Lesser Known Migrations

Pour Madame et Monsieur

Author's Note

The author wishes to acknowledge the invaluable assistance of the Editorial Dominatrix and her mentor, Monsieur le Chat.

Monsieur, graciously taking time out from his catblutions, instructed us thus: "Let your tale unfold briskly, in frenzied bursts. Have your cat encounter his mouse in the usual way. Your cat should see his mouse, chase it, elude the dog, pounce, and enjoy his reward. After dining he should perform his catblutions and nap, by which means you encourage your reader to nap in sympathy.

"In the next chapter your cat should arise, stretch, and straightaway conquer a new mouse. And so on, but with minor variations. In some chapters your cat should observe the abject humiliation of the dog. In others, your cat should savor the terror of the mouse. These touches of humor provide richness of detail and vary the exposition, which pleases the discriminating reader."

But at this point the Editorial Dominatrix, a person of exquisite taste, demurred on the question of explicit, full-frontal mouse-terror, which she deemed unseemly.

Whereupon Monsieur said, "If you didn't *want* my advice, you shouldn't have asked for it." And redoubled his catblutions.

But the Editorial Dominatrix was (as always) implacable, and so your author has endeavored to compromise. We believe that readers will find the story decorous and unobjectionable in all its particulars, but hope they will yet sense the ghost of a terrified squeak from time to time.

Genesis

In the six hundredth year of Noah's life, in the second month, the seventeenth day of the month, in the same day were all the fountains of the great deep broken up, and the windows of heaven were opened... – Genesis 7:11, from the true and accurate Geneva translation of 1599.

She tells me I'll need to start off right away with a little story if you're going to catch "the flavor of it." The flavor of what, I ask. She gives me most of a look her daddy left her and maybe half of the tone that came with it: the flavor of your *life* back then, about the time you started looking for me?

I tell her okay but it's not okay. My life had a flavor? I suppose my arm has a flavor but if I bit a chunk out of it I don't think I'd taste it. I think I'd probably just go into shock and even if I didn't, how I tasted would be the last thing on what would be left of my mind. I've seen a few people who were ready to eat their arms and I'm pretty sure they'd forgotten that flavor is even a word.

But she wants a story whether you do or not, and I suppose she's even right about you. She's usually right about most people and neither of us would still be around if she wasn't, so I'm not going to argue. Here comes the story of how Boronzee got his name, just as straight as I can tell it.

Every so many weeks our route would take us by the Crossroads of Grace Truckers' Wayside Refuge and we'd spend a few hours there, walk off the kinks, take at least one long hot shower, and fill up on name-brand comestibles, not to mention alms, alibis and e-karma. The night I'll be talking about, I had been on Boronzee's bus for a few months and in spite of all they'd taught me I was still mostly an empty vessel. Worse, I looked like one, barely eighteen with scarcely a single bluff left in me. I was the empty basket in the bulrushes and no baby Moses in sight. I was the uninscribed tablet no prophet ever stooped to read, I was the wall before which no king trembled because the terrible words writ upon me were writ in secret ink. I hung around the edges when I stood and when I sat I sat in the back. I kept the uncast first stone in my pocket where I could get to it fast and I waited for my daily bread with the best of them. These aren't bad ways to be once you see how it really is for the least of us. On the whole, Jesus gives pretty good advice to people like us, and as I see it we were pretty much his specialty, even if saying so in public is about the stupidest thing you can do. So I didn't look behind me at all back then and now that it would be safe to peek a little I find that it's too jumbled up to remember. Of course I was in that place for nine years and remember lots of things but the ones I remember best are the things they put into me on purpose just so I'd always remember them. I may not be a walking library but I'm a walking shelf from one. I can recite whole chapters from Augustine and Boethius and I can rattle off most of *Foxe's Acts and Monuments*. More to the point, I know who said "His work was to go and embrew his hands in the blood of men, to spill and pour out the blood of women and children, like water in every street," and I know that he said it because God *told* him, just as He told you and me, that *cursed be he that keepeth back his sword from blood* (Jeremiah 48:10 in the true Geneva version), and most of all I know that I was made to know these things so that I too would one day "go through with the work…when this is to be done upon Moab the enemy of God's church." If I'm now cursed which I'm almost sure I must be at least it isn't from failing that particular lesson. But from my own life just before the bus I mostly remember only a judge who really didn't like me. He didn't like any of us but I made his neck turn red whenever he had to check up on me, and by then he had to check up on me every couple of weeks. The last thing I remember is a cop who left a door unlocked and said, "If you don't belong here you'll know where to go. Or else you can just wait for it, and if you can't figure out what *it* is at least I tried." Then I remember Boronzee pulling the bus over, staring for a second and saying, "Well, maybe." I remember him getting up from the driver's seat and reaching down to haul me in when he saw that my legs had stopped working (I even remember that they didn't work and that it had to do with how long I'd stood still in the cold, but I couldn't tell you why I did that). I remember him waving a scanner at me, shoving me toward the back and hollering, "Get him dried off and warmed up. Check him out and be careful what he sees while you're doing it." I remember him checking his mirrors before he pulled back out on the highway, and I remember much of the rest of what happened on the bus that day like it was yesterday. But I couldn't tell you how I came to be standing by that particular stretch of highway, and anyway I would still need a reason I haven't got to try and start this story any further back than that. Let's leave it that in the beginning I was just about snow blind, I was also dizzy and half deaf, so the bus seemed even dimmer than it really was. I saw all the clutter inside the bus only as shapes and edges, and even when they started to get a little clearer they were just weirder shapes and sharper edges. I saw only the brethren right around me but I was aware of the rest. I don't remember how long it took to not feel the constant bus wallow – if sailors get sea legs then eventually I got a bus ass – but that day I kept flopping over and even before we'd been introduced my new family had to take turns holding me up.

Anyway, Boronzee hauled me inside and some of the others sat me down and hemmed me in. A seriously urban voice behind me said, "He's shutdown tight except for a three-Bible spread on idle. Nothing active at all."

The kid on my right was big all over but not like he'd been lifting. He was big like he'd been born big and wouldn't dream of having anything to prove. He had trustee written all over him, especially the way he held my wrist like he was afraid he might break it by accident, which went for both of us. "What about it, brother? Can you light yourself up or do people have to come and do it for you?"

"I have to say a thing but if I do I start sending my ID and grid, a full burst for like five minutes it feels like. If it's okay with you if I do that then you're nobody I want to know."

"Where is it?"

I stuck my left forearm under his nose. He saw the bump. "Graceful," he said, meaning it was anything but.

"Orphanage? Work farm?"

"Little of both I guess."

"Well, it's coming out or you're getting off and no offense but you're too cold to get off. Alright with you?"

"Hell yes. If you really know how to do it."

"I really know how to do it. Does it sniff drugs?"

"Hell yes. That's mostly what it's for."

"That's tough. We got stuff'll help you later but first we got to get it out. Want something to chew on?"

"I'm not a hero."

He gave me a paperback of *The Robe* but while I was still trying to chomp down on it he had my arm slit open and the capsule out and I was looking at it even before I started to feel the burn. "Where's your Bibles?" he asked.

"Under my right ear but hey, they don't bother me any."

He had a patch over the gash by then. Warm champagne washed over me and an angel was licking my ear. "Wow," I said.

"You get another one if you give up the Bibles."

"No man, I told you, I like them there. It took me forever to get the voices right. What *is* this shit?"

"Combat field dressing, barely expired. You call me Thumper, you call the fellow behind you Bluesbaby, and you can work on something for us to call you."

"Wow, Thumper, I swear I had a problem or two just a second ago. Call me anything you like."

The bus still pitched and swayed, but now I could see that it wasn't just me. Boronzee always took his driving seriously and this was my first taste of it. You've maybe seen *Ben Hur* in 4D, the chariots? Boronzee's bus on any city street. You've seen catamarans racing flat out in the roaring forties? Boronzee on the Interstate when he was bearing down on the automatic lanes.

"All right. You're Floppy till you change your mind."

"Floppy, sure, fine. When do I meet the girls?"

"Soon. Three or four years, tops."

"Huh?"

This Bluesbaby stuck his nose in. "What he means, man, you want a mutiny, let a girl on the bus. We'd tear ourselves apart to get to her."

Bluesbaby passed Thumper a rag and a chip reader with a couple inches of shielding around it. Other people debated questions for Thumper to ask his new friend Floppy. I thought, well, if girls are out, how about you ask me what I'd like for dinner? Thumper wiped off the bloody capsule, stuck it in the reader and set it to auto. In a couple seconds it beeped and started showing him data. His eyes opened wide. "Absolutely stone age. Jesus, it's putting out seven volts. What the hell is that for?"

"It's to fucking make me scream so I'll stick out like I'm supposed to when I'm supposed to stick the fuck out."

"And you sometimes make it do that by saying something? Why would you?"

"Sometimes I like to eat and some days a little electrical humility is the price of eating."

"What are the words?"

"They won't make a lot of sense to you. They sound like *add margarine day-ie glory um.*"

A couple of sharp laughs behind me and Thumper said, "Don't *tell* me you're a crow."

"No but they have crows on the brain. Others too but the crows really scare them, 'cause, see, crows can hide anywhere and pretend to be anybody. Not having to ever tell the truth or face the east or anything."

"Right, so they poisoned a password nobody's used in four hundred years. Really smart people where you come from which was where again?"

Understand, the whole time this was going on the world was breaking into my skull in irregular flashes of light, rushes of sound and waves of smell, if smell can somehow be combined with vertigo. Right about here I lost so much interest in the possibility of conversation that I can no longer piece together any of our words. I know that in my answers I had to say something about New Dispensation Custodial Ministries and I know I must have mentioned how my mother plea-bargained me over to them when I was nine. I surely told them how I was almost at the end of one eighteen-month Long Term Time Out and heading for a much worse one when that cop let me walk away. I know for a fact that somewhere in there I told them about my Biblical Educational

Development certificate because they all knew about it later – otherwise, I'd never have become Floppy the BED Man, would not later have split Loverbits' lip for him when he called me that once too often (or maybe just once, period) or would never have had to perform weeks of groveling penance for that incivility just to keep my place at the back of the bus. But that's all I know, and I'm not being coy when I stop telling you how it all went down after they pried the capsule out of my arm. I don't even know how it ended, except that at one point I got a bowl of cold hotdogs and beans, swallowed it all in three or four gulps, went to sleep and woke up to the pitching of the bus a long time after dark as an achy, bleary-eyed, bladder-gorged and sullenly bewildered probationary novice in crime. It was months later that Boronzee casually dropped that I must have been medicated for years. I'd never had the slightest idea. Just as if everybody is more or less conscious for maybe an hour a day, spends a couple more in their Remedial Modern Theology and Combat Theory classes and passes the rest of their time marching and hoeing the garden without a thought in their head. Boronzee had been planning to let me out and leave me somewhere warm if I didn't begin to snap out of it in six or eight weeks, which turned out to have been a very close thing.

So, the night a few months later when we met the poetry lover and I finally figured out where Boronzee got his name. We came off the Interstate at the Crossroads of Grace around six in the evening because we had been impersonating a grade school choir from Austin in the automatic lanes for the full twelve hour max. We'd have set off alarms in three states if we drove another mile before morning and one look at us would tell the dumbest cop on earth that we weren't who our electronics had been saying we were for several hundred miles. One thing we did at places like the Crossroads of Grace was prowl the bus lots with recorders in our pockets, borrowing telemetric identities that we'd use all over the country. Over time Bluesbaby cloned Evatars for high school bands, softball teams, seminary picnics, Charismatic garden clubs, vigiling nuns on pilgrimage, and sooner or later we used every one of them. All it would have taken to put us in a camp would have been one cop who looked in the damn window at the thirteen men and boys inside while his car told him we were a troop of girl scouts on our way to a Jamboree. It never happened. I never saw it happen, I never heard of it happening. I've seen trucks pulled over by the hundreds, I've seen countless cars swarming with cops and troops and militias of every sect, in my life I've seen more spread-eagled pedestrians than upright redheads, I've seen a houseboat boarded on the Mississippi and even a helicopter forced down outside of Akron, but I've never seen a cop look twice at a bus once it has made it to the automatic lanes. Buses are invulnerable when they're locked in and cruising, and Boronzee was the genius who noticed it first.

We parked and stood outside the door to the dining hall and did some *a cappella* psalms to pick up a little change and a lot more respectability. It was a pleasant evening and this routine works when it's sunny and mild, but it works even better in the rain and snow – people *give* when they catch you suffering for the Lord. Sometimes all they give is a sympathetic smile but the smiles of Christian strangers are a suit of armor in a strange place. No cop ever barges in to check out the troublemaker everybody's welcoming, and once you learn that you're on your way to being halfway free. But even though we did our caroling in the balmy evening breezes, people stepped aside so we could jump the line when we finally trooped in to spend our alms on pizza and Manna-dogs. We carried them outside and sat in a circle on the grass, Boronzee in his place in the center. Maybe we were praying, maybe we were studying our scripture, maybe Boronzee was preaching, but when you sit like that, in a tight enough circle, well-wishers and lonely servants of God just glance at you wistfully and don't try to join in.

But this time somebody did. He was a tall man in a dingy camelhair overcoat that had once been better than anything I'll ever wear. It ought to have had him sweating buckets and he had shaggy gray hair he'd tried to comb which was a mistake because it made him look even shaggier. Likewise, he wore clean and halfway polished dress shoes that would fall apart once he'd walked another five miles. He was trouble. He was a man on the run who wore a warm winter coat in pleasant weather because that was the only way he could take it with him, and he buttoned it all the way up so that, in his imagination, nobody would know what he wore underneath. We knew exactly what was under it, at least we could guess exactly how it smelled, and the fact that he didn't seem to realize he was a bum told us how far from reality he'd wandered. This happens to the unchurched gentry when they finally get flushed out and just start walking, but that doesn't mean they're not on a leash, fully wired and sent out on their last long walk to troll for the likes of us. By now Boronzee had schooled us thoroughly about that part of the staying alive trade, so we all took one simultaneous look and stopped as still as if he'd been Pilate himself.

Boronzee said, "Help you, Brother?" With a steady look that said help might possibly amount to a slice of pizza and a swig of soda from an almost empty bottle.

The old man cleared his throat a couple of times but he was hoarse anyway. He'd used his voice up with his shoe leather. When he could he said, "I'm looking for a ride. I can pay."

"You have to know that's not allowed."

"Not even if I'm going where you are?"

"Where would that be, friend?"

Brother now a thing of the past. Brothers have rides or wait to be asked if they want them.

"I have to get to Canada. I have real money. Real money in an account nobody knows about."

Of course he had to get to Canada. Canada wouldn't let him *in* but Canada wouldn't kick him *out* either if he ever found a way to get there – how could they, knowing what would happen next? Not unless he'd done some secular crime like they still care about up there. But that's a long way from being *welcome*, and this man was way past the age for a timber-cutting or hop-picking gang. He was headed for some kind of camp whether he knew it or not, and the way he said *Canada* like a believer says *Home to Glory* told us just how much he still had to learn.

Boronzee gave him a look that if we were being videoed no magistrate could object to.

"You have some very wrong ideas about who we are. Where did they come from?"

The man made a vague helpless wave toward the truck lot. "They told me…they sent me over. They suggested I ask you."

"Who are *they*?"

"In the maroon, the maroon cattle truck. The man and the woman. They said to try you, you help people."

Boronzee pointed at Thumper, me and Loverbits, and right then Thumper was off and marching with me right behind him and Loverbits running to catch up. We headed straight for the truck lot and nobody got in our way. The lot was packed with idling diesels and the breeze wasn't balmy there, it stank like it always does, no matter what the weather. Truckers were heading to the showers, to the food court, wandering back, standing in little groups and talking about trucker things but stopping to look us over when we came in view. Half of them at least would be bedding down in their sleepers and some of those who weren't already sacked out sat on the steps to their cabs and watched us come marching through. Thumper picked one out and asked, "Maroon cattle truck?" but the driver was already pointing to it, its ass end sticking out a couple of rows away. That night we and the overcoat man were already the whole show for lots of nosy people.

Thumper said, "They popular folks in your crowd?"

The driver who'd pointed spat. The driver next to him considered the matter and then spat too and said, "We mind our own business when people let us."

The maroon cab was a dusty relic. The man stood on the step with the door open and leered. The woman sat inside with a hamburger in her left hand and the right one under a jacket in her lap. Anybody who could eat sitting in that cloud of motor and cow fumes had to be too far gone to talk to, but that wouldn't mean she couldn't shoot.

Thumper said, "You get a kick out of siccing basket cases on people you don't know?"

"Who says we don't know you? Who says we didn't see you here in April with two shit-scared rich women in high heels? Who says we didn't see you again in Tulsa with a broke down old guy in a wheel chair and no ramp on the damn bus which was a church bus then but now I see it ain't no more.

Who says we don't know *exactly* what you are?"

They were staring straight at Thumper because Thumper is the guy you need to stare at and they didn't even see Loverbits follow me around to the other side. On the way back to the bus we passed the two truckers who'd directed us. Thumper said, "Pleasant evening, gents" without slowing down. The talkative one said, "Could be worse" to our backs. When we got back Boronzee was still talking to the old man, though they seemed to have gotten just a little friendlier.

Thumper said, "Time to move out" and everyone got up.

Boronzee said, "They going to wake up?"

Thumper said, "Probably."

Boronzee said, "Anybody else interested?"

Thumper said, "Probably not yet, but soon."

The old man didn't know what he was watching except that it had to be bad for him, but he lit up like Christmas morning when Thumper grabbed him by the arm and started dragging him toward the bus. I took the window seat in front, across from Boronzee. Thumper shoved the old man in next to me and took the aisle.

The old man said, "I–"

Thumper said, "Please shut up."

The old man said, "But I–"

Thumper said, "Please shut up or I'll shove your teeth down your throat."

From the seat behind and across from us Loverbits said, "Let me do it. I already had to break a woman's stinky teeth account of him." Bluesbaby sat next to him, wrapping a kerchief around his bleeding hand.

Boronzee took that in, looked at me, said "Talk," then turned back to his driving.

I said, "See, she had a gun and Thumper was wailing on her old man."

Boronzee looked back at me and said, "Where were you?"

Loverbits said, "He may have got the door open but I got in ahead of him for once. You know he always has to go first."

Boronzee had it floored and was staring in his outside mirror. When he was halfway happy with what he didn't see there he reached down and fired up an Evatar clone of a

Baptist youth group from Rhode Island. He'd had it out and ready because it was supposed to get us through Pennsylvania after the now-defunct choir from Austin took us to the border in the morning. The Interstate started pinging us back right away and the whole bus held its breath while the yellow light blinked. This is always the nervous part but tonight… The old man stared at that light as hard as the rest of us even though he couldn't possibly have known what it meant. Finally that prissy voice that I always think of as blonde said, "Merge to automatic lanes approved. Eleven hundred and twenty miles to next brake and steering test. You have fuel for three hundred and fifteen miles." The light turned orange and steady. Boronzee bore left into the merge lane and the highway grabbed us. The light turned green and the telemetry overrode the governor and took us up to 78.

When the steering lock clicked Boronzee slid his seat back and got up. He stood in the stairwell by the door and leaned over the old man and started talking in his weariest voice.

"We've got fuel for another seven hundred miles but that's one of our little secrets. This bus is twenty years old and it's picked up lots and lots of secrets. I'm not risking anything by telling you because you already know enough to put us in the worst kind of camp for the rest of our very short lives. Be quiet. We'd kill you right now but you've blown us already, back there. Be *quiet*. If you *won't* be quiet we'll *make* you be quiet and we'll make you *stay* quiet, and if the guys want to take turns making you quiet which they probably do I won't object at all. Just sit there. Just sit there while we figure it out."

I said, "He's scanned?"

Boronzee said, "While you were reconnoitering. He's what he says he is."

Thumper said, "Which is?"

Boronzee said, "Professor of twentieth century English religious poetry at Southern Ohio Polytech. Recently de-tenured, defrocked and dismissed after twenty-six years as the rose among many busy little abacuses."

The old man started and said, "That's Jacob Bronowski!" before he remembered he was supposed to be dead if he spoke.

Boronzee said, "Of course it is. What's the matter, is

Bronowski all yours? Nobody else could ever have read him and believed? Bus dwellers not allowed to know from Bronowski? Do *not* answer, Professor. Do not say anything more at all." I had never seen him that furious.

After the Professor left us we found another empty stretch of the same dirt road a little further on and we all got out and painted the bus green. We worked fast because we had no conceivable reason for being there – never mind being there painting a bus – and the hurry-up was a grim, nerve-chewing reminder of the precarious nature of modern life. It was the last paint job we had with us, so paint went onto the shopping list, and with this last coat it was getting kind of thick, so next time we were going to have to strip and prime it first. We'd been robin's egg blue for three or four months and for some reason turning green depressed us even more. We had one cloned Evatar left that we'd never used before and once it got us to Albany we'd have to park for a day or go out cloning again, neither of which you really want to do in a strange neighborhood – and that was *if* we made it to Albany, *if* a crew of trucker-muggers on a bus weren't finally a good enough reason to check out every bus that could be fleeing. All in all we were one sober crew by the time we got back on the Interstate and not all of us went straight to sleep like we pretended. I thought I had but I was only part way there. Words bounced back and forth in my head like tennis balls, and some of them changed between bounces. I was getting ready to wake up all the way and let the Geneva Bible's Ecclesiastes do its lullaby when I realized that "Boronzee" was turning into that name the Professor had used and then back again, Boronzee-Bronowski-Bronowski-Boronzee. I sat up straight. *Nobody else could have read him and believed? Bus dwellers not allowed to know from Bronowski?* No wonder he was so pissed. Boronzee was Bronowski just like Loverbits was Lefkevitch, except that Loverbits had once *been* Lefkevitch and Bronowski, whoever he was, was someone Boronzee had wished he could be. But it probably wouldn't have gone any better for the Professor if Boronzee had loved him just as much as Jesus did. He would still have never made it to Canada, and even after we left him we didn't even think about touching that account he sincerely believed nobody knew a thing about.

Exodus

Therefore go now, and I will be with thy mouth, and will teach thee what thou shalt say. –Exodus 4:12, from the Geneva translation.

Three years passed and then it was time for me to get off the bus and carry the word on my own back for a while. They threw me a going away dinner at an overnight rest stop, genuine ribs on the grill and a six-pack apiece for everyone, and in the morning I set out. Loverbits cried and didn't care who saw him. Ever since I zipped his lip up for him I'd been his sun and moon, and I don't think he ever realized that that was one reason Boronzee decided it was my time to go. But there were other reasons too and turning twenty-one was the biggest of them. Once you're twenty-one you'd better be somebody who's left traces and keeps on leaving them because if you don't then you're somebody else who's left traces you're running away from. You can keep your traces working while you ride on a bus but you don't pick up the kind of deep, old traces you need to start with that way. You pick them up by giving somebody a reason to give you some of theirs.

I walked into the Chariots of Fire station in Youngstown as John Michael Maguire. That's a Catholic name of course and Catholics do raise eyebrows, but we figured I'd be raising enough of them anyway. I'm way too dark to be pure Caucasian like my mother but I'm not dark enough to be anything else for sure, and no, I don't know what the other part of me really is. But what I *look* like is everybody's idea of a raghead, and if you *could* be Mohammed Somebody, then one way to get by is to *be* Mohammed Somebody, with plenty of fast-acting, righteous data in plenty of different databases to back up your claim that you're one of the good ones – but then you can still get stoned in the kind of places that the likes of me have to pass through. Another way is to prove, absolutely prove, that in your case appearances are deceiving and you've always been something else entirely. I was on my way to get that kind of proof, not to show it, so I was John Michael Maguire, dumped on New Dispensation Custodial Ministries at the age of nine when his mother was sent back to Tunisia and his Irish father gave up on coping with him. All I had to back that up were the mostly real State of Colorado ID of the John Michael Maguire who'd died of his wounds (we were promised) and been buried anonymously but with full benefit of clergy outside of a Second Amendment Camp in Minnesota, some paper any good hacker could have faked (and did), a nine-month-old Social Presence I'd been working a couple of hours a day, and the slightly altered capsule that was back in my arm. Of course it wouldn't stand up if anybody actually asked NDCM about me, but Boronzee figured that just the capsule itself and the sight of me whimpering and twitching like an epileptic when it went off would convince the average cop or vigilant busybody of my servant-class bona fides.

I got to the station an hour before my bus to Milwaukee, which was a good thing because the place was packed and I had to wait in line ten minutes just to trade my eticket in for a boarding tat on my palm. I had a cheap passive scan recorder in my sock – ten people check out your shoes before one of them looks in your socks. After half an hour I went to the john and checked it. It showed that I'd been scanned fourteen times in the waiting room, which had me almost ready to freak. But then I planted it in a dirty paper cup behind a seat near the door, wandered off to watch Bus and Train Network News for ten minutes, strolled back, picked it up, carried it back to the john, and found that it had been scanned five more times. Bus stations are definitely no place to be hiding out, though it seems that a lot of people don't know this or are too desperate to care, but at least nobody was looking at me in particular. I flushed the recorder and headed for the scope line. Once I'd flashed my ID, had my boarding tat read and been scoped I thought I could go straight through to the bus, but a fat TSA woman liked my looks, pointed her wand at me and said, "Just a minute, please, sir." Then I was on the floor and three very worried TSA drudges were bending over me, babbling nonsense and watching my arm fibrillate. The fat one was demanding *why, why did it do that, it shows clean, it shouldn't do that, I've never seen that,* and it seemed like it was up to me to shut her up. I told her that New Dispensation believed in discipline. I told her I was on my way to a job interview and that if I got in they'd promised to take it out and give me a real employment chip instead but until then there's a law, right? I offered to show her my appointment. She wouldn't let me and took all my papers out of my pocket. When she found it she told her buddies, "Yes, here it is, job interview tomorrow, yes, it seems okay" while they rolled their eyes at her and helped me up and got my papers back from her. One of them said, "This always happen?" and I told him it usually wasn't that bad but I hadn't given anyone a reason to probe me for three years so maybe that had something to do with it. Then they worried that I wasn't good to ride for ten or eleven hours and I had to lie for five minutes about how chipper I felt before they'd let me go. But everybody else who was waiting had seen it all and when I finally got on the bus I had the only empty seat next to me. They let me keep it for the whole trip and nobody tried to talk to me even once, which gave me all the time I needed to decide that this was exactly how Boronzee had expected my trip to go.

In Milwaukee I had a late check-in reserved at a motel three blocks from the bus station. The clerk was glad to see me because I was the last one in and he could close the desk up. He told me three times that I had the last room even before he gave me the key just so I wouldn't dream of demanding a better one, but I'd be very surprised if they had a better one. It was just the usual sanitized cube with a bed the size of house trailer and Reverend Williston lecturing from an old flat monitor because there was no room for his whole self. There were instructions for changing it to the Christian Athletic Network but of course there were none for turning it off, so I draped a towel over the good reverend's face and fired up the King James Book of Job to drown out his voice. The bed was my only problem: I hadn't slept in a bed in three years, and this one seemed to know it. Eventually I got to sleep and when I woke up Job had timed out, it was a sunny day outside and Reverend Williston, that tireless hologram who today was favoring the King James Version, was belatedly celebrating the new day by recalling his Mark: *And in the morning, rising up a great while before day, he went out, and departed into a solitary place, and there prayed.* And so he did, but then he went forth and cleansed that faithless leper who went and tattled on him, and who knows whether they'd ever have nailed him up if that leper hadn't started the commotion? But Reverend Williston wasn't interested in pursuing that notion which was one of Pastor Mike's favorites, so I took a shower, sat down to wait for my ride, and played over Pastor Mike's *The Leper Who Murdered Jesus* sermon from memory. I could do that because I'd heard it at least twenty times and I'd heard it at least twenty times because Pastor Mike thought orphans, especially orphans, needed to hear why in a Christian world it's usually the right people who get shunned.

Sarah Schilling picked me up out front no more than one minute late and drove me to an early lunch at a Paco's Tacoroni, which briefly made me wonder if she knew a bit too much about me since every food court in the Interstate system has one of those. But it turned out that she'd picked it because she never went there and didn't want us running into anyone who knew her, and I had to take her through the menu like I was really the host. I had a meatball tostada because you can eat it if you really lay on the red pepper and I tried to steer her away from the green chili ravioli but she just had to try it. When she took the first bite she froze for half a second or so: her face, her hands, her eyes, everything froze. Then they all started moving again in the directions they'd been headed, and she offered no further clues about how awful it had been. I'd *had* the green chili ravioli at a Paco's Tacoroni and I *knew* what she was going through, and the way she took the blow and carried on as if it was no blow at all told me something. She had frozen up for a tick in exactly the same way when I slid into her front seat and she got her first good look at my face, so now I knew exactly where vaguely brownish young people stood with her. But I'll give her this: she never showed it in any other way. She was a good enough liar to be lying in the league she'd promoted herself to, and not everyone who really should be able to can say that. She kept the chatter neutral and light and it was only after lunch, when we were approaching the Galilee Robe and Gown plant, that she got down to business and then only the next few minutes' worth – how I was to walk in alone and ask for her and she'd be ten feet behind me and would overhear and take over. Just then she came off as someone who took no more chances than she had to and that was more than fine with me.

We stayed in her office for an hour because that's how long it usually takes to decide to take a chance on a rookie traveling sales rep. I spent half that time asking questions about the record she'd faked for me. I was interested in that of course but not half as much as I pretended. Boronzee had told me that Sarah was a very greedy but only halfway imaginative crook who would either retire rich or die with half a face from testing cosmetics in a camp. Before I met her I figured her odds at 50/50 and nothing she showed me changed my mind about them either way. If it was the camp for her then of course they'd come straight for me, so no matter what Boronzee and I told her I didn't plan on remaining John Michael Maguire one day longer than I had to. But I couldn't let her suspect that or I'd never get onto the payroll at all. She had to know the risks she was taking at least as well as I did – they had to seem worse to her in fact, since she had only our word for it that I knew how to stay alive on my own. If I kept out of trouble and she could bank my salary for ten or fifteen years it would all be worth it to her. If I walked away in six months as I planned to she'd barely recoup her investment and if I got caught she was finished. So she watched me carefully as I laid the timidity on thick – *who* would hear *what* about me, what did they already think they *knew* about me, was she *sure* I'd never have to come back to Milwaukee, who would review my expenses, what would happen if say in five years… After a while I worried that I might be coming off as *too* cautious if such a thing is possible in the fraud and embezzlement trade, but apparently that idea belonged to the half of her imagination that was missing.

She showed me my record from my two summer jobs there, one on the dock and one in the stockroom. She brought out everything I had to sign and watched me practice my signature. She took my picture herself and sent it winging off to HR. She explained my quota and salary and commission schedule to me. She taught me the rules for expenses and the things that aren't in the rules that auditors look for.

She had me sign for the bank account I shared with a certain Gloria Hightower who she didn't even try to pretend wasn't her, and she showed me the card that if she'd let me keep it would have let me actually take money out of it. Then she put it away in her purse. She told me when my pay would be going into it and how often I should check to make sure it really did and how far I should run if it ever stopped.

She gave me six Social Presence personas I should start bonding with ASAP, three registered Social Aliases of John Michael Maguire I should turn into when I bonded, and a two page list of the code phrases we'd be exchanging and what they meant. She *did* feel she had to tell me to burn it once it was memorized but at least she said "of course" – "of course you'll want to burn this" – and I suppose I should cut her some slack about it: people do die for the silliest reasons after all.

And in that vein, and even though she couldn't have made it clearer that she and I would never be sending money to each other, I got a fussy lecture on how you can and can't do it without people taking an interest – *this* is too much to *keep, this* is too much to get or send, *this* is too many payments in or out, *this* is not enough. "They're *algorithms* John, they have to think they feel you *living.* They have to sense that if anybody looked closer they'd just find another lonesome robe peddler on his rounds." She never asked me what I knew, she seemed to assume I knew nothing. *This* was too regular a pattern but *this* was too *contra-profile* or some other police-like word for *unusual* that someone had once impressed her with. The ways I might mess up my money must have scared her half to death. Maybe when the night sweats came she could remember how she'd beat this part of it to death and think *At least I told him how to handle his money.* She didn't cover everything Boronzee had taught me years before but she came closer than most people could have.

She gave me a temporary badge and took me out to the shop floor and showed me the Lutheran women on the pattern line, the Catholic women on the stitching line, the Muslims and Jews not looking at each other from across the embroidery and tassel lines. She showed me the bolts of cloth in the stockroom where I'd once spent eleven weeks and she showed me the loading dock where before that I'd spent twelve. She walked me through order entry which seemed to go on for acres, and I noticed that the more important women seemed mostly to be dressed like her, in their tightly jacketed suits with the Pentecostal skirts hugging their asses and then flaring out to swing barely off the floor. On the way out we stopped in HR and she signed for my IDs.

Back in her office she dumped the IDs on her desk. *This* one was the company-issued driver's license, good for driving rentals and company cars in all 84 states. Sign it here please. *This* one was the airline pass that swore that John Michael Maguire had business in the sky. Sign it here please. And *this* one was the credit card that would never stop working as long as I remembered what expenses were and were not and if I ever rented two cars or two rooms at the same time which someone had done *twice* so far she'd find me and strangle me herself. Sign here. Please. Then came three more that "might not seem important John but they all add up" – the junior executive gym, the men's Bible study club, and the cafeteria pass, also good for genuine gumbo in the Baton Rouge plant where she'd better never hear I showed up. *Next*, and we're almost there John, *this* is your badge which you wear today and then on every call you make. There was my picture and name and "Galilee Robe and Gown" in fancy lettering and the Galilee Robe and Gown logo with the halo and wings in gold and the golden Cross of Jesus running up and down the whole right side. I took off the visitor's badge and put the new one on and when I looked up she smiled for the first time and said, "And finally here's the one you came for." And turned over a Corresponding Member's Identification Card from the New Canaan Baptist Church of Wauwatosa, Wisconsin, certifying that John Michael Maguire was a member in full standing and of impeccable reputation too and desiring that true Christians everywhere should offer him their comfort and protection in the course of his travels far from home. "The chip is real. Get it scanned in any church and your attendance shows up in New Canaan's database." She paused a second to let that sink in. "So does your absence if you backslide, which you won't, will you?" But I had ridden almost a million miles for this card since I left the orphanage and I knew I would never backslide again.

We took an elevator up to Medical Identity and Sarah turned me over to a Nurse Altermann, an older, much embittered woman who read my name and my golden Cross of Jesus from my badge, decided how much she didn't like the two together, and made sure I saw the blue cross of the pope on hers. She pointed to an empty cube, said "Suliman's up next, she'll take you over there when she's ready," and turned her back. In a couple of minutes a Nurse Suliman did indeed join me, pushing a cart full of bottles and instruments. She compared the printed label on a chip case to my badge and she didn't seem to like my Cross of Jesus any better than Nurse Altermann had, but I think that in her case it was because our skins matched perfectly and her badge bore the crescent she probably thought I was born to. That I'd clearly noticed she was pretty as a flower didn't help much. But when she pried the capsule out of my arm she was shocked and when she popped it into a reader she was more shocked and blurted out, "What kind of people..." Then she stopped herself, as a lifelong probationer will.

"It's the kind of orphanage that takes you because they get paid to take you, not because they want to. That thing's been in there for twelve years."

She looked at me a little peculiarly. "This monstrosity may certainly be twelve years old. But if anyone with my qualifications asks you how long you've had this one" – she nodded at the new chip she would imbed next – "I suggest that you tell them the truth. When we cut them out of you we can tell, Brother."

By the time Sarah came back for me my legs were steady enough to walk on again, but it was a near thing. What if I'd told that silly pointless lie to Nurse Altermann?

Sarah cut me loose in time to catch the evening flight to Birmingham. It was my first time in a taxi and it was my first time on an airplane. When you're finally churched at last you have lots of first times coming at you, one right after another and almost too fast to savor. Almost, but not quite.

On the plane I looked down on the lights and the black

spaces and thought about all the times I'd watched people like me soaring freely overhead. I listened to my sales training. I read my catalog of robes and gowns, trying to get used to the idea that it was an actual book, with pages. Sarah had said, "Of course it's a book. Remember who these people are. They only believe it if it comes out of a book." Then she laughed at her own blasphemous wit. If I'd ever had faith that she'd stay alive to spend my salary I'd have started to lose it right there. That was a laugh that could easily laugh itself once too often.

Proverbs

Sinner, you think the world has failed you but it is you who have failed the world, and now you want a different one. What are you to do? What *can* you do? The world is coming for you. The world is mounted up and ready to move out. Think. For God's sake, sinner, *think*.

You can't walk into Canada. Get that thought straight out of your head: you think it should be possible but it isn't. There are fences, walls, moats, minefields in some places, quicksand traps in others, there are sensors, cameras, sniffers, infrared-flooded zones of omniscience, dogs like you never imagined could exist, half-robot, half-psycho dogs that eat bears for fun, there are official guards and blood-happy militias and everything in between and they all keep score by piling their kill in heaps for the cameras, and where there are none of these things there are drones: drones that take your picture and check your blood sugar while they're at it, drones that leave you peacefully stretched out and fit for an open casket and drones that incinerate you entirely and then scatter the ashes out of respect for the habitat. The drones get everybody something else doesn't get first but say they don't get you: what then? Good question. *Then* is the Canadians, and they don't want you. *Their* drones only take your picture and call the Mounties. Canadians won't kill you right off, not unless they're locals who have had more than enough of people sneaking in to steal from their gardens and hide on their land, but even the rest of them *will* put you in the nicest camps they can afford to build in the parts of Canada where no Canadian wants to be. And they will put you there forever, which under the circumstances is kind of a flexible term. And if by some miracle you do make it to Toronto or Montreal which you won't you'll be picked up on the first or third day, sooner rather than later you'll get hungry or cold, and then you'll stand out and get a hot lunch and a five minute hearing and *then* you'll go into your camp. You don't believe that, I know. You've heard stories and watched 2D videos about people who walked to Canada and are happy Canadians today with happy Canadian friends to get them over the rough spots. And those things were true once but they've been over for twenty years now. The Canadians had their fill of us quite some time ago, and the things that makes them do to us just make them angrier and more determined to do them.

If you're somebody special you can fly to Canada but if you're somebody special there'd be nobody stopping you from leaving the country in the first place. Hell, if you could fly to Canada you probably wouldn't have a reason to go. Given the life you'd be living right here, I mean.

Likewise, if you're somebody special you could drive in, but if you're somebody special you could fly in, so you would. Special people *do* drive into Canada sometimes but only because they're in the neighborhood already, as special people so often are.

Freight trains are a different kind of pipe dream. Say you're equipped to make it through the tear gas bath – and hell, it doesn't leak into the cattle cars, so why can't you hide in there? Could there possibly be cameras *inside?* You bet there could be. I'm not saying that it's never been done. I am saying that nobody's written home to tell how, and that should tell you something.

Which leaves us with boats. Boats can make it. Boats *do* make it. Boats make it on the oceans but to get on a big oceangoing boat you have to show you belong on one, and getting on a small oceangoing boat is like getting across a lake, so I'll just tell you about lakes. There are people who can cross the lakes to Canada. True, lakes have patrols and sensors and most of all lakes have satellites and drones, but lakes also have *weather*. If the weather is exactly bad enough a good sailor can make it, and sooner or later the weather is exactly bad enough. The people who take people across the lakes don't always make it, but they always make it till they die, which in most ways is almost like always making it.

We know some of these people. We know where to find them and how to talk to them (and you may think you know these things too but you don't). We do business with some of them sometimes, and I'm going to tell you a couple of things about them we don't ever tell our clients.

First, not everybody who gets on a boat gets off it on the other side. Sometimes they get off it in the middle of the lake.

Second, most people who do get off a boat in Canada go straight into one of their lifetime arctic resorts. You've probably guessed that but if you did you've been thinking *bad luck* and *lack of preparation.* Those things do happen of course but sometimes they happen on purpose. Suppose you're let off the boat on some obscure Canadian shore under cover of weather that's bad enough to hide you. The weather won't stay bad enough to keep hiding you and you won't make it far on your own while it lasts. You know this, of course. You've taken this into account, which is why you picked the crew of sailors who told you about their friends on the Canadian side, friends who'll share in the fare you'll be paying, friends who can make people disappear into Canada once they arrive. Those friends are absolutely real and the things you'll be told about them are absolutely true but there is more than one way to disappear. Some people disappear into holes in the ground. Some people inexplicably run into a moonlighting Mountie just when they were expecting kindly old Pastor Bonhoeffer to pull up in the church van. And some people really, really do get to where they were told they would go. I can't tell you how to make sure you're one of those, except that a lot of offshore money and a solid protocol for delivering it is probably an odds changer. Is that you? No? Well, best of luck then. You may make it in the end but it won't have anything to do with you. It will be because you've met a whole lot of honest people and not a single one who wasn't, and honest people are found only where you find them.

One last word about this. Maybe you've received letters or postcards, real ones, on paper, with genuine Canadian stamps and old timey postmarks on them, dolled up to look innocent and sent to that innocent address nobody could be watching. And you've applied the right chemicals and revealed the secret message written in your old friend's own unmistakable hand. *We've made it, we're safe, we're free! Captain Jack was everything we hoped for and his friends were brave and wonderful.* That's why you go looking for Captain Jack, isn't it? I really don't want to rain on your parade, but I'll make you a bet. I'll bet you only got one of those letters, right? I'll bet that secret message even *told* you it would be the only one you'd get. *We can't wait for you to join us but I can't write you again. I'd be putting too many brave new friends at risk if I did.* Something like that, was it? Sorry to be the one to break the news like this, but it's better you hear it from somebody, and I believe I told you that I'll be telling this as straight as I know how: *Such are the ways of everyone that is greedy of gain: he would take away the life of the owners thereof* (Proverbs 1:19, the Geneva translation).

You can't walk into Canada but maybe some people can. There are certainly people who say they can, and we've never been without our savvy local smugglers, have we? I could name more than a few who start off for Canada with emigrants in tow and come back later without them. Do I think they can actually deliver them? Yes I do. They bring back birth control pills and science books and holovids from England so they're meeting *somebody* up there, and if they can do that then they can take people the other way. Do I think that really happens? No. Not in a million years. Not ever. Why not? Because they're killers to the man. I know they're killers because I know they have to be, which is the best reason anybody can have for saying he knows something. Every day they're risking their lives at the hands of dangerous people who are determined to kill them, and every day they've survived. There is only one way to do that for any length of time and that way is to kill those dangerous people when they try to kill you.

If that were you I'm talking about then you'd be the stoniest stone killer in six counties. So now people who no one in authority cares a thing about give you all their money so you'll take a big, honking chance for them that nobody could ever know if you really took. Do you take them for a very long, hard and tricky walk in the woods, wait for them when they can't keep up, hope they stay calm and quiet enough when the patrol passes by, hope they make every move it took you years to learn? Not exactly. You walk a little way into those woods and then you find a nice soft spot to dig, that's what you do. But it took me a while to figure this out, and before I did I met some of these people and sent some customers their way and took a nice commission for doing it. I'm not the only one, either. It's no excuse, but I'm not the only one.

Maybe you think you could go to Mexico. I know very little about Mexico. I know it's a dirt-poor country that has no good reason to love us. I know we've made Mexico miserable every way we know how. I know we used to let them sneak in and do lousy jobs for lousy pay and then kicked them out when we were done with them. I know we didn't mind much when they died of thirst in the desert trying to get to those jobs and I know we put up fences and then bigger fences to keep them out once we didn't need them anymore. I know they lost millions of people in the drug wars, and I know that the drug wars happened because first we got a taste for feeling good, and then we outlawed feeling good in the only way that Mexico knew how to make us feel good, and then a lot of people in Mexico killed each other over the money some of us still paid for feeling illegally good, and no matter how many they killed we didn't let it bother us much because hadn't they tried to make us feel good in that low down unrighteous way? I've been told that before we did those things we took the southwest from them which was right because we could do it and then went back a couple of times to make sure they still respected us like we deserved. I don't find it hard to imagine what Mexico thinks about all that today, but maybe I'm just a pessimist and Mexicans are more forgiving than the twelve apostles with a winning lottery ticket. Maybe so, but I do hear everybody who says they know anything about it say that Mexico is a horribly poor and desperate country that can't even begin to take care of its own people, and that was before we closed the border for good and stopped talking to them at all. And with that I'm about out of facts and opinions about Mexico. I *said* I know very little about the place. But I know enough to stay the hell away.

That leaves us with the place we're stuck in, and I'll give you some words of wisdom about it for free. Here they come: the most ignorant way you can talk about this country is to do what I just did and call it a *place*. I know what places are. I've been to places. I've been to two or three places that were a hundred miles wide or even wider but I didn't stick around because big as they were they weren't big enough for me and the people who got in ahead of me. There are fewer places like that than most people think. Most people think that way because all they've seen are maps or the scenery out the window when they're driving through. Real places, though, are easy to recognize when you're really there: you look around and it hits you right away, *this place is different from the place I was just in.* Most of the places I've seen that really are places are small enough to walk across in a day, two days tops. Some of the best and a few of the worst could fit inside a big-city airport. I've seen places that I'd never leave on purpose if only they'd have let me stay there, but just thinking about letting me do that would make them laugh all day long if they ever got around to imagining it.

So, yes – you *could* find a place for yourself between the oceans, somewhere south of Canada and at least a little north of Mexico. You *could.* But you haven't yet and what are we to make of that?

We make of it that it's time to come see me, and we both have to hope you haven't left it too late.

I promise a lot but I don't promise results. I promise that I know more about these things than you do. I promise that I'll risk my life for you. I don't say that expecting gratitude or respect. I say it so you'll reflect that I've been risking it for years and still have it, so what I'll be risking for you has shall we say a pedigree and may be beneficial unto you. I promise that if you have enough money I won't take all of it. I promise that when you stop you won't be where you started.

First Chronicles

And these described by name, came in the days of Hezekiah king of Judah, and smote their tents, and the inhabitants that were found there, and destroyed them utterly unto this day, and dwelt in their room, because there was pasture there for their sheep. And besides these, five hundred men of the sons of Simeon went to mount Seir, and Pelatiah, and Neariah, and Rephaiah, and Uzziel the sons of Ishi were their captains, And they smote the rest of Amalek that had escaped, and they dwelt there unto this day. –1 Chronicles 4:41-43, from the Geneva translation.

It had been noticed that I am a natural chameleon. When you see me with Thumper or Loverbits I'm a darkish white man. When I'm with Bluesbaby or Ebonystick I'm a lightish black guy. It's only on my own that I stand out. On my own I could be Greek, except among Greeks. I could be Sicilian, except among Sicilians. You get the idea. The only thing I can always be is a son of the desert as it were, but not the son of any particular desert. Arabs see me and think of Turkmen, Turkmen see me and think of Kurds, and the *first* problem is that sooner or later you will run into whoever you're pretending to be and the *second* problem is that even before then you could run into lily white locals who will take you at your word about where you came from but not about why you came. By the time I got off the bus we all knew this, me more than anyone, and afterwards we worked the chameleon bit for our own good every chance we got.

Two years after I quit the robe and gown trade for something with better long-term prospects I drove a rented car across Ohio in the automatic lanes, heading west and watching for a purple bus going my way. My lane was doing the Ohio maximum of 96 so I had a slower lane between me and the buses, but the traffic wasn't bad and I had no trouble seeing it and when I flashed the toy laser at it they had no trouble seeing me. Thirty miles ahead I came to a rest stop and hit *divert*, pulled off, parked and waited. A few minutes later the bus pulled in too and let everyone off to buy snacks and use the john. They all wore backpacks so Bluesbaby wouldn't stand out in his. I walked up to him while he was having a hard time deciding what kind of slice to order from a pizza machine and said, "You only had to get two of them. Does it really need to take all day?"

He ostentatiously punched two buttons without looking at them, took the two boxes as they came out, grimaced at one of them and held it out to me. "Pineapple, walnuts and cheese is *exactly* what you got coming for rushing a man trying to look out for *your* damn ulcer."

We went back out to the car we'd both so clearly come in without exchanging a look with anybody. When we got to South Bend I requested a downtown exit and we rode the groove right to our hotel. I punched out of the Interstate, pulled into the lot and we went inside to check in. Our passengers were supposed to be waiting but we wanted a good night's sleep before meeting them because after that they weren't getting out of our sight. These passengers were three men who did not have a heresy problem. They had fingers-in-the-till problems that were showing signs of closing in and even at church they were starting to get funny looks. It had taken them a while to find the right broker and then Boronzee took his time checking them out like he always does so we figured they'd be in the right frame of mind when we all met for breakfast.

In the morning we walked into the coffee shop at exactly 7:06. It was pretty crowded but as we expected there were only three men dressed for fish camp besides us, sitting together at a six-top in outdoor duds but with faces more fit for waiting for the power breakfast to start. As we got close we could see that their outfits were still wrinkled from the boxes they came in. Like them we were wearing boots and jeans and flannel shirts but it still took them a second to recognize us, partly because our clothes had actually been worn before but mostly because, you know, *black*.

"*There* you are," Bluesbaby said, pulling out a chair and sitting down.

"Sorry we're late," I said, sitting next to him, "you know

how he likes his shower."

Bluesbaby rubbed his hands together. "Never mind that, I'm here now and I'm *hungry*. Y'all looked over the menu already?"

All this talk was because other people need to hear it. It doesn't matter what they hear but they need to hear something because if two men sit down at three other men's table and nobody talks, then people can't help but notice the sudden air of surliness. These three were still stuck on bovine stare number twelve so we kept the patter going.

I said, "You're going to love this camp. My uncle was up there last week and caught the limit every day."

Bluesbaby said, "You change your mind about renting your tackle? I know they got it but man, that spinning outfit you showed me, I'd love to see you work that."

He said this to our least gob-smacked passenger, a fellow who seemed just a tiny bit worried instead of taking a standing eight count like the other two. That one was indeed groping for something to blurt back at us when a waitress barged in and said, "What'll it be gents?" in a tone that told me she'd been waiting way too long for Bluesbaby and me. What, had these fools shown up for their 7:06 meeting at 6:15 and expected nobody to notice?

Bluesbaby said, "I'll take the pancakes and sausage and two eggs up on the side with a large orange juice if it's the real thing? And all the coffee you got."

"Short stack or five of them?"

"Now do I look like a short stack kind of fellow?"

"Didn't think so sweetie but you know I got to ask. You, honey?"

I was honey and I said I'd take the same. At that the worried guy saw his chance and said, "Me too" and the younger of the other two hurriedly nodded agreement and closed his menu. That left the one who had to be Hammaker because he had maybe ten years on the rest. He didn't see any reason to put on a show for anybody.

"Does anybody in the kitchen know how to poach an egg? If so I'll have one, light, *light*, with dry wheat toast. And none of whatever you call orange juice because I already know what you think coffee tastes like."

Making sure she remembered him. Making sure the other two remembered who their boss was. Making sure Bluesbaby and I knew he was dumber than a stump. This paragon of fatuity sat right at that table in that very public place where we were all supposed to be the best of fishing buddies and announced before a whole roomful of nosy people that we'd do our talking to him and nobody else. This Hammaker was kind of pigeon-chested and carried twenty extra pounds that he'd soon wish he didn't and he thought he wore the outthrust jaw of leadership, but what he had was the pointy weak chin of chronic constipation and the glare of the too-often snubbed.

The other two were Armstrong of the worried look that I never did see him lose and Fuller who was already perspiring a little too freely and only sweated more as the day wore on. Whatever scheme they were in that was ready to fall apart on them, I was willing to bet that Hammaker had dragged Fuller and Armstrong into it. He clearly thought they owed him a permanent debt of obedient deference in all things. When the check came he pointed to his half-eaten egg and said, "If you think I'm–" but stopped when I handed the waitress the card I had ready for her and said, "Here you go" like a Rockefeller tipping the hat check girl.

At least they'd checked out as arranged but when they picked up their bags at the desk we saw that he and only he had ignored instructions and brought a carry-on bag instead of a backpack. Bluesbaby shook his head joyfully at that and said, "We knew somebody'd probably forget and bring one of those so we brought an extra pack along. You didn't really plan on carrying that thing did you?"

"I don't *plan* on carrying anything at all and if you don't yet understand that–"

I said, "That's all right but it's going in the trash and if you want anything inside it you can repack it now before we start. There won't be another chance." Fuller and Armstrong were still sweaty and worried respectively but I got the impression they enjoyed that. I wondered which of them was the designated porter and decided it was probably Armstrong since he was the heftier of the two. Hammaker balked again when we got to the car and I opened the trunk but when

Bluesbaby said "Okay" and reached for the bag he snatched it back and started pulling things out of it furiously. He somehow squeezed them all into his new backpack and I don't think that it occurred to him even then that he, the feeblest of all of them, had packed by far the heaviest load.

When Hammaker finally got used to the idea that he'd have to ride three across in the back, we pulled out of the lot with Bluesbaby taking the first shift at the wheel. I checked the Social and saw the message that told me the front half of the fare had been paid. Hammaker being what he was I'd grown a little worried about that. I figured the same thought had occurred to Bluesbaby so I turned to the back seat and said, "I see that everybody's finances are up to date."

Hammaker said, "For what we're paying—" and I cut him off again, which was something I was getting to like.

"For what you're paying you get to go to Canada. Take a load off your spleen and consider the alternative."

By then Bluesbaby was in the merge lane and the Interstate was considering letting us in the whole way. When we got the orange light he merged and the highway grabbed us and shuffled us to the slow car lane which that day was only doing 83. I'd been hoping for the fast lane but with that load I hadn't really expected it. When we were locked in and cruising I casually turned on some other electronics that the boys in the back didn't need to know anything about.

The truth was they *were* paying way more than the going rate but it was their own damn fault. We were cleaning them out of dollars and they'd left themselves way too many of those. From now on they'd be living on whatever they'd stashed offshore, out where dollars are worthless. *Anything* but euros is worthless in Canada and Hammaker had to know it. The fact that they had so many dollars for us to take meant not only that he hadn't known his time was running out but that he'd refused even to consider that it might. That, the exorbitant fee we'd been able to gouge them for that they knew they might as well pay because the money was useless once they left the country, was why we'd known all along we'd be meeting at least one idiot at breakfast. Because I was used to that idea I'd been able so far to not think too much about Hammaker and how I loved him. But I knew that would start to change if I had to keep on talking to him, so we drove more or less silently toward the Upper Peninsula.

By early afternoon we had driven up through Escanaba almost to Marquette and then turned east along the shore. We kept the windows rolled up through the Hiawatha Nondenominational Forest but nothing can keep the smell of those iron mines out of your clothes. Your clothes, your hair, the lunch you thought it would be smart to pack. A couple of hours later we got to the shore road just west of Whitefish Bay, where we turned left and headed north. As long as we were heading toward the little tourist town of Paradise we could be the would-be campers we pretended we were. If we passed through it and kept going we'd be flat out naked, five men in a car heading nowhere they could possibly belong, concertina wire and cameras on posts between us and the shore, Coast Guard watch towers every hundred yards and officious teenage sentries stopping cars at random in pursuit of their merit badges. We knew we probably wouldn't make it so we were meeting Animkii in Paradise instead and letting him take us the rest of the way overland, away from the shore and through the woods more or less as the crow flies. Bluesbaby and I expected that to be an eye-opening learning experience.

We pulled off into the lot of the Upper Room Café right outside of town and I told our passengers the plan and the reasons for it. Fuller just kept on with his sweating. Armstrong still seemed alarmed but said nothing. Plans that the likes of us could make meant nothing to Hammaker but he wanted to know what kind of bullshit name A Monkey was. I couldn't be bothered with him anymore so Bluesbaby explained.

"Well, it's tricky. Animkii which I believe you heard just fine means thunder. But see, it means it in Ojibwe, so it also means *give me any lip and I'll slice it off and use it for bait*. I just mention that in case you haven't kept up with the latest trends in Native American etiquette. Which would mean you'd best restrict your conversation to *please, thank you* and *how high*."

Hammaker, more and more the gutless back-stabber with every passing minute, took it sullenly and narrowed his narrow eyes and said nothing more. There were things that Bluesbaby and I hadn't had a chance to discuss, but I took his etiquette lecture as agreement that if things went south and we had to cut our losses, Hammaker would be the first one down. Animkii drove in a few seconds later in a muddy, dusty, beefed-up, camo-skinned pickup with an old-fashioned camper top that had met more than one low-hanging branch at a pretty good rate of speed. I looked around and couldn't see where he'd been watching for us but I knew he had been. The last time we'd Socialed him was before breakfast when we hadn't known within 90 minutes when we'd get there. We rousted the passengers out and hustled them and their gear into the camper. Bluesbaby leaned in after them and gave them his little speech about no talking and whispering is talking and moving around is as bad as talking so don't even scratch. Then he shut them in and went back to our car to get dressed. In the front seat of the truck Animkii gave me a floppy camo hat like his and just like that we were two Chippewa buddies riding off to tend their traps before supper, only this time followed for some reason by a car that belonged in nobody's north woods, especially when driven by a forbiddingly pissed off Major in the dress camos of the Missionary Prayer Warriors of Harlem. But it's probably best not to notice such things – wouldn't you agree?

Animkii took us down a little street of nice frame houses that got smaller and smaller as we drove a couple of blocks. When they'd shrunk to huts the street turned to gravel and when the huts became house trailers it turned into the kind of washboard mud that once gave somebody the idea for speed bumps. Then we were into the woods and the road became a rutted track. Animkii had the windows rolled down but we'd lost the breeze and the high summer humidity rolled in, carrying its usual complement of bugs and smelling of that sweet woodsy rot. I'd have rolled mine back up but I figured Animkii had his reasons. He drove in the ruts but Bluesbaby had to drive between them or he'd have lost his undercarriage, and keeping him in the mirror slowed us down. It was still bright afternoon but the woods closed over us in spots where I'd have needed headlights to see the road. Animkii didn't bother with them. He'd probably made those ruts or maybe his grandpa had. As we came out of the dark into one of the bright patches two teenage heroes-in-training stepped out in front of us with automatic rifles leveled and twitching. When we stopped they both said "Exit-the-vehicle-and-leave-the-doors-*open*-for-inspection" in memorized rushes like they were racing each other to get it said first.

Animkii leaned his head out and said, "When your officer tells me to. Get him."

The boys went bug-eyed and came around to the sides. The one by Animkii said "Exit-the-vehicle–" but Animkii cut him off.

"No. Not today. Yesterday was okay and maybe tomorrow but not today. Your officer. Now."

The boys glared death-dealing loathing but Animkii just gave them back a patient, bored look of *I'm putting up with this, but barely* and I aped him as best I could. Bluesbaby pulled up behind us. The boy on Animkii's side turned to see him better while his buddy sighted in on my nose. Animkii just shook his head. The boy on his side touched a throat mic and said, "Unit five to Blue Chief. Request your presence." The boys stepped back in front of us, their rifles shaking furiously. They could see the truck exploding. They could hear our screams and smell our blood running through the ruts. They were what you'd have to call thwarted, and being thwarted hadn't happened ever since daddy pulled his strings and finagled them into the troop.

We waited. A hardened veteran of maybe eighteen stepped out, took it all in, got an *oh shit* look on his face and said, "Stand down."

One of the boys said, "But–"

Blue Chief said, "Stand *down.*"

Unit Five lowered its weapons and stepped out of the track. Blue Chief glanced meaningfully back at Bluesbaby and looked a question.

Animkii said, "With us."

Blue Chief said, "Carry on."

Animkii said, "Peace be with you," and put it in gear.

We'd barely pulled away when we heard a brief shouted tirade cut off by a curt command. Animkii said, "That was the first spot you wouldn't have got through. Right now he's telling them about two brave boys just like them who woke up one morning with their hamstrings cut. Because they didn't think low rent people like us should be carrying pelts out of season which they decided they'd confiscate to make their point."

I said, "What makes you think we didn't know how much we all need each other?"

Animkii chuckled. "That's good. Mind if I use it?"

Twenty minutes later we came to a straight stretch and Animkii put on some speed, leaving Bluesbaby way behind. As the track began to curve again Animkii stopped hard enough to squeal the brakes and make a couple of big satisfying thumps on the back of my seat. He put it in neutral and revved the engine. A middle-aged sniper with a pair of night googles resting on his forehead stood up from a spot I'd only just decided had to be empty.

Animkii leaned out and said, "One car behind me with one man in it. He's ours. Any more than one car or one man, they're yours."

The sniper said, "Roger that." His voice was amiable enough but he was memorizing my face. It didn't take him long and he sank back into the earth while I was blinking.

When Bluesbaby caught up and we drove off in convoy again Animkii said, "That was the second spot where you always knew we needed each other."

"Who was he?"

"Unh uh. Who were *they*. All six of them."

"Jesus. Who were *they?*"

"Reconstructionist Militia. Premillennial orientation and kind of aggressive proselytizers. Very territorial, but they do know whose territory it really is."

"Who'd drive out here just to be converted?"

"They're not here for the local white people and we get along with them fine. They don't really approve of us but who does? They like that sweet smoked whitefish with the pepper on it so from time to time I bring them some and we pick at it and shoot the breeze. It's the idea of certain people coming south that keeps them here and on their toes. Not us, others. You'll see."

In another forty minutes Animkii slowed to a crawl and turned sharply between two pines and into a clearing I hadn't seen from the track. A cabin stood well back from any cover with two silent but very capable looking dogs sitting at attention on its porch. Pink and turquoise laundry dried on a line and a tire swing hung from one lone tree in the yard. A man who could have been Animkii's twin stepped out the screen door. Animkii nodded, which must have meant "all clear" because the man went back inside and the dogs lay down. Animkii parked with the truck pointed toward the cabin.

We got out. Bluesbaby had stopped in the entrance to the clearing and Animkii made backing up motions to him. When Bluesbaby was parked on the track Animkii opened the camper door maybe a foot. He leaned in and said, "First order from your new commander in chief. Step outside and don't turn or look around. Turning or looking around will be punished by instant death. Looking down will be rewarded with a two minute rest and further orders." He turned to me. "Is that right, former commander in chief?"

"That's exactly right," I said.

They staggered out fearful and squinting, Hammaker first of course. They had not had a pleasant ride bouncing around in the hot, closed-up dark.

Hammaker glared naked contemptuous hatred at Animkii. "*How* high, new commander in *chief?* I mean, how high can we *look* when we're obediently looking *down?*"

Sweating Fuller and nervous Armstrong stared at him with pure disgust. Their deference had vanished in the camper. Evidently there'd been talking after all and Hammaker had some slipping authority to reassert.

Animkii turned to Fuller and Armstrong and said, "Any objections if we let him bleed out here? Nobody'll find a trace if that would worry you."

Armstrong said, "No personal objection but he's got the codes on him. For the rest of the money. Nobody else, just him."

I said, "That's not really true anymore. I scanned them off him right after breakfast."

I let that sink in. It sunk into Hammaker first and he started to say something but shut up fast when Animkii casually pulled out a righteous bowie knife and started cleaning his nails with it.

Fuller said, "Then you've already moved it."

There didn't seem to be any point in denying that so I just nodded.

Fuller said, "But you brought us up here anyway." He was sweating more than ever but he was showing guts, and we needed that.

I said, "We have a deal. Deals matter. I keep mine. Animkii keeps his. You two are keeping yours. He isn't. Not if Animkii decides he isn't. My deal is pretty much over but his is just starting so he decides."

Armstrong turned a legal inch toward Hammaker and said, "Now do you finally understand how out of your league you are? Or do Executive Vice President and Deacon mean so much to you that you'll stand here watching your guts leak out? And don't look at Fuller or me because we're sincerely past caring."

Hammaker turned an illegal foot toward me and said, "I'm sorry he took it the wrong way. I promise to, to keep quiet the rest of the way."

I said, "I'm out of it. Convince *him*."

Fuller said, "And call him sir you overgrown pea-brained clown. Call him sir and apologize for your own sorry mouth because everyone here read you perfectly."

Hammaker said, "I—"

Animkii said, "That's okay, I know what you want to say and I can't stand hearing people lie to me. If you shut up and follow orders all the way to the boat I may think again and decide you mean it. I may, and I may not. From now on you do your promising with your feet. I'm sorry gentlemen but break time is over."

Animkii drove us in the car another few miles and parked it by backing into a spot he obviously had picked out. He left it with its nose pointed back down the track toward the way we'd come and I took that as a reassuring sign of good faith on his part. Then we got out and walked for several careful, muggy, itchy, weary hours.

Somewhat before midnight the moon rose and where it broke through the trees it seemed brighter than the sun had before it went down. The passengers were winded but not so much they couldn't keep up even though Hammaker had to stagger to do it. Nobody had said anything since we left the car, not even Hammaker, which had to be his personal best though gasping like a guppy on the floor had probably made it easier. At a spot that I know I wouldn't have recognized Animkii stepped off the track and into the trees and from then on we were climbing. After a little of that Animkii turned to us, squatted down and motioned the rest of us up close. He whispered, "From now on we take it real slow and when I stop you do and when you stop you stay dead still. Still like you're a dead tree because that's what we'd all better look like." He looked at Hammaker and added, "Heap big danger now."

It seemed to take an hour to crawl up that hill. The bugs were all over us and the passengers let it bother them, which I suppose was a good thing when you consider what they might have been worrying about instead. After a while I realized that we were crawling up a path, a miserable narrow twisty path that was only fit for crawling, but even so it was *possible* to crawl it, unlike the broken, overgrown ground to either side.

We crested the hill in a copse of trees thick enough to keep the moonlight off the ground. Animkii waved us down and then forward on our bellies so we could look down a steep treeless slope. He pointed to a track maybe sixty feet down the slope and almost straight beneath us, a track about twenty feet wide beaten into the brush, bright and clear in the moonlight, without a tree or bush standing in it but with the forest on either side except where it bordered the slope. This track wandered off to our right and disappeared into the dark and going the other way it turned just beneath us at a right angle leading straight away from us. Animkii made sure we saw it clearly, then waved us back a few feet the way we'd crawled. He put me on one side of him and Bluesbaby on the other where we could still see the track if we raised our heads. He put the passengers behind us and out of sight of the track no matter how they fidgeted.

Animkii turned to the passengers and whispered, ""We lie here for a while and nobody moves or talks unless I tell them to. This is what happens to any fool who talks or moves." He took out his bowie knife, showed it around and planted it in the dirt. He pointed across the track and said, "There's a settlement about a half mile that way full of some very unfriendly people who make sure everybody else stays out or gets dead. All night and all day they walk their perimeter which is that path down there. They walk it in platoon-strength units and I do mean strength. We're waiting here for their next patrol. It takes them half an hour to make a circuit and we're going to cross their path when they pass us."

Bluesbaby said, "And why the fuck do we want to do that?"

Animkii said, "Because our place is on the other side of their place of course."

I said, "And they don't mind you there?"

"They don't mind us long as we act scared enough which believe me we are. It's worth it to them since we give them fish for what they think of as rent and they couldn't catch a fish if it walked into their camp. It's worth it to us because nobody else can get through them. Anybody who comes looking for us has to go through them and that's not going to happen. Anybody following us now will die before they're halfway to the boat. They kill anybody who's not Chippewa, day or night, and they'll kill me too if they catch me with you which is why you gentlemen are very, very expendable. Sometimes people they catch take all day to die which is mostly for our benefit I think although they do like to see a properly roasted heretic."

The bugs had been bad before but now that we were lying still they peeled us and rubbed us down with horseradish. The crickets screamed in pulsing waves. Birds held urgent conversations that I suspected were all about us.

Animkii whispered, "Here they come." He was looking way off to our right through a scope I hadn't seen before. I saw nothing and I didn't exactly hear them except that the sounds I did hear seemed to change after Animkii spoke.

Half a minute later they came into view, just dark shapes bobbing up and down in the patches where the moonlight hit the path and disappearing again in the dark stretches. A few seconds after that I understood what I was listening to. They were chanting that ancient military common-cadence call and response. I couldn't make out any words from the first set but by the time they started the second one I could pick it out, one strong voice calling the cadence and forty more replying in unison.

"Bones of Judas in the tree
Swinging slow for all to see
Bones of Judas in the dust
Watch his shekels turn to rust
In the tree and on the ground
Thirty shekels scattered round
Sound off
    One two
Sound off
    Three four
Sound off
    One two three four – that's right!"

Now they were on a part of the path that swung wide of the trees and the whole group was in the moonlight. I could tell that everybody had some kind of rifle across his chest but they were still too far away for me to see clearly and they carried other things I couldn't make out much at all. Animkii put his mouth next to my ear and whispered, "You military trained?"

I whispered back, "Seven years of orphanage militia training and I maybe shot twenty live rounds the whole time. So no, not really."

"Still, you see how easy they'd be to ambush. Couple mortar rounds or a dozen grenades, it's over. So maybe you think they're idiots but they're not. They know nobody they have to worry about is bringing a team up here without them hearing. They're just spraying their boundary line like wolves do except they're meaner than wolves ever were."

Animkii handed me his scope. It turned out they had all different kinds of weapons, most of them genuine infantry. No two of them were dressed or moved quite alike. Most had beards down to their belts. Two or three carried rams' horns that they held over their heads and pumped up and down to the beat. A giant in the front held up two rough tablets the size of tombstones, one in each hand. The only things moving together were their feet, and their feet were the scariest thing about them. They weren't marching, they were stomping the earth to death. I passed the scope to Bluesbaby. They started up chanting again, the words much clearer now.

"Pilate running down the hill
Stink of death is on him still
Pilate swimming in the sea
He can't get away from me
In the sea and on the land
Blood still dripping from his hand
Sound off…"

I stuck my mouth in Animkii's ear. "Who the fuck are they?"

He looked a little surprised that I hadn't figured it out yet, but who would have?

"The last postmillennial militia in the U.P., survivors from all the ones the premillennials wiped out. They don't expect any easy rides up to heaven. They've all seen the antichrist and they figure they'll have to kill most of us to get there."

They were within thirty yards of us now. We took our last peeks and hugged the ground. The birds had gone quiet, or maybe every bird in Michigan was screaming and the pounding of those boots drowned them out. Their pace seemed much quicker than it had been. I knew that it couldn't really be any quicker at all and the show was working on me like it was supposed to. They had to be peering up at our ridge as they came on. They had to know exactly what shapes they ought to see and what shapes they saw instead. Behind me I could hear Armstrong's breathing and I reached back and got a hand in his hair and tugged it till he held his breath. They started chanting again and I let him go. They'd been marching and chanting for hours but they were bellowing it out. How can chanting men stomping in the dirt be too loud to look at?

"Ev'ry night and ev'ry morn
Some to misery are born
Ev'ry morn and ev'ry night
Some are born to sweet delight
Some are born to sweet delight
Some are born to endless night
Sound off
        One two

Sound—"

Fuller coughed like a firecracker. The chant and the stomping stopped dead. Bluesbaby moved like a striking rattler and had a hand over Fuller's mouth. Armstrong squirmed and I reached back again and pushed his face into the dirt. Animkii made a low lunge to hold down Hammaker but Hammaker stood up and took a blundering step back down the hill. He tripped, he fell, he screamed. A wild yell broke out down below and shrieking demons raced for the slope. Animkii was up and running, Bluesbaby right behind him and me a foot behind him. We leapt over Hammaker and plunged down into the dark. If Bluesbaby or I once lost touch with Animkii I knew we'd never find the path again and Animkii was flying so we flew too. We didn't care how much noise we made because we could never be heard over the screaming behind us. Well, no. We didn't care how much noise we made because we were running away in terror. I hoped that in the dark of the woods half of them would shoot the other half but with all their firepower not one of them pulled a trigger, which to this day I think showed great judgment and discipline. We made the bottom of the hill and started pounding down the track. Once on the track we could see Animkii clearly and didn't have to run up each other's ass but that didn't mean we slowed up any. The yelling was dying down but now there were different screams. Those screams were what we were running from now. It seemed like we ran for an hour before we finally outran those screams.

When we finally got to the car Animkii pulled out the activator, the activator to *my* car, which I never should have let him keep and which goes to show how much thinking I didn't do that day. He used it on the doors and we piled in and he turned the anti-tampering field all the way up to *kill* before he even started the motor. He drove us a mile down the track so fast that I thought he'd lost his mind to panic. Later I realized that he'd been thinking how the car might have been found and staked out. By then I'd completely lost track of how many things I'd missed and how many times Animkii had saved our lives.

The moon had set but he stopped in a dim patch of starlight. We just breathed for minutes on end and said nothing. Those were some of the best minutes of my life. Finally Bluesbaby started giggling and said, "I see that none of us has a hat anymore." We all laughed like it was the funniest joke ever told. Bluesbaby's face was a bloody mess from running through twigs and whipping branches. I felt my own and it was slippery as raw liver. Animkii's was almost unmarked. I pointed at it and at Bluesbaby's and mine and Bluesbaby and I broke up again but this time Animkii took a pass.

When we quieted down Animkii said, "Money."

Bluesbaby said, "Same deal now as it always was."

Animkii said, "Make it happen."

I got on the Social and made it happen.

Animkii drove us all the way back to Paradise.

Numbers

Take ye the sum of all the Congregation of the children of Israel, after their families, and households of their fathers, with the number of their names; to wit, all the males, man by man; From twenty years old and above, all that go forth to the war in Israel, thou and Aaron shall number them, throughout their armies. –Numbers 1:2-3, the Geneva translation.

That one had consequences and most of them were blessings on the tribe of Boronzee.

I wasn't joking when I said that Hammaker had left far too many dollars lying around and now they fell to us. Heaps of dollars are by far the worst way to store the wealth that honest commerce brings so Boronzee set out to invest them on behalf of the tribe. The bus got a thorough refit. Many of us went forth to buy up reputations and honorifics which Boronzee stored away for future use. We could afford to be pickier than ever before and we were. The treasures we brought home were few, but how they gleamed... Not satisfied with furnishing our own caravan, we sought out kindred nations and gave impressively. And we sought out enemy nations and gave even more impressively, with the result that chinks appeared in their walls, and many zealously hidden paths were revealed to us, and certain of the enemy's noblemen beheld us with eyes newly cleansed of their ancient disdain.

Thumper, already a Master of Divinity, went off to Harvard itself for his Doctorate. As young Puritan boys with a calling once went away to a *place* called Harvard, so every morning he went away into his Social to the modern Harvard and received the identical instruction – and I, as always, set out to follow in his path. I rarely spent less than three hours a day in the bosom of that honorable seat of learning, but since I rarely spent less than three hours a day on the road I had the time. The fact is that being brought up as I had been I already knew one hell of a lot more about divinity than Thumper ever would which I say with no disrespect to him at all, and I also began to surpass him in other ways simply because Boronzee found him invaluable as a fellow teacher and kept him close to the bus. But Thumper was big in every way. He never held it against either of us and even seemed to take great pleasure in my worldly victories, which began to make their way into the lessons he taught the newly bused younger boys.

But that was only one consequence of my trip to the Upper Peninsula and I'm starting to get ahead of my story. Even before I was back at work and Bluesbaby made it back to the bus, authorities of various kinds, every one of whom shared some responsibility for letting Hammaker, Armstrong and Fuller get away, moved quickly to salvage what they could of their careers. In itself this was probably not uncommon, but they were unusually loud about it and it quickly became a scandalous public titillation. There were good reasons for this. When the average lonesome atheist disappears the authorities go to every extreme to keep it quiet because any widespread belief in the possibility that the denounced or almost-denounced *can* escape them is their greatest fear. But Hammaker had raped that company thoroughly and several well-known congregations that had invested too heavily in it suddenly awoke to the horror of being dead broke, much to the clamorous glee of their rivals for Christ's affection. Furthermore the nature of the crime let the authorities off some hooks while leaving them publicly wriggling from others. Done as it was by solidly churched men purely for their own material gain, the theft *itself* was neither blasphemous nor an indecent affront to public morals. What *was* a matter of legitimate public concern was the authorities' demonstrated failure to protect the congregations they were after all appointed to serve. Therefore waves had to be made and most of all they had to be seen to be made.

Of course they got onto Bluesbaby and me at once but as we'd hoped they filled in the little they knew with so many lies that, if anything, they covered our trail for us better than we ever could have by ourselves. The first public witness was our waitress from the hotel coffee shop. She testified on the very best networks that *the Middle Eastern man* – me – had instructed her that no pork in any form must touch his plate, which *the darker foreigner* had strenuously reinforced, even specifying *no sausage, not a trace of sausage for us* (and thus do Satan's lies reveal the truthful seeds from which he grows them). Next, a fragment of recovered security video from Avis showed me checking my watch and then hurriedly kneeling next to the car I'd just rented, facing east of course. (It *was* me and it *was* the same car and we all had quite a laugh at the idea that I could have really done that and then made it out of that garage unmolested.) This of course was followed by day after day of theorizing by terrorism experts who – and we really liked this touch – were even allowed to argue quite vigorously with one another about the nature of the godless horrors that the stolen tithes of blameless widows would soon pay for, and about where said horrors would be made manifest, and about who among the righteous should take the greatest care to stay tuned in for their own safety because *their* righteousness was surely the righteousness most likely to attract our Satanic hatred. Then they arrested two or three secretaries at Hammaker's company, one of whom for all we knew really may have been sleeping with Fuller as they claimed. When the non-absconding executives were allowed to voluntarily enter a famously plush Congregational penitentiary we figured it was just about over and stopped following it, but the fruits of our good work continued to ripen and drop for some time. Animkii's people for example sent us several mildly ironical Socials thanking us for the upturn in their economy and reminding us of the benefits of our continued patronage. We and other likeminded tribes similarly saw increasing, and increasingly optimistic, interest in our services. You understand, it wasn't that anyone knew enough to name Animkii or us – they'd have done a whole lot more than name us if they had – but we had all been planting cautious little advertisements for years and suddenly these seemed to grow in credibility among newly hopeful unbelievers. And all because, and this is just delicious, all because those scurrying authorities were so desperate to take the focus off Hammaker, Fuller and Armstrong, and especially off their own negligence in not preventing the fruition of the crime, that they allowed the impression that the three embezzlers *had got away* and were thereby rendered inconsequential to the search for vengeance. And when they later realized their mistake and announced the fugitives' deaths while resisting arrest in Louisville, half the public had already forgotten them and those most likely to seek us out didn't believe a word of it – I mean, what the hell: run away to *Louisville?*

But somebody really did go to Louisville and that was us. Boronzee reserved a spot at a Reverend Williston Outreach Camp-in there in late October and the bus, newly covered in mostly green and purplish scenes of daily life aboard Noah's ark, drove in and not only I but all the rest of the surviving bus alumni straggled in from wherever we'd been to meet it. And it was fitting that we should go there, for does not Numbers 2:2 instruct us to? *Every man of the children of Israel shall camp by his standard, and under the ensign of their father's house; far off about the Tabernacle of the Congregation shall they pitch.* Boronzee had booked space for the bus and forty tents not fifty yards from the Holy of Holies, which was the most popular attraction at the fair. High above it he hoisted a pennant done in the exact shade of Reverend Williston's green and purple robes that showed the Ark perched atop Mt Ararat. With that standard as our beacon I and the other alumni had no trouble finding the place no matter how far away we'd had to park. My tent, when I found it, proved to be the only one on our lot of the style that Reverend Williston's tent-renters called Uriah's Battle Tent. Reverend Williston's people obviously felt that sleeping in Uriah's Battle Tent is an honor that comes with no omens attached, and Boronzee and Thumper assured me with straight faces that any forebodings I got from it came entirely from my own guilty conscience. At the time I actually felt good enough to laugh about this.

In the course of our travels we had variously disguised ourselves as hundreds of churches whose identities we borrowed electronically for a few hours at a time. But there was no way for us to impersonate any real church for the duration of the Outreach Camp-in and anyway that would have conflicted with our purpose for going – for this week was to witness our coming out as the Pilgrims of the New Wilderness, whose somewhat provocative name Boronzee had chosen precisely for its faint implication that there were still (or were again) patches of spiritual infertility in Jesus's America. Our new name was thus a bit on the disquieting side, for while there is scarcely a church in the country that doesn't think of itself as a mountain looking down on valleys of impurity, there are also few that don't realize how they themselves are falsely seen as such valleys by their deluded inferiors. Might our presence, just possibly, be suggesting that very thing? Well yes, it just might be, but certainly not with respect to *your* fine church sir. We hold *your* church in the highest of esteems and will be proud to sing its praises as we travel this land if only you will allow it. Will you sir? Will you ma'am? May we, as we seek to convert the benighted who dwell in the many dark places that still so despoil Jesus's beautiful country, tell everyone we meet that you have been true friends unto us? May we?

Such was our mission in Louisville, spreading that good message, giving ever, seeking never.

Now, holy vagabonds are theoretically welcome everywhere, but they do attract scrutiny. *Prosperous* holy vagabonds are mostly exempt from it since the bounty they're obviously used to receiving is pretty good evidence of their bona fides. So our first task was to demonstrate our well-earned prosperity, and our next was to make everyone forget about envying it. Boronzee contracted with a couple of local merchants who proved quite adept at the bona fides business. Ebonystick is by far the best cook on the bus and he has always favored barbecue. Now Boronzee put him in charge and turned him loose. He rented twenty grills. He ordered sacks and sacks of charcoal, bushel after bushel of corn and side after side of beef, and they got all the attention we could have asked for when they were trucked in every afternoon. Every night for the whole week Ebonystick supervised and we cooked and handed out hundreds of New Wilderness Burgers to whoever wanted one, New Wilderness barbecued beef ribs to elders and anyone in a choir robe, New Wilderness Fatted Calf Steaks to clergy and their valued guests. We poured hundreds of gallons of soda and grilled thousands of ears of corn and the corn we didn't grill we baked into cornbread that we slathered with New Wilderness Honey and Locust Butter (the locusts were really pecans and the stuff tasted a lot better than Ebonystick thought it would when he dreamed it up). You'd have thought that would have kept us too busy for anything else but some of us only worked the food about half the time. The rest of the time we spent admiring our new friends. We admired them fulsomely, verbosely, and with tangible proofs of our spontaneous esteem for them, which we explained away with the story that *we* alas had no permanently anchored church to carry with us on the road – so here we were, parked for a week among the trusted representatives of so many well-anchored churches, and with a whole year of tithing to make up.

Every evening at eight the rams' horns sounded their call and everyone sat back in their lawn chairs and looked toward Heaven. The lights went out bank by bank, children were hushed and then Reverend Williston appeared high and wide above us and gazed down with that beatific sternness that I've heard DreamWorks needed nineteen months to perfect. If you've only seen Reverend Williston in your home and in the mall you're not ready, no matter what you think, you're not *ready* for your first sight of him when he's glowing to outshine the moon, half a mile tall and pacing above you in the sky. When the sky-borne finger of Reverend Williston points down it points down only at you, no matter where in the camp you may be. Likewise, though he seems to stand above the Holy of Holies in the very center of the camp, and everyone agrees that that's exactly where he stands, he is always leaning down at that impossible angle toward *you*, he is always facing right down *at* you as he leans. I'm told there are students of holographic science who know how this works and I believe it but only in certain senses of what it means to know. The stern holy face of the Reverend Williston above you is the face that passeth understanding.

The fool hath said in his heart, there is *no God,* and maybe he did indeed, but I promise you as one who was there and saw it that no such fool has ever looked up at Reverend Williston and said in his heart that *he* isn't there.

On the night of the first day in Louisville I saw the Reverend Williston above me and I knew I had to make an instant choice. I could let it happen to me or I could remain sane and think about what I was seeing. But I didn't know whether I could really remain sane and I didn't know how well I could think and I had five more nights to do my thinking in and I was on the point of deciding that I should probably decide to forget why I was there and just let it happen to me for one night when I realized that it was happening anyway and I didn't have much of a choice after all.

That first night when Reverend Williston appeared the campground echoed with gasps. Small children screamed and were hushed. (Some of them took a while to hush but that's okay because now they know how to hush themselves, now they'll be hushed in many important ways for the whole rest of their lives.) Grown people said things too but not to each other. They said them to whoever we say things to when those things are just *Lord!* and *Sweet Jesus!* and *My God!* and they said them because they had to say them and just as quickly they shut up again like they knew they were supposed to.

Up in his sky the Reverend Williston knew exactly how long it took them to shut up. He waited until the last *Mercy!* had been expelled and then he spoke. "Friends," he began. When you're sitting there you know that he's speaking to you from speakers scattered throughout the camp but knowing that doesn't change the wonder of it. Of *course* he uses speakers: could we stand it if he had to boom it out through his own galaxy-wide mouth? "Friends," he began, "we are here to recommit our lives to our Savior whom we know as Jesus."

We is the Reverend Williston's most important word. He says *we* more than he says *Jesus*. Infrequently, very infrequently, he says *you*. He has never been heard to say *I* and he didn't say it here either. I know. You're getting this word for word because for a very small offering Williston Ministries will Social you any sermon he's ever delivered.

"We committed our lives to Jesus at our baptism. He knows this. He does not forget. He does not need to be told again that our lives are His. It is we who need to be told again because it is we who forget. Every one of us, in every minute of our lives, is prone to forget that promise, the most important promise anyone can ever make. We don't think we forget it. We think we remember, and whenever something reminds us we say we *do* remember. But what we remember are the words, and the words are not the promise. Words can be the empty shells of promises. The promise was hot and joyful and urgent and the words it came in were never more than the wrapping on the gift of our lives. If that promise is not hot and joyful and urgent to us now, we have withdrawn our gift. We have *exchanged* it, as if we had bought it at any ordinary earthly store, and we have done it for the same reason we trade any gift for another one: because, in the truest and most horrible sense of the words, *we have changed our minds.* We have changed our minds and exchanged the gift of our lives for the cares and rewards of our transient time in the world beneath Our True World. Will Jesus welcome us home to Our True World once we, with nobody's permission but His, have left this tawdry planet? When we offer Him an empty box wrapped in the pretty words that once contained our sacred promise? Or will He send us to that other true world, that dark true and eternal World ever burning in the flames that give no light? Will He say, You must go hence to that terrible true world, for My World is for my friends who have brought me the gift of their lives and the likes of you shall not dishonor it.

"Friends, every minute of every day we are liable to *change our minds.* When the baby fusses. When our boss is surly. When money is tight and the gutter is falling down, then without any sense that we are doing it we can *change our minds.* We change our minds, the minds that we *promised* as they were *when* we promised them, we change them whenever we think that our lives are less than the perfect gifts we once consecrated to Him. And when our luck turns good again, as it will, as it will, when the girl we adore says *yes* she'll go to the prom *yes* she'll go to the alter, when the baby smiles and goes to sleep and that surly boss offers us the raise we deserve and the gutter sags and we have money in our pocket to fix it, then we change our minds again. In our innermost thoughts we say, this life is all right, this life is *good,* this life *is mine.* And when we say that it truly *is* ours once again, it does indeed belong again to us, to us, who can do *nothing* with it, instead of to Him to whom we promised it, to Him who would give it back to us a thousand million fold *if only we could learn how to keep our promise to Him.*"

Reverend Williston's hair is askew and his voice has risen to match the clamor of the seventh angel's trumpet, but now he pauses and looks down upon us with concern. He runs his hand through that white mop of hair and its wildness reminds him that he is overwrought. He chuckles at how seriously he takes himself sometimes. He smiles. The transformation of his concern into compassion is a lovely thing to see, and by now his terrified and mostly stricken flock is ready for a good serving of that compassion, a very good serving and a second helping too. He seems to know this, for when he speaks again it is in a new and softer voice, that famous voice you've heard him use continuously in your homes, in the stores and while you work, the very same voice he uses to comfort the dying and the bereft and to welcome the chastened sinner's return to the fold.

"Friends, this evening, this very evening, we will remind ourselves again how our promise to Jesus was not only made but can be kept. We have come a long way to get here and we are weary with travel but before we sleep tonight we will once again regain the divine power to keep our sacred promise to Jesus. Let each of us pray silently now, pray that we're ready to receive this power Jesus is trying to send our way."

And the Reverend Williston bows his beautiful head and closes his beautiful eyes.

Suddenly we realize that a restful blue light has spread throughout the campground. It flickers in the dead October grass, here a little paler and there a stronger, deeper blue. Now that we see it we also see the mottled streaks of green shifting in and out. Wait, was that a fleeting patch of violet? Maybe it was but it's gone now, but look, there's another over here. This is beautiful. How can anything bad happen when everything's so beautiful? Listen! Was that a violin? No, not from there, from over here – no, maybe from there after all. A violin for sure, or maybe a flute… Are those roses I smell? I'm not sure, it's funny, now that I think about it I don't really *know* how roses smell, but I'm pretty sure they ought to smell like that.

"Friends, we will need all the holy virtues in order to keep our promise, we will need all of them at our command every day at every hour, and how is that possible, who is virtuous enough to never slip? We are if we but listen. In the earliest days of God's church the seven holy virtues were set down for us. They are chastity, temperance, charity, diligence, patience, kindness, and humility. None of them are easy and we are to master them all. It seems impossible, but two great secrets have been revealed to us.

"The first great secret is that if we but master one of them, the other six will fall to us. What virtue is so powerful that it commands the other six?

"It is the holy virtue of humility. Humility is the secret road that leads us to chastity, directs us to temperance, guides our way to charity, points our feet to diligence, escorts us to patience and even ushers our hearts toward kindness. To know that humility can do these six great things we need only remember simpler things that we've oftentimes known before. Let us recall them, one by one."

Now if you had been there you'd have seen the faces of certain of your fellow worshippers begin to glow, two or three worshipping faces glowing within sight of you no matter where you stood or lay or sat.

"To surrender to the sin of lust means, foremost among many things, that we put our pleasure and our will above our regard for others, and especially above the particular other whom we pretend to ourselves that we love. To those in the grip of humility the sin of lust is impossible, and thus they achieve the holy virtue of chastity."

They glowed like old ivory lit from within, like a candle glows beneath its flame in a dark room, not the flame itself (Reverend Williston was the flame that lit us all) but the candle *beneath* the flame, as certain old masters of painting from time to time captured for our reverence.

"Temperance is loyalty to something better than our own impulses. To be loyal to something we must see it as being above ourselves in our most private, most honest estimation of things. To place something higher than ourselves by *raising* it is sometimes impossible. Some wise men have said that it's *always* impossible. But to place something higher than ourselves by *lowering* our *selves*: that is no more than the

55

everyday work of humility."

These few glowing faces, every one of them, were not the faces of people who had a thought left for themselves. These were the faces of people hearing the voice of truth and feeling it spread within them as they heard. How did the light know who they were? Who commanded the light? Who was watching us so attentively?

"The third holy virtue is charity, which means not only benevolence and generosity but also sacrifice. With pride it is possible to give gifts. The proudest men who ever lived have given astounding gifts purely in the service of their pride. There isn't a particle of charity in such things. When humility conquers our pride, we cheerfully make the sacrifices that God has demanded of us since the earliest times. We make those sacrifices because they are the obvious thing to do. We make them, in other words, in the true spirit of charity."

The illuminated ones did not know that they shone for us. The light they felt was not the light we could see. The light they felt was the light carried by the Reverend Williston's words, the very light of Jesus himself. It struck their souls and reflected outward, but those from whose souls it reflected saw only the far greater light that dazzled them from within.

"The fourth holy virtue is diligence, which means no more than working hard in all the work we should be doing. The opposite of diligence is the sin of sloth. Some people think that sloth and laziness are the same but they are not. Laziness is an *impulse*. Sloth is *surrender* to laziness. Laziness is something we all have in us, and sometimes we are well advised to use it. Humility tells us when it is time to do that."

Now, one by one, the illuminated faces slowly faded, while other faces close by began to glow in their stead. And these too were only faces that revealed an inner rapture.

"The fifth holy virtue is patience. Some people think patience means waiting. It doesn't. Slothful people wait all day. They never consider *not* waiting, but they are not showing patience. The opposite of patience goes by many names: wrath, aggression, antagonism, intolerance. Humble people are patient, in that they withhold their wrath, they withhold their aggression, their antagonism, their intolerance. Therefore they hate truly when they hate, because they hate only when and what God tells them to hate, and when God does tell them, then they don't wait any longer."

And the fading and the glowing began to quicken, and in the space of only a few of these wise words there were many faces inspired by memories of God's righteous hate, and the rest of us waited patiently for the illumination to come to us.

"The sixth holy virtue is kindness. Do you imagine as some people do that opposites of kindness are wrath and intolerance? They are not, my friends. We have just seen that wrath and intolerance are failures of patience, not of kindness. The opposite of kindness is worse than both of them together. The opposite of kindness is the horrible sin of envy.

"When we are envious we want what others have. Because we want what others have, we despise what we ourselves have. We *must* despise it, we can't *help* despising it – envy sees to that. And what do we have that we despise? Oh, nothing much. Eternal life amid the incalculable pleasures and treasures of Heaven – that's all. So much wiser to trade it in for *this* neighbor's new truck or *that* neighbor's new hairdo, don't you think? Wouldn't wearing those perfect curls be worth burning eternally? What? You disagree?

"Then what you *really* want is the humility to accept what Jesus already *gave* you when you promised him your life – the humility to say *I have already been given a joyous life eternal and I will not burn with envy for any lesser thing.*

"When our humility has defeated our envy we feel our kindness shining through. We see it in the faces of those who are kind to us. We see it in the hands of Nurse Brankovitch who bandaged eighteen skinned knees this morning alone. We hear it in the voices of the New Montgomery County Gospel Singers who sang their hearts out for us on stage six all afternoon. And this evening we felt it in our mouths and in our stomachs as we accepted the delicious victuals so kindly offered to one and all by our new friends, the Pilgrims of the New Wilderness. Truly, with kindness come all good things, and with humility comes kindness."

I felt heads turning to look behind me and I looked too and I beheld for the first time the glowing face of the prophet Boronzee, his features gripped in a rapture of kindness and bathed in the pure sweet light of grace. And when I turned back I saw other faces looking back at me, ordinary faces, unilluminated faces, lean faces and bloated faces, many of them still smeared with hamburger condiments and all of them twisted from the strain of exuding willful kindness from every greasy pore. And I knew from their stares that I had been chosen and my own visage glowed with the light of true conversion and meat-benevolence, and I smiled at every one of the wretched suckers, and I thought I could keep on fooling them forever. It was a difficult thing to look away from my adorers and back up to the rest of the sermon but I did it, and if this story is going to make any sense to you then you had better hear what I heard.

"So we've seen that just as the first Reverend Williston Hour was brought to you by Paco's Tacoroni Restaurants so many years ago, so these six great and holy virtues are brought to you by the seventh virtue we call humility. But is just knowing that enough? If it isn't then we are just as far as ever from knowing how to keep our promise to Jesus. Can *knowing* that the essential virtue of humility will save us be enough to *bring* us to it, or is even humility as elusive as the other holy virtues when we bend down and try to grasp it?

"Friends, yes it is. Indeed, humility is the hardest of all the virtues to just reach out and grasp. But there's good news, friends. The *power* of humility was only the *first* of the two secrets Jesus brought for us this evening, and the second secret *will* save us all. Here it is, friends, here's what Jesus wants us to know tonight.

"He has a program we can follow, an easy to learn and easy to practice *method* that is *guaranteed* to summon humility and put it to work for us. His program is *The Solution* to every problem that stands between us and an eternal place at His Table. And it's so uniquely simple that it *ensures* our place on the very first airlift home, because anyone, anyone *at all* who wants to take that trip can learn and *master* it right now on this very night right here in Louisville Kentucky.

"Friends, this great program is called Obedience. Now we've always known that Obedience to Jesus is what will get us home, but sometimes it seems like much too hard a way to go. Jesus told us *If ye love me, keep my commandments.* We listen to these divine words and they make sense to us. Of course they do, they're the words of God Himself! *If ye love me, keep my commandments.* And we *do* love Him, and we *understand* these words, so why can't we *obey?* It ought to be simple, so why is it so hard? If we obey Him we live joyfully forever. If we disobey Him we die eternally in torment. *Why do we who love Jesus find it so fatally hard to obey Him?*

"Friends, the answer is simple. It is the simplest thing in the universe. It is so simple that it has eluded great minds throughout history. Great minds are easy to fool. They're easy to fool because they think the world is complicated. They are confused by all the complications that come directly from their own great minds. But the world is simple. God made it for us, and He would not have made the world so complicated that only a few great minds could understand it. He made a simple world with simple answers to all our questions and then He *told* us what those answers are. *If ye love me, keep my commandments.* But sometimes we can't obey Him, and because God made a simple world for us there's a simple reason why, and here it is: *we can't obey Him because we're out of practice.*

"Say it to yourselves again. We're out of practice. We can't play baseball like we used to because *we're out of practice.* We can't play the saxophone like we used to because *we're out of practice.* We can't obey Jesus like we *need* to because *we're out of practice.*

"Think about it, Friends, think with all your might! We're out of practice. What does that mean? When we're out of practice in our saxophone playing we can no longer play *Amazing Grace* as we used to, but we are not out of practice in *Amazing Grace,* we still *love* that song and remember every note. We are out of practice playing the saxophone. We have lost our command of the *instrument* and it no longer plays *Amazing Grace* for us as it should. When we're out of practice in obeying Jesus, we are not out of practice in loving Him. That could *never* happen to us, we're Christians, we will *always* love Jesus. What we are out of practice in is *Obedience.* We have lost our command of our holy *instrument of Obedience* and our attempts to obey Him no longer work as they must, as our eternal lives depend on them to work.

"When our skill at playing the saxophone grows rusty from disuse and we want it back again, we take the instrument down from its shelf and we begin to practice it again and in due course our power over the saxophone returns to us. When our skill at playing the holy instrument of Obedience grows rusty, also from disuse, we must do the same thing. We must *practice our Obedience,* we must take the holy instrument of Obedience down from its shelf and practice it every day, practice it *throughout* every day, practice it every minute of our lives from this hour forward.

"How do we practice on the holy instrument of Obedience? We practice it by *doing what we are told.* That's the secret. That's the amazing secret that Jesus wants us to learn tonight! We live in a great country, Friends, the only country on this planet where our place in eternity is safe if we always do what we are told. Think about it! There are countries where we would be *told* to limit the number of children we have, *told* to worship the false god of the state, *told* to deny Jesus Himself. How could anyone practice Obedience in such places and still find themselves in Heaven when they leave? Let us pray for those poor people, Friends, let us never forget their misery and the darkness of their lives, but let us *also* never forget that we live in the one place on earth where Obedience means safety to our souls and to our eternal happiness, the one place, the *only* place where we can never for the blink of an eye run out of safe and holy opportunities to practice our Obedience.

"Yes, Friends, safe *and* holy. Now, we may wonder how it can be *holy* to obey our bosses at work when they order us to do something we're sure is a mistake. It *is* a holy thing to do because what we're *really* doing is perfecting our command of the instrument of Obedience, so it will be fit and ready when we need it to fight our way into Heaven. Think about it. A young student saxophonist must learn to play simple songs he hates, stupid songs, ugly songs, the *Mary-Had-a-Little-Lamb* songs and the *Old-McDonald-Had-a-Farm* songs he outgrew long ago, when all the while he yearns to wail out *Amazing Grace.* But after a few years of practicing those *Row-Row-Row-Your Boat* songs night after night, suddenly beautiful music begins to flow from his horn, suddenly he can play *I'm on My Knees in the Chapel on Prom Night Because Jesus Asked Her First* as it deserves to be played, as he has always dreamed of playing it. Just so, Friends, just so will the glorious melody of Humility one day begin to flow from *our* holy instrument of Obedience, if we but practice, practice, practice diligently enough on the simple scales and homely tunes that our worldly life in this great land offers us every day. And after the heavenly strains of Humility have begun to flow from us, next will come the harmonious chords of chastity, of temperance, of charity, of diligence, of patience and of kindness, and then, Friends, then: Heaven itself is ours. All because we have finally, finally, after thousands of years, learned the only lesson God has ever required us to master – the lesson of Obedience.

"Let us pray."

As the Reverend Williston's familiar, comforting benediction rolled on, every soul in the campground mouthed every word of it – after you've heard it six times a day for years and years there's not much you can do but recite it with him or scream and I was long over screaming at it, screaming at it was how I completed my fall from grace in the orphanage. While the words spoke themselves on our lips we were free to pursue our own prayers and reflections. At some point the lights came slowly on and with a smile and a wave Reverend Williston receded into the Big Dipper, but most of us sat a few moments longer to bask in the awe of the moment.

As for me, I sat there watching the campers in their basking and I studied the God that Reverend Williston was building all around me.

The fool hath said in his heart, there is *no God.*

The fool wasn't watching his neighbors very closely. The fool never saw Pastor Mike's sadistic little bully god play with me inside its ant farm. The fool never saw Major Joe's drill sergeant god run us up and down the obstacle course till we puked in submission, never heard it order us to die for it when someday Major Joe would pass the word. The fool completely missed the two or three different versions of the god of infinite cruelty that I hoped I'd just left behind me on the Upper Peninsula. I can understand the fool missing various gentle and undemonstrative gods of philosophy and compassion that I've encountered from time to time because sometimes it has taken me hours and even days to see them working quietly inside their authors and I know I probably only saw them in the end because I already knew that *some* god had to be in there since some god always is. But to miss those others – that isn't *foolishness,* it's utter blindness, and it's a blindness that I've often thought about. I think it comes from accepting the infantile notion that gods aren't something people make, or the other one that holds that any god a person could make is somehow not *real.* Those are two of the most baseless ideas that anyone can think and still be said to have a mind. Leonardo da Vinci *made* the Mona Lisa so *therefore* it was never *real?* I get it, I really do, but I don't *want* to get it and I swear I will never want to get it.

So now the fool would be missing this new god growing all around me on the campground lawn. He wouldn't see its power increasing as, worshipper by worshipper, it strangled the few remaining seeds they carried of every worthwhile thing that humanity has ever done for itself. I know who my enemies are and that god is sure to grow up to be a big one, but the fool is the greater enemy by far because the fool stands by and lets it eat its fill.

The fool hath said in his heart: that was Psalm 14:1 by the way, from the Geneva Bible. It happens coincidentally that on paper the words in the King James Version look identical but that's only because you can't hear them. They are the same but they are not the same. The King James Version is recited – I insist on this word – by the Reverend Emancipus Healy, late of the New Bethlehem Church of God in Christ somewhere in Georgia. As far as I know he never actually recited the whole book for posterity but he left more than enough recordings for me to sample in the sound lab. I was maybe 15 then and still "in good odor" at the orphanage as I once heard a Unitarian refugee from Connecticut put it, and in my free time they let me play with scripture in the sound lab all I wanted. It took me eleven months to complete the Emancipus Healy King James Version and parts of it still give me goose pimples. *The FOOL hath said in his heart there is NO God.* It roars, it thunders. The Geneva Bible is *spoken* in the plain and lovely voice of a woman, in a style so simple and direct that many who have no ear for these things would say it's no style at all. Getting her right took me the next two years and I barely finished her before the sound lab went on the list of privileges I was to be forbidden forever. She started as a sixty/forty mix of an old-time 2D actress named Katherine Hepburn and believe it or not a Frenchwoman named Piaf, who as far as I know never said a word in English – but when you're building a voice the words you build it from don't matter all that much. I let the Hepburn lady say the words and used the Piaf voice to fill them up. They made for a good start that told me I was on the right track. I cannot remember my mother's voice in any usual sense but I'm pretty sure I was rebuilding it.

Item. When I was building her I could always tell instantly whether I was getting closer or further away from something I wanted.

Item. Even now hearing her read Ecclesiastes is the most restful, calming thing I can do for myself.

Item. That voice has driven me to do things nobody can explain in any other way.

I have a third Bible nestled under my ear. It's the New American Dispensationalist Bible for Everyday People. For Psalm 14:1 it says *Stupid people don't believe in God.* The voice that says it is the voice that came from the factory. It's not hard to imagine that the voice didn't like it much in the factory because he always sounds just a little pissed off, any book, chapter or verse you pick. I used to wonder whether Pastor Mike liked that pissed-off tone and copied it on purpose or whether it's something that happens to you when you become a New American Dispensationalist preacher. I kept it buried in the top of my neck to remind me of how things were back there in case I ever forgot them but I've learned that I don't really need it to remember all the wretched moments I could ever want. Sometimes I play it anyway and lately when I do it sometimes makes me think of Boronzee.

The rest of the week went by mostly as we'd hoped it would – I won't say as we planned because we couldn't really be sure we'd pull off all of the bridge-building stuff. After Reverend Williston's plug for the Pilgrims of the New

Wilderness eatery, more churches than we'd ever hoped to sound out took it upon themselves to sound us out instead. That makes sense, especially when you reflect that practicing your obedience usually means practicing your sucking up as well, but it doesn't mean we weren't frantically busy setting up contact protocols with all our new friends. We put in early mornings and late nights, and after we became official paragons of virtue all the money we didn't have to spend on tithes anymore we spent on more food than we'd ever planned to cook. At times the boys had a hard time maintaining the true face of humble kindness now that the whole camp showed up every night for supper. Even people who'd eaten their fill at their own campsites wandered over for an ear of corn just to get a taste of its invisible Holy Spirit sauce, and they all felt the need to add their blessings to Reverend Williston's. We had to work hard reminding ourselves that we were only fagged out and ready to drop because we'd already been far more successful than we'd dreamed we could be.

I don't know about any of the others but I grew intensely curious about how much of our unexpected success was really unexpected. I couldn't ask anyone but Boronzee. Thumper would know but he'd feel equally bad about telling and not telling, and I didn't want to do that to him so I bided my time. Sometime during the afternoon of the third day the three of us were out of earshot of anyone else and I put the question.

"Boss, I'm wondering if you were every bit as surprised as I was when Reverend Williston put in the good word for us."

Boronzee grinned wickedly. "Floppy, you have a devious mind."

"Yes I do. Also it's a sunny day and I hear the stock market is up and look, I'm still wondering."

"You want a yes or no."

"Either one would do."

"I can see how it would but it wouldn't be honest. We greased people. We had hopes. Nothing was certain. As it turned out the hopes we had weren't quite big enough, they were more like, some of the right elders would walk around the camp saying nice things about us where other right people would know they were supposed to hear them. And we still had a lot of work to do here if that didn't happen and I didn't want to set everyone up for feeling disappointed so Thumper and I kept it to ourselves."

It didn't exactly satisfy me but I couldn't figure out why so I let it drop. I'd have had to let it drop anyway because it was time to go back to hustling the campers, and we all stayed busy doing that till the end of the week. But at odd moments it still nagged.

I suppose that from what I've told you about us you've already realized that our long-term plan was to someday park the bus and turn our roving brotherhood into a no fooling, firmly planted, out in the open certified and fully protected, no-questions-ever-asked-again *church*, to be plunked down in the middle of somewhere pleasant on a big parcel of fallow Lammas land where maybe a bowling alley or a VFW hall once grew wild. You probably won't be the least surprised to learn that that year's working name for the project was the New Pilgrim Wilderness Fellowship, nor that we had come to Louisville to gather soon-to-be-ancient fragments of what we hoped would become our respectable past, much in the way that a thousand years ago we'd have bartered with returning Crusaders for martyrs' noses and pieces of the True Cross. Having gone this far I may as well paint you the rest of the mural, even though by now you can see it as well as we ever did: how Bishop Boronzee would navigate the rarefied ecumenical politics and also their secular offshoots while Pastor Thumper knocked 'em dead on Sunday mornings and Co-pastor Floppy presided over the most prestigious and select little Bible Study group ever to meet of a Wednesday night; how a bewildering number of curates and canons and deacons and presbyters, all of them seeming to have somehow known one another since childhood, would occupy a correspondingly bewildering variety of arcane ecclesiastical offices; how the pews would be packed with only the luckiest of the locals, but only after they had pulled every string they knew how to pull to get admitted to the congregation; how this flock would brag to all and sundry of the rectitude of our pageants and the orthodoxy of our doctrines and most of all of the pirate's treasure that would fill those little yellow envelopes every week; how the prettiest maidens in the shire would scurry forth to marry us, each with her father's villeins and serfs dragging her dowry in her wake, and how said maidens would retain their youthful figures while raising enormous broods of secure and happy children who would never once cast a single worried eye on their futures and only very rarely wonder why no grandparents or aunts or cousins from their fathers' sides ever came to visit them.

It's one thing to have a dream like that and know it's a dream. It's very different once it starts to get real, and it started to get real in Louisville. Of course it was still years off in the future but now we were working directly on it, on the dream itself, and not just on the things we knew we had to do to get there, the ugly, scary things that would be past and done with once the dream was real. And I still had to go out and do those things and I had had it up to here with the Reverend Williston and his flock of fat pink zombies and I couldn't shake the feeling that they and especially the he who was really an it were turning out to have a bigger place in our dream than I'd ever considered – not considered *possible*, just never considered *at all*.

I thought about it more and more every day and when I was all packed up at the end of the last day I let Boronzee walk me to my car and I brought it up again.

"Remember I asked you if you expected we'd get this tight with Williston?"

"I do indeed. Still have questions about how it happened?"

"I suppose not. I've got a different question. Do you hate what you see here as much as I do?"

He looked a bit surprised and started to answer so I rushed ahead.

"Because I always figured you did but this horror show has seriously creeped me out. And here we are getting friendlier and friendlier with them and we're doing it on purpose. And it's not just us doing it, it's coming from the other side too. So I'm feeling insecure and I need you to tell me you hate this every bit as much as I do."

We were out from under the awnings now and onto the fringe of the parking lot and the illusion of being in Williston's world vanished abruptly with the shade. It was early evening but it was still at least a hundred and five and since most people were waiting for dark to make the trek to their cars we didn't have too hard a time staying out of everyone's earshot.

"I'd love to reassure you Floppy but the truth is I've been way too busy trying not to give away how thrilled I am and it hasn't occurred to me to spare these people much thought. The kind of thought you're talking about I mean."

"Understand, I don't have a problem riding any horse we have to ride."

"That's good. *But.*"

"*But* I was hoping to get off this particular horse someday."

"And now you're thinking that maybe we won't. You're thinking that maybe we'll ride it all the way."

"Yes I am. That's exactly what I'm thinking. I can see the sense in it but I can also see *that.*"

I pointed at *that.* *That* was a melting family of five, wallowing hopelessly toward some distant car and dragging things through the burnt up grass. One of the things they dragged was a poster of the Reverend Williston up in the sky. Off to one side Jesus looked on approvingly, but he was much shorter than the Reverend Williston.

"Floppy, we've always known we'll need a congregation. Most congregations look a lot like this one."

"And I've just seen this one trade in their old god for the god of do everything you're told to do every minute for the rest of your life and they don't even know they made the trade. So what kind of god are *we* going to sell them?"

"The god that's in the book of course." He smiled. "The one true god who changes on every page."

We could see my car now and I used the activator to open the doors and start the air going. Did he get me or did he not? When, before, had he ever not got me?

I said, "I remember a speech you made us. It was the best speech I ever heard. You told us how once people made gods for everything, every good thing, every bad thing. Gods of wine and gods of rage and gods of sex and dancing and thunder and war, and most of all gods who loved people and made them happy and other gods who hated them and made them suffer and die. You told us how these gods fought among themselves like the world fights. You showed us how that all made sense. You showed us how people who thought this way really were *thinking* because in those times we didn't have any other facts to think with.

"Then you told us how people got just a little smarter and ruined it all. How people realized there couldn't really be all those squabbling little gods and wouldn't it make sense if there was just one of them, one big god who did it all, like there's one big world and one big nature and one big sun and one big moon. You told us how ever since that day nobody has been able to figure that god out. Nobody knows if it wants us to be happy or miserable or dead or smart or stupid or kind or vicious because at one time or another it seems to want it all. And then you told how most people don't even try to answer that question. How they pick the one part of that god that makes the most sense to them and hold onto it and throw the rest away, and how after they do that they'll do whatever their little piece of god says to do from then on."

If you can't tell, I was pretty worked up by then. We'd reached my car so I stopped and took a deep breath and asked him one more time.

"So. It all works out for us. We're all where we want to be which is wonderful but also puts us in the god selling business. These people, these zombie idiots, are filling our pews and we're telling them what kind of god they're going home with because we already know that they *will* buy the one we sell them. And I can't get that off my mind and I want you to tell me what kind of a god it will be."

He thought for a second and then he smiled. "I suppose," he said, "they can have any God they want."

I thought, *Oh no no no no no. Oh no no they won't. Not in my damn church they won't.*

And I thought, *This is what happens to smart people when they forget that the gods in people's hearts are the very realest things they own.*

And I thought, *This is a good, smart man starting to turn mean and stupid before my eyes.*

And I thanked the God Who Serves the Godless which is the name of the god that lives within me. I thanked her that our pilgrimage was over and it was time for me to drive out into the wilderness again. And I said my goodbyes and got my orders and said I'd be in touch and I got in my car and drove.

Second Chronicles

If I shut the heaven that there be no rain, or if I command the grasshopper to devour the land, or if I send pestilence among my people, If my people, among whom my Name is called upon, do humble themselves, and pray, and seek my presence, and turn from their wicked ways, then will I hear in heaven, and be merciful to their sin, and will heal their land: Then mine eyes shall be open and mine ears attent unto the prayer made in this place. –Second Chronicles 7:13-15, the Geneva translation.

Now that we had done it with Hammaker and friends and seen that it was possible we went looking for the big money every time. I understood the principle of the thing but I didn't have to like everything it led to. The principle was that one big score could take five years off the dream and three of them could make it happen. I had no argument with that – who could? – and I saw how a man with Boronzee's responsibilities would be wrong to play it any other way. In a way I had already gotten used to telling people we couldn't help them if they couldn't come up with the cash. Sometimes it was up to me to do it because sometimes we didn't know for sure that they could pay what they'd promised until I showed up and asked for the cash. But, as I said, I only got used to it *in a way* because you have no idea how rotten it feels to say that and walk away. When I used to have to say it I had to say it because it was true: we were a shoe-string operation and we were dead if we ever went broke. But now I was supposed to say it to people who had just enough cash that we'd have taken them a month before, and sometimes I said it and felt terrible, and sometimes I didn't say it and felt worse than when I did because the only people who had never betrayed me expected me to say it and walk away. This put me in a surly frame of mind that I didn't shake for months. I got used to it and sometimes I didn't remember that it was there but I didn't shake it.

i

I did a couple of quick and easy jobs and then Thumper Socialed me to meet him in Boston so he could brief me on a pickup in the area. Twice a year Harvard throws a kind of job fair on the site of the now-abolished apostate imposter-university of the same name. Paid-up students like us can rent caps and gowns and get holographed in front of the last remaining ivy-covered wall. Then we can kiss recruiters' asses for two days. It's all a scam since no church really hires that way, so your time is your own and nobody notices who you talk to. At least that was the theory but it was the week after Thanksgiving and while there may be worse times to be in Boston there are also better ones. It rained, it snowed, it rained again, then it all froze hard and anybody standing outside talking would have stood out like a woman's knees in church. All the indoor party places were too loud and too crowded to hear anyone unless they were shouting at you (which everyone was) and what we had to talk about didn't go too well with shouting. Finally we took my car and locked into the Old Boston by Car tour, twenty miles at five miles an hour, but at least this way you get your own private holos of whatever they had to bury to build the thing you're crawling past. Plus if you turn the sound up you get the authentically reconstructed voice of Paul Revere telling you all about it, especially the part about the tea, and you just can't put a price on that.

This job I was there to be briefed on was unusual in a few ways that taken together meant I had to meet Thumper in the flesh. First, there were props to be handed over. Second, the passenger wasn't trying to leave the country. What he wanted was a ride to a private clinic in Freer New Hampshire, where the word *private* is a redundancy. The place specialized in replacing faces and not necessarily the deformed or burnt-off ones they spoke so touchingly about on the Media. Quite a few of the faces they replaced were perfectly fine in some ways but inconvenient to their owners in others. Since there are a lot of ways for your face to become inconvenient the place was forever denying hurtful, baseless rumors about the

71

kinds of patients it took, which was of course the best advertising it could get. It was called, not very imaginatively I thought, Freer New Hampshire Facial Re-imagination. FNHFR, as they liked their friends to call them, also did some things they didn't advertise much that weren't entirely about faces, and it was for one of those specialties that the passenger wanted to go there.

This brought Thumper to the last way the job was unusual, which was that the passenger was on the Connection, had been Connected for nineteen years and yet was totally unmonitored and therefore couldn't have been more illegal. Probably more from a screw-up than from any kind of scheme he–

But Thumper wouldn't be able to finish that thought for a while because I had freaked. The whole *point* of being Connected (I ranted) is that you're never *alone*, you're even being sampled while you *sleep* which after all is how the Roll Keepers know you're *dead* when you *die*, and they know where you *are* every second, and they know who you're Connected *with*, and what you *see* and *hear* and *feel* and *smell*, and *part*, a big part, of what they'd be seeing and hearing if we took this lunatic commission would be *me*, and what I *say*, and where we *go*, and how we *get* there, and every little trick I pull along the *way*–

Thumper, grinning like he really had me this time, held up his hand, summoned every ounce of fey, disappointed, murmuring meekness he could fake, and said, "Well of course dear Floppy we *do* have a plan."

At which masterpiece I surrendered and said, "Okay, Thumper, you're going to tell it and I know I can't stop you. But that doesn't mean you don't have to make it good."

Thumper said, "Oh, it's good Floppy. You can't imagine how good it is till you hear it. So sit back and enjoy your country's history and I'll tell you a little story."

We were only at the Faneuil Hall Megatower so Lord knows we had plenty of time. I waved him onward and sat back as he suggested but with, I hoped, a look on my face that said I did not expect to believe a single word I heard.

Thumper leered agreeably. "Once upon a time, dear Floppy, the Connection was invented, and people started using it, and right away we had the Head Police – because, of course, how could we not have them? But we don't have them anymore and do you know why that is? No, it's a rhetorical question. We don't have them anymore because Connectioned people look goofy while they're Connectioned-up and after a while they look goofy all the time. And what good is an undercover headcop who looks goofy, and what good is a headcop sitting at a desk who *is* goofy. Which it turned out they all were pretty damn soon since the reason Connectioned people look so goofy is because they really do become goofy through and through and being goofy they're useless for being cops of any kind. So they shipped all the headcops, the goofy ones and the ones who weren't quite goofy yet, off to one of the usual places and they stopped making new headcops and closed the headcop office and that's why we don't have the Head Police anymore.

"But for as long as we had them we had to have two ways people could be Connectioned. Ordinary idiots who sign up of course go on the Roll, and the junk in their brains tells the Roll Keepers all those things you whined about, grid coordinates, hormone levels, but mainly it copies them with every feed you put out and take in and *that's* how you are monitored, and because it's good to have *some* people monitored because then *their* eyes and ears are *your* eyes and ears, the Connection has stayed legal even though it does what it does to people. But *also* when you get Connectioned and go on the Roll everybody else who's Connectioned can see you there, which after all is kind of the point, isn't it? You *see* somebody you want to get inside – you see them because there they are on the Roll – and you go knock knock and then you're in their heads unless they unConnection with you which if they do it the Roll Keepers know about too. But the Head Police couldn't *go* on the Roll, could they? Because then people could see *them* and go knock knock and get inside the Head Police's heads. And *they* meaning the Head Police wouldn't be able to stop *them* meaning everybody else unless they unConnectioned with everybody else on the Roll, and then who would be left to police?

"And that's why there had to be another way people could be Connectioned, another way just for the Head Police.

So in those days Connections-Iz-You made two kinds of brainware, one kind for selling to just anybody and also a special Head Police model that did not go on the Roll and did not send out those perpetual feeds to the Roll Keepers. And *that's* the kind of brainware Connections-Iz-You mistakenly installed in our passenger lo these nineteen years ago. Because of which he can see and use the Roll as well as anyone, but nobody who's not Connected-up to him can see him or anything he does. And that, in a nutshell, is everything."

Thumper sat back to smirk while I seethed.

I took it point by point. "Not so fast. For nineteen years this freak has been walking around with modified brainware which is a death sentence, right? And nobody noticed. How is that possible?"

The smirk intensified. "You'll love this. It turns out that the Roll Keepers genuinely believe the Roll to be infallible. So much so that as far as they're concerned if you're not on the Roll you're not Connected, and if you're not Connected then you're no concern of theirs. But, and here's the good part, everyone else *also* believes that the Roll is perfect and trusts the Roll Keepers to look after it. So all they're concerned about is people who disappear from the Roll. That's why they check to make sure you're dead when you stop sending and that's why they make you dead if you aren't dead when they get there. Because what *does* worry them is people getting their brainware altered so it stops feeding the Roll Keepers, which has been tried but I wouldn't recommend it. Since they know exactly where you were when you went under the anesthetic and all that. But not our boy. They won't know a thing about him when he gets dis-Connected."

"Oh. When he gets dis-Connected. So that's what he's going to do."

"He's counting on it and so are we. You're taking him north to get dis-Connected, which it turns out is one of FNHFR's less well-known specialties. Which I find fascinating. Because in theory they have to report the death of any Connected patients to the Roll Keepers and then they have to prove it, and if anybody stopped sending their feeds while on their premises and the Roll Keepers didn't right away get a report and a holo of their head split open with the serial number in plain sight there would be paratroops and commandos and a bloodbath in the recovery room, Freer New Hampshire or not. Because the Roll Keepers will go to war rather than tolerate illegal Connections. Since this would be well known to FNHFR and to any prospective candidate for dis-Connection surgery, it's kind of hard not to conclude that FNHFR is prepared to participate in illegality, which I find absolutely shocking. Imagine, *illegality* in Freer New Hampshire, the self-declared country within a country that likes to brag that it acknowledges nobody's laws at all…"

"But no such problems for our guy."

"None at all, except of course it's also death for any doctor caught removing brainware. Which is why FNHFR advertises their services so discreetly."

"So how do they usually get around the problem?"

"Well, Floppy, I didn't ask, but if *I* were them, I'd kill somebody else and split his head open. Then I'd remove the brainware from my patient and shove it into the mess I'd made in the other guy's head and I'd holo it to the Roll Keepers in the usual way. That's what I'd do. If I lived in Freer New Hampshire I mean."

I was getting dangerously close to believing he had all the answers. I got grimmer and grimmer.

"Okay, then tell me this. Our boy's not on the Roll. How do people Connection with *him?*"

"Now that's what I asked, Floppy, and it turns out that it's very simple. It seems that your *address*, I mean if you're Connectioned of course, your address, the code that other people Connection with, is in your own brainware. And there's a shortcut to it on the Roll, so when people see you on the Roll they can ask for you and poof, they get your address. But they also get it when you Connection with *them*, which means that anybody you've ever Connectioned with can Connection you back. And you can even send your own shortcuts to people on your Social. Apparently our boy did this all the time."

"And nobody you're Connectioned with knows you're not feeding the Roll Keepers?"

"That's right. Because you can't see your own feeds or else you'd have infinite feedback, and nobody you're

Connected with can see any more than you do."

"But when I pick him up anybody he's Connected with will be sure-enough monitored, which means that everything they see, hear, smell or touch is going out on *some* feed and possibly on hundreds of them if our guy is popular enough and there I'll be and—"

On and on, feebler and feebler as we went. We were all the way to the Old North Church Arcade before I ran out of objections and gave in. And *then* he went back to mocking Freer New Hampshire, where nobody who doesn't have at least one serious offshore stash of hard money can even *visit*. But by then I knew he was only trying to provoke me and I let it go. As far as he could see I let it go. But lowest common denominators have been my lifelong study and Freer New Hampshire was one place I'd always promised myself I'd never even think about trying.

This fool was named Liam Gallagher and amazingly for someone who'd been Connected for nineteen years he lived alone. Most of them can't do for themselves after five or ten years – living many other people's lives in your own body will do that to you if you let it. He obviously hadn't let it. He must have forced himself to eat his own boring food when he could have had forty ten-course dinners at the Ritz every day. He must have made himself spend time in the bathroom and take out the trash. Maybe he was one of the few who had to work for a living and had found a way to do it – that could teach you to stay in your own space just a little I suppose, though why your Connections would want to feel with you while you wash dishes or smell with you while you clean toilets or participate in anything else the Connected can barely do is beyond me. One thing I was sure of was that after nineteen years he no longer had his own sex, but maybe the Media exaggerate even about that – but those videos of four-hundred pound men in diapers lying in rows on the Connection Hostel floor, twitching and moaning with their useless eyes bulging – surely they're not faked. Nobody in the world would be sick or cynical enough to fake *that*, and besides it's known that a third of the people who sign up to be Connected are registered exhibitionists so *somebody* must be tuning in to them. I swear, if I'd had to pick him up at a hostel I wouldn't have done it, no matter what anyone was paying.

Liam lived in a pretty nice – nice for what it was – apartment house in Bedford that turned out to be called Connection Manors, which explained a lot. Mainly, how his neighbors could not be too creeped out to tolerate him when he meandered past them with that tilty-headed zombie stare. Two of them were standing in the lobby when I went in. One was facing the door leaning forward a little and her lips were moving to some song that of course I couldn't hear. The other was facing the elevator with a sack of groceries in his arms. He'd been ready to push the button – it was an old building with an old elevator that had kept its buttons – when someone had Connectioned-up with him and in spite of the fact that maybe he'd been promised kayak trips down the Grand Canyon or front row seats at the Red Sox simulation or who the hell knows what, he was now engrossed in somebody's cat sniffing the aspidistra.

I took the steps two at a time just to put those freaks behind me and more or less quick-marched to apartment 26. I saw that the door was an inch ajar as arranged, took a deep precautionary breath, held it and stepped inside. The place was only halfway a mess and had been dusted sometime during the year. This was encouraging. He was sitting across the room from me, facing the wall as he'd been told to. I clapped my hands. I don't know what kind of voiceprint they can get from a cough or a harrumph but I could have got a good one once and I wasn't taking chances. He raised his head maybe an inch, held up a hand, and a faltering wheezy dead flat voice said, "Look Caden I'll catch you later but I got to go. Unless you want to help me take a dump." He kept his hand up. I let my breath out and took a small one to replace it. The smell wasn't that bad, mostly just musty and no trace of body stink which since I'd be in the car with him half the day had worried me. He let his hand drop. The voice said, "I'm alone now. I mean we are." Did I believe him? It didn't matter if I did or didn't, I was already busted if this was a trap and if he'd lie about that then it was a trap.

I said, "Don't turn around."

The voice said, "I know. They told me."

I gritted my teeth and walked up behind him. He was a skinny guy which is one of the two ways they get and it looked from the back that he could be the 38 years old he was supposed to be. He needed a haircut but he hadn't needed it more than a few months and his clothes seemed to fit. So long as I didn't have to see his face I thought I might get through it.

I pulled the Williston Goggles and the noise-cancelling earmuffs out and got ready to slip them on him because once he stood up he was *not* going to see anything but the Reverend and he was *not* going to hear anything that didn't come from inside his own damn head. But then I lowered them and asked him the question I couldn't stop asking myself.

"Liam, why did you do it?"

He was still for a couple of seconds and then the voice said, "To have friends." There was just a hint of incredulity in the voice then, like it wanted to add *Who wouldn't know that?*

I said, "That's not what I meant. I meant why didn't you turn yourself in and holler when you didn't see yourself on the Roll? They wouldn't have done anything to you if you'd told them right away."

The voice said, "Yes they would have. They would have taken it out. And it was just so wonderful. I couldn't give it back. I put it off. I put everything off. Then later…the business. After I had the business…" He let it lay there like the rest was too obvious to say.

I said, "What business, Liam?"

He stretched out his left arm and pointed to a heap of junk in the corner. He didn't turn his head and I give him credit for that. I walked over and looked down on a dusty black box and a tangled dusty pile of wires and electrodes. Electrodes in gloves for making your hands feel what somebody else is touching. Electrode-sandals to fool your feet into thinking they're doing foot things. Sticky electrodes for the rest of your body, slimy electrodes for shoving up your nose, and finally the cap that's one big electrode for overriding your eyes and ears.

I stared at it till I thought I understood what I was staring at and I said, "What kind of *business* is that, Liam? Who pays you to feel what they feel, and why would you need that gear at all once you're Connectioned?"

It took him maybe ten minutes to tell it. It felt like days. Twice the voice stopped in mid-word, the head snapped up, and he was Connectioned-up again. Each time he told his rude lie and was soon left alone to his defecating in private. The hardest part for him seemed to be his amazement that I didn't already know how *the business* works.

The black box was a sensory storage unit that held petabyte after petabyte of feeds that Liam himself had broadcast. It had recorded them in the usual way, from a Connection Receiver just like the one in Liam's skull. Liam had bought it on credit so he could play parts of his weekend walks back to himself during the week. He'd hop off the back of the garbage truck he rode around on all day, half-walk, half-run home to his apartment, put on his electrodes while still stinking of overripe trash and until he fell asleep in his chair he'd be back in his mountains feeling the breeze and smelling the pines.

His mountains were the southern part of the White Mountains of New Hampshire (in the merely ordinarily free part of New Hampshire) and they were *his* because he'd been hiking them since he was twelve. He knew trails and streams only the locals knew. He knew how to look at them in summer, and in the fall when people drove by in convoys to look at the colors but only from what to Liam was an unacceptable distance. He knew where to look in winter and in the spring when the ice and snow were halfway melted and choked the streams so the water had to race. He could walk all day because he'd been walking there all day for years, and once he got Connectioned and bought his box he would Connection-up with it while he walked. Then he could go home and put on his electrodes and do his walk all over again while sucking engine fumes through his window, which overlooked the busiest, ugliest street in Bedford.

He found out about the business when he got a spam Connection from somebody offering scuba diving in the Caribbean for only a few thousand dollars a minute. At that price he could afford to buy an hour on his lunch break and since he'd never gone scuba diving, much less in forbidden waters, he took a chance and Socialed them the cash.

Afterwards he thought to himself how pleasant it would be if he could afford to visit new places all day long. After he'd been thinking that for a couple of days it dawned on him that maybe other people who felt that way might like to go walking in the mountains. He asked around and found a spam agency that quoted him a price. He saved his pay for six months – no more scuba diving or sailing, sailing was something else he'd found that he liked a lot – and then he retired from the sanitation business and spent all of every day electroded-up and reliving walks in the mountains while his customers listened in until the shortcut they'd rented timed out. On the weekends he took off the electrodes and went back to the mountains for real, recording new walks as he went. He did this for three years. Maybe two – he could have been mistaken about three. Anyway he did it for a while but then, sitting all week as he did, he started getting winded on his hikes and who's going to pay to feel that? Also his agent had complained from the start that the feed wasn't up every day and although that had always annoyed the hell out of Liam, suddenly he saw the sense in it. He felt he was growing up and taking responsibility even if it did mean being wired to a box twelve hours every day of the year.

In the evenings he went out, walked the kinks off and ate pizza or Chinese standing up. He didn't Connection so much with his friends anymore because they were used to all-day hookups like normally Connectioned-up people have and they started to see him as an opportunist and kind of an intruder. But he found he didn't really care and made a few casual friends who didn't mind doing their Connectioning in occasional brief visits. He told me as if no one would ever believe it that his Connection was probably idle for at least two or three hours a day.

"So Liam – why did you stop?"

The voice was shocked into silence. Then a shaky finger pointed to the box and the voice said, "It broke."

It was as simple as that. One day his box stopped working and when he had someone check it out they told him all his walks in the mountains had leaked out into the ether and would never leak back in. Didn't I see? His life was over.

"Okay, you lost your business but why get yourself dis-

Connectioned?"

I thought he really wanted to turn and face me then and had to work hard to stop himself. The voice, weepy with frustration at my obtuseness, hissed it out. "So I can go back to the mountains of course. Look at me. How I can go back to the mountains like I am? You ought to know that. You can't be in the mountains when you're like me."

I knew the rest because Thumper had told me and a pathetic little tale it was, but I made Liam tell it again anyway just to hear how our act had worked on him. I said he must have gone broke pretty fast so how could he pay to be dis-Connectioned? He said it was all because of a great humanitarian, a great doctor. He told me how he'd been hinting around here and there to people he'd Connection-up with but nothing came of it and just as he was about to give up hope this wonderful young man had found him, had come right to this room, this doctor who lived to help people like Liam. And this doctor told him there's a charity fund that goes for dis-Connectioning only the very worthiest cases. And Liam qualified. This wonderful doctor who looked so very young turned out to have been practicing medicine for years and in all his time doing it he had never seen a more deserving case than Liam. And neither, for that matter, had I.

I slipped the earmuffs and the Williston Goggles over his head, helped him up, and with his disgusting quivering hand on my shoulder I led him out to the elevator and into the car.

The Interstate took us through the crowded towns north of Boston and up into New Hampshire. We went through a couple of grimy old cities whose names I recognized and then we began to see some scenery. I could look to my left all right but I couldn't look right or I'd be looking at Liam. I took the first rest stop, got out, hauled him out with both hands and threw him in the back. I lifted one of the earmuffs and told him if he took the Williston Goggles or the earmuffs off I'd shoot him in the head and leave him by the roadside. I told him I'd be watching him in the mirror, then I let the earmuff snap back hard. After that I took care never to look at him once.

We started climbing. The Interstate cut through dense

woods. Mountains closed in on either side. The Interstate shrank to two lanes, then to only one and it slowed us down to sixty. I saw scenes I'd seen in videos and as holograms in store windows at Christmas. I saw vanloads of pilgrims turning off to visit the spot where the ancient rock that looked exactly like Jesus had stood forever and then one day fallen, leaving behind the inscription that reads *I can no longer watch over you until you reclaim this land for me.* I saw signs that ordered me not to hit any moose. In a while I saw signs for Freer New Hampshire: just the three words, the distance, and a skull and crossbones, in spite of which I requested the Freer New Hampshire turn-off. The blonde in the transponder said, "Clearance to exit granted. Exiting is not recommended. The Interstate System accepts no responsibility for persons entering Freer New Hampshire. To cancel exit touch your steering wheel once. To confirm exit touch it twice." I slapped it twice, left-right. The blonde said, "Exit confirmed. The Interstate System hopes you know what you're doing."

We swung out down a wide ramp that ended in a bumpy pitted road. The Interstate abruptly let me go, it didn't even try to help me drive. I drove the decrepit road through the woods for a few miles I was too busy missing potholes to count. The road turned into a serpentine track. I followed its twists at ten miles an hour for a hundred yards and stopped at a barrier. Up here there must have been two feet of snow but the road was clear. Just short of the barrier there were billboards on either side that read "Warning! You are leaving the protection of the State of New Hampshire. Turn back now or proceed at your own risk and may God have mercy on you if you do." I had to look back and forth between the billboards to read the whole message because someone had shot them both up pretty thoroughly. The exit holes were all on the New Hampshire side.

There was a delivery truck stopped at the barrier. I pulled up behind it and watched two men in crisp green fatigues and combat boots walk to the back of it. The car said it was twelve degrees outside but neither man wore a coat. One of them threw open the tailgate and ducked while the other knelt and aimed a Close Quarters Personnel Killer into the interior. If he pulled the trigger he'd put 5,000 uranium flechettes into it in a second and a half but the hanging sides of beef inside didn't shoot, so neither did he.

When the truck moved through the barrier I moved up. One green soldier type walked to the right rear window and put a sidearm on Liam. One went to the right front window and put one on me. A third who appeared to be unarmed walked to my window. I lowered it. He said, "Identify yourself" and pointed to a black button in the middle of his chest.

I said, "Arbuckle, party of two."

The button said, "Full name, mister."

I said, "Cyril Winslow Arbuckle the ninth."

The button said, "Right on time. Pull through the barrier, stop and wait for your escort. Stay in your mangy heap while you wait or we'll be doing our business with Cyril Winslow Arbuckle the tenth."

I expected the escort to be a car but a youngish guy who carried his green uniform like a civilian walked out from behind some trees and got into the front seat. The first thing he did was look back and sneer at Liam, who was lolling his head around and wearing that drooling Connectioned grin. The young guy shuddered and turned back to me.

"God, that is the ugliest thing I've seen since I dumped off grandpa at the nursing home. Welcome to the land of the freer, Arbuckle. I'm Davidson."

I looked at his name tag. It said he was Davidson. If I hadn't known that it couldn't possibly be true I'd have guessed that his name might be Davidson.

I said, "Tell me something Davidson. How come you people can walk around undressed and not look cold?"

"Because our hearts are full of hot love for Liberty. Also, our shirts and pants cost more than this car and are good for thirty-five below but mainly, Liberty."

Davidson may have carried himself and his expensive shirt and pants like a civilian but now I saw he was a civilian with responsibilities. On his belt he wore one of those compact flechette projectors that can shred an elephant and aren't all that much use for smaller-scale work. He wore it casually like he wore it every day and I was pretty sure he hadn't done anything to make sure I saw it. He directed me down neat, winding little country roads, all of them swept clean of snow, all of them heaped with it on both sides. The trees were as dense as in un-freer New Hampshire but had a kind of manicured, landscaped look to them. There were plenty of picturesque frame houses scattered in clearings in the woods. Every one of them looked like the day it was supposed to have been built two hundred years ago. Every hundred yards or so there were a couple of coatless, green-fatigued sentries standing on one side of the road or the other. One always had a sniper rifle, one a shotgun with a fifty round drum. Davidson seemed to be wearing a fairly long-range badge because the sentries always waved us on before we got within forty yards of them.

Davidson never directed me anywhere where I'd get close to anybody who wasn't prepared to shoot me. We skirted a pretty little village and then a larger town that looked like a sappy Christmas Social. Then we turned into a curving, climbing drive and pulled up in front of a neat, smallish, and very modern hospital with a sign reading "Freer New Hampshire Facial Re-imagining. Walk-ins will be shot on sight."

I said, "I think I'm picking up on the flavor of the local humor."

Davidson said, "That's good. So many just don't learn in time. Let's go in, shall we?"

We hauled Liam out of the back. I lifted one of the earmuffs and said, "You Connectioned-up?"

The voice said, "No but where—"

I said, "Shut up" and let the earmuff snap back. Davidson and I walked him in and we did get stares. A white-coated doctor hurried over with an orderly in tow, nodded to me and said, "Dr. Jaspers. We'll take him now. Davidson will show you where to wait."

I said, "Wait?"

Jaspers said, "Yes, wait. Until we check him out. If the gear is other than as advertised you're taking him back – didn't they brief you?"

They'd briefed me enough to know that Jaspers was making it up on the spot but there didn't seem to be much point in saying so yet. Right then a ticket out of there sounded pretty good, even if it was Liam. I said I'd wait. Jaspers said he'd thought I would. Then Liam started struggling feebly. He said "Hospital." He said, "Dr. Ebonisticker? Are you here? That's you isn't it Dr. Ebonisticker. We're in your hospital." His earmuffs were down tight, all he could have seen was Reverend Williston, but he knew anyway.

I wondered how and it must have showed. Jaspers looked daggers at me and pointed to his own nose. Liam had smelled a hospital. Jaspers lifted an earmuff and said, "No, Liam, this is Dr. Jaspers. It would seem I'm a colleague of Dr. Ebonisticker. Let's get you to your room."

Liam's knees collapsed and Davidson and the orderly had to fight him into a wheelchair. Jaspers watched disgustedly. Once Liam was chaired and buckled Davidson said, "Jesus, he's all over my hands" and took off running for the head.

Jaspers pointed to a square of facing couches, said "Wait there, Arbuckle" and walked briskly off beside Liam as the orderly wheeled him away.

I sat. I've sat in hospitals before and usually there are a lot of people sitting, bored people, anxious people, dead tired people, fidgety people. Here I had to be all of them because I was the only one waiting. There was a low square table in the middle of the square of couches and on it was what looked like a menu. I opened it to see what the choices were for dinner and learned that it was really The Story of Freer New Hampshire, Last Refuge of Liberty. I thought *oh boy* and with the shittiest of shit-eating grins I leaned back to read. I was just about through it when I caught the reek of disinfectant and Davidson's voice said, "You ready to apply for a visa yet?" He smirked down on me, his confidence restored by household chemistry.

"Not really."

"That's good because we don't issue any. You know, you just read it – no government and all that."

"My gilt-edged portfolio would be my visa?"

"Something like that. Let's walk outside."

So I exchanged my warm couch for the cold steps outside. The sun was beginning to go down and the temperature seemed to have fallen in the few minutes I'd been indoors but I had to admit that the view was a big improvement. I looked back toward the lobby and said, "The walls have ears?"

"That ain't the half of what they've got. What did you learn about our glorious little nation?"

"Freedom-loving rebels swarmed in, outvoted the locals, abolished the government, put up fences all around, declared independence, and it's been a paradise ever since. I think I got the order right."

"You did indeed. You just passed the civics test."

"Any idea what really happened?"

"Something not too different from that I suppose, I'd guess for about a year or even two. Then the real money would have started to show up. You know, those rebels were mostly our age and that was only thirty-some years ago. You'd think I might have met just one of them, wouldn't you? In the three years I've been working here?"

"Uh huh, you would at that. So if there's no government who, you know, governs? Officially I mean."

"Officially it's whoever signs your paycheck. But unofficially, it's whoever signs your paycheck. See those people?"

He pointed back down the road we drove in on. An orange truck was parked by the side and a small crew, five or six men and women in blue coveralls, was sweeping up snow that had blown back onto the road.

"I wondered how the roads were so clear. Who are they?"

"They're called Guests. It's kind of an inside joke. Notice anything peculiar about them?"

"Not really, except they aren't wearing hats and they seem a bit on the elderly side."

"No gloves either. Studies have shown that you sweep faster without hats or gloves. Yes, our older Guests do like to keep active and we try to accommodate them. What was it you said? The rebels "outvoted the locals," something like that? I wonder what happened to those locals after that."

"You have any other Guests?"

"Sure, they keep arriving all the time. They usually think of themselves as immigrants when they get here but we explain it to them. You have to work hard if you hope to save up enough to buy in."

"And do they?"

"Well, they're kind of shiftless at that. Of course they have excuses. They say it's hard to save when you're paid in oatmeal, work clothes and a bunk. Plus this beautiful scenery of course."

"But they keep coming."

"Like I said. Just drive right in and don't drive out again for some reason."

He was enjoying himself way too much but there didn't seem to be much I could do about it. In a few minutes he got a message on his Social.

"Your Mr. Gallagher's gear checks out."

"Of course it does."

"They're going to operate now."

"That's quick. I suppose you'll be riding back to the gate with me?"

"I suppose so. These things don't usually take that long and I suppose I'll still be on duty when it's over."

"That's nice but I think I'll just leave now and beat the rush."

"Well, that would make sense except that if Dr. Jaspers doesn't call the gate and clear it, all it will get us is dead. Me too, so I won't be getting in your car just yet. Let's go get some dinner, okay? What shall we talk about, sports or our investments? Neither one will bother anybody unless we really whisper."

We ate in the cafeteria, Davidson paying because I could have flown to Miami for what they charged and besides they only took euros. But if any cafeteria was worth what they charged it would have been this one. People waiting around for their discretionary new faces seem to have expectations in the food and drink department. I saw what I took to be a few of them across the room from where Davidson had led me so I wouldn't get a good close look. They sat alone or in small groups, they wore the kind of casual but super expensive what-*this*-old-thing? clothes that are one more way the rich love to mock us, and they were just interested enough in me to look me over once and then dismiss me from their world forever. The cafeteria would have sat a hundred, there were maybe a dozen eating there at dinner time, and the staff of twenty or so stood by as nervously attentive as if the place was packed with dignitaries. We were lingering over our desserts and cognac when Davidson's Social summoned us back to the lobby. Whatever happened it didn't look like I'd be allowed a look inside the hospital itself and I took that as a good sign, purely because I didn't want to think it was a bad one.

Dr. Jaspers stood by my couch with a couple of sentry types a few feet behind him who wore very small side arms that didn't cover up more than their whole thighs. Jaspers gave me a look of perfunctory condolence.

He said, "We did everything we could but your friend Liam didn't make it."

I said, "That was quick."

"Mercifully, yes. He was very weak you know. But sometimes I think it's actually better for them if they don't make it. You know, it takes months of therapy before they can live on their own. It's nothing physical, it's that they suffer a catastrophic loss of sensation and stimulus when they're suddenly returned to the normal sensory world. They can see what you see, hear what you hear, feel what you feel, and they are still driven mad from sensory deprivation. I honestly believe that none of them ever has a happy moment again. But we are doctors and we take an oath and when the patient can pay for the treatment it is not for us to substitute our own judgment."

His mocking smile told me he was playing with me, seeing how I'd take it when he turned his sententious comforter act up to high. He was showing me that sometimes he had to make this speech to people who actually mattered.

"Dr. Jaspers, I wonder if you would answer a layman's question for me. How does the dis-Connectioning operation work? I've been wondering."

He leered delightedly. "Well, there are two ways. The first, which is very arduous, is suitable for only the strongest patients. In it, we carefully destroy the implants into the brain. This preserves the brain but destroys the Connection apparatus. The second one, indicated when the patient may not be able to tolerate the rigors of the first, is much simpler. In it, we destroy the brain but preserve the brainware. Unfortunately it's a new treatment and the survival rate is still much lower than we'd like. Any other questions?"

As a matter of fact I did have some.

I wanted to know how much unregistered brainware would sell for.

I wanted to know who would pay to have it installed and who they would want it installed in.

Somebody planning to create the perfect spy, a secret witness sending out feeds of secret conversations? An expendable spy, one who can be allowed to go as mad as Liam once his mission succeeds...

A hotshot Media producer with a plan for infiltrating gatherings of newsworthy celebrities who'd never dream of performing in front of a crew? *Miss Poppycock and her "friend" don't dream that this mere waiter is capturing their every indiscretion...*

Or just obscenely wealthy people with a hankering for the kind of experiences that Connectioning is known to offer, people whose social and professional positions forbid them from going on the Roll? And so greedy for those experiences that they tell themselves they can handle the consequences?

But the two sentries didn't look like they wanted me to ask those questions – in fact, they hadn't liked the first one much at all – so I just shook my head and said no, my curiosity was satisfied.

Jaspers said, "That's good to know. Mr. Thumperson said you were getting close to other candidates for dis-Connectioning who have your late friend's peculiar qualifications. Is that so?"

The sentries were now *very* interested.

"Yes it is. I'm hoping to run one down next week in fact."

"That's very encouraging, Mr. Arbuckle. I'll not detain you further then. Mr. Davidson will escort you back to the border."

The sentries deflated like kids just told they'd be kept after school. I silently thanked Thumper as I'd never thanked him before, and I did so remembering everything else he'd ever done for me and how I'd already thanked him for them. Walking slowly and calmly and casually out to my car was the hardest thing I did that whole day.

When I got back to the Interstate on-ramp the blonde in

the transponder said, "You are now under restraint. Please remain in your vehicle while your request for re-entry is evaluated." She drove me off onto the shoulder and cut the engine. The yellow light started blinking faster than it had ever blinked before, and it kept it up for two and a half minutes; I know because I counted off every second. Then it turned to blinking orange, my engine restarted, my car pulled into a gap and accelerated, and the blonde said, "Your request for re-entry from Freer New Hampshire has been evaluated and approved. Welcome back. Approval of this request was not automatic. To apply for automatic approval of future re-entry requests touch your steering wheel once. To agree to future one-time evaluations such as you have just passed, touch it twice. To agree never to visit Freer New Hampshire again, which will prevent future exits into Freer New Hampshire territory, touch it three times." My hands went *slap, slap, slap* before my brain finished telling me what it had heard. "The Interstate System congratulates you on a wise decision and offers a prayer of silent thanks for your unexpected deliverance. Enjoy your trip."

Driving south I saw snowboarders come flying down the mountains, cutting through wide gaps between the trees, leaping ridges, kicking up rooster tails of snow as they swirled around jagged granite boulders. I don't know how they did what they did but I know they didn't feel one bit freer than me.

ii

In mid-winter a broker nobody trusted named Aiden MacAndrew tried to put me onto a woman named Ava Sonderborg who he said was a gold mine waiting for the right miner to stumble in. According to Aiden all his prospects were undiscovered gold mines or diamonds in the rough or piles of bearer bonds under a mattress but few of his mines ever panned out. But Aiden was a deacon in a gigachurch in Phoenix and well enough connected that not only was nobody looking at him for his hobbies, he could also get you limitless tankfuls of water anywhere in the southwest. Since water is the bedrock, can't-get-around-it price of travel out there

Aiden was not a man you could ignore, and while I'd never yet bought a passenger from him, I'd given him a few free of charge – solid prospects all, but people who for one reason or another we'd decided to take a pass on. Those people had made him money and they were the best part of his reputation, so he was always happy to see me. Sometimes when I had to have water and didn't already have my own I had to see him too, whether it made me happy or not. Water was why I'd come to see him this time and I needed it badly.

I let him pitch me the Sonderborg woman before getting down to my business because buyers are so much more congenial than supplicants. I had to admit that she sounded okay. Since it was Aiden talking *sounded okay* means that I couldn't see what was wrong with her yet but I had faith that I would soon enough if I bit. But I had to seem to go along and I told him she sounded good but I had this other passenger to deliver first. He let me put a deposit down on her and in exchange for a tankful of two hundred gallons of drinking quality I agreed that it was non-refundable. He said he'd stall her and keep her from jumping which made me a little uneasy, but then again two hundred gallons would get me all the way past Bakersfield so I didn't see a choice. We shook and I went back out on the road.

I took my passenger through the Arizonas up to Las Vegas, then down again to LA and back up to Monterey, six states in all and an average of thirty gallons at every state line. In Monterey I sold him to a fishing boat captain who probably really did take people up to Seattle – at least we'd never heard proof to the contrary. Anyway, there was no choice. The passenger said he had friends in Seattle from the days before Seattle moved to Canada, friends who were sure to take care of him and would know how to do it, and unlikely as that was he wouldn't listen to alternatives. We didn't know anybody who said they could get him there other than this captain, so that was that. I took half his money for getting him to Monterey and left half for the fisherman.

Half, in this case, was a lot. This passenger was a dentist from Tucson who had been raking it in for years and feeling pretty good about himself while he raked. He felt so good about himself that it did things to his critical faculties. It let

him believe that no one would care if he got himself
unchurched for screwing the pastor's wife, and it let him
believe it for much too long. He was red hot by the time he
ran. We had to make the trip in easy stages with a different
story for each one. He burned up a pretty good alias at every
stage and complained every morning about how hard I made
him work to learn the next one. It was nine days before I was
free of him in Monterey and I hadn't liked him much when
we started. The Sonderborg woman lived in Carmel, where
Aiden and I had left her dangling, expecting me to show up
any day. She was on my conscience and what I'd scored off
the dentist put me way over quota and what I'd put up with
from him had earned me some time off. So I figured what the
hell, let's at least see what she's got herself into, and I popped
in a clean alias and headed off toward Carmel right away so I
wouldn't have a chance to come to my senses. I'm telling you
this so you'll understand how it happened that for the first
time ever I went to check out a passenger who Boronzee
didn't know a thing about.

I Socialed her when I got to the edge of town. Aiden had
given her two responses to give me, one that meant now and
another that meant later – nothing else because Aiden has
never seen a reason to take no for an answer. People who
actually do the work don't ever think that way. *Later* is just as
likely to mean "hold on a bit because the militia isn't here yet"
as anything else, and if I got anything back from her but *now* I
wasn't planning to hang around. What I didn't expect was to
get her *now* in less than a second, but I did. I got an uneasy-
making image of a woman staring at her Social for nine days
with the response loaded and queued. I overrode the
Automap and stepped on it.

I thought business was looking up when I pulled in out
front. This was the heart of rich old Carmel and it was still as
rich and old as ever. Her address was a neat yellow two story
cottage with a sunken balcony all the way across, brick
terraced flower beds for a yard, a flagstone walk, and a trellis
full of live roses over its little front porch. It was January. Live
roses in January aren't flowers, they're a fuck you to the whole
world, and for what a trellis full of them would cost you could
have your pick of house trailers in Monterey. And even

without them this house had to have gone for a couple of million or so way back at the turn of the century when as the old people are always telling us a million was *money*.

She had the door open as soon as I parked and she stood in the doorway with a half pint of unfiltered anxiety on her face and a small suitcase in both hands. She held the suitcase in front of her and from the way she was straining it seemed to be much heavier than it should have been. She held most of her anxiety in her eyes but I also had the impression that her cheeks were vibrating. As I was halfway up the flagstones she called out to me. "Do I have room for another one? It's bigger but it doesn't weigh as much."

I took the one from her, winced, and said, "I can see how six more wouldn't weigh as much. What's in here, gold?"

"Almost. Books."

"Books? On paper, with covers?"

"Yes. Real books."

One of *those* people, then, but why not? It wasn't any less realistic of her to think she was driving off with me with her books than without them.

I said, "Can we go in and discuss this?"

She said, "Of course we can if we must but you've cut it a little close. He'll be home in half an hour."

I took another look at her then. The anxiety on her face wasn't the mindless panic I'd thought it was. The anxiety on her face was all because I had taken my sweet time and *he'd* be home in half an hour. "Your husband?"

"Yes, my husband. And since I'm leaving him and since he won't like that at all I'd have thought you'd want to be underway as soon as possible. Considering who he is if that doesn't sound like bragging which it is anything but."

I could see her point. If this was his place and he wasn't the one who needed to get out then I already knew all I needed to know about who he was. Taking her away with me on the spot was crazy but it suddenly seemed not as crazy as still being there arguing when the kind of man who belonged in that house showed up.

I said, "Let's go get your bag."

She led me to a hidden closet under the stairs, the kind that has a false panel. The panel lay on the floor with a heap of ice skates and tennis rackets and a French horn on top of it. She ducked into the closet and dragged out a bag you *could* take on a cruise but not even check on an airplane, then nodded at the heap of junk. "I had the bags hidden in the back. They've been there a while." That was as close to a reproach for my tardiness as she ever got.

I said, "We going to clean this mess up?"

She shook her head. "There's no point. You don't know my husband. If I'm simply gone when he gets home he'll call the police and report me missing."

"He calls the police whenever you're not here?"

"I've never not been here."

Uh oh. "We really don't want him to do that, you know. In time, sure, we can't stop that, but not right away."

"That's why we're leaving the mess. The mess will make him look around for what else is missing, and he will find things and they will slow him down. He won't call the police till much later, believe me."

That was a lot to ask me to believe but time was short and it was shorter if she was wrong. I carried both bags because it would look better to the neighbors. Limousine drivers do *not* make you carry your own luggage. Of course, limousine drivers don't usually wear jeans and camo jackets either but perhaps she wanted to travel incognito to the yacht. At least I'd had what I'd like to think was the foresight to wash the car that morning. I put the bags in the trunk and held the curbside rear door for her. She slid in gracefully and with so little interest in anything around her that maybe I *was* a limousine driver to her, or maybe she was just thinking like I was about the neighbors. I got in and started away at a dignified pace.

She said, "Where are we going? If it's not indiscreet to ask."

"Somewhere we can talk in private. Any suggestions?"

"We can't talk on the way?"

"I don't know where the way is yet. I wasn't planning on starting out so soon."

"Oh. Am I rushing you?"

"Not anymore. But you rushed me about a week's worth back there."

"Then I suppose I should apologize but it would be insincere. I'm too happy about getting away."

"Uh, about getting away. We haven't exactly done that yet."

We were coming up on a vulgar touristy shopping mall. I pulled in, parked out of sight of the street and turned around to face her. I took my first real look, long and slow. She was at least forty-five and possibly quite a bit older than that but she'd kept the looks she'd had, which was lucky for her since they'd been on the meager side and mostly confined to her eyes. The rest was just a face – a well-bred face but then it would be, wouldn't it? She was dressed for anything from afternoon tea to boarding a cruise ship to an afternoon in somebody's box at the track. She was dressed for anything except riding around with a guy in jeans and a camo jacket or going anywhere he'd be likely to take her. I did like her hair. It was that pale blonde that is never that far from white and now that it had some real white mixed in it only looked paler. She wore it straight with a long braid in back and had probably worn it that way when she was ten.

"Is Sonderborg your married name?"

"That's very observant of you. My grandfather brought it all the way from Denmark. He had a lot of money once and spent most of it around here. Sonderborg was useful to Wockenfuss so he let me keep it socially. Wockenfuss is my husband. Where do you *think* we'll go once we actually start out?"

"Mrs. Sonderborg, I have–"

"Ava. Or Miz Sonderborg if you must. Or hey lady, believe it or not I've been hey lady before. But no more missus for me, please."

She was beaming like she was the happiest woman on earth. I supposed there could be reasons why I might just have been able to drive her to the desert and bash her skull in while she slept but there was no way I could leave her in that mall.

"Ava it is. The man who owns this car is named Babcock. Lucas Babcock. That's also what some of the papers I carry say."

"I understand. I mean, I understand, Lucas."

"Call me Luke. Do you think your husband will make San Francisco too hot for us if we spend the night there?"

"I think that in a few hours San Francisco will be in flames."

"This presents a challenge. I have twenty gallons of water left and I can get to San Francisco on that. Also to Oakland and Berkeley but not to Sausalito, and any place further off is out of the question till I can get more. I know how to get it in San Francisco but—" I stopped because she was looking at me in a very quizzical way.

"There's a water depot right over there."

I shook my head. "Babcock lives in Missouri and so does his car."

"I don't."

I shook my head again. "It's the car that matters, Ava. Out of state cars give water, they don't get it."

She could shake her head as well as I could. If there is such a thing as a sorrowful grin, then she gave me one with her shake. "For a Lucas Babcock a car does matter, but it doesn't matter for everyone," she said.

I fueled us up and drove over to the water pump and Ava leaned out her window and said, "Can you fill us up Rafael? My husband meant to use his permit but he's running late."

Rafael already had the hose connected. "No problem, Mrs. Wockenfuss."

Rafael never looked at me once. What could there be to see in the front seat except another Rafael?

Ava said, "Could we use some extra?"

I said *fuck yes* but only with a look.

Rafael wrestled three thirty gallon ponies into the trunk. He'd have kept on bringing them but that's all he could fit. Rafael, Rafael, where have you been all my life?

When we pulled away from the pump Ava checked the time. "He's home. He's found the pile of all his old junk from summer camp that he never took out to look at and would never agree to throw out. He's puzzling over it now. In a minute he'll remember the suitcases in the back. He'll hate to get dirty but he'll look anyway. Then he'll go into his office because the first thing he'll worry about is that I've taken something, some business thing that some people can't ever see. Instead he'll find the note. It's a long note because I had quite a few things to tell him but he won't read much of it now. He'll get to the part about how he'll never catch up to me and then he'll stop. Then, right about then, he'll finally remember my jewel case. When he runs upstairs and sees it lying open with nothing but my Social inside, that's when he'll take his out and Social the pastor. What a glorious afternoon for mid-January. Three, two, one, now. Ring ring."

I stopped just short of the coast road so she could get in front. I put it to her. "Can we get to Monterey before he pulls the plug on you?"

She considered. "I'm probably still a citizen till late evening. He'll have to persuade the church and that will take some time. It was Grandfather's church and my parents are buried in the churchyard. He's a big man in some places but he's always been the Sonderborg son-in-law to the church. He'll have right on his side and they'll know it but they'll try to talk him out of it anyway. They won't give in until they're sure they can convince our little world that they did all they could. And until they unchurch me the police won't do much for him except send him crawling back to Pastor."

"You know, Ava, what the police are supposed to do and what they'll do for a Wockenfuss…"

"I know that, Luke. I also know what they won't do around here to a Sonderborg without a warrant signed by six deacons. But what good does getting to Monterey do? That warrant will be signed by midnight and this car has been scanned a hundred times since you picked me up."

"I'll tell you what good it does us but let's make sure of something first. Not that I'm doubting you." I pulled out into traffic and requested a lane to Monterey. The blonde in the transponder reminded us that if we were continuing south there would be a thirty gallon water tax we could pay anywhere before Bakersfield. When the highway had us and the light turned green I turned back to Ava.

"Well, well. Cleared to Monterey, just like decent folks. I'm so glad you know your locals, Ava."

She simpered prettily. Maybe I'd been wrong about the meager looks. I decided to tell her the next few stages of the trip, which is something you never, ever do.

"Once Mr. Babcock exits in Monterey something kind of like a small electrical storm happens. When it's over Mr. Babcock and his car have vanished. Right about that time a Mr. Ethan Davis and *his* car resume their long day's journey. Mr. Davis, whose best friends call him Two Ears, drove up from Bakersfield this morning to do some business. He was recorded the whole way of course so nobody will be surprised when he turns around and heads back. When he gets to Bakersfield he'll reserve the sleeping lane clear to LA and since that's a trip he regularly makes the Interstate won't mind that either. In LA there will probably be some electrical problems again. Depending on some things we have to decide that we've got plenty of time to discuss."

She leaned back, stretched, and yawned delightedly. "I've never met anyone named Two Ears before. I hope he's half as nice as you."

Along the way we reviewed her assets. They amounted to around ten pounds of jewelry, of which only a couple of pounds were worth more than a good dinner out. She was worth a lot on paper – hell, that house had been only part of her dowry – but it was all under Wockenfuss's control now. She had some cash with her, a lot of it in fact, but once you've filled up on hamburgers what else can you do with it? She still had plenty of stocks and bonds in her own name but those are registered and once you're unchurched...

But Wockenfuss had had a weakness. He liked to show her off and especially he liked to show her off in diamonds. Not discreet tasteful diamonds confined to the extremities. Great glittering swaths of diamonds spread across her chest and in her hair and drooping from her wrists. Who knows what they said to him? You're the man who bought a genuine Sonderborg at a bargain price and then renovated her? See people, see how things have changed around here? Behold this year's New Improved model of the Wockenfuss-Sonderborg, watch how it gleams as you tremble at my power and don't you even dream of fucking with me.

Whatever those diamonds said to him, she hated it and them. Until the day she realized that diamonds cost a lot of money and what costs a lot of money can be sold for a lot of money. And they're not *registered*. You don't have to sign any *proxies* on them. They can't be reduced to electronic pulses. All you have to do is have them, and she had hers. The day that thought struck her she started hinting around and a while after that she ended up talking to Aiden.

We were well into the Arizonas before I was sure I'd asked every question but one. Now there was nothing to do but ask it and I dreaded the answer.

"These diamonds. Are any of them famous, even a little bit?"

"I'm afraid not. My husband went in for quantity."

I let out a long-pent up whoosh of relief. She looked me a surprised question.

"See, we'd get nothing for them. Nobody'd buy them because nobody could sell them. Plus, any honest dealer would already know they'd been reported stolen, so even to get turned down we'd have to talk to people it isn't all that safe to call on."

"They aren't trash. He wouldn't show me off in trash and besides it was my money he was spending."

"Better and better."

She gave me a long thoughtful look. "No, it's not. I've seen more ways to lie than the old-time churchmen had names for and you're telling one of them now. The lie of the missing *but*. What's the *but* that's missing from *better and better?*"

I took a breath. "It's kind of a long one."

"Fortunately we seem to have time for even the longest *but*. Trust me, you'll feel better when you get it over with."

"There are lots of pieces to it. You miss one and you miss the whole thing."

"Then tell me all of them, but tell me the last one first. I'm not going to Canada, am I?"

I tried to think of ways to say it that didn't sound like *no* but no matter how long they were none of them came out *yes*. "No. I just don't see how."

She let out a little sigh and said, "Well, I won't deny that I was hoping. But I wasn't really counting on it. I still have everything I really wanted for a little while at least. I *do* have a little while, don't I?"

I stared. "Yes. Maybe a bit more than a little."

Then she *smiled.* "Thank you. And thank you for telling me the truth. Why is that so hard for people to do? From what I used to read it hasn't always been that way."

I should have said something but I couldn't stop gaping at her. This is the part where, if you have to get to it, people fall apart. Some just shrivel up, some throw fits, some argue and a surprising number threaten, people who haven't owned a threat they could back up for years. What they never do is *smile.* She *smiled.*

She said, "I interrupted. I've broken your train of thought. I think you were going to tell me how Wockenfuss's diamonds are going to buy me a little time. In little smidgens that have to be taken one by one."

So I got back on track and smidgened her. I told her how we could sell all her diamonds in one place but only at a discount so heavy it would be a crime. (She smiled again, this time I think at my idea of what a crime amounts to.)

I told her that whatever any one of them was worth, it was the bottom number on a list of three. The top number being what Wockenfuss or any other buyer would pay for it. The middle number being what any jeweler could buy it for wholesale without having to deal with us. The bottom number, ours, being enough less than wholesale that buying from us made sense.

I told her that the only people who'd even pay the what-it's-worth number owned jewelry stores and that because they owned jewelry stores they didn't sell a lot of diamonds every day because only wholesalers sell a lot of diamonds every day and we'd already eliminated them.

I told her that because they didn't sell a lot of diamonds every day, they'd only buy one or two at a time – any more than that and we were back to discounting them away for peanuts.

I told her that because they'd only buy one or two at a time I'd have to visit a great many jewelry stores. I told her that that would take me a certain amount of time – probably weeks if not months. Because I had no excuse for taking two or three weeks off in some place where there are a great many jewelry stores and that even if I had the time I didn't have a cover for that kind of expedition. And for those reasons I'd have to sell them intermittently, in the course of my traveling around. Which to sum it up was why it would take weeks or months.

She said, forgive her, but it didn't sound like I thought of selling her diamonds as a *job*.

I said no I didn't. I said that that's why she wasn't getting to Canada. Because there wasn't a *job* here. Because for there to be a *job* here we'd have to have all the money at one time, so we could pay the people who'd have to be paid to get her there. But that didn't mean that each piece I sold wouldn't keep her going for a while.

She said ah, she could understand that, it was getting clearer, she was catching up to me. So my selling her diamonds would be a part-time job, what she believed is called moonlighting.

I got mad, and I didn't have time to wonder why, and moreover I did *not* feel like explaining that I'd finally had enough of shitting on people because they're not rich enough for Boronzee. I tried not to show quite how mad I was. I tried to say *Oh, sure, yeah, I'll sell your diamonds and pocket a week off your life as a commission every time I sell one,* but in a reasonable and inoffensive way. It didn't work.

She said, "Please don't be angry, I'm only trying to understand. From what Mr. MacAndrew told me this would be a commercial arrangement. You're being unbelievably good to me and I'd never have dreamt of expecting you to do it without compensation."

I got over being mad and got exasperated instead, so now I had to fail at not showing *that.* "Yes, it started out as a commercial arrangement. You had hopes and so did we. But sometimes things don't work out and this is one of them."

She got a little exasperated herself. She said she could understand that but she'd been under the impression, and purely because Mr. Wockenfuss had explained it anew at dinner every night for a very long time indeed, and by the way he did so because he, Mr. Wockenfuss, couldn't stand to live with somebody who might have carelessly forgotten how stressful and challenging his life away from home was every day which possibly was not *quite* to the point but she brought it up so I'd understand how she could think she really knew how commerce is done: anyway, she'd been under the *impression* that *usually* when commercial arrangements fall through they fall all the way through. With no obligations from either party remaining, unless that party is the party Mr. Wockenfuss had hoped to take for everything they have. But those residual obligations are only *moral* obligations and, more to the point, in the present case they would all seem to be liabilities on *her* moral balance sheet, since she was the party who had not delivered. So she was still unclear as to why I now seemed to believe that taking care of her was my responsibility.

I asked her if her question was complete yet, or did she think she might still have a little more to add to it.

She said no, she believed it might tolerably stand on its own without amendment. But to reiterate, why did I–

I cut her off and said I had my reasons. And there was no way I wanted to go into it with her, so that's all I said: I had my reasons.

She thought that over, then said, "Two Ears, that's either a truism or a tautology – I used to know the difference but I'm afraid I've forgotten. But yes, the reason you won't take any pay for what you do for me is indeed your reason. Which I do not doubt. I don't doubt that you have many reasons in fact. I promise to be satisfied with just one of them."

I gave up. I said, "No I do *not* have many reasons, I have one reason and here it is. I have things going on in my life and I've decided that this is a bad time for me to turn into a Wockenfuss."

That rocked her more than it should have. She got contrite and misty eyed. She said, "That's true, isn't it? I've been unforgivably insulting, haven't I? I tell myself I'm civilized but..."

I told her to forget it. She said I was asking way too much and she would never forget it, how *could* she forget it? I told her she could forget it because if she didn't I wouldn't and if she made me keep thinking about it then it would be a terrible and undeserved unkindness on her part. For some reason that answer delighted her. She asked me if I'd ever read Jane somebody. I told her I was pretty sure there was no Book of

Jane in either Testament. She laughed a little but not enough
to offend me if I hadn't been joking. She thanked me again
but kept it tolerably brief and non-specific. We drove.

I said before that I'd asked her every question but that
isn't really true. To show you what a blue funk I was in,
consider this: I never even *tried* to ask her if when she planted
that lovingly-worked-on-for-weeks *note* she'd also thought to
grab "some business thing that some people can't ever see."
What we could have done with that! Knowing as I did and as
Boronzee would just how much of her money Wockenfuss
had. By now we knew people all over the country, second-tier
churchmen, ambitious and impatient for their big break,
who'd have taken one look and paid us twenty, even thirty
percent of street value on the spot. Of course we'd have kept
most of the proceeds but we'd have kept most of anything she
could have walked out of Carmel with anyway. The point is
that she *would* have made it to Canada, I'd have seen to that,
and after the very proper people who bought Wockenfuss's
secrets from us had sold them back to him he probably could
have been persuaded to send her enough of an allowance to
keep her out of a camp.

But I never even brought it up. I knew what would
happen if I did. After she got over the shock she would stare
at me with pure cold hurt. Then she would summon some
words, something like *Thank you very much, but I will* not *become
what I am fleeing.* Then she would despise me forever and
probably not even speak to me again.

And knowing this, having played this out thoroughly in
my head, I'd still gone ahead and accused her of trying to turn
me into Wockenfuss. I'd never imagined that disobedience
could ever be so complicated.

I saw a mall near Gallup and I got off and bought Ava a
clean Social, and she amused herself for a while dreaming up
Social Aliases from books she'd read. I didn't see the harm in
her having a little fun but when it came time to populate it for
real I was going to have to lay down the law and make her
pick something innocent and unremarkable, maybe *Heathen
Killer 8492*. I bought a room for her at a motel outside of Taos
that I'd never used before but which had the unmistakable

look of cautious corruption. The owner gave me a name that I naturally didn't believe. After one look Ava renamed him George Wickham for reasons she said were "too flimsy to repay their windy exposition." George Wickham and I exchanged some very polite threats and promises and I paid him a week's worth of rent by Social and we agreed on how it would work after that. The truth is I had no idea how long *after that* might last but I let him think it might be years and years if he kept his end of it up.

Taos in the summer is one kind of brutal and sometimes Taos in January is another kind, blustery rain chilly enough to make your teeth chatter even if you're used to genuine cold. But at least while I was there it was just moderately windy and not even all that gray. Still, it made neither of us regret the disrepair of the swimming pool or the absence of any halfway appealing place to sit outside. The inside wasn't so bad, the most serious exception being a fairly new and quite clean carpet that perfectly matched the shade of those electric green spots you get on moldy potato chips. Without that carpet the orange curtains would probably have gone unappreciated. The refrigerator worked, three of the four burners on the stove worked, the shower worked, and Reverend Williston probably worked too except I'd paid extra to have him disabled which of course is supposed to be as impossible as it is illegal. George Wickham told us that the Reverend had to go back on when the maid was in but, see, at least that way Ava, who George Wickham believed, or more likely didn't believe, was named Scarlett, would know the maid was coming when the good Reverend materialized in mid-homily. So – George Wickham, a man with no faith in the loyalty of his employees: a good thing to know about a man as far as I'm concerned. I pretended to be curious about how George Wickham was able to turn the Reverend off but at least he drew the line at spilling that – we'd have moved on if he had. Of course George Wickham had no bookcases lying around but he brought in an extra table for her books and, without being asked, a reading lamp and a not-broken-down easy chair. He supposed out loud that she wouldn't want the sports hooked up but what about the Salvation News Network? For no extra? She managed not to shudder and said no, her books would be more than enough for her. George Wickham didn't believe that of course but he was tactful enough not to pursue it.

George Wickham told us about a market down the road that being out in the desert was said to accept cash if she wanted to preserve her privacy (and what the desert had to do with that I have no idea) although George Wickham wasn't sure they always took it but anyway cash probably didn't matter because he was going to do her shopping. Ava said she'd walk there when she needed something. George Wickham said no she wouldn't even before I did, which earned him some unexpected points – he really had done this before. He said she was to give him a list every day and he'd get what he could from it and he'd pay for it and it would go on the bill. She said she didn't care what she ate and anyway she didn't eat so much that George Wickham had to shop for her every day. He said that he went every day anyway so she might as well take advantage of the service. This went on till I thought I'd scream.

Eventually George Wickham couldn't think of any more ways to be nosy or impress me with his dedication and he left us alone. I gave Ava at least an hour's worth of instructions. I was as stern as I could make myself be with her and whenever I suspected I wasn't being stern enough I regrouped and bore down harder. Ava found those parts particularly hilarious but she found something amusing in all of it. I could have sworn she didn't listen to half of what I said but when I questioned her she gave it back to me perfectly, even down to the fractured grammar which she enjoyed mocking gently and only by using her right eyebrow.

Before I left she laid her books out on what she called George Wickham's library table. There were somewhere between forty and fifty of them. At the time I was pretty sure I'd seen holovids of two or three of them but now I couldn't tell you which they were. She never stopped mocking herself or taking pleasure in doing it. She told me she'd probably rearrange them at least once a day. She told me she'd stand over them with a kitchen knife to protect them from the maid ("dusting a well brought-up book is like whipping an obedient dog"). She told me that she'd almost certainly spend an hour or more deciding which of them to read first and then pick one at random which she really ought to do right now since she'd been waiting for the chance for years. She told me that when the church reluctantly caved in to the campaign of shaming secular book idolaters and Wockenfuss insisted that she throw them away to protect his business ("although for him he was very gentle about it") she was so numbly devastated that she almost had, and it was only after she'd packed them to put out on the curb that she thought of the closet under the stairs. She told me that every day for thirteen years she'd resisted the temptation to haul them out and read for just a few minutes. She told me that at first her fantasy of an ideal life, a sublimely perfect life, had been to live hers out alone in the company of those books, but over the years it had shrunk as impossible fantasies do. She told me that even in the beginning Canada had been an afterthought, the unnecessary dessert after a filling meal. For several years now her impossible dream had been to just read them through once again. She believed that if she could stay there in the motel for three months she could do it without hurrying and she'd like that because it would be a shame to have to hurry. But there she was, thinking only of herself again while I would have to—

I allowed her to think she had bored me. I fished through her suitcase and took out her diamonds, which she'd stuffed any which way into a plastic bag. They made a compact tangle in my jacket pocket. I zipped it up, said a few words, and left.

iii

In late winter Boronzee Socialed me instructions for a rendezvous at a Paco's Tacoroni near Omaha. When I got there he and Thumper and Bluesbaby and Loverbits already had a table, four people with five plates of untouched food waiting impatiently for an almost tardy friend to join them. Because they wanted their friend to see them they sat way off by themselves, away from the other patrons, and waved me over with hungry relief when they saw me walk in. I took the empty chair, watched them dig into various things they'd seen me halfway enjoy eating with them in the past, and looked down at my plate of green chili ravioli.

I took up my knife and fork and said, "Fellows. You shouldn't have."

Loverbits said, "It's okay, we're docking your retirement."

Boronzee said, "Is there a joke here? Because they all swore it's your favorite."

I turned to Thumper. "These two I understand, but you? A Doctor of Divinity?"

He said, "You're right. Nobody should dock anyone's retirement unless I get a cut."

Bluesbaby said, "Bits and I are going with you so I hope you cleaned out your car."

I said, "Don't worry, the trunk is spotless."

Loverbits said, "Good. The bishop can ride in there."

Bluesbaby said, "How many times do I have to tell you? He's only an archdeacon."

Loverbits said, "You should still want him to have a clean trunk. He is a warden after all. Someday he may get to pick out your cell."

I said to Boronzee, "All right, I think it's time you told me or I might accidentally believe something they say."

Boronzee nodded at Thumper. Thumper said, "Well, they haven't lied much yet. You're finally going to the grownups' prison. You three are breaking in. In, not out. And then you're sending the warden to Halifax. But as BB says, he's only an Episcopal archdeacon. His name is Jackson Hogarth by the way."

I said, "Well, the first part sounds simple but we've always said that Nova Scotia is a stupid place to run to. Our Coast Guard won't let you near it and theirs won't let you land. If you do sneak onto a boat that belongs there they ship you straight back to Bar Harbor as soon as they pick you up, not even to a camp and not even a hearing. No matter who you are. Tell me you've forgotten this stuff. Tell me it's changed."

Thumper said, "Hasn't changed a bit as far as we've heard. But he's expected and he's not staying long in Halifax. He's flying to England the next day. As the personal guest of the Archbishop of Canterbury. Who is paying for his trip. The *whole* trip."

"Including our part of it?"

"Especially our part of it. Would you like to guess how much he's paying?"

"Enough so the three of us don't mind going to prison?"

"Well, maybe not that much. But enough that the rest of us don't mind seeing you go there."

They had quite a bit of gear with them and all five of us had to haul it to my car. It overflowed the trunk and filled up half the back seat. There was no room left for this archwarden or whatever he was so maybe we really were going to leave some of us inside. Normally I wouldn't have worried much if the plan had called for me to spend two or three months relaxing in a four-star Episcopalian lockup – I'm as fond of prime rib and sleeping late as the next man – but I had parked Ava's diamonds in an unlicensed storage unit in Kansas City that Boronzee rented by the year and which nobody but me ever visited. I'd sold four already for pretty good prices but they were smaller pieces and her rent was only paid five weeks ahead. So this time I did worry a little but since I couldn't tell anyone why, I kept it to myself.

This prison was outside of Iowa City. Being the kind of prison it was – mainly a sanctuary from far worse places for the well-connected miscreant who still has a few friends – getting somebody out wouldn't be that tough, especially with the gear we were bringing. Getting the warden himself out should be easier yet, and if all he wanted was to step outside he could just do it like he probably did every day at quitting time. But getting him from Iowa City to Nova Scotia after he'd well and truly disappeared was something else again, and so we had a job.

After the briefing we drove more or less directly to Iowa City even though it put us there a week early. We wanted to prepare at our leisure. All three of us felt we had good reasons for being well prepared. The International Congress of Anglican Clergy to Report on Conditions in America – ICACRCA for short – was to open in Halifax on Thursday, February 24th, some 1500 miles and a wide-enough patch of ocean away from Iowa City. Hogarth's Europe-shaking, Africa-shaking, everywhere-but-America-shaking speech was set for Saturday afternoon, although for obvious reasons few people knew it yet. Personally I thought that was cutting it a little close since we weren't going to assassinate him until Wednesday evening, and that was going to be the easy part. Still, I suppose that if anyone is going to have faith in his own plans it would be the Archbishop of Canterbury and he was paying so we'd agreed to do it his way.

We rented a spotless new van, which put an end to the "why Floppy will have to stay behind" jokes, and a garage to park it in. We took out the rear seat and installed van-type shelves in its place. When we were done all our gear was stacked neatly away and the van bore the proud name and logo of the famous Next Millennium News Network which you ignorant people have doubtlessly never heard of. Loverbits was especially proud of the lightning bolt that flashed down from the angry heavens to scorch a smoldering city below. The boys had costumes with them but I had to buy a suit and the turtleneck to go under it, also a trench coat. We tried our act out on each other and had a certain amount of fun with it – at least they had a certain amount of fun with my impression of an aspiring junior super anchor.

Early Wednesday morning I Socialed Hogarth's PA to confirm "our 9:30" as we in Media like to say. He or she (I mean, with an Avery you just don't know) Socialed back 800-some words of Instructions for Visitors and a demand that we show up precisely at 8:00AM for *inspection and entry protocols*. We left for the prison at 7:45, drove through the nine miles of gray winter flatness dotted with corn stubble and, there being nothing in it to hold our attention, got to the prison early and parked outside. A den of luxury it might well be but from our view it looked like a lot of dirty concrete walls broken by a few chain-link gates topped with the usual razor wire. At 8:00AM we drove up to the visitors' gate, were directed onto a scanner pad and kept waiting for forty minutes. During this time the scanners presumably counted the live bodies inside, listened to what we said, cataloged the signals all our gear was putting out even on idle, and interrogated the van's Vehicle Identification Chip which Bluesbaby had taught to send out "Next Millennium News Network" when anyone asked it the name of its owner. I didn't like it that Bluesbaby had had to do that: my life (not to mention the bus's) would get a lot more complicated (or maybe just a lot shorter) if it came to be known that it's possible to reprogram a VIC, and since very soon it would be obvious to the world that there never was a Next Millennium News Network, some unusually bright cop might ignore the experts for once and start thinking that very thing. But given the plan we were stuck with there was just no way around it. At least the forty pounds of thermite in our last bomb would melt that chip along with every other trace of us so there'd be no way for anyone to know for sure.

I had no such worries about the signals our gear was putting out. Their real processors were shut down cold. Over the last few years Bluesbaby had recorded what they were sending from real news vans parked at rest stops – it was just a small part of his collection of electronic aliases for more kinds of machines than most people know exist, the same collection that made my life in the wilderness possible. And he'd supervised every step of Loverbits' work on the gear we were carrying so I knew it was as solid as the rest of everything Bluesbaby did. Still, these guards had no way to know how good it was, so they it would seem needed forty whole minutes to collect their samples, ship them off to whatever quasi-governmental data-cruncher would analyze them, and then read the reply that said "standard news media holovid recording and transmission gear on idle."

When they'd received and read that message a couple of them finally walked over, got us out of the van, scanned us just as if the robots we were parked over hadn't already done it, had us certify that we agreed to the statement of Visitor Rights and Responsibilities Avery the PA had sent us – and then escorted us inside so we could wait some more. To get us to the proper place for waiting they walked us through a fifty-yard corridor of screens that effectively kept us from seeing anything of the prison and any of the prisoners from seeing us. Everything they did – how they spoke, how they walked, how they opened doors ahead of us and how they closed them behind us – was slow and regular. It was a prison. The only speed allowed was slow and regular and these were men who had adjusted perfectly, as I suppose everyone in prison does in time.

When the clock on the waiting room wall said 0925 the door opened and another guard motioned us through. He led us down a hall that could have been part of any clean new office building in the country, onto the elevator you'd expect to find in that building, and up two floors. We arrived at an ornately carved wood door at 0929 according to the clock above it. The door announced in tasteful gold leaf that through it one would find *The Reverend Archdeacon Jackson Hogarth, Warden, Saint Giles House of Penance for Refractory Men, Administered by the Episcopal Diocese of Iowa on Behalf of the People of the Sovereign Independent States of America,* which I've always felt is kind of a long-winded way to say *the Interstate.* The guard stood before the door for a second, two seconds, twenty seconds. The clock clicked and the 29 became 30. The guard rapped sharply three times, opened the door, stepped inside and said, "Your appointment, sir." He stood aside for us to enter and then waited easily at parade rest. At the dimly lit far end of the room, which by the way was almost certainly Henry the eighth's largest library assuming he had more than one of them, a longish-haired man was bent over the first Episcopalian's favorite desk and writing something out by hand under a low lamp. Without raising his head he said, "Thank you, Mr. Charles. You may leave us."

The guard turned and at that precisely unhurried standard prison speed he walked out and closed the door behind him. Still without looking up the man at the desk said, "I'll be with you gentlemen in three shakes but first I must get this thought down. It's for our interview you see." Then he did look up, and not even in a mirror have I ever seen a look that was more wickedly pleased with itself. The man carefully and noiselessly put down what I believe is called a fountain pen and with a slow and elaborate gesture that at one point wandered a full two feet further away from his face than was strictly necessary he put an elegant finger to his lips. Then he picked up a small gold cylinder, held it out for us to see, put it gently down next to his papers and tapped its top. As those little gold things do when you tap them, this one began to speak. It spoke in its master's voice and in exactly the same tone, cadence and volume as the man himself had spoken a few seconds before. I believe I told you I know something about voices. So did this guy. He was *good.*

What his voice said was, "Let's see, I believe you'd be Mr.

ah, Mr. de Truth. Interesting name. Assumed for professional reasons, possibly?" He tapped the cylinder and beamed. He motioned me encouragingly to speak, moving one long finger in a hurry-up circle.

"Not by me," I said. "My great-great-grandfather took it because von Wahrheit offended some of the patriots of his day. But I admit it comes in handy in my work."

He applauded soundlessly, roared silently with joyous laughter, winked, and tapped his cylinder again. It said, "And you'd be Mr. Pennyfeather and you, ah, Mr. Cherry? So good to meet you all. Now, before we start I suppose I ought to tell you something of our work here, as what I believe you people call *background*. It's no secret that our denomination, the Episcopal denomination, has sometimes been accused of excessive leniency toward the criminals we are regrettably called upon to care for. You will see for yourselves that there's not an ounce of truth to these slanders but there *is* in fact a reason why this misunderstanding so often occurs. You see, when dealing as we do with the worst of society's dregs, we believe it is essential to preserve even the smallest scraps of humanity and faith that these wretched scum may still have clinging to them when they are committed to our care. And it is in pursuit of that goal that we..."

The archdeacon in the little gold cylinder was off and running. The one in the chair gathered up the papers he'd been writing on, stood, and walked silently around the desk. He wore the high church priest's horse collar and cassock and he was very tall. He had taken off his shoes, and impishly mimicking the exaggerated comic gait of a child he tippy-toed to a small green carpet in the center of the room. There he slowly sat down on it, crossed his legs, and motioned us to join him, nodding a gleeful invitation. He was having the time of his life and he wanted us to know it and join in.

From his desk his voice was saying, "...every form and variation of depravity known to sin, Satan and secular subversion..."

When we were seated in a circle Hogarth took the page off the top of his pile and gave it Loverbits, who read it and passed it to Bluesbaby, who read it and handed it to me. It seemed that he'd first written it out in that old-fashioned, run-together way you see in holovids that nobody except it would seem archdeacons and maybe bishops can read anymore, and which always reminds me of the recordings they make of earthquakes. Of course he knew that the earthquake writing wouldn't do for us so underneath it he'd repeated it all in legible printing. I suspect that the earthquake writing was one of those affectations, like his horse collar and the bishops' miters, that only exist to separate the high church from the low. The part that was printed (at least that part) read, "My hideous monologue will last another 13 minutes. I believe that will be enough if we don't dawdle." One by one we nodded. Not "13 minutes" but "*another* 13 minutes." I liked that. A man at the top of his game and showing it.

...crimes that sometimes threaten us with the despairing notion that Our Lord and Savior perished in vain for us...

The second sheet read, "Can you make your moving holograms in here? Is the light good enough? My idea is that we'll do them while you pretend to interview me."

Loverbits showed it to Bluesbaby and me but held onto it. Then he pulled out a pen and, using his thigh for a desk, wrote: "Better outside. We're equipped for that. We'll be doing other things out there anyway. And we have a lot of gear to bring up. Is that what you're planning too?"

Hogarth nodded twice, once for each of Loverbits' messages, and passed out the next sheet.

"When my diatribe ends and if you haven't strangled me for what it says, I'll take you down to your truck. We'll be able to speak in places on the way. We'll supervise the loading of your equipment and the guards will bring it here. Acceptable?"

We all nodded. I don't know what Loverbits and Bluesbaby were nodding at but I was nodding at his clairvoyant answer to Loverbits' concern about bringing up the gear.

...monsters in human form who would deserve no pity or comfort from us were it not for the bare possibility that in one out of a hundred the Light of Jesus may not be utterly extinguished...

The next sheet read, "Then we shall eat lunch with some of the guards, whom you will impress and gratify with hate-filled observations concerning the inmates. They will reward you with dreadful anecdotes which Mr. de Truth will promise to incorporate in his remarks."

...and so we grant even these worthless animal shells an opportunity for contemplation and repentance. And thus, every few years a miracle occurs and one of them will...

Hogarth passed out the last sheet. It read, "Before the 'interview' I will take you on a tour, the excuse for which is that you will observe things you will then ask me about during our performance. You will inspect the prisoners' garden shed. You will meet my murderer. Then I will lead you to my balcony where, after your departure, I will take my fatal stroll. It is on that balcony that we will have our last free conversation, which can be made to last as long as ten minutes. Will that be sufficient?"

This time we passed it around twice. We each thought it out in our own way. Loverbits and I looked at Bluesbaby. Bluesbaby bit his lip and thought some more. Then he nodded. Hogarth beamed.

...this faint, forlorn hope, the hope that one unspeakable, depraved sinner out of so many, many unspeakably depraved sinners such as you will see here today can be snatched, if only in his last moments, from the pit of hell: this is the great cause to which we have committed our lives, and so it is the height of irony that we should be accused of...

Hogarth stood up and tippy-toed back to his desk. He tapped his cylinder just as it said, "...will take your questions now." It went quiet. The living Hogarth said, "Mr. Pennyfeather, perhaps you'd care to go first." The blending of the voices was still a masterpiece.

Bluesbaby said, "As you know Reverend Warden sir my department is the sound and lighting. I wonder if..."

To get to the guards' cafeteria we had to pass through the prisoners' dining hall, and since we hadn't seen any prisoners yet, and since we were to entertain the guards with *hate-filled observations* about them, Hogarth took his time and let us look our fill. I hadn't really expected to be filled up with hate but it was surprisingly easy to pretend that I was. On the one hand it was definitely a dining hall, with rows of long tables that all together sat a few hundred men – but everything else was on the other hand. The ironed linen tablecloths, the china, the wine glasses, the *cutlery* (not a word I associated much with prison). As for the men themselves… I had an impression of one of those airport club lounges, if not the Pastor Class lounge, then at least Elder Class. Well-but-casually-dressed men who formed tight little groups even though they'd all been thrown together, men who kept their separate conversations low but not secretive, but paused them and waited with resigned patience as we menials moved into earshot. Not hostile about it, no sense that we *intruded*, no sense even of annoyance. Just the in-bred discretion of the elect coping with worldly life's petty burdens in Augustine's City of the Devil, the look that isn't really a look at all that says "nothing you could think or do could ever bother us but at least we let you walk among us, don't we?"

Hogarth watched me watch.

I said, "Is there somewhere we can wash up before we eat?"

Bluesbaby said, "Amen."

Loverbits just gawked.

Hogarth led us out.

We helped a dozen guards put away a lot of very starchy food that maybe had more appeal to men who'd been standing out in the cold all morning than it had for me. They put it away at prison speed, slowly and ponderously. Only two of them talked to us, but that seemed to have been arranged since the others followed the conversation with interest. One of the talkers was a big florid redhead of maybe fifty. The other was a short wiry black-haired man who was a little older. He was the one I'd have worried about in a fight. Most of the rest were quite a bit younger.

Loverbits said, "These inmates seem, I don't know, like a whole different kind of people. I got the feeling that if I said anything at all to them they wouldn't take it very well."

The big one said, "That's the first thing you learn. They don't have no use for anybody but their own crowd and not too much use for them."

The short one said, "Nasty mouths on them all. Can't say anything that isn't meant to cut you." It seemed to make him sad, not angry.

Bluesbaby said, "You meet people like that out in the world but not so many together. Must be tough not being able to just walk away."

The big one said, "You get used to it. Inside here, you can get used to anything because there's just no choice. And it ain't like we ever had their advantages."

At that the short one stopped eating and thoughtfully studied a forkful of instant potatoes. His face turned even sadder and he said, "And we still don't."

We made our way back out through the general population dining hall. Second service was just starting. This time one of the inmates, an irritated middle-aged man in corduroys and what I took to be a cashmere sweater, held up a hand to stop us.

He said, "Hey, Warden, I don't like to complain but much as I like spaghetti carbonara this is the third time since New Year's. Not that it isn't primo but come *on*."

Hogarth said, "Now settle down Benjamin, you'll ruin your digestion. I just had succotash in the guards' room. If you'd prefer it I think there's probably some left."

Benjamin said, "Aw, don't take it like that. It's just..."

I never heard what it just was because Hogarth patted him on the shoulder and led us off. But I did get to see the man next to Benjamin start to tell him something. I guessed that it was something personal because he had the look you used to wear on the playground when you finally got alone with the kid who'd just been snitching to Teacher.

I told Hogarth, "Now that spaghetti did look pretty good but from the stories I've heard..."

Hogarth nodded and said, "Over there."

We headed *over there* which was a corridor at the far edge of the dining all. It was lined with closed doors with lights above them glowing either red or green. Most were red but a guard was wheeling a cart up to a door with a green one. On the cart were covered dishes, a lot of them. The guard checked a list, then knocked. The door opened and he wheeled his cart inside. We waited. In a few seconds the door opened and the guard wheeled the now-empty cart out. The light turned red.

Hogarth said, "The private dining rooms. Is this more like what you've heard?"

Bluesbaby said, "What's that take that Benjamin hasn't got?"

Hogarth said, "What does it always take?"

Loverbits said, "That's just so true, isn't it?"

Bluesbaby and Loverbits carried duffle bags full of gear while we toured. Since I was the super anchor my hands were empty, but every so often Hogarth stopped and he and I put on a little show. The boys would pull strange bits of gear from their bags, fondle them expertly, then nod. I would then ask Hogarth incisive super anchor questions like "What kinds of changes to this sinister place have you seen during your tenure here, Archdeacon?" Hogarth would give me back a few sincere platitudes and the boys would examine their gear with professional concern, nod an okay, and we'd move on again. When we got near the inmates' garden shed Hogarth waited till we were sure to be overheard and said, "Here, let me show you this. This is some of what we do to help the men keep busy."

He put his palm on the lock face and the door swung open. He said, "We have to keep it locked I'm afraid. The inmates have some valuable tools in here and the guards, you know… Why subject them to temptation?"

We went inside and Hogarth shut us in. Loverbits slapped a suction lock across the doorjamb and flipped the lever. He and Bluesbaby emptied one of the duffle bags and sorted through the gear. I put my gloves on and picked up the scorched pipe with the sight and the pistol grip at one end, stripped off the plastic skin and held the pipe out to Hogarth.

"The murder weapon, is it?"

"Yep."

"What is it?"

Bluesbaby said, "It's *supposed* to be a hand-held, multi-gigajoule, one-time laser cannon after it's been fired and burnt itself out. It's really Mr. Cherry's hobby for the last few weeks. I particularly admire how the melted wires spread out and fuse with what's supposed to have been the battery, see?"

Hogarth peeked down the tube and said, "Very impressive workmanship."

Bluesbaby took it from him and carefully stuck the

receiver/speaker/bomb assembly about halfway down the barrel. He said, "It'll be more impressive after that thing goes off. This is where we need the prints."

Hogarth held out an envelope that Loverbits took and opened. While Bluesbaby held the weapon Loverbits carefully applied a dozen strips of clear tape to the pistol grip one by one, removing each one after it stuck for a second. When he was done he held the biggest one up to the light and studied it. "Nice palm. I was worried you wouldn't be able to get a good palm. We really need it where he'd have had to grip it here."

Hogarth said, "That's what I was told. I took it off that hoe right there. It's his and he won't let anyone else touch it."

Loverbits said, "Selfish of him not to share. The kind of thing that can get you punished in a true and just world like this one."

Very careful, so as not to spoil the prints or leave any new ones, we backed out of the shed and propped up the cannon where the tip of its nose kept the door from closing just the last few inches.

On the meandering walk to the first class lounge I asked Hogarth how he'd chosen his killer.

Hogarth said, "He met my three criteria. First, he fully deserves it. Second, it will do the world good to see him defamed. Most importantly he has the voice of God in a very bad holovid, you know it, the voice that surely would have left Moses a useless wreck with shattered eardrums."

I said, "He has it coming more than the rest of them?"

"He does. He, the Reverend Rockofpeter Gable if you will though I won't, *has it coming* because he's here for unchurching old people, most of them old women, for having fallen into penury."

Bluesbaby said, "How is unchurching bums a crime? I mean a going-to-prison crime?"

Loverbits said, "Yeah, I thought having money and being churched kind of go hand in hand."

Hogarth said, "You cynical young men are right of course, although I will point out to you that there *are* still churches that embrace the poor and actually care for their material needs. Reverend Gable's so-called church is not one of them.

Reverend Gable's so-called church preaches that money is a sign of God's favor and more to the point they preach the loathsome inverse of that proposition. But so do many churches. And you're quite right, nobody goes to prison simply for unchurching paupers."

He had us now. We waited.

"But Reverend Gable's former parishioners were paupers because they'd given all they owned to Reverend Gable. Specifically, to his Down Payment on Paradise Crusade. In which those approaching what he called their Hour of Homecoming were offered the certainty of preferred immigrant status up above in exchange for their last penny. And the corresponding though unspoken threat of exclusion were they to demonstrate too much affection for that penny at such a critical stage of their life's journey."

Bluesbaby said, "Jesus. Forgive me Padre but *Jesus*. He picked them clean and then he kicked them out?"

Hogarth said, "And why not invoke Jesus? If His name isn't for this then it isn't for anything. But yes, that's exactly what he did, often on the day he received the final payment. I suppose he felt he had no choice. It might have unsettled his congregation to arrive for church on Sunday mornings and find their old friends homeless and starving in their midst. There might even have been calls for actual *charity*, and that is not what the Down Payment on Paradise Crusade was for. But that's not what he said at his trial. At his *trial* he testified that he knowingly sped them on their heavenly way because he knew that they, of all in his flock, had achieved unimaginably perfect spiritual credit scores. Therefore, and by the most foundational of all laws, they alone were assured admittance to the Pearly Gates. He described the cheering throngs, the parades and banquets that awaited them. And he added, I would normally say as the cherry on top…"

Loverbits alias Mr. Cherry said, "Go ahead, for some reason it doesn't bother me."

"Well then, as the cherry on top he offered this: that even spiritual credit scores are subject to change and perfect ones most of all. All that a continuation of their life as material beings could have offered them was the opportunity for some last, disqualifying sin – after all, the materially poor are so prone to envy, to gluttony, every pastor knows this... Might they not sin so grievously that even the immense treasure they had on deposit in Heaven was forfeit? As their shepherd he could not presume to take such risks with their souls, so he prayed hard and, with God's help to make it through the terrible temptation to cling to their beloved presence just a little while longer, he did the right thing."

Bluesbaby said, "But the jury didn't buy it for once. Who screwed it up?"

"A Tarrant County prosecutor. Reverend Gable made the grievous error of judgment of dispatching the man's favorite great-aunt to a Jumping-off Camp near Laredo. The nephew didn't learn of it for almost a week and by then she had indeed jumped off from a few of the usual causes. Her very substantial last contribution to Reverend Gable was to have put this prosecutor's three daughters through Baylor."

I said, "And this place is all he got? They had *that* on him and they let him off with spaghetti carbonara?"

"Oh no, but his appeal went up for auction in the usual way and his church bid the sentence down to two years in this compassionate institution. And it has continued to support him in style during his residence here, of which only a month remains. And do you know why they do it? They do it because ever since Reverend Gable's highly publicized testimony at his trial, the Down Payment on Paradise Crusade is taking in more than ever before from elderly queue-jumpers all over North Texas. Now do you see what I meant when I said that his defamation will do the world some good?"

For the first time Hogarth had lost his bantering playfulness. He was showing some quality hate, honest hate that had real weight and depth to it. That was the first reason I'd seen firsthand that seemed strong enough for him to give up what he'd be giving up just to make a speech and go into exile. But I wished I hadn't asked. I was going to have to talk to this Gable and make nice to him just a little and now making nice wouldn't be as easy as it could have been.

We passed through the common room where we saw prisoners relaxing in front of first-run holovids, most of which did not seem to me to be all that penitential. We did not run into Reverend Williston anywhere at all – think about

that, please, try to fit it to your notions of *prison* and *penitent* –
but we did stop to kibitz a poker game. Gable was getting a
massage in the first class lounge. Hogarth introduced me to
him and told him that this was his chance to air all his
grievances to a nationwide audience. He'd been right about
Gable's voice. It wouldn't have to be altered much at all for
his big scene, and I got a good drawn-out "Satan" from him at
one point and a fine "in the name of my beloved Lord Jesus
whom I serve in all things" at another. As a bonus he did a
splendid job of denouncing Hogarth for capriciously denying
him the live-in conjugal handmaiden to which his position as a
class AAA Felon entitled him. I was able to use almost all of it
with only minor improvements here and there.

We could understand why Hogarth said he spent so much
time pacing his balcony, even in winter. Though the whole
compound was spread out below us it was far enough away
that the balcony was an utterly private place, of value only to
someone who had very old-fashioned ideas about his privacy.
Moreover it had a low solid wall that Loverbits and Bluesbaby
could hide behind while they set up the tableau. There were
chairs at the back of the balcony that were out of sight from
the compound, and the boys *might* have been sitting in them –
might. But it would be a true freak who'd want to sit out in that
cold. When I said so Hogarth said that he was often that very
freak and people were used to it so why wouldn't his
professionally sycophantic guests enjoy it too?
The boys had the rest of the gear out of their duffle bags
and explained its use as they worked. Loverbits unrolled the
explosive mat. "The orange layer on top is the flash. Now
here's what I see as our only weakness but Blu– Mr.
Pennyfeather that is has convinced me that it probably won't
matter. The problem is that the flash has to go off several
milliseconds before the big bang or else the H. E., the high
explosive, will just disperse it before it does much. And no
flash, no laser, right? And if they have a good enough long
range shot they can slow down the video and see that gap and
then they'd know."
Hogarth said, "I see. And why *doesn't* it matter?"
Bluesbaby said, "It doesn't matter because one the shot

they have of us up here is probably too low res to slow down that much and two they'll figure it out anyway when they find the explosive residue on the rubble. Which they will but only a few days later when they've sucked it all up and sent it to a lab. And three, most of all three, it only has to fool them for not quite three days because in three days they'll sure as hell, sorry, know they've been taken anyway."

Hogarth said, "That makes sense and by the way Mr. Pennyfeather it is presumptuous to apologize for the certainty that hell exists."

Loverbits had Hogarth do a bit of his standard pacing. I ducked down behind the wall and all three of us shot Hogarth as he paced so we could get him from every angle. Loverbits insisted on about twenty slow trips back and forth because he said that the eye records everything and if Hogarth started repeating the exact same moves over and over people would notice. They wouldn't know what they were noticing but they'd sense something wrong anyway and then they might decide to take a closer look. I got worried about the three of us being out of sight for whole minutes but Loverbits poo-pooed it. He said see, this was what he was talking about, people were *used* to the Warden pacing like this so they weren't seeing anything to make them pay attention. He was probably right but I still felt better when we stood up.

We chatted for the minute it took Loverbits to merge and load the holo images – did I mention that Loverbits was *fast?* – and then he laid out the projectors along Hogarth's pacing route. "The charges in the base will blow them a couple hundred yards and mangle them good. Sooner or later somebody *could* find them and figure out what they were. Especially if they're looking for bits of…you know, you. Mr. Pennyfeather is betting me they won't bother and like he says by the time they could do a search like that they'll know anyway."

By then Bluesbaby had the foot out of its sack. He set it down toward the far end of the balcony, several feet from the explosive mat. He said, "I wonder if they'll really put it in your coffin."

I felt distinctly queasy even though it looked like nothing more than an unusual lump of coal.

Hogarth said, "Where did you get it?"

I was expecting that question but it wasn't the one I expected first.

Bluesbaby said, "Bought it off a cadaver seller near the medical school in Rochester. The one in Minnesota."

"And they'll really think it's me?"

That was the one I'd been waiting for.

"One. Cooked to a crisp, no useful DNA left. Two. Right size, shape and age. Three. Johnston and Murphy two-toned Oxford wine and brown, size 11-1/2 triple E. Which trust me will be a whole lot easier to identify than the foot."

"And we really need this morbid little prop?"

Bluesbaby said, "You see there's always something left. Don't know why but there always is. Suspicious off the bat if this is the one time there isn't."

I said, "Plus this is what'll make it real to them. We'll see it on the Media for sure. They'll lay it on a velvet pillow and weep over it."

Hogarth said, "At least I shall be spared the sight of that."

Loverbits said, "Uh, we're ready for clothes and the..."

Hogarth said, "Oh, yes." From one deep pocket of his capacious overcoat Hogarth pulled a wad of torn-up cassock and half a pair of tighty-whities.

Loverbits said, "I'd have put money on boxers." Hogarth and Bluesbaby laughed but not me, I got queasy again at the thought of what was coming next.

From another pocket Hogarth pulled the two red plastic bricks, frozen solid but it was still blood all right.

Bluesbaby carried the scraps and the blood bags to the near end of the balcony, the end by Hogarth's office door. He took a knife and slit and stripped the plastic off the frozen blood and tossed it into an empty duffle bag. He wrapped the bricks in the rags and said, "Be enough DNA left from this to identify you ten times over. And *that's* why nobody'll be looking for tricks."

I tried to not look like someone who might be about to faint.

Loverbits said, "How long did it take you to do that?"

Hogarth said, "Only twice, two weeks apart. I regularly give blood, I'm used to it. My standing donation came due at the same time. I had to fake a cold to explain why I missed it and the hardest part was remembering to sniffle and sneeze all day."

I said, "I think we should get back inside. We still have a lot to do you know."

For that I got two telling grins and one mockingly raised eyebrow. When it comes to blood I can't fool anybody.

Loverbits and Bluesbaby pretended to set up their mobile holoset while I worked on Gable's voice. Hogarth asked them curious questions – what does that one do, why does this one blink when I approach it – and the boys stretched their answers out so even whoever was listening in probably understood them. I write this as if I saw and heard it all, but I saw little because I mostly watched my equipment and I heard none of it because I had my headphones on. But I knew the plan and so did they and I did see enough to know they were sticking to it. What I heard was the real Gable through one earphone and the changes I was making to him through the other. They both played out on my monitor and it took me half an hour to splice them together. In spite of what I'd been swearing up and down to everybody I was a little worried that my lack of practice would slow me down. I needn't have been. Those three years building my Bibles were never leaving me. Once I got used to the controls of this new unit I flew. Before the boys were finished setting up there was only one voiceprint on the screen and it was all Gable. I spent a minute transmitting it to the speaker in Gable's cannon and we were ready.

The interview itself took exactly the forty-four minutes allotted for it, sixty minutes less commercials. We didn't actually holo it of course but we did leave the world the Warden's final words, just as he'd written and practiced them. Even if they routinely recorded over the bugs from his office they'd be holding on to this set. An hour or two after this set of bugs was finished it would be playing in more offices than you could count, and then it would go onto the bugs flowing from *those* places. I asked my questions, he answered them, and what an ugly little toady for our masters he was. If I hadn't seen the real man already I'd have sworn that nobody could be faking that kind of unctuous corruption. It would go out on the Media all right, maybe with archived videos of the archdeacon at his desk or walking the yard, his infectious smile and confident stride bringing tears to right-thinking citizens throughout the land, while his official smarmy lying voice slandered the very idea of civilization.

We packed up and tried to say our goodbyes but Hogarth, still pumped from his performance, insisted on walking us to our van.

With the Warden leading us the guards skipped the usual exit scan. He even insisted on helping us load the van back up and the one guard who'd hung around to watch backed closer and closer to the warmth of his hut. Hogarth walked beside the van shouting loud farewells as we crawled through the gate, then turned to walk back into his prison. We drove next to the wall at the regulation five miles per hour and when in fifty yards we got to the fire door with the disabled alarm Hogarth was waiting outside it and not even out of breath. We barely slowed at all as Loverbits slid the door open and Hogarth dove in, and then we showed back up on the monitors right when we should have.

I was driving since my part of it was done. Loverbits was on the console with Bluesbaby watching the time and directing his moves. "Reverend Hogarth walking up the stairs... First landing... Second landing and *in*. Hit it."

Loverbits hit it, and in Hogarth's office a small directional speaker made door and footstep sounds, then made door sounds again, then disabled itself to sit inconspicuously until the first real search maybe on Sunday or even Monday would prove that it wasn't really the black queen's rook's pawn that had sat on the Warden's chessboard for the last seven years.

Bluesbaby said, "Reverend Hogarth out on the balcony and walking. Hit it."

Loverbits hit it again and the holo of Hogarth started pacing for his observant minions below.

The real Hogarth said, "How the wretch is savoring his moment of fame. It's nine degrees outside and he's basking in the sun of the public's love. How gratifying to look down on the drudges he commands. However will he pass the hours till his face shines out in homes throughout the country, till his voice speaks directly to the people's hearts? Perhaps a steak tonight, even though it is only Wednesday. Yes, a great bloody steak, and until then he will walk to build up his appetite. Walk, you reverend archdeacon, walk. Walk for your public. Walk for us."

Fourteen minutes to go. We fell silent. I kept it under ninety because this was no time to not fit in. When we got to our garage Bluesbaby jumped out, opened it up and drove our car out. I backed the van into its place. Loverbits grabbed his console. I waited for him to reach the car and get in the back before I took the safety off the charge because the alley was icy and a dropped console could get ideas of its own. Then Hogarth and I got out and I shut the garage.

Four minutes to go. Bluesbaby got to the Interstate ramp and asked for clearance to the fast lane at once. The blonde told us it was snowing in Minneapolis but traffic was moving. The light turned orange and we were cleared to Duluth. Eighty-seven seconds to go.

Loverbits said, "I wonder what Gable's doing."

Hogarth said, "Taking his before-dinner nap. Nobody's actually watching him but they *will* wonder how he made it to the shed and back unobserved."

Bluesbaby said, "That's another way they'll know he had outside help, that plus his cannon of course. They'll torture him for days to find out who."

Loverbits said, "For three days to be exact. Time to blow the van." He pressed a button. I looked back in the mirror but we'd made it too far to see the garage go up.

Loverbits said, "Time to say goodbye Warden."

Bluesbaby said, "Let him push it himself."

Hogarth said, "Yes, please. I'd like that."

Loverbits put Hogarth's finger on the button. Hogarth said, "Back to hell, you fraud" and pushed.

The rest we had to imagine, but after all the work we'd put in imagining was just like seeing. Probably I was the only one of us to hear Gable's hollering just as it was really heard then and as we heard it on the Media for weeks thereafter.

Archdeacon you so-called archdeacon you have trampled upon the Law. You have denied a man with a triple-A rating his lawful concubine. You've pushed me too far you so-called archdeacon and now you die. In the name of my beloved Lord Satan whom I serve in all things I send you to him.

Then: the charge in his toy cannon exploding – or, rather, the flash of burning air from the discharged battery extending thirty yards out of the shed, the Warden pacing on his balcony two hundred yards away. Does he see that flash in his last instant? No he does not because at two hundred yards there are no instants between the departure of that concentrated laser fire and its arrival, so the Warden has already had his last earthly look at anything. The brighter flash on his balcony – and then the terrific blast of his superheated body and the concrete that surrounds him obliterates all traces of the Warden from sight. It shakes every building in the compound and deafens every ear. Pieces of Warden (imagined) and balcony (real) fall for several seconds, and then fall again for weeks as the Media makes sure that an aroused citizenry never forgets.

When we were sure that the last lump had fallen Loverbits opened the cooler and asked if anybody but him was hungry. He'd packed it himself and assured Hogarth that there were three big tasty sandwiches for each of us.

It was early Thursday morning and not yet light when we pulled into the Ojibwe fish camp outside of Finland, Minnesota. Finland lived up to its name that morning. A fog of bitter swirling snow was blowing in across the ice all the way down from Thunder Bay, and even though Thunder Bay is in Ontario no border patrols on either side had even tried to stop it. Animkii hustled us into the biggest tent and showed us off to his Ojibwe colleagues from this end of the lake. They thought we were pretty funny even before Hogarth and I took off our coats. Hogarth was still in his cassock and I still wore most of my suit. When they saw that they really cracked up, which being Ojibwe meant they grinned noticeably. One of them told Bluesbaby that no offense but he was the blackest Indian anyone had ever seen and since it wasn't exactly tourist season selling this one was going to be tough. Animkii told him Bluesbaby and Loverbits were staying in the tent and they only had to worry about selling Hogarth and me.

They all wore insulated coveralls with fur-lined jackets

and hats and they had extras for us. I'd been worried they wouldn't have an outfit for a man as tall as Hogarth but Animkii had been briefed as well as we'd been. We had most of an hour to wait and they fed us and lied about how good their fishing had been. Then six of us headed off for the ice while two of the Ojibwe kept Loverbits and Bluesbaby company, purely – we'd understand – so that people used to seeing six men go out to fish every morning wouldn't have anything new to come check out while we were busy in the ice hut.

The wind and what it blew in our faces was brutal and even in the boots they'd given us I had a hard time staying upright on the ice. Hogarth did just fine, though. We got to the hut and one of them lit up the heater. With the door closed we warmed up almost fast enough for me, and then it got way too hot. The hole in the ice was maybe a foot and a half across and it had to get bigger. Animkii started a gas auger and began boring fist-sized holes. After he had the second one done one of the others got the chainsaw going and connected them. Between the auger and the chainsaw the noise was close to unbearable, and I thought *ah, observe the stealthy woodcraft of the red man, see him at one with nature herself*... After five minutes of this the hole was a seven foot square and we were standing on a short ledge around the inside edges of the hut.

Animkii took up an ice-fishing rig, hung a little round gadget on its hook, and said, "Bait." He pushed a button on the gadget and a small red light started flashing. Then he gently lowered it into the hole and let some line out.

One of the men picked up a fish finder, dropped the lead in, and he and one of his friends began to study the display. We'd all have joined them but the ledge of ice was too narrow for a crowd. In about five minutes (but only by my watch) one of them said, "Something coming."

I said, "You see it?"

He said, "What I see are fish running like they've never run before."

The other one said, "Here he comes. Mama, would I like to get a hook into that one. We could eat on it till June."

In a minute we heard a muffled commotion from below and then a gray oval can like two oil drums stuck together rose slowly through the hole. When it had risen a foot it stopped, its top opened up, and a sandy-haired young man in a dark blue turtleneck popped his head and shoulders out.

"Sorry to drop in unannounced gents," he said, "but we've carelessly mislaid our parson and we wonder if you might have one you can spare."

It was a voice from an English holovid. I knew that was coming but it was still a thrill.

Hogarth raised his hand and said, "That would be me, Commodore."

The Englishman said, "Welcome to His Majesty's submersible Sleeping Beauty, Padre. I'm sure you'll meet many a Commodore presently but just for now you'll have to content yourself with a handsome left-tenant and his grotesque and surly cox'n. Grunt for the Padre, Jenkins."

From a foot or so beneath him a voice called out, "Never mind the little shit, Padre, he's an officer and can't help himself. You and me'll get on fine and that's what matters on this boat, Admiral Porter here and his opinion of himself notwithstanding. You've got Abbot's chair as we've only space for three so he's pining for me at home, poor love. Mind your noggin as you go."

Porter, assuming that was his name, said, "Well, yes, I suppose we oughtn't hang about. If I could just have your feet, Padre?"

Hogarth had stripped to his cassock. This was the last tricky part, at least for us. Hogarth was almost four feet from the hatch – three feet, really, but it looked like nine to me – and if we dunked him now we might as well have blown him up back on his balcony. Animkii took one of his armpits and I took the other and we swung him out over the hole. Porter caught his ankles and Animkii and I leaned over as far as we dared and then gave him an upward shove. He straightened up teetering and wobbling but then Porter had him by the thighs and got his feet planted on the ladder. Porter disappeared and we watched as Hogarth followed him down. He looked at us as he ducked his head inside and gave us his best grin but he didn't even have time for a brief good luck and thank you. Then Porter reappeared one last time, said "Splendid work, gentlemen, His Majesty's Navy thanks you all" and reached up and lowered the hatch.

After the Sleeping Beauty blew some rude bubbles and disappeared we watched the hole in silence for a minute. Then I said, "How long till they reach shore?"

Animkii said, "Probably not till late tonight. Our side has Thunder Bay pretty well sensored up so they'll come up further east. And even under the ice they'll want to go slow and quiet even if they do have the minefields charted. Which they do or we wouldn't have got to meet them. But they'll give him a spell of rest before they fly him east and I suppose they'll let him get some sleep on the plane."

I said, "So can we go back now?"

Animkii said, "Jesus. You come all this way to see me and you don't even want to fish?"

On Saturday afternoon I made sure to watch the Media but the story didn't change then and it hasn't changed yet. In case you're wondering how you missed it, nobody ever let a peep get out here about Hogarth's speech but I'm sure the rest of the world enjoyed every minute. Two months later when Gable stepped off for Hogarth's murder they were still sticking to our story word for word. Of course they never pinned anything on Gable's church, probably they were afraid to because somebody out there – us – knew better and might be tempted and able to spoil any story they made up, but they had them on the dead old people scam and every last member of the congregation belatedly followed Gable's suckers out to Jumping-off Camp. It made quite a stir and the holos of the weeping and carrying on as their kids were brought in for the formal goodbyes played on and on for days. It feels *good* to have one's work appreciated, you know?

iv

One more thing. I've been saving it up but I may as well tell you now. It turned out that that was the last one I pulled with any of the others. I didn't expect things to move so quickly but this business of chasing the big money changed things in ways that none of us foresaw. The truth is that my game had become almost obsolete. If Boronzee hadn't had my next big score already lined up I suspect that he'd have probably brought me in and tried to set me up in an office somewhere; he already had a couple of them going and they were bringing in more than my kind of job was ever likely to again. And with Ava stuck in that motel there is no way I'd have gone along, so the split would have come much sooner. But that's hindsight and none of us felt any premonitions at the time. Except maybe me a little bit and Boronzee a little bit more, but I only say that because it might help explain how we both acted later.

And still another thing. Later that day after Loverbits, Bluesbaby and I had a nap Animkii came looking for me. He took me out for a slow walk in the woods. It had warmed up some and turned into a nice day and I was glad for the walk since even the best kept tent gets kind of close after a few hours. We walked without talking for a little way and then Animkii said, "You remember my cousin, the man whose cabin I left my truck at that time?"

"I remember a man but I didn't get a good look."

"Well that was my cousin and he's dead. His wife and kid too. My godson. They were shot and I didn't shoot them but I killed them just as dead as if I had."

I stopped and stared. "Jesus. Who?"

"The postmillennial army of Jesus. Three or four days after they chased us off and caught our cargo. After they had all the time in the world to make those three sorry fools tell them everything they knew. And everything they knew was just a clearing and a cabin in the woods. You know what I did to kill my godson don't you?"

I sighed. "I suppose I do but let me hear it your way."

"I killed him and his folks and even their fucking dogs by not gutting that big-mouth asshole the second he smarted off. I knew I was going to. I knew it. But I figured it might spook the other two if I did it before we made it to the boat. That was the stupidest thing I've ever done, and I'm not criticizing because it was my call but it wasn't too bright of you either."

"Yeah. You're probably right. Someone still could have coughed."

"The militiamen weren't sure. They weren't sure till the big asshole broke and ran."

"Animkii. What about your village, your people?"

"Never made a move, never said a word to us. My cousin was their word to us. They probably thought about it but then who'd bring them their fish?" He took a couple of steps and said, "I never told Boronzee."

I thought about that. There could be a couple of reasons for not telling Boronzee and I didn't care which one counted the most with Animkii, only that my life was simpler because he hadn't.

"I never told him because—"

"You never told him because it's none of his business."

Animkii took a few more steps. "I was hoping you'd see it that way. I want to move across to Ontario so bad. Every time I go it's harder to come back. But there are forty-two people living on what I make for us. Forty-two. And I'd never get them all across."

We walked for a while longer. I said, "I won't tell Boronzee. I won't tell anybody. I'll get you what business I can. I can't promise anything."

Animkii said, "You just did. Only it wasn't what you wished you could promise. But it's a better promise. It's the one I wanted. The only promise worth having is one a man can keep no matter what."

And in a little while I was back in the tent with Bluesbaby and Loverbits and then there was the very last thing. At the time I didn't think it was a thing at all and I'm still not sure how much of a thing it really was, but it feels like I ought to mention it.

Bluesbaby gave me an *ahem* noise, the one that means "I've got something to say that kind of matters," and Loverbits stopped his packing and looked at him like he knew what it was.

Bluesbaby said, "So, this new us. The new us that rents offices and takes on full-grown jobs from the people who wanted us dead this time last year. This bother you any? Reason I ask is you've always been one of us misfits who do our own thinking when we can. Now and then. And seen it pay off. Now and then. But maybe I'm wrong and you're tight with this, so I'm asking."

Loverbits turned my way now.

I said, "It doesn't *bother* me, it scares the living shit out of me."

Loverbits said, "We saw you talking in Louisville. You tell him?"

I said, "Told him as in said some words. Didn't tell him as in made him hear them."

That seemed to be the end of it. I got the sense that they didn't have an argument with me but that they'd been hoping for something a little more – what? Satisfying? Comforting, at least? Anyway, we still had a few hours left together with nothing to do but drive, we still had several hundred miles left together which was plenty of time to bring it up again and talk it through like it mattered, and not one of us even tried.

Lamentations

How doeth the city remain solitary that was full of people?
Thy Prophets have looked out vain, and foolish things for thee, and
they have not discovered thine iniquity, to turn away thy captivity, but
have looked out for thee false prophecies, and causes of banishment.
The Lord hath done that which he had purposed: he hath fulfilled
his word that he had determined of old time: he hath thrown down, and
not spared: he hath caused thine enemy to rejoice over thee, and set up the
horn of thine adversaries. —Lamentations 1:1, 2:14, and 2:17, from
the Geneva translation

I dropped Bluesbaby and Loverbits off at a rest stop in
Ohio. It was as smooth a hookup as we ever pulled: the three
of us walking to the Paco's Tacoroni and by coincidence,
look, a boisterous crowd just off a bus meandering toward the
same place and swallowing us up. Then I, freeing myself from
the noisome throng and on my own again as I'd so obviously
been all day, was through the door and hurrying to the head.
Out of the head I walked to the tail of the line where I was
hailed, as wayfarers sometimes are, by the hearty fellow just
ahead of me who was stopped at this oasis even as I was and
sought as his kind will do at such times to pass an idle
moment in travel-gossip.

Thumper said, "Say, Brother, do you know what's good
here?"

I said, "Try the green chili ravioli. It's my favorite."

"You having it then?"

"Too messy for the car. I'll have to settle for the Tuscan
meatball burrito."

"Well if I see you again I'll let you know how I liked it.
They have these places in Orange you think?"

"They probably have them on Mars."

"Well I hope they do. Have them in Orange I mean. I
have to be in Orange a month from today. I'd hate to be stuck
eating fish."

He turned back to his kinsmen, leaving me to contemplate that I had a month on my own till my next job was ready, and that when it was ready it would be ready in Orange. I'd known before I went to Iowa that it was still being negotiated and I knew that we now negotiated at a statelier, more church-like, more *prison-like* pace than we had when we were riffraff and I sometimes did three jobs a week. So I wasn't surprised, not about my instructions. What surprised me was how much they disgusted me and also the tingly surge of relief I felt at being cut loose for a month. I decided I ought to think a little about those feelings and maybe try to pin down where they came from. I decided that for years we had lived by our reflexes and now we had given them up and I seemed to be the only one who noticed. Instead of living by the hour and day we were living by the month and year. Your daily bread doesn't stretch that far. It never has for anyone. The world doesn't slow down just because we choose to. Boronzee had no idea what we'd just given up and now I was beginning to have doubts about Thumper, too.

I took my burrito and fled like the hurried traveler with a deadline I was supposed to be and suddenly felt like.

I asked for clearance to Chicago which was the first place that popped into my head, and with the car emptied out I got the fast lane which was up to 96 today. Even so I had a few hours to think and I realized how much I'd been looking forward to thinking, but I also remembered how foolish it usually is to look forward to being alone with your own head right after a job. The first stretch of time alone after a longish job has a way of turning uncomfortable. Things have built up that you didn't know were there. When they arrived they saw how busy you were and they politely sat down to wait their turn. By now they've read all the old magazines in the waiting room and they're growing antsier by the hour. They watch for the moment when at last you can't claim to have anything better to do and when it comes they jump up and sprint to beat the rush. Each trying to elbow the others out of the way, they barge in without so much as introducing themselves and demand to be heard.

That's something that always happens. On top of it I

already knew that my obligations were backing up and had to be put in order. So now I had a month, and what could I do in a month? I could do many of the hundreds of things that we used to do in a month but now I'd have to do them by myself because I was the only one of us still moving at day and hour speed. Now I had a few hours of sitting ahead of me: how much could I do in that?

After a few seconds' thought I decided that in a few hours I could worry thoroughly about my name. I used many names of course, on a good long trip I might run though half a dozen of them, but those were throw-away names that were pretty useless for anything but traveling. Once you get out of the car your name needs to stand up and at any one time it's more than just hard to keep even one stand-up name in good working order. My look-into-me-all-you-want name of late was Connor Alexander, which I thought was a fine name as far as it went. My problem with it was how far it didn't go. For instance, it was Connor Alexander who attended Harvard as a divinity student, so it was Connor Alexander who would become a Master of Divinity. And that made old Connor a little more permanent than I'd have liked. Of course Harvard lets its graduates sell their degrees and so Connor's successor *could* also become a Master of Divinity and probably would someday. But Harvard being Harvard they charge more than most for that courtesy and more to the point the name Connor Alexander would have to show on the bill of sale. For another instance, it was Connor Alexander who held down the best job I'd ever had, one that had cost Boronzee a pile of cash to line up. So along with the security of owning a respectable, accomplished name like Connor Alexander came the difficulty of replacing it. It wasn't that I couldn't start over, it was that starting over would just *be* starting over and where was the profit in forever doing that? But still, living as I did had always made keeping the same name for very long a reckless thing to do and nothing about the bus becoming respectable was going to change that. Patterns emerge whether we want them to or not and sooner or later enough data about Connor's travels was bound to pile up, and high enough that some lonely machine on the late shift would notice how well it fit a few heretics' last recorded sightings. So

I was more secure than I'd ever been but at the cost of constantly increasing danger. It was a paradox and a dilemma and seemed likely to stay both.

Since the problem of my name didn't seem to be yielding to a frontal assault I thought I'd get tricky and try to outflank it. I decided that maybe I ought to figure out why I was going to Chicago. And it turned out that that was an easy one. I wasn't halfway through my burrito before I'd nailed it cold.

I was going to Chicago to pull a fast one on my boss.

I haven't told you about the bosses I'd had since my days of hawking robes and gowns for Sarah Schilling. There were a few, each of them dull as dirt and each just marginally more respectable than the one before. My current boss, now that we could afford him, was different. He is a smooth piece of work named Jayden Delgado and of all my bosses his distinction is that he doesn't try to hide a damn thing from anybody. He is a proud, up-front broker of respectability and the world salutes him for it. You pay him his fee every month and he pays you back sixty percent of it as salary, less whatever you've run up on your Jayden Delgado and Associates company credit card. Of the part he doesn't pay you back he keeps a quarter which is ten percent of the whole. Since all his employees are successful and highly paid and since he has a lot of them, his ten percent has made him something of a wealthy man.

Another ten percent of your fee goes for your tithe. Jayden is a rep for several top-drawer ministries, so you have a choice. I, for instance, was a corresponding member of the New Hope Gospel Church of the Wayfarer, Reverend R.T. Pettigrew presiding. Reverend Pettigrew's church doesn't have an address in the usual sense. It exists purely on the Social. Your statutory attendance requirements are fulfilled by Socialing-in an hour a week, and you *do* have to do that because his logs go straight to all the proper places. I often attended three or four times a day, especially when driving. Reverend Pettigrew takes his ministry seriously (especially when you consider what he has to be taking in) and he records two or three services a week, plus you can always pick an old one from his archive and get full credit for it. There are a lot of churches that will do this for you if you can manage the tithe but I applied to New Hope because Reverend Pettigrew does first-class old-time fire and brimstone in a voice and manner much like those of Emancipus Healy himself. Also he plays a lot of the best gospel singing you'll ever hear and when I'm hearing gospel, I *am* in church.

That leaves twenty percent. Half of that goes for your fees, which are for your Jayden Delgado and Associates Driver's License and your Evidence of Gainful Employment Waiver and so on. I have no doubt that a little of your fee deduction finds its way back to Jayden but ten percent is industry standard so it's pointless to let it get to you. It's the other half of your last twenty percent that makes Jayden stand out in a crowded field, because that part, ten percent of what you pay him, goes straight into your retirement fund – and Jayden's retirement fund is a big cut above the usual. Not just big but huge. Because a merely big cut above would mean only that Jayden doesn't pocket it all up-front. Jayden really does save it for you and you really can take it out, subject to two restrictions. The first restriction is that the fund is non-transferable: whatever name you have when you contribute, that's the name you still need to have when you take it out. The second restriction is that it really *is* a retirement fund and you can't claim yours until one of the three doctors Jayden lets you pick from runs some tests and certifies that you really are at least sixty years old. And these guys are top of the line and can afford to be incorruptible.

These restrictions, burdensome as they may seem, are what make the fund legal – legal for you, I mean. Once the State of Chicagoland has certified as a matter of public record that your retirement fund really *is* a genuine retirement fund and it really is *yours*, you have a bullet-proof defense against a vagrancy indictment anywhere in the country. When you need something like that you can't put a price on it, and if you travel around enough sooner or later you *will* need it. And also, because it's a matter of public record that you can't touch it till you're sixty, cops and judges and other lowlife know they can't expect you to use some of it to grease your way out of the kind of trouble strangers in town can get into when they show up looking well supplied with lubricant.

But that's not what makes Jayden's retirement plan really special. What makes Jayden's retirement plan really special is how your money grows. The way it grows is simple, but it's the simplicity of pure genius. As soon as you go off salary – that is, when your fee stops arriving for any reason at all – your retirement is forfeit, and it's split among the remaining contributors in good standing. Now take someone like me, who signs up in his mid-twenties. How long does his name typically last? Two years, three years? How many people who *need* a service like Jayden's are going to make it the whole thirty-five years till they're sixty without even trading in their *name?* Not many, and that's not just a guess. My own fund, though still small, had grown rapidly in the short time I'd had it – hell, in a few months I'd be eligible to vote – so it was obvious that the forfeiture rate is big. And what that does for Jayden is it keeps you as a client for as long as you can hold out, and what that does to you is it gets you thinking *about* holding out. It can change your whole outlook on life. It can get you to consider maybe scaling back those vague long-term dreams you have of cashing in big in some way you haven't quite figured out yet, and start you thinking instead of just hustling up Jayden's fee every month (which, face it, is really how you have to live anyway) because then you'll walk away clean as a very rich and respected man the day you turn sixty. And hell, you know you're never going to make it but you know you're never going to get there any other way either, so you pretend because we all have to pretend something for as long as we can. So why not pretend *this?* And that's what keeps people paying Jayden's fees when it might be easier to switch identity merchants, and that's why I say the scheme is genius.

Now I don't want you to think I'd fall for something like this, but I do want you to consider that Jayden didn't know me all that well and wouldn't have been surprised at all if I did fall for it. Didn't his business *work* because most people fall for it? So I knew something he didn't know – namely that I wasn't buying what most of his clients bought – and it seemed to me that there simply had to be a way to turn that around on him. I was almost through the Indianas when I figured that way out, and when I figured it out I realized I'd need a few days before I actually spoke to Jayden. First I'd have to pick up Ava's diamonds in Kansas City, which I'd known I'd be needing to do soon anyway. But here was the hard part: I was going to have to ask the lady her age. For that I was going to have to go see her. Asking "By the way, exactly how old are you?" was the one thing, silly me, that I'd left out of our protocol of prearranged code phrases for the Social.

Now that I had to head south I diverted at the Northeast Indiana border and bought two hundred gallons of pure Lake Michigan semi-sewage and made sure they put in enough AquaSpoof to get it by all but the most dedicated of water-tax collectors. Then I requested a change of clearance to Kansas City, continuing straight on to Taos after what had better damn well be a very short stop. It was.

I Socialed Ava with the *let's-pretend-to-be-old-neighbors-and-chat-out-loud* code when I was about an hour out from Taos. I started to feel a little worried when she didn't get back to me right away but then she did and apologized for not noticing because she'd gotten too wrapped up in planning Elizabeth and Fitzwilliam's wedding for them. I made an exasperated mental note to remind her again how it really *is* safest to make up chitchat about people whose names have actually been, you know, *used* since the Middle Ages. I filed it away with its predecessors and said I was thinking of dropping in for dinner. She said oh dear the cupboard was almost bare and I told her not to worry and I'd pick something up. She said to *please* this time make it something *light* for her. I agreed of course – why would I want to see Ava if I wasn't going to *agree?* – and I signed off. Then because I hadn't eaten since a corn dog in Kansas City I started thinking about what would go well with a very light standing rib roast.

I'd had plenty of time to think and over dinner I underplayed it pretty well. I said there was a way that she might possibly be able to make me a lot of money without costing herself very much. I told her some things about Jayden's retirement fund that were true. Then I told her two things about it that were lies: I said that I had a lot of money lying around in mine and I said that if she also enrolled as an employee it would be legal for me to sell her my retirement. Then when she reached sixty she could cash it in and give it to me. I was careful to put it that she'd give it *all* to me, as if I hadn't even thought about cutting her in. I pointed out that if

I lived till sixty it sure as hell wouldn't be by keeping my name, so she was my only chance to ever get my own money out. Finally, and I counted on this for the clincher, I said that I was pretty sure I could buy her into Jayden's employ for only a few of her diamonds.

She gave me the fish eye and tried to break me down, but this time my story held. She admitted to fifty-eight and a half, which was even closer than I'd hoped. That gave me a lot of confidence when I slipped in the bit about oh *that* should work, she should be okay from her diamonds for five or six months yet and I could carry her for the extra year no problem, it would be a cheap investment. She said she knew what I was doing which of course I knew she would but I had her cornered and no matter how she tried she couldn't find a way to tell it where it really wasn't the best thing for me – and how can you accuse yourself of taking advantage of somebody when you're making him rich? At the critical point I asked how the reading was going. She knew what I was doing then too and even said so but she was weak and had to tell me how last week she'd rediscovered that somebody named Dickens had made Wockenfuss up about two hundred years ago. I didn't get all of it but the parts I got did sound like she might have been onto something. Pretty soon she said she could see I was tired and shooed me out early so I could get back to the Interstate for some sleep in the automatic lanes to Chicago.

I stopped in St Louis because I had twelve hours or so to kill if I was going to show up in Chicago early in the morning. I spent some of my time there selling two diamonds and eating the roast beef that of course I hadn't inflicted on Ava but which I'd driven myself half-crazy imagining as I munched my salad with her. In Chicago I Socialed Jayden's office and asked for a very brief appointment, apologized sweetly but *confidently* for the short notice, and because I confessed that I could only stay in town for the day I eventually got a 2:45 out of his PA with the stipulation that if his 2:00 ran over I might have to wait. I signed off, reflecting as I always do on how I hadn't believed a word of it when I first heard Boronzee's standard lecture about how showing confidence makes people want to please you. This time I amended the memory with the further reflection that so much of how I now thought had come straight out of Boronzee's head that he probably knew exactly what I was doing right then. *That* of course I didn't like thinking, so I resolved to get busy. I bought a long shower and shave at the parking garage, found three eager jewelers and sold them eleven stones (!) and walked to the State of Chicagoland Building. I spent an hour and a half there feeding money into the public access terminals and learning exactly what *public record* meant in practical terms when it came to Jayden's retirement funds. Those terminals had to be thirty years old but they revealed enough about Connor Alexander and especially his finances that I scared myself shitless in no time. Then I reminded myself why I was there and copied most of the information on thirty women into my Social. They weren't the richest by a long shot because I figured that the richest had probably learned way too much about surviving but they were all at least what I've heard called *comfortable*. Of course even by thinking that way – thinking of their money as *theirs* – I was falling into Jayden's con, but I figured their bogus Jayden-wealth had to be *some* indication of their real prosperity and competence. When I left I was satisfied with my work so far and treated myself to a first-class steak for lunch, reminding myself as I often do that there will be enough meatball burritos out on the road. At 2:40 I walked into Jayden's outer office and didn't have to fake my confidence at all when I gave the receptionist the name she knew me by.

Jayden stood up to greet me and he shook my hand. There are lots of ways to assert superiority and Jayden's way – treating you like an equal when you both know you're not – has to be one of the very best.

"Been well, Connor?"

"Can't complain, and you?"

"No complaints here either. I'm sorry if we're a little rushed today but I think my PA explained. Are you here on behalf of Mr. Boronzee?"

Translation: *No small talk for the likes of you Brother and are you playing your own little game here as I think you must be?*

"No I'm not, I didn't even tell him I'd be here. I happened to be in town for the day and I thought this might be a good time to ask you a couple of questions I didn't know enough to think of before. It shouldn't take up much of your time."

I'm thinking of playing a little con on my real boss and because I'm careful I want to make sure it doesn't offend you. Because I do understand that you get to say no.

"Well then, ask away."

"I suppose it really boils down to just one question if I can figure out how to put it. I thought I was clear on the retirement fund rules but now I'm not quite sure. I get that nobody but Connor Alexander can claim his retirement and that he can't do that till he proves he's sixty. My question is, what does he have to do then to prove that he really is Connor Alexander?"

Jayden's eyes got big and he showed me all his teeth. He leaned forward, put his hands flat on his desk, and gazed at me with astonished and I thought somewhat paternal pride.

"Whatever *are* you thinking, Connor? What *is* your delicious little brain considering?"

"Oh, nothing big. I was just wondering what would happen if in the next year or two Connor Alexander showed back up here and this time he was sixty years old and didn't look a whole lot like he'd ever been me."

Jayden's face relaxed into a merely delighted grin.

"Well I'll tell you Connor. Apart from the fact that he wouldn't take out a whole lot of money unless he did wait a couple of years which you *do* know, right? Yes. Well apart from that, *if* he had identification that would pass the usual kind of scrutiny, and if we *did* find his age and appearance surprising, then we would try to reach every reference we have for Mr. Alexander, starting with Mr. Boronzee. And *if* those people told us that the Mr. Alexander we used to know seems neither to be among us any longer nor known to have departed this world, *then* I suppose we would pay him. And announce that another happy long-term client had collected on his wise investment. But only, Connor, only after making it very, very plain to the Mr. Alexander we paid that if the *other* Mr. Alexander, the one we've always known as you, should ever materialize again under that name or any other, then there would be dreadful and vindictive consequences for both of you. Consequences which I'll leave to your fertile imagination. Does that answer your very interesting question?"

"Yes Mr. Delgado it does. It's even the answer I was hoping for."

"*All* of it Connor? Even the last part?"

"Especially the last part, Mr. Delgado. Especially that."

Oddly enough six of the women on my list were supposed to be working out of New Orleans, and I decided to head down there next. I like what's left of the old city, I like the food, and even out in public you can still catch traces of a way of looking at life that would seriously displease Reverend Williston. But my main reason was that I had to go *somewhere* and spend the next three weeks or so proving to myself that this would or wouldn't work, and New Orleans is the best place I know for just wandering aimlessly around without anyone wondering what you're up to.

At this stage the plan was simple and I'd be surprised if I'd gone any deeper into it yet than what you've already guessed. That's what New Orleans was for – to take the plan further, not even all the way, and certainly not to do it. I couldn't *do* it until Ava was actually sixty or almost there, assuming we both lived that long. If I was to find one of those women *now* and make her go away *now*, I'd have to find a way to keep paying Jayden her fee for the next eighteen months just to keep her retirement fund alive. Jayden's fee for three or four months was enough to get Ava to Canada, so if I could come up with that kind of cash Ava could go straight to Canada and there would be no point to the whole thing. And if I even identified the woman now and stopped right there, what were the chances that in a year and a half she'd still be alive and using the same name and would be not only where I could find her but where I could *get* to her?

When I left for Orange a little less than three weeks later I'd accomplished all I had hoped I would. Assuming I could keep going myself, I'd already saved Ava's life for the next year and a half and had a good shot of buying her a decent life in Canada at the end of that time. I was feeling pretty damn good about it if you want to know the truth.

Still, except for selling diamonds, New Orleans was pretty

much a drawn game for me at best. On the plus side three of the women were actually where their money's public records said they were. I'd been hoping for one and expecting none at all. Finding three of them meant that I was looking at people who were different from me. You'd never find *any* of six people like me if you only look where we're supposed to be. I'm not sure if women who need and can afford to turn into other people tend to survive differently than the men I know, or if Jayden's clients in general are just that much different from us, which could very well be true given how much I couldn't begin to afford him for most of my life. *Or* – and I didn't want to think about this but I had to – whether I was a victim of my own beginner's luck and would never catch up to one of Jayden's people again. Whichever it was I was surprised and pleased to find my three.

One of them was a wife and mother or more likely was doing a very good job of impersonating one. With a family depending on her (or at least having to look like they did) she could not be made to disappear quietly even if I'd been okay with making orphans. Jayden hadn't come right out and said that there'd better not be a manhunt on for whoever Ava said she was when she showed up to collect, but I thought he'd expect me to take something like that for granted.

But the other two would have been possibilities if this had been more than a dry run, and that's where my confidence came from.

One of them spent all of the two days I watched her floating from café to coffeehouse to restaurant to park to café again and then to tavern and club, running some kind of business the whole while on her Social and staying just a little further away from other people than she would if she was really legitimate.

This woman was possible.

The other one left home only once in the two days I spent watching her building and as it was I almost missed her. I was debating gospel music in a café across the street with her picture loaded in my Social and the Social aimed at the door to her building, but even though my unit was top of the line, asking it to match a 2D picture to a real face at thirty yards was asking a lot. It had already claimed two hits but I'd ignored them because these were women who were just walking past. When it went off this time she had just stepped out of the door. She walked off briskly and I couldn't follow her, not without all my new café-friends knowing exactly what I was doing which is only one of the reasons why people who follow other people for a living don't work alone. But that was okay. Mainly, I'd just wanted to find her, and I had. She had left her apartment empty-handed but she came back in an hour with a big bag of what had to be groceries. It was a ritzy building and I saw any number of delivery men pull up in vans and give bags and boxes to the doorman. But not her. What did I want to bet that she never used the same store twice in one month? I'd have to make sure she lived alone of course but she had the look of a woman who did.

This woman was very, very possible.

That was the plus side. Here was the minus. Whatever woman I ended up choosing in a year and a half, one of these or somebody else entirely, she would have to disappear more or less exactly when I wanted her to – and then she would have to stay disappeared long enough for Ava to get away. There is one and only one very good way to make sure that happens. I couldn't use it. I'm not claiming scruples I don't really have, I'm not pretending to believe in my own moral code *all* the time. I had no problem with either of these women dying for Ava but I couldn't kill them. She would know if I did.

I don't mean that she's psychic or talks to God and he tells her things. I mean that the day was coming, the day right after the woman I picked disappeared or at the latest the day after that, when I would have to tell her I'd been lying. I would have to say, forget that story about me selling you my retirement for a dollar. I lied about that. It can't be done. Instead, tomorrow you're going to walk into an office in Chicago with this ID I bought for you for a lot of money that you now owe me on top of your rent, this one here, take it, read it, memorize it, it has your picture on it, see? And you're going to swear you are this woman and you're sixty years old and now you want your own retirement money. And then you're going to go through holy hell for two days but you *will* walk out with that money. And then a friend of mine is going to take you up to Canada and friends of his will set you up there, and you will use the part of this money that I didn't take and they didn't take to live on for the rest of your life which the Canadians will let you do simply because you have it. And no I won't tell you why this real woman is giving you her retirement except that she wants to do it. I didn't steal it, I didn't hurt her, I didn't kill her painlessly like I wanted to. I found a way to make her want to give it to you and that's all I'm going to tell you.

If every word of that isn't true she will *know* it, and the whole thing will stop right there. All of it, including this Jane Dickens and all her pals. Including, pretty soon, Ava. You don't have to believe me. I'm the one who had to believe me, and I did.

Even if I could make it all happen up to that point, I put the odds of convincing her at no better than 50/50.

And to even get to that point I was going to have to deliver a tricky pitch to the woman I finally found and picked, and she was going to have to buy it. So far I had only this rough draft of it in my head but I doubted it would get much better:

You have a lot of money, a lot *of money, tied up in a retirement account with Jayden Delgado and his nonexistent associates that the odds say you're never going to see. You know it and I know it so let's not pretend it isn't true. Because you're a smart woman you don't expect to ever see one dollar of it. But I'm going to offer you the deal of a lifetime. I'm going to buy that retirement account from you today and in a week I'll give you a third of it, in euros, in whatever offshore account you want it in. In return you're going to leave with me now and go with me where I take you and sit tight for that week. After you have the money you'll have to go somewhere other than Chicago and buy a new name the same way you bought the last one. And you can't ever use the old one again or one of Jayden Delgado's nonexistent associates will show up and kill you. I know because he, Jayden, promised me it would happen and we both know he always keeps his word. So – need any help with your packing?*

I also put the odds of pulling that one off at about 50/50.

50/50 and then another 50/50 aren't really great odds, so maybe I exaggerated when I called it a draw. And I knew perfectly well that if either of my pitches failed, the one to this imaginary woman or the one after it to Ava, it would be my fault.

And this thought oppressed me mightily until I finished up in Orange, but then it didn't matter anymore.

I detoured only a little on my way to Orange and stopped again for dinner with Ava. I'd sold all of her diamonds and gotten enough for them that she was good for seven more months. She wanted to know about taking that stash of seven months' rent and trying to buy her way across with it. By now I was pretty sure that Animkii would take her across for his cost and not say anything to Boronzee about it, but there'd be almost nothing left for her to live on once his people on the other side turned her loose. She'd end up in a camp for sure. It would be the kind of camp she could survive in and even have a marginal kind of life but twenty-some years of that is the kind of last resort you don't take till the only alternative is a camp here. To keep her from jumping at it anyway I was careful to put Animkii out of my mind completely, so I was truthful and what's more I looked it when I said that the only people who'd take that little for the job would put her in a hole an hour after I delivered her.

She did tell me something that I knew was coming and that I hated to hear as much I expected to. She said that in a year and a half she'd have read all of her books at least twice and some of them three times over. She said that she'd enjoy doing it but that she didn't *need* to do it the way she needed to read them once. She said that the only reason she could see for *staying* that long was to help me get my money out. She figured she owed me at least that much. But she didn't linger over it and she didn't get dramatic. She just said it and then she made me turn my back so she could make me dinner which was going to be a surprise and I'd better not peek. I looked over a couple of her books while she cooked. They were very strange and I can't imagine reading a whole one but what was interesting was that I'd be going along trying to make sense of what was happening and what people were really trying to say when out of the blue there'd be something that was clear as day and sometimes even so funny that it had to be intentional.

When she had dinner on the table she told me to turn

around and look. I'd almost figured out what it was when she announced it: scratch-made green chili ravioli. I'd have guessed it sooner especially since it was a *surprise* but the ravioli were five times the size of Paco's Tacoroni's.

I said, "Uh, I *did* tell you about me and green chili ravioli didn't I?"

She said, "Of course you did, and one day when we were chatting I told Maria the maid whose Navajo name is Mosi if you're curious. She was appalled. She said 'That can't be real green chili he hates because nobody ever hates real green chili.' And the next day she brought me some of this and now she makes me a big pot once a week. Neither of us had ever made ravioli though. She Socialed a recipe for me and I wrote it out. See?"

She waved a food-stained paper at me and I swear, I *swear*, it was an incomprehensible tangle of earthquake writing – *for a recipe...* It was one of those things that maybe seem to explain more than they do – hi, I'm Floppy and my calling in this life is to save the earthquake-scribblers...

But she was talking again. "...took us about five tries to get them to stick together and not burn but we finally did. You do like them don't you? Even if you don't please say you do because I promised to tell her tomorrow and you're the one who does the lying here."

It turns out as I'd suspected that New Mexico green chilies really *aren't* the color of radioactive limes and *don't* taste like spinach boiled all day in disinfectant and just this once nobody had to do any lying.

But all the way to Orange I kept hearing her, over and over.

One day when we were chatting...

That can't be real green chili he *hates*...

I promised to tell *her tomorrow*...

And sometimes I would whimper and sometimes I would scream and sometimes I would just calmly tell myself that she'd never live another month if I didn't get her out of there.

Isaiah

And according as God gave them understanding of things, they applied the promises particularly for the comfort of the Church and the members thereof and also denounced the menaces against the enemies of the same: not for any care or regard to the enemies, but to assure the Church of their safeguard by the destruction of their enemies. — The Geneva Bible, edition of 1599, from the "argument" to Isaiah, a prefatory distillation of the book's meaning inserted by its translators for the benefit of laymen, lest they fall prey to incorrect or unlearned interpretation.

Boronzee flew into Blessed John Wayne and checked into a business hotel in Laguna Niguel. The next day I paid fifty gallons at the border outside Anaheim and got a pass for meeting him. When you're an outsider going to Orange you fly in, or you drive in to meet somebody who's registered an invitation to you with the Interstate, or else you're a trucker with provable business. There's just no other way, which is why we'd never worked in Orange before. Buses will definitely not get in and peddlers can just stay home.

He was waiting in the approved business way, meaning in the lobby and almost at attention. He looked at me quizzically. I looked at him confidently.

I said, "Mr. Boronzee?"

He said, "Pleased to meet you Mr. Alexander," and shook my hand. Somewhere he'd learned the businessman's power bone-crusher. That too would show up on the lobby video if anyone ever looked hard at it. "Mr. Boronzee" and "Mr. Alexander" are another thing about Orange — they do deep checks, so when you go there you'd better be you and there'd better be a lot to the you that you are.

Boronzee showed some more manners. He escorted me to the concierge for my retinal scan. Now that the Interstate knew I'd arrived it would be waiting for me to leave. It's not a foolproof system because none is but it does slow you down and cramp your style. That's why they do it. Orange slows you down so much that when they finally decide to take you you're just about standing still.

Room service brought us bloody marys for two and fresh fruit for ten. I had the passivescanner-scanner since Boronzee would never have gotten through airport security with it. It showed a hot bug sucking up our every word but it didn't show any active video. We had a fallback ready in case it had but that would have cost us another few hours.

Boronzee took out a briefing document for me to read while he talked nonsense but he laid it face down on the coffee table, meaning that what he'd start off saying was as much for me as for the State of Orange. He laid out two pads of quick-dissolving paper and two pens so we could converse when we got that far. He seemed to be enjoying himself and I was thinking *What a way to have to work*. He gave me a big grin and started in.

"As you know we have a client here who we believe would benefit from the services of Jayden Delgado and Associates. He is Mr. Mason Thorkelson who is the majority owner of Thorkelson Industries which I'm sure you've heard of. Needless to say he is a highly respected and thoroughly upright man in no personal need of your company's services..."

I will spare you. Minute after useless minute about how some of the troops in this great man's army of salespeople are being harassed, hijacked, railroaded and a couple of times even disappeared way off in trailer-park-world which I will realize (he hopes) is far, *far* away from the unfailing civility and not-to-be-questioned rectitude of Orange...

Oh, hell, maybe I won't quite spare you.

Item. Mason Thorkelson did send forth his servant Oliver Gunderson into the hinterlands of Pennsylvania, where he was set upon by the malign inhabitants of that rude place, and robbed of his chariot, and stripped of his clothing, and his other possessions were taken from him, so that next was he beaten for the crime of poverty, and left by the wayside, and must surely have perished had not a kindly Samaritan of the Interstate Patrol discovered him, and bound his wounds, and given him food and drink and such other gentle succor as befitted his need, and conveyed him to the land of Ohio, for which good service the Interstate Patrol did demand of Mason Thorkelson shekels exceeding Oliver Gunderson's keep and recompense for nine full seasons of toil.

Item. Mason Thorkelson commanded his servant Abigail Dunham to journey to the land of South Virginia, that she might sell his wares among the people of that place. But arriving there she was taken and brought before a Magistrate who demanded proof of such wares, and if she did prove it, then more proof that the wares were hers to sell. And Abigail Dunham besought the Magistrate to make inquiry of Mason Thorkelson, who would answer him and provide assurance. But the Magistrate said to Abigail Dunham, wherefore should I trouble myself to seek out thy accomplice, that he may lie to me as thou hast? Whereupon Abigail Dunham was thrown into his prison, and abused most shamefully for the sport of the Magistrate's soldiers, until such time as all her comeliness was spent and the soldiers of the Magistrate besought him to remove her from their sight. And so the Magistrate at last made appeal to Mason Thorkelson, saying behold, I have recovered thy serving wench from ruffians who took her and used her most rudely, and now I will restore her to thee for the gift of many shekels, which she sweareth thou hast power to bestow. And it is fitting that thou should offer this gift, seeing as thou hast taken these shekels of our people in exchange for diverse trifles such as no lawful Magistrate of ours hath granted thee leave to sell. But if thou givest not this gift I will feed thy serving wench to the swine, for they are precious unto us and hunger much for the flesh of my captives. Therefore let the choice be thine, for it is all as one to me. And Mason Thorkelson did pay again, though his nostrils strained at the passage of such a treasure.

Item. Mason Thorkelson bade his most excellent servant Jacob Hall to go into the land of the Wyomingites, that he might make commerce with them. And no word of him coming thereafter, Mason Thorkelson sent ambassadors to make inquiry. And his ambassadors were bold men and fearfully armed, and such Wyomingites as they encountered were sore afraid and spoke honestly with them, saying, Your quest must come to naught as Jacob Hall, having not the means to pay the tolls that on some Thursdays are demanded of the travelers here, was made to vanish into the place called Return to Sender Camp. And journeying to this place the ambassadors found many wretched prisoners starving there and many heaps of bones and many pits wherein scattered limbs and torsos were given up to corruption, but of Jacob Hall they found no particular trace.

Item, or is it *nota bene?* Mason Thorkelson then sent spies into the land of the Wyomingites, to gather him knowledge of the place therein that is called Return to Sender Camp. And returning they did relate how the living inhabitants of that place numbered nine-hundred and forty, but the people transported thereto were multitudes beyond numbering. Wherefore Mason Thorkelson despaired, at last perceiving that Jacob Hall was lost to him. For even the shekels his nose so oft spewed forth in great abundance lacked Our Lord's power to restore a servant who has surely perished.

How all this upsets Mr. Thorkelson.

How he has tried so hard to take an unfailing paternal interest in the welfare of his people.

How he grieves that the benevolence in his heart and the treasure in his vault cannot protect his people as, to pick an instance at random, Jayden Delgado protects his clients with mere cocoons of inaccessible wealth and vaguely rumored promises of retribution should that wealth be disrespected. But how, also, Mr. Thorkelson has studied this lesson, and is now determined to procure such a shield for those he can't protect in any other way.

Has Mr. Boronzee already mentioned that every one of Mr. Thorkelson's people is an honest son or daughter of Orange? Well in case he hasn't, let him tell me again so that when I go to see Mr. Mason Thorkelson on behalf of my employer Mr. Jayden Delgado of Jayden Delgado and Associates which as I know is the company I work for…

Occasionally pausing to pluck a strawberry from the platter and *mmmm* and *ahhh* at its perfection.

Occasionally pausing to glance meaningfully at said platter so I would realize its significance which first of all I couldn't begin to guess and second I didn't believe it could possibly have any and third I wouldn't have cared by then if it was the

Grail itself.

I gave him grimace after grimace and all the *yeah-yeah-yeah* nods in my sample case. If he hadn't yet established that we were working for a local political powerhouse and that the trouble he was hiring us to make would happen more than half a continent away, then the people he was performing for were too priggish or too dense to be persuaded by more talk. But I got more of it anyway. Maybe Boronzee was cleverly painting a picture of us as the dullest, most prudish sycophants in town, men the silent protectors of Orange should definitely avoid if they were not to perish from boredom. If that's what he thought he was doing then I couldn't agree. I thought that if anybody ever bored me the way Boronzee had to be boring them I'd take it personally and hold an itchy grudge for weeks. I thought Boronzee had been on the bus too long and then had been schmoozing with churchmen too long and that the time we were wasting was mostly ours and furthermore we were wasting it in a dangerous way. I was beginning to think that maybe he'd gone so far down the road to dither-and-schmooze land that we'd never do anything right again. Then he picked up another strawberry and held it up and gave it several glances of pure stark desperation, and I saw what he was up to. *He was only trying to make me eat my fruit.* Eat my rare and excellent fruit before we got started for real, eat it because it would do me good and this was the only chance I'd get to eat it for years and years and years. Thoroughly boggled, I shoved a hunk of pineapple into my mouth and made my teeth go up and down on it. I had the impression that it was one of the best things I've ever eaten but I had a much stronger impression of *so what?* Disregarding what he didn't know I thought, he grinned and mimed mopping a steaming brow with the back of his hand. Then he turned my briefing papers over and talked a much easier strain of gibberish while I read.

I read that Mason Thorkelson had a difficult willful daughter named Lily. I read that Lily was "all girl" but in every other way "would have fit right in on the bus." Lily loved every luxury and privilege she was born to and hated herself for loving them. In the grip of her hatred she said reckless things and she did reckless things. Every time she did them

Thorkelson paid to get her off the hook. He paid more and more every time. That was all right with him because he had plenty more to spend but she had reached the age where soon there would be no more getting off. Soon his only choice would be to cut her loose or go down with her. Thorkelson would tell me how that was. If I didn't stop him he would tell me all night how that was.

If Lily was going to stay alive she would have to go live in Canada or Europe. She'd been all over both before and every time she went he'd hoped she'd stay but she wouldn't. She'd have a nice week or two and then she came back and said her place was here with the rest of the vultures. She said that when the other vultures got their fill of her then she'd have finally earned the right to join the carrion people, her true nation. Now that her own vulture class had lost almost all its patience with her they'd even taken her passport away and that made her *happy* because now maybe Thorkelson would shut up about sending her where she couldn't embarrass him anymore.

Boronzee wrote that Thorkelson and Lily understood each other thoroughly and not at all. He wrote that each was resolved never to understand the other, because they knew that if they did then they might very well begin to think alike, to see things as the other saw them, and with that would come the destruction of everything they hoped they were.

Thorkelson had made a plan. Boronzee said it was a pretty good one. Boronzee and Thumper took it and made a better plan out of it and sold it back to Thorkelson. Like all of their plans it was the essence of simplicity. All I had to do was con and then kidnap an unwilling passenger and carry her off to Canada and make sure she burned all her bridges along the way so she'd have no choice but to stay and live there safely in lifelong wealth and comfort. The really creepy part of reading the plan was realizing that it would probably work.

With the end of my reading came the end of my official public briefing. Boronzee Socialed Thorkelson, confirmed that I'd show up in an hour and forwarded him my pass. Thorkelson amended it with a Class II Invitation to spend less than 24 hours at his residence and sent it back, copy to me.

Boronzee and I sat and watched it glow: the State of Orange does have just the prettiest seals and gizmos. Thorkelson had simply ignored the Purpose of Visit section but still in under a minute it turned from pending-yellow to fully-approved-green. Boronzee gave me a look: *See? I told you he was somebody.*

If you ever get to make the drive from Laguna Niguel to Costa Mesa you'll understand why Orange has the highest water taxes in the country. What wasn't sunny green was shady green and what wasn't any kind of green was screaming in other colors. I don't know many of the names of the flowers I've seen in my life but I know for sure that I'd never once seen any of the thousands of kinds I passed on that drive. There were reds and yellows too bright for a holovid starlet's shoes at the Oscars. There were purples and blues too deep for any 4D nighttime shot of the Milky Way. Of *course* the streets were cobblestoned and all curves without a straight stretch anywhere. Of *course* there was a horse-and-carriage lane – how could there not be? Of *course* the velvet curtains of the carriages were drawn, of *course* the horses wore high-arcing plumes of feathers from every bird known to every jungle on earth, and of *course* the silk-hatted coachmen looked down on me and sneered. The sea breeze was everywhere, even where some mansion blocked your view of the water. Every palm and every patch of color and all the horses' feathers swayed in that breeze. And in the midst of all this Thorkelson's estate still stood out.

My official pass had told the street where to take me. The street drove me up to a weathered wooden gate in a flinty granite wall. The street told the gate to open and let me through and the gate complied leisurely and with a kind of haughty grace. As the gate closed behind me the drive took over from the street. The drive kept me at five miles an hour so I could take in the greenest lawn I've ever seen and fully appreciate its hillocks and trees and arbors before I turned my attention to the house at its far end. It was low, no more than three or four stories in most places, but it did sprawl a bit. It was mostly made of the same granite as the outside wall of the estate, which I thought went well with the faded orange tiles on the roof and the half acre of flowering vines crawling up the building. I tried to decide whether it really was bigger than the orphanage I grew up in but I couldn't make up my mind because the landscaping kept throwing me off whenever I tried to guess a measurement.

When the drive decided I'd had a good enough look it parked me under a weeping willow. I was grateful for that because of the hundred or so trees along the drive and on the lawn that weeping willow was the only one whose name I knew for sure. A man stood waiting for me, a tall lean man in his fifties with a rich man's long hair and a craggy hawk-like face. From bottom to top he wore polished leather sandals, pale cream wool slacks with a crease you'd find useful in a bar fight, a soft silk shirt one shade darker than his pants that was open at the collar and rolled halfway up his arms, a tan on those arms that made them at least two shades darker than mine, an unsmiling mouth that was used to being obeyed but mostly without speaking, and skeptical pale blue eyes that hadn't seen much they liked for at least a couple of decades. Although he hadn't looked like a man given to superfluous banter he nodded a hello at me and said, "I'm Thorkelson. Let's walk."

We followed a winding stone path through maybe eighty different kinds of flowering bush, crossed a long narrow patio, and walked out to a low wooden catwalk that ran straight and true over about four hundred yards of pristine beach. Thorkelson turned left onto it with the decisive air of a man who takes his pacing seriously and knows exactly how it should be done. Every forty yards or so we passed little outcroppings in the walkway where three or four deckchairs were arranged for proper ocean gazing. Out past the surf sailboats darted in toward shore and then darted back out to sea again. On the outward leg the smaller ones swung in to pass close alongside one or another of the gray-hulled patrol boats, I figured to check in so there'd be no questions when they sailed back again. The larger sailboats didn't bother. I supposed they were the kind of well-connected vessels that patrol boats take their orders from and not the other way around. They were quite a sight and so was Thorkelson and if I were capable of knowing my place then strolling with him down that catwalk in my plebian suit and tie would have put me in it for sure.

We'd gone at least fifty yards before he said his first real words to me. "The hardest part of this for me is knowing that once she goes it will be years before I can go visit her. And I won't even be able to say goodbye or she'll know she isn't coming home again. That's mostly what I'm thinking right now and you ought to keep it in mind."

I saw no reason to cut him any more slack than he had coming. "Why years? A man like you goes where he wants."

"To my face they'll believe she's really dead. Maybe they really will believe it too, but they'll watch where I go anyway. Until they're sure I couldn't have stood to stay away from her that long."

"But you'll stand it."

"I'll have to."

"What about her mother? Will she?"

"Her mother doesn't see her. Her mother knows what my wife and I tell her and I don't tell her anything and my wife does what she's told. And my wife will be happier to see the last of her than anyone else in Orange and the rest of Orange will be pretty damn happy."

I wondered how people as successful as Thorkelson don't learn that tantrums never earn you anything.

"Why? I get that Lily speaks her mind and according to Boronzee her mind works a lot like mine does. So that makes her obnoxious but she's rich and spoiled and spoiled rich kids are supposed to be obnoxious. It's what making allowances is *for*, so you've got something to give the rich kid who has everything else. I'm having trouble understanding what she could do to stand out in a place like this. Stand out enough to get into real trouble I mean."

He stopped walking a second and gave me a surprised look of unfeigned admiration.

"Damn, kid, I *like* you. Last thing I expected to be saying."

"I don't give a flying fuck what people like you like."

"And that's why I like you. Because with all we've got to talk about that was the first thing you made sure I understood."

"After I make sure people know where they stand I get persistent. Here, let me show you. Why does everyone in

Orange hate your daughter so much, mister? What makes her so much worse than the kind of wretched brats people *try* to breed around here? And why if she *is* that much worse which would really be something to see would you lift a finger to stop them from carting her off to the dump?"

Just then we reached the end of the catwalk and turned back. Turning gave him the chance I wanted for him to see my face and know how much I meant everything I said.

He saw and said, "Look, I already told you where you stand with me so you don't have to keep trying so hard. I won't let them take her to the dump because I love her more than everything else put together. You question that and I will definitely change my mind about you.

"As for how she gets under people's skin, it's simple, she really is like you. Other kids make a show of all the things they pretend they do and don't believe in and you're right, people make allowances. She doesn't act up at all, she just shows you what she thinks and leaves it laying right there. You say *God has a plan for my prom dress* or *Wasn't Reverend Williston just precious this morning* and she just curls her lip and sometimes, not always, *sometimes* she says 'Oh *please*' or 'What a crock' and not like it could ever matter one bit what you think. Wherever she is. At somebody's wedding, in front of somebody's grandmother, in the middle of a hot slow dance with Prince Charming, nothing but pure contempt and the worst part is they know she doesn't care who sees it. She–"

"*Okay*, right, I got it. She's the honest mirror nobody can stand to look in, she's the doctor who should have waited till after your vacation to tell you the tumor isn't shrinking, she's got no more use for people than the rest of you but she doesn't have the sense to not show it. The point is made, can we move on?"

I was wasting my breath.

"Oh but she has all the use in the world for people, so long as they aren't paid-up citizens of Orange. That's what she runs her mouth about and that's the part I can't buy her out of anymore. Shit-kickers and hilljacks can do no wrong, their ignorance is all our fault, underneath the lies we've sold them they're the salt of the earth. The Levellers and the atheists are the only honest people in the world and it's a crime what we do to them and someday when she grows some real guts she'll stop talking where it's safe to talk and go where it isn't and *do* something about it. And she means it too. No matter what kind of trouble she gets in, she says she's a gutless parasite now but maybe not forever.

"Sixty-two felonies quashed to date and believe me I *have* been told what happens on the next one and I *have* passed it on to her. And all she'll say about it is *so what* Daddy, we all have it coming but at least I'm going to earn mine and I'll take it standing up. And the part you have to believe is that she absolutely will. I had trouble convincing Mr. Boronzee too but in the end he—"

It was time to put a stop to it. "Yeah, he told me. He said I'd have to let you go on about it for at least an hour before I could shut you up but that doesn't mean you have to prove him right. I have an advantage over Boronzee. You already convinced him and when he's convinced about something that means it's true, so I believe it even when I don't. And you believe it because you're too upset to be faking and you'd know what you're talking about so now I know it's true for a second reason. Are we clear on this? I believe? No more?"

He stopped and studied me for a long minute. Then he said, "You *asked* me how she's different and now you say you knew it all along. Why would you do that? Do you think I *like* saying these things and feeling like this?"

I shrugged. "I told you I don't care what you like. I did it to see how you are when you're telling the truth. So I'll have one more way to tell when you lie."

"*When* I lie?"

"Right. When."

We sat in one of the outcroppings and turned the chairs around to face the house. It had cooled down and a vaguely Asian houseboy in a white linen jacket came out and served us hot coffee from a silver service. He stepped back a few paces to wait but Thorkelson told him to leave the pot and not to bring the sandwiches till he waved.

I said, "I hear she's been all over the world."

"Not all over it. All over Canada and most of Europe. Never anywhere else."

"And I hear you hoped she'd take to it without having to be convinced."

"It's been clear since she was twelve that she can't live in this country. Of course I had hopes."

"But she never found anywhere she liked."

"Not true. She loved it all. Other kids from Orange get their week of playing in the snow in New South Quebec? Hell, at any one time half the fools in Stowe, in *any* expensive enough place in *Vert Mont,* are from Orange. They fly there and then to *Keh-beck* City and *Mohn-ray-al* just to order dinner in French, and then they're off to Toronto or Seattle or Portland for the pub crawling and the gutter puking. *She* goes to little villages and learns how to make cheese. *She* goes to other little villages and learns how to catch salmon. *She* wanders into a lumber camp and learns how to sew and make flapjacks. It's okay to cook and sew if no man expects you to. Wherever it's been, she's always loved every minute."

"Then why the *hell…* You know what I'm asking."

"She'd come home and look me in the eye and say *Someday I* swear *I'll deserve to go back and live there.* And then she'd go off and get herself booked for incitement to public blasphemy."

I started. That one would have saved us some time if he'd said it at first. That's not one anybody can make up.

We drank our coffee. I worked on my question. When it was ready I asked it.

"Boronzee told me she won't be coming back this time because I'm going to burn her bridges. What bridges are those? What kind of bridge is there that if she burns it she'll deserve to stay away? And by the way deserve to live very well off your money which the Canadians will insist on for a good long while?"

"Oh God that *is* the question isn't it?"

"Uh huh. And you called me and I'm here so that means you have the answer."

"It means I think I do anyway. You're not going to like me much when I give it to you."

I grinned. "Who says I like you now?"

He grinned back. "Right, you told me that and I forgot. Here goes. She's not coming back because if she does she'll be killing me which might not count. But she'll also be killing twenty-six of the kind of people she thinks of as halfway innocent, and that's one thing I don't think she'll let herself do."

I sat and looked over the house. I thought for the first time that just maybe Thorkelson hadn't inherited all of it and maybe none of it at all.

I said, "I see. You know, I did read over the plan. And I don't remember any people getting killed at all much less twenty-six of them. Not if I get her there I mean."

He nodded. "That's right. Twenty-six people dying is not part of the plan as you've seen it and it won't be if you and your boss-on-paper Mr. Jayden Delgado do your jobs. And make sure she sees you do them, make sure she understands what you've done, and make sure she knows that it's too late to undo it, *that now she has no way to back out.* I admit that sounds like a lot, but Mr. Boronzee said that if anybody could pull it off it would be you. From what you've been showing me, I'm inclined to see what he means."

The light was fading and it was a little more than cool when Thorkelson waved just once at the house and the houseboy trotted out with a linen-draped tray.

Thorkelson said, "Keep your sandwich in your hand or it's seagull dinner for sure. Even then you have to watch for them because they're sneakier than you think."

"I'm surprised you tolerate them."

"You think you're joking but every year *somebody* brings up how nice it would be if we could just poison them all and be done with them."

"And then you nature lovers talk him out of it?"

"Hell no. Then we nature lovers commission another study to show him how high his taxes would have to go up."

With the sandwiches came a millimeter-thick sheet of shiny black plastic. Thorkelson pressed a corner and it came to life. He tapped it a couple of times and handed it over.

"Here. Give it a nice strong password you can remember."

"Okay but you know they'll just scan it."

"It'll be harder than they expect. This one costs a little

more than most. It has a dedicated q-processor just for the terabit encryption key. It won't stop anybody with a decent lab but no mere cop is going to get anywhere with it."

The sandwich was prime rare beef. A pissed-off gull did everything he could to get it away from me and then tried hard to ruin my meal when he saw he couldn't but I didn't care at all. Thorkelson had his own gull but he didn't seem to notice it or the sandwich in his grip.

I chewed on my dinner and examined the tablet. There was a patrol boat just off to the side behind us and a pretty good ways off shore and I fidgeted my deckchair around so I'd be between it and the display.

Thorkelson said, "They don't watch us."

I said, "How could you possibly know that?"

He considered. Then he moved his own chair so we were side by side. "Why do I believe you? I *know* better. They're *patrol* boats."

"Yeah, everybody's only one thing, like you're a famous businessman and I'm a chauffeur, so how could we be hanging out eating supper? But here we are and here they are and what they do and what they're for is to watch."

"Sometimes they do a little more than watch. Laser aft and Gatling gun fore, strictly line of sight but nothing they can see could possibly get past them. Not since we drowned the navy in that famous old bathtub."

"Other people still have navies."

"And we have a treaty with Nebraska and Nebraska still has the nukes so other people's navies are the last thing we have to worry about. For what matters to us those boats do fine."

"They do fine or they look fine?"

Thorkelson pointed down the beach. "Ex-neighbor of ours, you can't quite see his place but you can see the end of his beach. His widow's beach now. Liked to fly his own plane, old military jet restored to cherry. One night he takes it out to sea a few hundred miles, turns around and heads home and half his electronics go dead including his beacon. Fool Socials his wife, tells her he'll be a little late because he wants it looked at when he lands. Wife says but what about the patrol? He says they know him and anyway he passed them on the way out, they're expecting him back. Wife says, still, the beacon – shouldn't she Social the patrol? He says Jesus Christ for what he pays in taxes they'd better know where they get their beans and biscuits and anyway if anybody's going to Social them it'll be him. Which he isn't going to do because he doesn't need to which he could swear he just explained. Over and out. He liked to hear himself say things like that. Over and out.

"Taylor and I are out here with another couple, Logan and Zoe. Beautiful night, clear as a holo. We hear a whoosh building out to sea and I say, 'Here comes Ryan.' Then comes one thin red flash, sea to sky, straight as an arrow but over in a blink, and then a huge white flash overhead. We just look at each other. One second, two seconds, we hear the rolling boom, just like thunder. It passes but now the whoosh is gone. Five seconds, six seconds, then *tick tick tick* on the deck, little bits of something glowing like hot red hail. Logan who's sometimes a little slow asks what the hell is that? Taylor says, 'I believe that would be Ryan.' Maybe you had to be there but we simply cracked up. I should probably mention that we'd had a little bit to drink and nobody ever really liked Ryan. Widow's okay so we let her keep the place. But the gardeners were picking BBs out of the grass and sand for a week."

Maybe I had to be there but I'd never been anywhere else.

I brought up the first page on the tablet, a certain Jacob Navarro.

I said, "Navarro, doesn't sound too much like Orange to me."

Thorkelson said, "Shows what you know. Old Spanish, cartel people from way back but come down in the world a little since then. Salesman of the month three times, I met him once, nice fellow. From Anaheim of course, he does okay for us but no better than Anaheim. That's true of all of them in fact, they're all Anaheim. We have some snobbish people here, I don't deny it, who will tell you that Anaheim isn't the real Orange and we should just give it back to LA. Well of course it isn't the real Orange, but how are we supposed to get the people we need to work for us? Let them in from outside? You can't *have* an Orange if you don't have an Anaheim. You can have a Beverly Hills with a fifty-foot wall around it, but you still have to let *some* people in to do the work, and how can you really control that? You can have an Anaheim and you can be careful and control who lives there, and then you get good people like Jacob Navarro. Or you can lock them all out at quitting time, and then you take who you get. You wouldn't believe the people who sneak in when you try to do that, I've heard stories that would–"

"Mr. Thorkelson. I know. I *am* one of those stories, remember?"

He thought that was pretty funny, almost as if I'd been joking. "Yes I guess you could say that, couldn't you? But the focus for this meeting is that Anaheim only works inside of Orange. When we send them out to work for us anything can happen to them and sometimes–"

"Mr. Thorkelson. I *know*. Surviving out there is what I *do*."

"Well, yes, so you do. So you understand. To be safe and do business you either have to have real money or you have to have something that looks so much like money most people can't tell the difference. But I suppose you'd know that too."

"Yep. Sure as my name isn't Connor Alexander."

"So we're in the same holo then. You and Lily go see your employer of record and buy us twenty-seven small but fictional fortunes. Armed with which Navarro and the rest of my salespeople can roam the land in safety."

A thought struck me then and I laughed out loud. Thorkelson was somewhere between surprised and annoyed.

"Care to share it son?"

"Sure. I'm wondering whether Jayden Delgado has ever sold anybody their own real name before."

That got him grinning too. "I wish I could have been there to hear Mr. Boronzee explain it to him."

"So which one's Lily?"

"Number 14, Layla Solberg. Solberg for the Scandinavian DNA and Layla for Lily."

I called up number 14.

"You gave them different birthdays I hope."

"Ten days apart. Close enough to get by any test they can run on her."

"Good because that's the first thing the Mounties will do.

How deep is she?"

"Excuse me?"

"How deep is her history, her past?"

"I made her up four years ago and put her on the payroll. Since then she's been a good worker especially for someone who hired in at seventeen. Couple of bonuses but not a hotshot. I admit I was tempted to make her one."

"Good that you didn't. Travel history, medical, that kind of thing?"

"Medical, any time Lily had something done, I paid for it in Layla's name. Since the company was right and the payment cleared nobody ever checked. I suppose they thought Layla Solberg was a rich girl's incognito."

"If they thought at all, which they probably didn't once they had the cash. That's good. Curious people buy her billing records, they match what any doctor sees. Travel?"

"Layla hates to fly. She prefers to drive and has had two company cars. She puts in a lot of miles and always files her expenses. Hotels were trickier. She makes lots of reservations and then cancels at the last minute, when it's so late she has to pay anyway."

"That's probably good enough, at least for Jayden and he's all we care about. There are better ways but they only work because people like you wouldn't know about them. Banking, mortgage, rent, clothes, other things people buy?"

"Covered."

"Boyfriends, girlfriends, other lovers?"

"Layla is the soul of tact."

"Family?"

"Dead, or so she believes. Last seen vacationing in Idaho four years ago. It's why she needed the job."

"And you gave it to her, Thorkelson Industries is all heart. That's good, no people in her life. People you're supposed to know are the amateur's weak point. Nobody ever lies for you like they say they will. So what if anything does Lily know about Layla and her life?"

"Not a damn thing, because she doesn't know anything about the other twenty-six. Layla's as real to her as they are, no more, no less."

"Not quite. Layla will have Lily's face. I assume this *is*

Lily's face?"

"Of course. What would be the point otherwise?"

"Well then Lily will see it in Jayden's office if not before and boy will she be surprised."

"I cooked up a story, tell me what you think. Lily's going to Chicago because I don't trust you so well that I'm not sure you wouldn't cut a deal with this Jayden, split the money and leave my people as naked as they are now. And there's hardly anybody I can trust to watch you because how do I know you won't persuade them to just split the money with you?"

"I know. It's the plan. Boronzee told me. It doesn't explain Layla's face."

"I'm getting there. When I told Lily how much I don't trust you it rang true to her because I don't trust anybody, which is one of the things she hates about me. What also rang true is the idea that, consumed as I am by guilt and fear, I won't send her off under her own name with a dubious man like you. A name that could be worth a lot to a kidnapper in a place where kidnapping is almost a legitimate business. So she'll have to be Layla to you and everybody else for the whole week. Now, she isn't capable of respecting that combination of paternalism and timidity *but*. To be sent off incognito with, pardon me, a crook. To meet another crook, and to participate with them in their crookedness, and all for the noble cause of protecting my exploited wage slaves? That seemed to appeal just enough."

"I can see how it might. How does Layla get her face back?"

"I told her Delgado will substitute the pictures after you give them to him. I told her I already sent him Layla's real picture."

"You could send *one* picture and not the whole thing? She bought it?"

"I had to wrap it up in all kinds of silly crap. I also had to promise she'd get to meet the real Layla. God only knows what she plans on telling her. She wanted to do it before you leave, but I explained that Layla's in Kentucky. But she should be back in Orange when Lily gets home."

Thorkelson was looking just a little ill. The memory of his lies to his daughter was working on him. The fact that those lies would be the last thing she'd remember him for probably didn't help. The evidence said lying bothered him more than I had thought it would, since with all the chances he'd had he hadn't lied to me yet.

It was downright cold now and I was grateful for the feeble warmth of my suit coat though Thorkelson in his open shirt seemed oblivious. It was also fully dark. Japanese lanterns had come on all by themselves and lit the way back to the house. They beckoned. We had talked it out and I was ready to go and he looked sick of me and sicker at the idea of what my going meant. I stood up and said, "Come on. It's time to do it."

We went up another path, across the patio again and in through a pair of French doors. They opened in on an ornate living room that I didn't have time to take in because Thorkelson led me down a hall and into a bright, comfortable and practical kitchen.

She was waiting for us at a table like the hired help she was supposed to be. He had shown me a picture of a pretty girl. It had mostly looked like the picture that belongs on anybody's badge. He had said so much about her but he hadn't told me she had the body of an athlete or the kind of hair girls in Orange just don't wear, hair that was all one color and what's more was probably the color it came in, which was red – blondish red, but not blondish enough to be reddish blonde. There was nothing modest about that hair. She wore it aggressively as if daring the world to comment. After managing to notice just that much I looked only at her face because I seemed unable to look anywhere else.

Thorkelson introduced Mr. Connor Alexander to her and Miss Layla Solberg to me. She simpered prettily, expertly, sarcastically. That simper started to work on me in ways I'll tell you about soon. What matters for this part is that it shut me up and Thorkelson did most of the talking which was the way I should have planned to play it anyway. I let him go through his pep talk one more time and he leaned heavily on how much danger his people were in on the road. Hearing him tell it I got a new impression, something that should have occurred to me before: that his people really were being picked off like flies and until he needed to pull a con on this girl he hadn't tried to do a thing to help them unless they were already half dead or worse.

She interrupted and looked at daddy and pointed to me with a backhanded thumb. "What does *he* do, *Boss?* When he's not doing this I mean?"

Thorkelson said, "Mr. Alexander specializes in–"

I said, "Usually I smuggle atheists and heretics out of the country one step ahead of militias and lesser authorities."

A kind of glow spread across her face and settled in like it planned on staying awhile. "You wouldn't lie to your Layla about that?"

"Sure, I confess all the time to capital crimes that it's a whole other capital crime to confess to."

She liked that answer too. She seemed to think it proved she'd made a smart decision and now she was sure to have fun for a whole week. She said she'd just run and get her bag. Thorkelson tagged along behind us to the car. You see people at funerals walking like he did, especially those last few steps to the hole. His face would have sunk the plan on the spot if she'd glanced back even once but I guess he knew she'd never think to do it.

Song of Solomon

I am black, O daughters of Jerusalem, but comely, as the tents of Kedar, and as the curtains of Solomon. Regard ye me not because I am black: for the sun hath looked upon me. The sons of my mother were angry against me: they made me the keeper of ye vines: but I kept not mine own vine...

Behold, thou art fair, my love: behold, thou art fair: thine eyes are like the doves: among thy locks thine hair is like the flock of goats, which look down from the mountain of Gilead...Thy lips are like a thread of scarlet, and thy talk is comely: thy temples are within thy locks as a piece of a pomegranate. Thy neck is as the tower of David built for defense: a thousand shields hang therein, and all the targets of the strong men. Thy two breasts are as two young roes that are twins, feeding among the lilies. Until the day break, and the shadows fly away, I will go into the mountain of myrrh and to the mountain of incense. –An Excellent Song Which Was Solomon's, 1:4-5, 4:1, 4:3-6, from the Geneva translation.

When I walked behind Thorkelson into that kitchen everything I had in mind changed on the spot. I know what that sounds like, but you can take your love at first sight and tow it to the fairy tale junkyard we start growing in our heads about the time we turn six. Didn't I tell you how old I am? Do you imagine I'd never seen a beautiful girl before or thought what it would be like to be the one she wants to be alone with? But I was going to be alone with this one. I was going to be alone with this one because the people who could have kept me away from her, the people who had always done everything they could do to keep me away from her, those people now wanted me alone with her instead and what's more they had told me so. That had never, ever happened before. It changed things. It changed them so much that my first thought popped up in one whole piece and moved in for good.

This one is not going into anybody's camp. This one is not going into

*a hole in the woods or into any lake. This one is going to get free and I'm
the one who'll get her there.*

Make of that what you will. Think anything else you want
to think of me, but do not think that after what I've already
told you I'd turn into the lying fairy godmother who once
upon a long time ago sold you your love at first sight and your
happily ever after.

And don't expect to hear any more about this from me. If
you don't know what it's like nobody could possibly tell you
and if you do know then I don't have anything to add.

Daniel

And the King spake unto Ashpenaz the master of his Eunuchs, that he should bring certain of the children of Israel, of the King's seed, and of the princes: Children in whom was no blemish, but well favored, and instruct in all wisdom, and well seen in knowledge, and able to utter knowledge, and such as were able to stand in the king's palace, and whom they might teach the learning, and the tongue of the Chaldeans.

And the King appointed them provision every day of a portion of the King's meat, and of the wine, which he drank, so nourishing them three years, that at the end thereof, they might stand before the King. Now among these were certain of the children of Judah, Daniel, Hananiah, Mishael and Azariah. Unto whom the chief of the Eunuchs gave other names: for he called Daniel, Belteshazzar, and Hananiah, Shadrach, and Mishael, Meshach, and Azariah, Abednego. But Daniel had determined in his heart, that he would not defile himself with the portion of the King's meat, nor with the wine which he drank: therefore he required the chief of the Eunuchs that he might not defile himself. (Now God had brought Daniel into favor, and tender love with the chief of the Eunuchs.) And the chief of the Eunuchs said unto Daniel, I fear my lord the King, who hath appointed your meat and your drink: therefore if he see your faces worse liking than the other children, which are of your sort, then shall you make me lose mine head unto the King. –Daniel 1:3-10, from the Geneva translation.

We got in the car and I started driving, which in Orange means you tell your car you're ready to go and then you're basically off work.

Layla-Lily said, "Are we–"

I said, "Excuse me, I know this is rude but I have to think a little."

I shut my mouth. I had plans to reconsider. I had my whole life to reconsider. By the time we got to the gate and the drive turned us over to the streets of Costa Mesa again I'd reconsidered it two or three times in every variation. There was only one way it came out anywhere close to right.

She watched me make up my mind. She watched me very carefully and apparently she saw it happen because just when it did she kind of backed into the corner of her seat like people do when they suddenly get nervous about who they're riding with. When that was done she opened her mouth to speak.

I wasn't ready for her to speak her mind so I said, "How long before we get to the water depot?"

She said, "The car knows, why do you care?"

"Because until we take on our water and pick up some steam I'll probably start lying if you make me talk very much."

"You're either a prick who lies or the man you say you are. What the fuck does it matter where we are?"

"Right now I'd probably lie because if I don't you'll want to run back and have it out with your father. And if that happens while we're taking on water or crawling like this you'll try to jump out and take off. But not after we really start moving, not when it'd mean a high-speed road rash on the LA side of the line. That's when you start hearing the truth from me."

"Then shut the fuck up and drive."

I shut up but the car and the road did the driving. I just looked at my passenger. Looking at her suited me fine. It seemed to suit her fine too because she looked back just as hard. I've called her a beautiful girl and right away you thought *Of course, twenty-one year old girl from Orange, when are they ever not beautiful?* She wasn't like that. I suppose she'd probably had her teeth straightened and for all I know she got her chest rightsized like they all do there but she hadn't changed her face. It was the face for which Thorkelson's had been the rough draft before he ruined it by being Thorkelson. Thorkelson's grown-up face was nothing but appetites and calculations. I hadn't seen that clearly before but with Lily's to compare it to it was obvious.

In four minutes the car darted behind the false front of what looked like a block of old mission-style houses and we were in line for water, fuel and anything else you might need for your trip. My pass had four hundred gallons on it, Lily had packed only one bag and there was plenty of room in the trunk so I asked for four thirty-gallon ponies after I filled the tank.

Lily said, "What's that for?"

I shook my head. "That would be the truth and we're not ready yet."

She sniffed. "I hope you realize that this truth you're advertising had better be really special."

I grinned as I may have never grinned before. "I can promise that."

In Orange the streets not only drive your car but they also do your talking to the Interstate for you. We were still meandering at horse and buggy speed when I told the winding boulevard where I wanted to go and it asked for clearance to Las Vegas. The light flickered yellow for a fraction of a second, there was no orange at all and then it was green. The Interstate blonde came on and said, "We hope you've had a pleasant and productive visit to Orange, Mr. Alexander. Please notify the Interstate of your travel plans upon reaching the Las Vegas area." The car moved to the far lane and began to pick up speed.

Lily said, "Truth time yet?"

I could see the Interstate ahead. We were already up over forty and there was nothing to stop us before the ramp.

I said, "Why not?"

She said, "Why the extra water and why no clearance to Chicago?"

I said, "Why so suspicious? Layla and Connor really are going to Chicago exactly as planned. It's just that Lily and Floppy will be making a fairly significant detour."

Her eyes got big and then she howled with laughter. Then, "Detour where?"

"South first. Where we'll need the extra water we bought. And then north again, where there's more water than anybody could want."

She stretched like she'd been riding for hours. "Daddy doesn't know about this, does he?"

"Nope."

"So many questions I have! First, how do you know I'm Lily? Not that I mind. I think."

"Two ways. One is, at first glance your face isn't all that much like your father's but it's pretty much the face he could have had if he'd wanted it."

"I figured you'd have to be dumb as dirt not to see that but since Daddy hired you I just assumed you would be. What's the other way?"

We were on the Interstate now and heading for the fast lane like we meant it. I started to answer Lily but the blonde interrupted me and said, "Your travel pass to Orange is now in completed and closed status and a new pass will have to be obtained before your next visit. *Bon voyage* and *au revoir.*"

I watched the traffic and said, "I'm afraid we'd better not count on that return pass to Orange. The other way I know is your father told me. He had to. He couldn't very well hire me to kidnap his daughter and carry her off to Canada without telling me who she was, could he? But you said you had some other questions?"

This was a good time of day to get out of Orange. The fast lane was up to 108. I turned to Lily as though about to make a remark about that and was gratified to see a full-grown dumbstruck gape. We shot under a fancy orange and green arch. I said, "I think we're over the border into bad people country."

She was good. She could take a punch without going down and she knew how to cover up. She said, "You wouldn't have told me if you meant to go through with it. You wouldn't tell me if you meant to kill me either. Unless you're a sadist. You wouldn't be a sadist would you?"

"Not much of one. I admit I'm having a good time here but I don't mind at all if you have one too."

"And Layla and Connor are still going to Chicago?"

"Yeah but they're taking the slow route because Lily and Floppy ran out on them and up and drove off to Taos."

"*Floppy.*" It was a snort. "*Floppy.* If our affair wasn't Platonic I'd worry about that name. What's in Taos for Floppy and Lily?"

"You haven't figured that out too? Maybe I overrated you."

"In your dreams. Let's have it. What's in Taos?"

"Not what, who. We're going to Taos to meet a lady who'll be going to Canada instead of you. And by the way living on your money when she gets there."

"That could be kind of a problem for her. I don't really have any money. Not *money*-money. Of course she could have it if I did. Not that I know her but as I always say, any friend of Floppy's is a friend of mine."

"That's nice to know but you're wrong about you not having money. Technically it's Layla Solberg's and Layla has a heap of it, all safely offshore and all in her name. Enough so that when you, Lily, get to Canada you can live like a queen on it for the rest of your life. As Layla of course. Go ahead. Ask me why you'd have to be Layla forever."

That didn't even slow her down. "Because if Lily gets away they'll go after Daddy."

I nodded approvingly.

"But if it isn't Lily who gets away, where is she? I mean– Oh. Shit."

I nodded again. "It's the only way. Three days from now Layla is fully and irrevocably documented but she still doesn't know she's going on a long cold boat ride across a corner of Lake Superior. Which is how she'll have to travel because with all her money the one thing she doesn't have is a passport. She doesn't know it because I haven't sprung it on her yet, so she still thinks she'll be back in Orange in three more days. But that night Lily has another fight with her father and flounces off to her room. Rooms plural I suppose. From the evidence she leaves behind it seems that instead of going to bed she takes half a bottle of her stepmother's happy pills and goes for a walk in the ocean. At first the police won't like it that her body never washes ashore even though they admit that this does happen sometimes. The rest of Orange will be having too much fun with the news to care about bodies and after some thought the police will come around to that view. They'll come to see that Lily is gone for good whether she's alive or dead, and gone is where they've wanted her for a long time. And this way they don't have to take down a dangerous man like Mason Thorkelson. So to the extent that they suspect your father they're also grateful to him. Show me another way he could have worked it so everybody gets off."

She no longer pretended to find this amusing. "Did Daddy come up with this?"

"Not exactly. He had a similar plan that was needlessly

and dangerously complicated. We simplified it for him."

She thought. "He was going to kill some girl wasn't he? Kill her and say it's me."

"Not himself. He figured we'd be happy to do it for him."

"Would you have? If it wasn't dangerous and there wasn't a simpler way?"

"No, we'd have passed. We don't kill people for money. At least not on purpose."

"You don't kill them *for money*."

"Right. We don't kill them for money."

"Who is *we?*"

"That's not as simple as it sounds. When your father hired us *we* meant somewhere between forty and a hundred and forty people depending on whether you only count the full-time we-people. But since then *we* has shrunk and now there's only three of us."

"And they are?"

"They are Floppy, Lily, and a nice lady named Ava. Who's waiting for us in Taos though she doesn't know it yet."

She got pensive for a moment. Then she said, "That sounds good. I mean it sounds like it should sound good, but Lily's having a little trouble getting used to being dead. Do you suppose everybody does?"

"Some more than others I'd think. Which reminds me, we get to Taos, a couple of things happen and one of them will hurt a little. You've got a chip in your arm?"

"Of course I do. State of Orange Exempt from Employment chip. Something *you'll* never have by the way."

"Which every passive scanner in the country will be looking for once you walk into the ocean and don't come out and one of these days we *will* walk past one. It has to come out."

"Out?"

"Out."

"Think Ava has any tequila?"

"No but I bet I know who does. Fellow we call George."

"Then I'll think about the tequila and not the medical degree you don't have. You said a *couple* of things will happen in Taos. That me being dead reminds you of. Necrophilia, perhaps?"

"Never heard of it. The other thing is Lily's Social goes onto the pavement and we drive over it four or five times. The police can track them you know. But once you're dead you can't answer anybody anyway so I don't think you'll miss it at all."

"Yeah but think of the messages I'll miss."

"Uh huh. There's the police. 'Uh, Lily, if you're alive, call us.'"

"Plus the Media. 'Uh, Lily, if you're alive, call us *first*.' Then there's all my old classmates. 'Die bitch die.'" She fell over laughing at her own wit.

"That's the spirit. Then there's the usual looneys. 'Have you seen my Charley in Heaven yet? You two will make such a handsome couple.'" Which earned me a happy shriek, so I went on. Given, I said, her father's standing and the publicity she would be getting, there'd be at least a thousand of the bought-and-paid-for *Mourning Mementoes* every dead person gets since Reverend Williston took Hallmark on as a sponsor. And good thing she'd never see those. The words will gag you in their own right but exposure to just one of the embedded holos has been known to induce diabetes.

"You know," she said, "there are people in Orange who think that water, oxygen and the Social are what make life even possible."

"Not just in Orange, O Princess. But Lily will be okay. We'll pick her up a virgin Social on the road and I've got a couple of unused Aliases she can pick from. Which one's more *Lily* do you think? Jacob's Stepladder or The Risen Leper?"

"You're joking, right? Tell me you're joking."

"Not this time babe. Your first awful truth about camouflage. When you're trying to fit in, then you do what it takes to *fit in*."

The sierras turned grim and gray and dusty in the headlights and the sky above grew clear and starry as we raced toward Las Vegas. Lily said, "Why all the way to Lake Superior? Why not just head up the coast and sneak Lily across the Oregon border?"

"One, she wouldn't stay put if she doesn't go to Chicago

first. Two, nobody sneaks across the Oregon border."

"I've crossed it a dozen times and flown over it a dozen more."

"Carrying the passport of a citizen of Orange. Don't you know how much difference that makes?"

She waved that aside with an *everybody knows that* motion and then proved that she didn't know much. "Sure but if you have to sneak in somewhere, why not there?"

"Because there are only two kinds of borders, hard borders and impossible borders and Oregon is as impossible as it gets."

"You drive up to the gate—"

"You die a hundred yards after you crash the Far North California passport control and that's three miles from the Oregon gate. Three of the hardest miles for people like us to survive in anywhere on the continent. Didn't they teach you about the Battle of the Cascades?"

She went little-girl eye-rolly and sing-songy on me. "The greedy Godless Canadians were jealous we had Portland and Seattle which in old times were called Sodom and Gomorrah and they wanted them for themselves so they could have sex before lunch and when the 204th Amendment disbanded the Army of the Interstate and turned it over to the militias but the militias weren't ready to fight yet that's when the sneaky Canadians saw their chance and dropped their paratroops and—"

"For a while it looked like you might be happy to take a ride with somebody who smuggles people over borders."

She let that lay a minute. Then she said, "Okay. That's fair. And?"

"And while it looked that way it occurred to me that *maybe* it looked that way because you might like to hear how people-smuggling gets done. But it's no big deal. I'm used to boring people with facts."

"Facts? You think *no-you're-wrong* is a *fact*? You think *passports-make-life-easy* is a *fact*? A fact Mr. Truth-teller is when you tell me something I never heard before."

"Want to know why we can't just walk into Oregon? Most people find it kind of boring I suppose or more people would bother to learn about it, but it *is* the kind of thing I'd think you'd want to know. If you're really going into the heretic rescue business with me."

That earned me a blink. "Did you just proposition me?"

That earned her one too. "Am I going too fast for you? I thought I explained that we're stealing Layla's money and using it to send another woman to Canada."

"Yes. Ava. Though before you called her a lady. Lady Ava de la Pueblo."

"And I thought, I was under the impression anyway, that you approved and wanted to help. Because any friend of mine is a friend of yours and you don't want to run away yourself and you don't want the money for yourself and you could have objected and you didn't. Did I jump to a conclusion there?"

"I see. You thought you'd *already* propositioned me. I could have objected?"

"I know you could have because I kept waiting for you to do it. And you never did."

"I see more and more. When you proposition a girl she accepts you if she doesn't fight you off on the spot."

"What's with all the proposition talk?"

"Well maybe if you'll finally tell me some facts about heretic smuggling it will get my mind out of the gutter."

"Really? You're ready?"

"Anything to distract me. The Oregon border, walking across, difficulty of. The true history of the Battle of the Cascades, relevance to said border and said difficulty."

"Talk like that all you want. You think I only have a General Biblical Development Certificate but I'm a month away from a Master's of Divinity from Harvard. I read stuff like that three times a week."

"After the Bill of Faith which contains the 204th Amendment to the Constitution of the Interstate which before that was called something else was proposed and ratified and the Air Force went over to the states and the Army was—"

"Okay. Here's the story. It's not seventh grade history and it's not a joke. It's ugly. If you're not ready for ugly I won't tell it. If you think you're ready but change your mind halfway through you won't get the point because the point's all at the end. Do I tell it?"

"Is it something I'll need to know when we go into business together?"

"I wouldn't go that far. But it's the *kind* of thing you'll need to know."

"Okay then. You know I'm spoiled. You know it because I'm from Orange and because my daddy told you that even for Orange I'm extra-special spoiled, which is why I can't live there anymore. And you're trying to see if it's possible to un-spoil me. Un-spoil me in my twenty-first year. That's good thinking, Mr. Floppy. A princess of Orange isn't going to be much good to you as a partner, is she? And Daddy told you I'm reckless. I know he used that word because that's almost all he ever calls me anymore. So you kind of like my looks and you kind of like the idea of having me around or you wouldn't have propositioned me which I'm still not supposed to notice, but you're not so far gone it doesn't worry you – can I really shock her all the way from reckless to careful, careful like a people-smuggler has to be? Because if I can't this could be a very short partnership, no matter what she can do with those legs I keep looking at."

Now *that* wasn't fair because I'd barely peeked but she was on a roll and I wasn't going to interrupt.

"But there's more to me than you know, Mr. Floppy. You think I'm just a naïve little rich girl from Orange which you may not know is also the Land of the Truly Free, but what you don't know is that I'm so spoiled I want to be more than Truly Free. I've always thought that merely Truly Free purely sucks. So tell me some of the ugly things I need to know to get beyond it."

I took a few seconds to arrange it and then I told it. In a way it was a strange experience. It's all been in my head for a long time but I'd never really heard it told before, not all in one piece. When I finished telling it I realized it had changed somehow just by being said out loud all at once. I mean that even in my memory it had changed into the way I told it but even so it was all still true. I don't understand how that can be but I do know that it really did change. Here are some parts of it, pretty much as I told them.

In the orphanage where I grew up, a man we were supposed to call Major Joe started making killers out of us as soon as we turned ten. One by one as each of our turns came up he told us that our easy life of childhood was now a thing of the past and on that day our hard lives as men were beginning. We were orphans and Major Joe knew we were and he could still talk about our easy lives that had lasted till the day we met him.

Major Joe always wore a hat when we drilled, a strange old thing with a stiff flat brim that stuck way out all around. It and his whistle were his staffs of office. We all felt that if only we could steal that hat he'd lose the will to eat and breathe and we yearned to do that to him but try as we might we never found a way. But sometimes Major Joe would take that hat off and hold it under his arm – while saluting the Cross or standing at attention to pray for instance. At those times we could see the bent twisty cross tattooed on the back of his head. It was faded and misshapen but most of us had seen that kind of cross before and we knew what it was supposed to look like and we knew that this one had come a long way.

One night when I was sixteen Major Joe told me and a couple other Senior Cadets about the twisty cross and how he got it and how a long time ago it made him the free man we knew him to be. We'd been on a hide-and-seek hike in the hills and the three of us found every one of the twelve-year-old heretics who thought they could hide and ambush us. We cut their throats with burnt sticks so that when Major Joe came after us to tally the score he could see the black stripes and make sure they were long and wide enough to do the trick. Not one of the heretics heard us coming and they all kept quiet after they were dead because they knew what would happen if they didn't. So there was no yelling at all. Major Joe told us that while it was going on and he wasn't hearing anything he thought we couldn't find them and when he finally saw what we'd done it was the happiest he'd felt in years. He didn't usually talk like that but it was the first time we'd ever been *good enough*. It was a true spiritual experience for him and he said it called for a celebration.

He sent the younger cadets off to make their own camp and sat the three of us around a fire he built for the occasion, the kind of fire we were never, ever to build in hostile territory. Then he brought out a bottle and announced that we were about to taste liquor for the first time in our lives. Being careful of his feelings as we were we said nothing to correct that unimportant misunderstanding. The bottle went around two or three times and then Major Joe was ready to break it to us about life.

These kids we get here, lying around playing till they're ten, their brains turning to jelly when they should be up here learning. Then they come into the militia way of living way too late and they think they can just catch up. I go to bed every night and I wake up every morning and I don't know how I'll ever make real soldiers out of them. Only I know that trying to do it is the only calling that measures up to killing trash-people and Jesus-haters up on the slopes. You guys done good today. Today you were good enough to work the border and still get back home again later, so let me tell you what that means.

I was militia when I was six. That's when I got the cross on my head. You know the one, I seen you looking at it, but you don't know what it means. It's called a swas. Some people gave their kids play swasses called swas-stickers that you could peel off before they got you in trouble at school, but my daddy gave me the real kind that lasts for life and never lets you forget who you are. A real swas means three things. First one is people should stay with their own kind. Hard for some of you to do I know but a long time ago it was simpler. I don't think I can explain how important that part was to us, so I'm not even going to try. Second thing it means is that you're militia for life. Because if you wear it and aren't in a militia everyone'll know you deserted. Last thing is surrender is not an option. When you wear the swas you can't ever get taken or you die for sure and you die hard *and if you're going to die you may as well die fighting. That's why they put it on me, because of those things, so I wouldn't ever have to be* taught *them and couldn't have no second thoughts when I got older.*

When the time came the militias got together and we swept the trash-people clean out of our part of Oregon. We charged up the Cascades cleaning them out as we went and we didn't have to start fighting for real till we reached the passes. Understand, I was still six and didn't actually fight. I just followed behind with the women and the other little kids. But I sure learned what fighting is about.

When we got to the passes the trash-people realized we meant to keep going so they finally grew balls and stood their ground. And they

183

fought pretty good considering what they were. Up there on the slopes the ground's like these hills only a lot rougher, and there was no end of places for them to hide and pick us off. That's why we train up here, so you'll know what to do when we go back up the slopes someday. We spent a lot of time bogged down, then we'd break through for a mile or so, and then they'd stop running and we'd be bogged down again. You understand? They could slow us down but they couldn't stop us. Their kind will never stop us, which is what they brought me here to teach you.

We were almost all the way through the passes when their Canadian friends decided they didn't like how it was going. We were supposed to have our piece of the Interstate Air Force on our side but they went right on banging their barista-girls and their tree-hugger girls and whining oh no they couldn't fly *they didn't have no* fuel *and they didn't have no* parts *and they'd gone and left all their* bombs *in Colorado. Except for a handful who didn't last long they all sat it out, but the Canadians knew nobody'd fight them in the air, so gutless as they are* they *didn't sit it out, not at all. They hit us with fifteen gunships just after dawn, came up the slopes behind us from the east at treetop level with the sun in our eyes. It was a massacre. I've told you what Gatling guns do to infantry but until you see it it's all just words. They caught most of the men in the open and that was that.*

The men they missed and the rest of us took off fast down the slopes the way we came, gunships and trash-people on our heels. Soon enough we were in the trees and the gunships couldn't touch us but then we heard their planes up ahead and we knew it meant we were running toward paratroops. We thought they were ours and my momma said Good, they'll show the bastards. But they weren't none of ours, were they? Ours *were on the ground in Idaho getting told that Idaho didn't have a fight with Canada unless Canada crossed the Idaho line. And we know how that turned out don't we? Now that Idaho has what was two thirds of Oregon* and *Washington and never fired a shot to get them. Because they made that cowardly deal with the Canadians, and for once the Canadians kept their word, which they did because it only cost them* our *land to keep it. You boys know the idea of pretending the Interstate could be a country was a terrible mistake that it's good we finally got over, but the one part of it that ever worked was the military part. If they'd have held off getting rid of it for a year, for just as long as it took us to clean out the trash-people, Canada would still be where it belongs and a lot of good people wouldn't be dead and a whole lot more trash-people would be. Would be dead I mean. Dead back then and no more born since.*

After they rounded us up the paratroops made a big pile of our weapons and sorted us into groups. I never did see my daddy but my momma was led off with the rest of the women to one group of grown-ups and all the men to another. All us kids were in the third group. Then we sat there for hours. Trash-people, full of swagger now like it was their gunships and their paratroops that snuck up on us, were arguing with the paratroop officers and pointing at us and the women. We could see the officers give in bit by bit. First the boys over twelve were taken out and put in with the men. Then the bigger girls went off to the women. They didn't ask them anything, they just picked by look and size. Then some of the women started screaming and pointing over to the men. The trash-people cut loose with a couple of old machine guns and all the men went down. Then individual trash-people, mostly women, walked up and started shooting our women one by one. The Canadians didn't do nothing. They just stood and watched but you could see they liked that it was happening. After about half the women and girls were dead the trash-people brought up twenty or thirty little trash-brats to shoot the rest. The kid who killed my momma was about my age. He didn't even know how to hold a rifle, he was as spoiled and useless as they all are, but a trash-man held the weapon for him and the trash-kid pulled the trigger. Then the trash-brats tried to come over and kill us too but the trash-troops dragged them off. One of their sergeants came over to me because I was screaming the loudest and he talked to me real pleasant like he was telling his own kid how the grass grows. He said, "See, your filthy pig of a daddy and your diseased whore of a mommy killed their parents, so we thought we'd let them get a little even. And now just think, they want to do you too. Personally I don't see why not but our Canadian friends say no. 'Cause, see, they don't know you like we do." Then a paratrooper came and shooed him away.

By then the Canadians had landed helicopters and paratroops started hauling us off to them. One of them had a headlock on me and my hat fell off. I bit his arm and he swung around and saw my swas on the back of my head. He hollered for an officer and one of them came over, took a look and said, "Not in my fucking helicopter. Not in my fucking country. Leave the little pile of puke."

By the time they took off there was ten or so of us tied together in a little group. Nobody buried any of the dead. Nobody untied us or gave us anything to eat or drink. The paratroops ignored us except a few who came over to spit on our swasses and one who pretended to pull the pin on a grenade and toss it at us. They didn't hang around they just marched

185

away up the slope so they'd get to the passes before dark. Towards midnight a party of militia showed up and found everybody who was dead and found us and saw our crosses and cut us loose and made us tell what happened. They talked it over out of our earshot and then came back and told us we were walking with them back to northern California which was still the old name we called Far North California then and if we were all real brave and strong we just might make it. And most of us did, and that's how the swas is the only thing that let me grow up a free man in a free country, which is something I never forgot.

A month later Canada and Idaho divvied up Washington and Oregon and the wire went up and the minefields went down. I wound up here but lots of us are still back there. And every once in a while one of us sneaks over the mountain and brings back souvenirs, just to remind them how it will be when we come back for good. And every once in a while we catch a party of Jesus-haters trying to get through our lines so they can live happily with their own kind. When that happens we make sure the friends get to hear them one more time because they sure as hell ain't never going to see them again. And one of these days you boys are going back with me to find that little serpent who shot my momma. I'll bet he wets his bed every night thinking how it'll be when we do.

I said, "And that in a nutshell is why I never recommend walking into Canada from Far North California, never mind from Idaho."

But all Lily wanted to do was say she was sorry about some vague thing she wouldn't spell out that seemed a little bigger than just smarting off like she'd been. I never quite figured out what it was but if I'd known it would take her that way I'd never have told her that story. To lighten the mood I told her about easier places like New South Quebec where all they did was shake hands for the last time, drain the Connecticut River, build a fence in the riverbed and lay down quicksand on both sides of it – but, see, the best laid plans and all that, because the good people of the former *Vert Mont* had never even dreamt that once they succeeded in seceding their new Provincial Government would ban the speaking of English in public places and require that anyone who didn't want to walk around mute must learn French... In a while Lily brightened back up and I felt like I'd dodged a bullet that somehow I'd fired at myself.

A couple of hours before dawn we were heading south through the Arizonas on the same route Ava and I took to Taos. I was too keyed up to sleep. The difference between the two trips had me almost singing. Then I was driving off to bury Ava. Now I was coming to save her.

Lily woke up and slapped me on the arm. "I want to know. Did Daddy tell you not to have sex with me?"

"It was the one thing he didn't mention."

"Would you have listened?"

"I listen to everybody, always. What I do after I listen depends."

"That's a good answer. For somebody who bothers to listen I mean. I usually don't. But even if I don't listen to Daddy very much I still don't think we'll have sex right away unless that messes up your plans."

"My plans all take vows of abstinence. I insist on it. I like them boring and dependable."

"Boring?"

"My plans. Only my plans. What I do with them hardly ever bores anyone."

In a few hours I Socialed Ava and told her I'd be bringing a friend by for lunch and we were hungry, no-salad-this-time hungry. She said I'd better stop and get something then because all she had was a whole pot of green chili and a big stack of pretty fresh tortillas. I said that in that case we'd come straight there.

Proverbs

He that speaketh truth, will shew righteousness: but a false witness useth deceit. The lip of truth shall be stable forever: but a lying tongue varieth incontinently. The lying lips are an abomination to the Lord: but they that deal truly are his delight. –The Proverbs of Solomon, 12:17, 12:19, 12:22, from the Geneva translation.

First of all you should know that when the sun rose it was Friday, and everything depended on it being a Friday because Jayden Delgado and I suppose his Associates too took their weekends off. The plan said that Layla and Connor would arrive in Chicago on Friday evening, which Layla was supposed to think was meant to give us two days to rest up before the Monday meeting with Jayden. The real reason was so Layla would be off the road and provably far away from Orange when Lily Thorkelson drowned herself. That amateurish silliness was all Thorkelson's. Boronzee tried gently to talk him out of it but Thorkelson held firm, and to budge him he'd have had to be told some unpleasant truths that he was happiest not knowing.

One thing Thorkelson was happiest not knowing was that until Layla reached Canada she'd never be safer than out on the Interstate with me because just about any hotel anywhere looks at its guests much more closely than the Interstate ever does. People like him – and to be fair, people with a lot less money than he has – misunderstand how the Interstate works every day. They think the Interstate watches them. It doesn't. It watches their car and who their car says it's carrying. They get in their car to drive and their driver's license (or something some Bluesbaby cooked up that says it's a driver's license) tells the car who they are and the car tells the Interstate and that's all it knows and that's all it gives a damn about. Or if they're rich enough they get in the back seat and their chauffeur tells their car who he's carrying and the car tells the Interstate that too. That only happens because they're the people who obey all the little rules when it feels good to obey them and obeying this rule feels good because they're the good, deserving people who can go wherever they want. But all the car really cares about is does it have a legal driver who can drive it because if it doesn't and gets caught it will be stripped and sold off for its parts, and all the Interstate cares about is does the car look like a good honest car that deserves to live another day – so unless a passenger has a custodial chip in his arm like I used to have and somebody probes it, passengers who want to be anonymous can be until they step out of the car. But *that's* where the trouble starts because now they're none of the Interstate's business, are they? Now they're some state's business, and states care a lot about who is walking around in them, and people like Thorkelson forget that part too because don't they have the *right* to be wherever they want? Face it: states are just flat out nosy, aren't they? And even the nicest hotels are in *states*.

Something else Thorkelson wouldn't want to think about was the general principle that our kind of work is always safest when you don't hang around anywhere for very long. Every day you spend working is dangerous because everything you do while you work is a capital offense. Even sleeping late or munching lox and bagels from room service is a capital offense because everything you do to advance a crime is also a crime. So the total danger you face on any job pretty much depends on how long it takes you to do it, and the safest plan would have put us in Chicago early Monday morning.

Which, Thorkelson be damned, was exactly when I intended to put us there.

And which, to finally get to why everything depended on that day being a Friday, is what allowed us to make the detour to Taos and still keep our appointment with Jayden.

Ordinarily I couldn't have counted on that working because we wouldn't really *be* at the hotel where we were supposed to staying. But when Thorkelson told me how he fabricated Layla's biography he let me know that the hotel records he could read were only the billing records – and the billing records could be made to show that we were there. Almost the last thing I did before we got to Ava's motel was Social the hotel in Chicago, confirm our reservations for four nights and tell them we'd be arriving late. That meant that on Friday evening the hotel would charge us for our rooms just as if we'd checked in and when they charged Layla's Thorkelson Industries company card Thorkelson would see it and unleash a hopelessly deluded sigh of relief.

I said that that was *almost* the last thing I did. The last thing I did was give Lily a lecture about truth and lying. As far as I was concerned it was by far the most dangerous thing I'd do that weekend and I told myself I was putting it off not because it scared me as much as it did but so that Lily would have as many hours as possible to get to know me as an apostle of truth. Before I let her see just how good I am at lying. And how much lying matters to me. And how much it would have to matter to her from now on.

Half an hour out from Ava's I was off the Social and I told Lily I had something to say to her that she needed to think about. I said I had already told her quite a bit about Ava but now she needed to know just how much Ava had had to be fooled into letting me keep her alive. I told Lily all I had done to fool her so far and I told Lily that we were going to keep right on fooling her. I told her that we were *both* going to convince Ava that she was getting away to Canada now because the price for two was the same as the price for one and Lily had agreed to let Ava tag along, and that we were further going to convince her that Lily would have major influence in Canada on account of her wealth and how she already knew all kinds of people there and that she, Lily, was pretty sure she could get her, Ava, a job in a library in Toronto. And believing that lie was the best chance Ava would ever have of living out her life, so that's why Lily needed to help me tell it.

We were now twenty minutes from Ava's and I had to take over the driving because just then the Interstate turned us loose. I'd been counting on that. I knew what Lily had to be thinking and I didn't want her looking into my fear-crazed eyes while she thought it.

Oh I see. He decides what's best for people and then he tells them stories they'll believe. And they do believe it, this very smart woman he's gone on and on about bought it whole. Just like I'm buying that I'm his new partner. His new partner who is now going to pretend *to run away to Canada just like Daddy by coincidence* paid *this man to make me do. His new partner who will willingly go along with this lie but who never would have agreed to go to Canada any other way.*

I mean, how could she not be thinking that?

She chewed on it for a good long while. Then she said, "Just to humor me. Does your Ava believe every lie you tell her, every time you tell her one?"

"Ha. If you knew how hard I have to work…"

"So you're saying she knows you lie to her but she pretends to believe you anyway."

I considered. "Yes I suppose so but it isn't that simple. She knows I leave things out and that I do it because she wouldn't be happy to hear them. But I've got her convinced I do it so I can use her for business reasons and she buys it because she can't figure out how I wouldn't be making money out of what she can see me do. Which makes it okay with her because then I'm getting paid. See?"

"I see what you're saying but I don't believe it. It's much too complicated. I prefer it that she'd rather pay her debt to you by letting you have your way. You did call her a *nice lady*, didn't you?"

I started to argue just because I didn't buy that Ava would ever accept charity from me. But I swallowed it when I realized that Lily was working from the ridiculous notion that my lies could never be believed. Which would mean that I'd told her the truth so far because hadn't she believed me? Which meant–

With a smug look she interrupted my thought. "Mr. Floppy, I saw how you looked at Daddy and I see how you look at me, especially certain parts of me, and if you're really as worried as you look that I could think you'd throw me away for his sake, then you're not half as smart as you've led me to think.

"Get used to it. I want in. You want me in. So I'm in, and there isn't a thing your conscience can do about it. Stop trying so damn hard to get what you've already got and start thinking about what you want to do with it. And, if I may make a suggestion, when you want to get started doing it."

That deserved some kind of answer but at that moment the well of truth and honesty had gone dry. All I could come up with was, "So you're in. And that means that as far as Ava is concerned you're letting her ride along with you to Canada. Right?"

"Right. That's an accurate statement of my partner's beliefs of the moment. Right."

Esther

...and let the King give her royal estate unto her companion that is better than she. –Esther 1:19, from the Geneva translation.

The table was set, the green chili was steaming, the tortillas were hiding under a hot towel, and three mismatched chairs including Ava's armchair were drawn up and ready.

Ava beamed at us and said, "Two Ears my dear, who have you brought me?"

I said, "Ava meet Layla. Layla has to take a trip, the kind I usually conduct, and it turns out she has room for—"

Ava said, "I'm pleased to meet you, Layla, welcome to my manor such as it is. Though I mustn't deprecate it since Two Ears so thoughtfully found it for me and on such short notice. Please be seated, you must be exhausted."

Lily took the easy chair since Ava was holding it out to her and I took one of the others.

Ava said, "This is *so* nice" and took the last chair. "Layla, if there's anything I can get you please speak up. I don't have much here but what I have is yours. And Two Ears' too of course."

I said, "Maybe she'd like a book? Layla darling, Ava has a book collection that—"

Lily turned to me and said, "*Two Ears,* dear, I'd like you to shut up for a while now because I have something important to say to Ava."

A certain amount of foreboding began to creep up my spine.

She turned to Ava and said, "Don't you think he should shut up while I say it?"

Ava said, "Well, it *is* what the moment seems to call for."

The feeling reached my neck and began to climb up past my ears. Ava was beaming at Lily. I tried to beam too.

Lily said, "That's exactly what I think. Mr. Floppy here, and would you believe that that's his real name? I'm actually

193

his new partner and he hasn't lied to me yet, so I know. Mr. Floppy here thinks you'll run off to Canada with me if we make you think I'm a timorous soul who needs companionship. And I do need it but the companionship I pine for is his. So I think it might be better to tell you the real plan."

I got ready to catch Ava when she collapsed in horror.

Ava said, "I couldn't agree more. I've been waiting to hear the real plan for quite some time now. And to think, I'll be hearing it from someone he hasn't lied to yet."

I gave up on the collapsing in horror part. I started searching for things that would be worse than collapsing in horror because one of them just had to be coming.

Lily said, "I thought that might impress you. The real plan is for you to escape to Canada by yourself but with a huge sum of money that my wicked daddy expects me to spend up there living a disgusting life of ease and guilt. And I'll stay here with Mr. Floppy, and you'll send tiny bits of that huge pot of money back to us whenever we need it which we hope will be often indeed, and that's how we'll smuggle worthy heretics and blasphemers like yourself to safety from now on. Instead of what we have to do now, or to be honest I should say what he has to do now, which is just picking out rich ones and then taking all they have. Now don't you think the real plan is a better plan all around?"

Now Lily was going to see what she'd done. I only hoped that I could somehow–

Ava said, "An infinitely superior plan. And he thought I might be too high-minded to accept such a wonderful offer?"

Lily said, "*Isn't* he a dear sweet boy? *So* overly generous in his judgments of those he cares for."

Ava said, "Exactly so, I've been searching for those very words for weeks, how clever of you to put it that way. You cannot believe the awful things he's made me pretend to think of him from atop this towering pedestal he's built for me out of... Oh dear, what's an unmixed metaphor about what pedestals are usually made from? One that corresponds to 'whole cloth'?"

Lily said, "Hmm. Rough blocks of marble? Sacks of cement? Insufficiently felicitous, I know, but better ones elude me at the moment."

Ava turned to me and said, "Mr. Floppy dear, I wonder if I ought to go visit George Wickham for an hour or so. I believe Layla here wants very badly to take you to bed."

I gave up. "Lily. Her name is Lily. And nobody's going anywhere till I've had my lunch."

Ava and Lily talked about books and schools. Ava was thrilled to learn that Lily had been expelled from Amherst, Bennington, Wellesley and Vassar, all while carrying straight A's, all while her fees were fully up to date which I would have thought was the same as straight A's if my experience at Harvard was anything to go by, and all for submitting assignments that would have had her professors executed for multiple capital offenses if they'd so much as read past the first paragraph.

Lily was thrilled to learn that Ava had spent two years at one of the last pre-Social colleges where they actually had *classes* and *dormitories* and a *library*, especially a *library*, where she'd spent…

I was thrilled to eat four excellent day-old tortillas heaped with green chili.

Ava was thrilled to report that George Wickham had hooked up an audio feed for her that played only Beethoven and Mozart, and that just that morning she'd listened to the Exxon Ninth Symphony *twice* all the way through, once with Somebody conducting and once if Lily could believe it with Somebody Else himself.

I was less than thrilled to ask just how much time Ava had been spending with said George Wickham.

Ava was more than satisfied to report that *just* like his namesake, George Wickham was charm itself in his relentless pursuit of the fortune I'd convinced him she possessed.

Lily was moved to slap her forehead and blurt out a string of very short questions that went something like *Namesake? Wickham? Elizabeth's Wickham? His name was George? How* could *I have forgotten?* And didn't wait for an answer after a single one of them.

Ava was equally moved. "After all these years. Are you *sure* you won't go to Canada with me?"

Lily seemed unnaturally pleased with herself for no good

reason I could see. She stuck her tongue out at me.

I'd been worrying about how to bring up a problem that concerned luggage and small boats. I gave it up as a lost cause and instead asked, "When does Maria get here?"

Ava said, "Maria's the maid, Lily. I'm not to tell her things, but in spite of that she leaves my room till last so she can take her time trying to worm them out of me. She doesn't get to me till around three on Fridays because she has to get all the hourly rooms ready for the Friday night rush."

Lily howled. It's barely possible I blushed because Ava gave me her simper which made Lily howl again.

Ava said, "Allow me to guess. I'm to tell her I'm going away for a few days but will be returning."

I said, "No, that's what I tell George Wickham. He'll guess the truth but he won't say anything to jeopardize a month's paid up rent. But Maria has to get the truth because if you lie to her she'll know you did when she sees your books are gone. So *try* to convince her to keep it to herself and–"

But I had to stop because Ava had turned into a holovid queen whose handsome trillionaire beau has just popped the question. "*My books?* I can take them?"

"We can *try* but if a man tells you they can't go in his boat then they can't go in his boat, okay?"

"But we can try?"

I knew then that I was about to get kissed but I was too focused on bracing for Ava and never saw Lily coming at me from the flank.

An hour before Maria was due Lily asked Ava if she could help pack the books and I immediately knew it was past time for my visit to George Wickham. Not all my intuitions are wrong and when I got back a half hour later Ava had a few clothes and other things laid out on the bed next to a laundry bag and six books were in the leather suitcase and the rest had all been opened and lay scattered on the table. I got two guilty looks and no ahem was necessary.

Ava said, "It's all my fault. I just couldn't resist showing her."

Lily said, "Nonsense. We have nothing to apologize for. Not everybody carries their books around in their heads you know."

I looked at Ava. She said, "Well, she mentioned that you don't seem to have any books and I didn't want her to think–"

Lily said, "Don't cover for me, Ava. I said he doesn't seem to *care* about books and you said–"

I said, "I didn't know Bibles count as books around here."

Lily said, "Maybe you'll play them for us after Maria leaves?"

I said, "Uh–"

Ava said, "About Maria. Do I still have any diamond money left? If I ever had any at all I mean."

I said, "Almost six months' worth and of course it's real. What could I do with your diamonds except sell them?"

"And I won't need it in Canada because I'll have Lily's trillions? And anyway it's no good up there, is it?"

"Nope, it's all on-shore and in dollars. How is this about Maria? You're thinking what I think you are?"

"Well, she's desperately poor after all. It would make such a difference and she's been such a good friend."

Lily gave me an evil look and said, "Besides, it'll give her a reason to keep her mouth shut, won't it?"

Ava said, "Oh Mr. Floppy. You're such a difficult person to know and I'm so happy you've found someone who understands you."

The last book was going into the suitcase when Ava pointed to the corner between the doors to the outside and the bathroom and said, "Hush. I feel the presence."

Reverend Williston popped to life and said, "–as the holy season of Easter–"

Lily jumped and yelped.

"–pulls into view. But is it really enough to sit and wait? Is there nothing we can do to hasten it?"

Lily said, "Talk about your holy ghost. Jeezus."

I said, "Not used to it are you O Princess of Orange."

"Of course we get him, but not like this. How do people sleep?"

Ava said, "Fortunately he appears only when Maria is due, and he departs as soon as she does. Mr. Floppy arranged it with George Wickham. We're used to him. I know it's hard to believe but you do get used to him even in a tiny place like this."

I said, "I was only in your daddy's house for a minute but I didn't hear a peep out of the good Reverend. Another privilege?"

Lily said, "Certainly not. He has his own auditorium with a pulpit even. It's just, the doors are kind of thick."

I said, "The inspector doesn't mind?"

Lily said, "He sees it all the time. Girl I knew in school? No-conscience little brat, *she's* your princess. *Her* father put the Reverend in a tiny room, no lights, no carpet or rugs, no furniture, just bare walls. Inspector shows up, sees the room, leaves glowering and muttering. Everyone thinks it's a big joke, didn't they put *him* in his place, the intrusive, vulgar little man. Four times a year from then on, and a bigger joke every time. One day a new inspector shows up. 'Who are you, where's Mr. Gibson?' 'Gibson retired, I got his route. Where is he?' They take him to the room and he opens the door. He turns to Madison's old man and says, 'You simple son of a bitch.' Two years' penance at Pebble Beach Penitential Retreat, cut down to three months when he paid the appeal. Just enough time to work on his short game. In a little while the Media reports Retired Williston Inspector Gets Life for Dereliction. At school Madison says, 'He had it coming, he broke the law.' I say, 'Which of them, Gibson or your daddy?' She hisses at me. 'My *daddy* isn't a *nobody* from *Anaheim.*'"

I thought about saying something a little bitter about that story but decided there was no point to taking my own life out on Lily. But it turned out I was only saving it up for later.

Maria came and wept and left.

Reverend Williston said, "In His name do we—" and de-substantiated.

Lily said, "Now I want to hear a Bible."

Ava said, "Lily dear, if he'd really rather not…"

Lily said, "Unh uh. If I'm going to *be* with somebody as we're supposed to put it, I want to know what he's hearing when he should be hearing me."

Ava said, "Well, Mr. Floppy, she does have a point."

I know when I'm beat. I went out to the car and got the portable scanner. When I got back inside they had the three chairs set up in a row with the middle one left empty for me. I sat down, turned the scanner to *listen* and balanced it on my right shoulder. I tried a random burst of Reverend Healy. The voice that came out was a wretchedly distracting echo to me but of course they couldn't hear what I heard. I played them some of the King James Job.

Emancipus Healy said, *Then Satan answered the LORD, and said, Doth Job fear God for naught?*

Ava said, "Wonderful."

Emancipus Healy said, *And the LORD said unto Satan, Behold, all that he hath is in thy power.*

Lily said, "Okay, I get it."

I turned Reverend Healy off.

Lily said, "If I was ever going to repent that's the man who'd make me do it."

Ava said, "It's as though I've never read it."

Lily said, "Let's have the others."

I said, "You'll love this one. It's the same passage only from the New American Dispensationalist Bible for Everyday People."

The peeved little man said, *So Satan says, Of course Job sucks up to you. Don't you give him every little thing he wants? You take some of it away and he'll badmouth you till the cows come home. So God tells him, Okay, Tough Guy, go break his toys, I'll let you–*

Ava said, "Make that stop right now!"

Lily said, "Why the *hell* is that *thing* in your *head?*"

I said, "I thought I might need reminding where I came from. Turns out I never did."

Ava said, "Play the one you like so much. When you want to go to sleep."

Lily said, "There's one he likes best, and he didn't play it first?"

Ava said, "I'm sure he wanted it for the finale."

Lily said maybe that was it but not like she believed it. As I reached for the scanner she added, "And do make sure it's your very favorite part."

I said, "Ecclesiastes from the true and correct Geneva Bible, edition of 1599 but actually translated between 1557 and 1560. It's the version John Knox used when he–"

Lily said, "Play it."

The voice said, *The words of the Preacher, the son of David King in Jerusalem. Vanity of vanities, saith the Preacher: vanity of vanities, all is vanity...*

Lily jerked up straight and gaped. I was as startled as she was. I hadn't heard it from a speaker since I'd made it. The voice playing in my head mostly drowned out the voice Lily and Ava were hearing but I could tell there was something very strange coming out of the scanner.

The voice said, *The wind goeth toward the South, and compasseth toward the North: the wind goeth round about, and returneth by his circuits. All the rivers go into the sea, yet the sea is not full: for the rivers go unto ye place, whence they return, and go. All things are full of labor: man cannot utter it: the eye is not satisfied with seeing, nor the ear filled with hearing. What is it that hath been? that which shall be: and what is it that hath been done? that which shall be done: and there is no new thing under the sun.*

By then I'd got it. I turned it off.

Ava looked at us both nervously and said it was lovely and how lucky I was to have it.

Lily boggled at her. Then she took a couple of gulps and said, "I understand how you might not be sure. I understand you but not him. People don't always recognize their own voices when they hear them but *other* people are fucking supposed to. Why is he carrying *your* voice around in his head and why didn't he seem to know he's doing it?"

Ava didn't say anything. She didn't look like she could say anything.

I mumbled something about how I'd never heard it before like it was outside of me.

Lily said, "You really didn't know?"

I said, "No." But it was a funny no. It was true enough as far as it went but it left too much out to be really true. I told them, pretty incoherently, that I'd always suspected I'd tried to make the voice from my memories of my mother's but I couldn't be sure. I couldn't be sure because I couldn't really remember her voice, but I was sure anyway because somehow I knew when I'd got it right.

Lilly glared in pity and disbelief. She said I'd been nine years old, how do you forget your mother's voice when you're nine years old?

I got nasty. I said doctors can do lots of things she might not understand. I said that sometimes they do them when having a mother is a recognized medical condition. I said that after ungrateful patients have been cured of that condition they might go off to the sound lab and try to get it back, but fortunately for the health of the community and for medical science itself they can't really do it.

Ava said, "My *voice*. So that's why…"

Lily said, "Of course that's why but is it true?"

Ava said, "True? Is what true?" Her eyes widened. "Lily, dear, I was married off to a man named Wockenfuss well before Mr. Floppy was born. At first he didn't want children and after I got to know him I didn't. So no, dear, I'm afraid it isn't *true*. Not that I'd be sorry if it were."

I said, "Princess, if we're going to have this out then let's have it out." I was rushing because I knew I'd regret saying it and I needed to get it out while I was still mad enough to do it. I said that she'd told her story of the distasteful and plebian horror that is Williston and now I'd tell her one that wasn't quite as elegant and witty. I said that for one month when I was nine I'd had a brother who being a baby cried a lot and wouldn't go to sleep. And that we lived in one room, the four of us, me, my mother, my brother, and Reverend Williston. And that nothing could make Reverend Williston shut up and let my brother go to sleep but my mother figured she could at least keep God's Own Holo from shining so much when the lights were out. And so she hung a sheet from the ceiling in front of him. And it didn't really work but she kept hoping it would so she didn't take it down. And she got used to it being there and forgot that it was and when it got light out she put the window shades up. And we had an upstairs neighbor named Mrs. MacPherson who didn't approve of my mother and didn't like the baby crying and Mrs. MacPherson saw the sheet from the front walk and ran and told on us. And my mother was lucky enough to have a friend named Mr. Schmidt or Mr. Schultz or something who used to come to dinner and later came to see the baby a couple of times and he was a fully ordained lawyer and he went to court with her and made a deal and she got off lightly with five years on half pay and permanent surrender of familial privileges and the rest of her life on the no-child-within-fifty-yards-of-you list. And the social workers came and I told them it wasn't fair because my mother was only trying to put my brother to sleep, and so they told me how Reverend Williston does his *best* work while you're sleeping because that's how Satan works too, and how both of them work hardest on you when you're in the cradle. And my brother went off to a good Christian family that wasn't named Schmidt or Schultz and I went off to New Dispensation Custodial Ministries, but how is it, does anyone here know how it happens, that medical science can make me forget my mother's *voice* and my mother's *face* but I can still see and hear Mrs. MacPherson like she's standing in this room?

Ava said "Oh Mr. Floppy" and then Lily was on me. Two people hugging violently on a kitchen chair is a precarious thing but somehow we managed it.

Somewhere around midnight Ava said something Lily found witty and Lily was about to answer back when something struck her and she looked like she might start sobbing instead. It took her a few seconds to fight it off and then she said, "I can't believe my daddy tried to let you die."

I said, "Lily, your father never even heard of—"

Ava said, "Lily, dear, I'm sure he did no such thing. I'm sure all he thought about was saving you."

Lily looked wildly from one of us to the other for several seconds. We were people she had decided to like and respect and here we were talking nonsense and missing the biggest point of all. Finally she said, "What difference does any of that make? Why would you have to know about somebody to not give a damn about them? How does it matter if you're trying to do something *you* want to do when you kill them?"

In time we got her off it. Ava told her about some of Wockenfuss's kindnesses to her – how if she told them just so, she'd sound like a very fortunate woman, but how telling them *just so* would leave out all that had been true in her life, all the things Wockenfuss denied her and mostly without even knowing it while he offered up those thoughtful little bribes in compensation, one after another. I told her how Boronzee rescued me from the orphanage – not that he got me out but how he kept me from being caught and sent back – and how for so many years I couldn't imagine not doing what he told me, couldn't imagine not *wanting* to do what he told me but somehow I'd gone and wandered off the reservation anyway and so here we were together, the three of us, weren't we? All in all we didn't give Lily all that much except maybe, just maybe, that we saw how you can find yourself at war with the people who really do try to love you the very best they know how.

In any case she did get off it whether we did it or not, and when it was plain that she had I pulled out George Wickham's pint bottle and asked Ava if she happened to have a sharp knife. Lily said she had a knife of her own and would do it herself and I could save the tequila for another time or else let everyone have some. I didn't argue. I'd been wondering how I could cut the chip out of her arm without seeing the blood.

Afterwards we sat around and talked all night. I had it timed for us to leave at dawn and we knew we'd get all the sleep anyone could want out on the Interstate.

Hosea

At the beginning the Lord spake by Hosea, and the Lord said unto Hosea, Go, take unto thee a wife of fornications, and children of fornications: for the land hath committed great whoredom, departing from the Lord. –Hosea 1:2, from the Geneva translation.

Jayden's receptionist recognized me as someone who'd been admitted to the inner sanctum before. She favored Ava and Lily with smiles that said it was her job to smile. She favored me with one that said see, she really did know who counted. When we were ushered in to see Jayden he rose as he always does and said, "Mr. Alexander, will you do the honors?"

I said, "Jayden Delgado, please meet Miss Layla Solberg, one of your new clients."

Ava, looking very much like a woman who is bearing up under bad news, said, "How do you do?" and she and Jayden shook hands. If I hadn't been looking for it I'd never have seen Jayden realize that the program had changed completely.

I said, "And this is my own associate, Miss Williston McGee."

Jayden said, "Indeed? And what do you do for Mr. Alexander, Miss McGee?"

Lily said, "I keep him focused on the little details. Left to himself he's pretty much a big picture kind of fellow."

Jayden looked at me and said, "That's true, I've noticed."

When we were properly arranged around his little round conference table and coffee had been poured and business was officially happening I turned on Thorkelson's slab of files and slid it over to Jayden. "On behalf of Thorkelson Industries, your twenty-seven new clients."

Jayden said, "Yes," and put on a professionally somber mask. "I heard some very sad news on the Media this morning about Mr. Thorkelson's family. It seems that his only daughter has disappeared under ominous circumstances and the authorities fear the worst."

I said, "Yes, we were shocked to hear it. But now more than ever I'm sure that Mr. Thorkelson would wish us to proceed."

Jayden looked directly at Lily and said, "I have no doubt at all that he would."

I said, "Miss Solberg and Miss McGee are with me today so we can straighten out a small wrinkle in our submission. It seems that when these documents were prepared Miss Solberg was off selling Mr. Thorkelson's wares in a remote corner of New Mexico. The holo in her file was ah some years old" – a sad and delicate blush on Ava's part – "and Mr. Thorkelson, remembering your stipulation that only recent holos are acceptable and facing the problem that the document-building e-monad you provided refused to proceed with incomplete data, asked Miss McGee if she'd mind posing for a temporary one. Which of course she was more than willing to do."

Brilliant smiles from Lily and Jayden.

"At which point your document builder also demanded a new retinal scan, which Miss McGee also provided."

Ruefully amused shake of the head from Jayden, who sees where this is going. Ah yes, isn't it always like this? More so and more so every day, our robot servants are becoming our masters.

"Whereupon your faithful e-monad noticed an apparent discrepancy between Miss Solberg's birthday as Mr. Thorkelson had copied it from his files and the ah apparent ah age of the face in the holo" – politely feigned embarrassment all around – "and forced Mr. Thorkelson to *correct,* as it put it, the data he had accurately copied from Miss Solberg's true records. So you see he had no choice but to substitute Miss McGee's birthdate for Miss Solberg's."

Serious shaking of Jayden's head now. What a needless and embarrassing snafu! He said, "I know what comes next. Miss Solberg returned to Orange but when Mr. Thorkelson obtained a new holo of her, the officious e-monad refused to let him edit her profile."

I nodded. "Exactly. It told him that after 24 hours the only editing allowed is deleting all profiles and starting over. Which Mr. Thorkelson would have done except that some of your new clients had in the meantime left Orange to go back out on the hard dangerous road of salesmanship."

Jayden said, "I assure you, Miss Solberg, that we only do that for your protection. So no one can obtain the password through trickery and alter your records for nefarious purposes."

Ava smiled sorrowfully and nodded. The *trouble* she was putting people to, and all from vanity, the vanity of pretending that the old holo in her file and on her badge still looked like her! And at a time like this, too…

I said, "So Mr. Thorkelson asked Miss Solberg and Miss McGee if they would accompany me today so you could ah see them before you in the flesh while he Socialed-in to this meeting and asked you to correct the record on his behalf. And they both graciously agreed. But then, last night…"

Jayden said, "Yes, last night. One can hardly disturb the man at a time like this, can one?"

Ava said, "She was such a lovely girl. When she was little she used to come to the office with Mr. T and…" But then she choked up and Jayden reached across to pat her hand.

He said, "Under the circumstances I feel I must be accommodating. But I have to be sure. Miss Solberg. Is it your belief, as Mr. Thorkelson's employee, that he will wish us to proceed as Mr. Alexander has asked?"

Ava, in her grief, managed a weak "It is. Anything to spare him more trouble at this…"

Jayden turned to Lily. "Miss McGee. Do you confirm that it is your wish, your wish and no one else's, that your holo and retinal scan be removed from Miss Solberg's record, and that her birthdate replace yours?"

Lily said, "Of course. I'm not really her, am I?"

Jayden's look got a little harder. "Oh, I never supposed that you were. But you understand that if these records remain unaltered you'll soon be able to prove that you *are* her? And knowing that, you still wish all traces of yourself to be removed from them?"

Lily said, "Indeed. That's what's right and that's what I want."

Jayden said, "So be it, then. We'll proceed as you ask."

Ava went down the hall to be holoed and to have her

retinas scanned and to get her ID chip reprogrammed, which she'd told us she'd been looking forward to since *Layla Solberg, Miss, Employee of Jayden Delgado and Associates* would be a far lighter load to carry than *Ava, Married Property of Caleb Wockenfuss* had been all these years. She came back and Jayden entertained us with a long, witty tale of his own mishaps on the road "when I was just an ignorant young man." A clerk came in and gave Jayden an envelope. Jayden held it for a second and looked at me thoughtfully. This, the delivery of Layla Solberg's documented identity, was the moment when Lily was to have discovered the trick we had played on her. This was the moment I was to earn our fee, somehow contain her explosion of rage, and in Thorkelson's words, make her understand *that now she has no way to back out.* Jayden had to be wondering how much of his part of the act I expected him to go through with now that someone had rewritten the script. I gave him an encouraging nod. I wanted them both to see it all, just as Boronzee and Jayden and especially Daddy had set it up. I think your hard-earned hate is something you should be willing to share, or you have no business walking around with it.

Jayden opened the envelope and removed a glittering holocard and held it out to Ava. "We're sending the rest back to Orange of course but I think that since you're here there's no reason not to give you yours now."

Ava said, "That's very thoughtful of you, Mr. Delgado."

Jayden said, "Well, Miss Solberg, we do like to think we understand the difficulties that the modern traveler faces every day. And we do like to think we anticipate as many of them as possible."

Ava said, "I can see that you do."

Jayden said, "I hope you always think so, Miss Solberg. Not everyone does, at least not all the time. We have a great many clients, and while they all seem to appreciate the measures we take to accommodate *them*, some, unfortunately – but also understandably – tend to resent the measures we take to protect and accommodate our clients as a *whole*. Let me give you an example of what I mean."

He turned to Lily. "Looking at you, Miss McGee, the tragedy of Miss Thorkelson's disappearance seems somehow more real to me. I can't help thinking that the two of you must have been very much alike. It occurs to me that in the days to come others may fall prey to the same false impression, and I'm somewhat ashamed to admit that, simply because of that, I'm a little relieved for both our sakes that *you* will not be our client. Merely, you understand, because of the interest you would be bound to attract from the innocent and coincidental facts of your resemblance to Miss Thorkelson and your employer's association with Thorkelson Industries.

"If you *were* my client, I would be obliged to offer you a stern and unpleasant warning. What I'd be obliged to say to you would go something like this. I'd have to tell you that if, despite all our efforts to prevent such a thing from ever happening, you were somehow shown to *be* someone other than who you have convinced us that you are, you would thereby invite scrutiny into the lives of every other client of Jayden Delgado and Associates. By doing so you would, inevitably, subject them all to serious embarrassment and some even to actual danger. And that is something we tell our clients we will never permit.

"To prevent it we would be driven to some highly distasteful measures. We would be compelled to tell the authorities exactly how you came to be our client. I'm afraid that under the circumstances the consequences for your twenty-six colleagues would be simply disastrous. I'm afraid that their innocence in your imposture would avail them nothing. They would be condemned as your accomplices and would therefore suffer the ultimate penalty for it. Naturally, we would feel terrible, but the rest of our clients would be protected, and in the only way we could possibly protect them.

"So, Miss McGee, you see how relieved I am to not have to deliver this warning. And *you* see, Miss Solberg, how happy I am that there are no reasons to say anything similar to you. And I'm sure that Mr. Alexander is the most relieved of all of us. With that it remains for me to wish you all success and happiness in each of your respective journeys – success, happiness, and most of all, Godspeed. I believe our business is now complete."

We filed out and walked back to my car. I asked the street

to put us on the Interstate. Lily waited until the street put us on course for it before blowing up, which I appreciated because I'd been worried I'd have to fight her off and drive at the same time. All things considered her explosion was on the muffled side, I think out of respect for Ava who after all was innocent in my deception and didn't deserve the blast I had coming. She merely asked me if upon reflection it might not have been the decent thing to *warn* her a little, to give her just a little *hint* that her daddy *and* Boronzee *and* Jayden *and* I had *all* agreed she should be threatened with responsibility for the deaths of twenty-six–

"Yes," I said, "it would have been. The decent thing to do. It also would have been the stupid thing to do, seeing as how I, I as in me alone, was responsible for getting us out of that meeting with Ava's ID in her hand. And not knowing for sure, which I still don't by the way, that you could have pulled off your part of it if you knew what was coming. That almost-flirty act with Jayden I mean. Which was perfect pitch by the way, that *yes-I'm-lying-but-not-in-any-way-you'll-mind* undertone was very pretty to watch. But could you have done it if I'd told you? Maybe but maybe not and the maybe not part counts, so I didn't tell you."

She chewed on it for maybe a block and a half and then she said, "All right, that's fair. Yes it was risky to tell me. No I wouldn't have blown it. And someday real soon you *will* understand that, Pardner."

Ava said, "Forgive me, Lily, but I have to ask this. What will your father do to those twenty-six people when he learns that the Layla Solberg living happily in Canada isn't you after all?"

I knew the answer but I let Lily do the talking. "Nothing at all. He's not the kind of monster who thinks about wicked things and does them. He's the kind that doesn't think and lets them happen. The better question is, what will he hire somebody to do to you when he starts imagining that you killed me for my money?"

I said, "He's never going to imagine that. When Ava gets to Ontario she sends the message and all the money is cut loose. Including Jayden's. That's when Jayden, that trusting soul, sends everyone's new identity back to daddy precisely according to the letter of the deal and that's when daddy learns that Layla isn't Lily anymore. And daddy has Jayden on the Social in about four seconds and Jayden gives him the speech he's working on right now if he isn't done with it already. Why of course he saw Mr. Thorkelson's daughter. Why of course he made sure she was acting of her own free will. Why of course he just assumed the plan had changed, what else could it have been? Wait a minute, would Mr. Thorkelson like to hear Lily *tell* him so? Here she is in his office, listen to her say *what's right is right and I'm here to do it.* Isn't that her own voice Mr. Thorkelson? My *goodness* this is terrible but what else was Jayden to think, what else was he to *do?*

"So that's what Jayden says and that's what your daddy hears. What's right is right. He'll get that, won't he? You outfoxed him, you're on your own now, and any move against Ava is a move against you."

We were on the ramp now. I asked the Interstate for Sault Ste Marie. The blonde came on and said traffic was moderately heavy through the Indianas. She went away and we sailed off through the fumes and haze to meet Animkii up where the air is almost clean on the days the wind blows down from the land of caribou and libraries.

This time nobody was pretending to fish or camp. We were going to Sault Ste Marie on business and six days earlier I had reserved the motel room that proved it. There used to be a bridge across the Saint Mary's River that connected Sault Ste Marie with the Canadian city of the same name but that came down a long time ago. Instead there is a fifty yard wide minefield right down the middle of the river that nobody gets through. Submarine nets dangle from floats and get fouled with fish and the fish rot because it would be suicide to try to clean them up. Patrol boats race from Isaac Walton Bay to Sugar Island, turn around and race back again. The only time they stop racing is when they see anything at all in the water on the Michigan side of the minefield. Then they stop and shoot the shit out of it. Drones take off from the Round Island Point Freedom Preserve and float over the whole length of the river but all they see is the shot-up flotsam the patrol boats leave behind. Nobody gets across from Sault Ste Marie, nobody at all, and as far as destinations on Lake Superior go it's the most innocent one of them all.

When the bridge came down and the life of the river went away most of Sault Ste Marie's commercial reasons for being died on the spot. The only one that didn't die was tourism and it got pretty damn sick. It's recovered a little since then because a certain kind of person likes standing in front of the wire on the shore – the wire itself is a thrill to some of them – to watch the drones soar and the patrol boats waste ammunition. And people who live around there still drive in for a restaurant dinner and a night in a bar where your neighbors don't tell your pastor and your wife what you got up to. And where there are cheap whores there are somewhat less cheap whores and people come from a little further off to see them. Still, tourism is a long way from what it used to be.

But another kind of business has slowly built itself up there. It takes several thousand people to man and tend and maintain the minefield control points and the patrol boat base and all the technical wizardry at the Round Island Point Freedom Preserve. Those people are only rarely allowed to visit Sault Ste Marie but they have their needs, most of them boring and predictable, and since they can't come to Sault Ste Marie, specialists in various kinds of need-filling have to go to them. Miss Williston McGee and I were heading up there to wholesale inspirational holos of Lot's daughters to the local peddlers – did I mention that most of these several thousand people are young men who spend weeks and weeks at a time on duty, or that the way they carry on when they do get to town is the reason so few of them are allowed free in Sault Ste Marie on any one night? Miss Layla Solberg didn't need a reason to tag along. When you have her kind of money the people who can demand that you explain yourself are few and far between.

Lily thought she should talk a bit about Miss Layla Solberg's money, and especially about how she should and shouldn't find it a new home as soon as she got to Ontario. "Say you just walk into Barclays and–"

Ava said, "I and my bodyguard, you mean. Wockenfuss

always said that you don't *ever* walk into a new bank without renting the most sinister bodyguard you can find at the biggest agency in town, and you make sure his suit is hand-tailored and he has the right shoes. Wockenfuss says bankers always notice the shoes, and after they notice them and you're talking business and he stands behind your chair wearing those holovid sunglasses that record *everything*, people who might otherwise see a profit in selling you to some other customer – why, suddenly their minds just go blank. And they can't imagine why they ever thought that not doing exactly what they're promising they'll do for you might ever have been a good idea. Is *that* the part you want to tell me about?"

That was my second business-wisdom-according-to-Wockenfuss lecture and since I was well up-range from this one when it went off, nothing got in the way of enjoying it to the full. I almost passed out from laughing and for some reason Ava and Lily seemed to think that was very rude of me.

We were passing safely to the west of Kincheloe, with its rumored population of half a million moribund blasphemers and its signs warning that *Stopping for Hitchhikers Means Summary Execution This Means You No Exceptions*. I made some conventional remark about how those who had made it through the winter so far would probably last till fall. Ava shuddered and Lily looked a little pissed at me for bringing it up but hell, it's right out there to see.

Ava said, "Why on earth don't they at least try to keep them alive? Where's the profit in letting them starve?"

I said, "States get paid to take them, not to keep them."

Lily said, "I wonder how many we could bust out."

I said, "Probably hundreds but they'd never get more than a few miles. There's no way to take more than a handful across the lake and the first thing Michigan would do after a breakout is shut down the Interstate. That's why it's up here, no place to walk to. And not many of them could walk very far anyway."

Lily said, "I wonder how many my daddy could just buy out?"

Ava gave us both a look that meant *please stop making me hear this*.

Possibly to take Ava's mind off it Lily said, "I wonder if Archdeacon Hogarth came this way." I tried to pretend I hadn't heard that but she read me all right and gave me a delighted "My, my, my."

Ava bit at the change of subject and said, "Archdeacon Whom? I'm afraid I haven't heard of him."

Lily said, "Mr. Floppy has though. Look at him, he knows something. Mr. Floppy. My partner. Who is maybe a bigger man than even I gave him credit for."

I figured there was no point in pretending. I told them that it's a very big lake and Hogarth had left from the western end of it. I reminded Lily that Ava had asked a question and that talking past her was rude. I said she should tell us what she knew and how she heard it. I said I really hadn't heard a thing since I dropped him down the hatch of an English submarine.

Lily said that I *would* tell them and there was no use trying to get out of it. I said that she was going first because I was more curious about what Hogarth did after he left me than she was about how he left. She said I was the most selfish man *ever*. Ava said no I wasn't because she had been married to the most selfish man ever but she agreed that I do get cranky sometimes so Lily should really go first. Lily said she'd do it for Ava but not for me and started in.

Apparently the latter stages of Hogarth's travels were very well known to the upper classes of Costa Mesa "if the term is not redundant which it isn't" and his adventures were even discussed somewhat openly. Her father for instance heard it on his you'd-better-be-*damn*-rich-if-we-catch-you-with-one-of-these-things Hyper Low Frequency receiver on which he picked up the BBC's weekly feed to "what they persist in calling America." He didn't hear it *right* away of course because on Hyper Low Frequency you have to record a feed for days before you can speed it up and get a single bulletin out of it. But he *did* leave it running for days which is how he and then her stepmother and finally Lily heard the four-minute bulletin about Archdeacon Jackson Hogarth's daring escape across Lake Superior and his sensational speech at the International Congress of Anglican Clergy to Report on Conditions in America.

The speech, being a sensational speech, caused a sensation. But the announcer had used up so much of his time saying *sensational* and *International Congress of Anglican Clergy to Report on Conditions in America* that he had no time to more than mention that it was a scathing indictment of *American* (that word again) penal practices that had shocked people who had imagined themselves to be beyond shocking, so let's get on with the story shall we (here Lily seemed to be mocking something and said that we "know how the BBC is" which was generous of her since I had no idea *what* it is). Upon taking off from Halifax on Sunday night the Archbishop's plane was pursued by three unidentified aircraft that were thought but not proven to belong to the Maine Air Militia. His RAF escort drove the intruders off and believe they shot one of them down. Arriving in England to a tumultuous welcome Hogarth was invited to address Parliament "on the Tuesday." As his procession approached the Palace of Westminster (which I know about because Cromwell spoke there) officers of the Special Branch (and your guess is as good as mine) apprehended three heavily armed members of the illegal Christian Patriots of England, more commonly known as "The Willistons," just before they could open fire on Hogarth's car. These terrorists, two men and a woman, are being detained indefinitely under the Intolerance Suppression Statutes. And that was all Lily had heard, except for a deadpan rendering of the French President's comment that "the mere existence of the Intolerance Suppression Statutes would be sufficient to turn England into what she hopes to defeat, were it not that in spite of them England miraculously remains a country."

Then I told my side of it. I kept it moving and stuck to the facts and when you do that you make yourself sound masterful and in control whether you mean to or not – and the more modest you are the more you sound like David saying *Oh yeah then there was this big guy named Goliath but I got lucky with him*. They didn't interrupt once. I was a hero. I wondered how I'd ever recover my self-respect.

I did manage to make one little point as an afterthought. The man who organized the Sleeping Beauty's welcome out on the ice was the very Animkii who would take Ava and Lily to the boat, the very Animkii who led the men who would take Ava across in it and then deliver her safely to her destination, the very Animkii who after Ava's departure would doubtlessly save Lily's life fourteen separate times on their ride back to Sault Ste Marie. So his word was to be obeyed in all things, wasn't it?

Which earned me agreement, both wholehearted and grudging agreement, and I'll let you guess whose was which. The main thing is I hadn't had to say *books* even once. It seemed to me that I might be learning just a little about this leadership business.

It wasn't a bad looking motel but it was in an ugly place. It wasn't the motel's fault. There are no good looking places left in Sault Ste Marie to put your not bad looking motel in. This place was on a narrow rutted road, half broken up asphalt, half dirty gravel and maybe an extra half of mud. Across from it was a bricked-up, boarded-up warehouse that hadn't been used in fifty years and still stank of fish. There were a couple of what had once been small frame houses that were now shacks. Everything was landscaped with mud and trash and last year's brown weeds. There was one ramshackle little store surrounded by several beat-up trucks. In its windows were signs for six different brands of beer and outside it a small group of slow-moving men milled around solving the world's problems and drinking from paper sacks. As we pulled in all heads turned our way and we looked to become the problem to be solved next.

I eyed those men up and down, then parked halfway down the motel. Lily and I left Ava in the car. I didn't like leaving her alone with that audience watching but the reservations were for two and Boronzee would see any changes I made to them. I found a luggage cart outside the office, wheeled it back and loaded it up with all our bags: look, guys, nothing left to steal. I set the anti-tampering field and turned it up to *serious injury* in case those fellows saw Ava and thought they sensed another kind of opportunity. Lily and I pushed the cart to the office, checked in, beckoned Ava out of the car and we all walked the cart to our room. I shooed Lily and Ava inside, told them to lock the door, and looked around for Animkii's truck. It was parked about five rooms down from me, almost at the end of the motel. The plan had been that he'd drive a Chippewa hooker up for a week or two of work and it seemed that she was already doing business because in spite of the chilly damp Animkii was sitting on the stoop.

I walked over and said, "You locked out?"

He said, "Kind of. The lady is busy."

I said, "How busy?"

He said, "Maybe five minutes ago he looked like about ten minutes worth of busy. Millie doesn't mess around."

I said, "Come on down and meet my ladies."

He said, "Ladies? As in more than one?"

I said, "One to travel, one to see her off."

He got up just slowly enough to tell me he would have to think some more about the extra lady. We headed off toward my room but halfway there he stopped and turned to me. "Plan was you and one lady. You changing it?"

"Yes."

"Boronzee know you're changing it?"

"No."

"Good."

I wanted *good* explained a little further but he started walking again and it seemed that my curiosity would have to wait.

I introduced Animkii as Animkii, Ava as Ava and Lily as Lily.

Animkii said, "Where's Layla?"

Lily said, "That's a little complicated. I used to be Layla but now Ava is."

Animkii waited just long enough to be sure she wasn't going to add anything. He walked to the door and looked back at me. "Let's go check on Millie a minute."

Lily said, "Who's Millie?"

I said, "A whore who's dying to meet me" and closed the door behind me.

Millie's door was now cracked open a couple of inches and a big sloppy fellow in a red checked jacket was waddling back to his buddies by the store. Animkii sat us down on his stoop.

"Girl's kind of proud of having a smart mouth isn't she?"

"Yeah but she doesn't know it. Where she was brought up they think of it as conversation."

"But she's the one Boronzee told me to take."

"That's right."

"And now I'm taking the other one."

"That's right. You mind?"

"I don't know yet. I have to think it out. Like she said, it's complicated. Since Boronzee pretty much told me without saying it in so many words that he'd consider it a favor if she has a bad accident once she's over the water."

I should have thought a lot of things when I heard that but what I thought was *Well that's that. You're an orphan again.* I was groping for an intelligent question to ask when the Jesus Patrol pulled up in a cart, four big dolts in camo with immobile sullen faces and crosses on their armbands. Their cart stopped right in front of us with a little squeal. They stared but only at me. Animkii seemed to be invisible.

Animkii reached back and slapped the door twice with the flat of his hand. The door opened and Millie stood on the sill. She was maybe seventeen and hadn't quite ruined a pretty face with whoring yet. She wore only long black braids and an olive tee shirt that came down just far enough. She took in Animkii and me and then the staring JP's. She nodded down at me and in a patient, nothing-surprises-me voice told them, "He's next in line but I can take you gentlemen right after. If you don't mind waiting a few minutes." The JP dolts didn't move or change expression but their cart lurched off with another squeal. I don't suppose anybody had ever taught them about grease. Animkii looked up at Millie and she stepped back inside and shut the door all the way this time.

I said, "How do you ask somebody to kill somebody for you and not come right out and say it?"

Animkii said, "Myself, I wouldn't know how. I'd like to think you wouldn't either. But if you're Boronzee what you do is you tell me over and over how this girl has to *get* to Canada and tell her daddy she *got* there or else we don't get paid. But then, like maybe you changed the subject and now we're just talking about the weather or how the fish are biting, you mention about twelve times how isn't it funny? Funny how the one thing we know for sure about this girl is she just won't shut up no matter how much trouble it gets her in? Her and everybody else? Like, who knows, us? But yeah, she really, really has to *at least* get to Canada. And oh by the way there's no reason to mention this to Floppy because, you know, he worries about stuff. Tell me you think I'm wrong to take it like I did."

"When did this happen?"

"Day before yesterday. You think I'd take the job if he put it like that up front?"

"What'd you tell him?"

"I didn't *tell* him anything because he didn't *ask* me anything. I just uh-huh'd and oh-yeah'd and said well that *is* something to consider isn't it. But I'm telling you because I don't think I can work for Boronzee anymore. Not after I know he'll kill people who depend on him. And I don't think I *can't* work for Boronzee anymore because how will I take care of my people if I don't work? But now you're telling me you're changing the plan and he doesn't know it and that's the best news I've heard in two days. Right now I got what's left of my hopes pinned on the idea that you're up to something."

Half my mind was still on *Boronzee the man I worship is trying to kill Lily*. With the other half I said, "Well let's go talk to the ladies because if we're all going to be in it then let's all be in it."

Back in my room I saw that Ava and Lily had the suitcase of books sitting right at the end of the bed where it would be the first thing we saw.

I looked straight at Lily and said, "Animkii and I are in a terrible surly mood and don't anybody joke with us. Let's get this one out of the way because believe it or not it's the easy part. Animkii, take a look at that suitcase and tell us if it can go with you."

He hefted it. He set it down and opened it. He took a step back when he saw what was in it. He asked, "May I look?"

Ava said, "Of course you may."

Animkii took one out, felt the binding like he was petting a kitten, opened it in the middle and peered at a page. Then he put it back. He said, "I'm sorry but we can't take this."

Ava's face fell briefly but she rallied with an

understanding smile while Lily got ready to fight.

Animkii said, "It'll be storming when you go. These books'll be soaked through and ruined and packed all together like this they'll spoil the trim of the boat. We can wrap them in plastic, put some in the bow and some in the stern, but we just don't have room for your suitcase. Sorry ma'am. I can see it's a nice one. Someday I really got to teach Floppy about boats."

I sent a look Lily's way that said *I'll kill you dead if you laugh.* She turned it around and sent it back only now it said, *I'll kill you deader if you really think I'd insult this man.*

Ava went pink on us. I'd heard about people turning pink with pleasure but I'd always thought it was just an expression. She said, "Oh thank you so much! The suitcase doesn't matter, it was just to carry my books and I can get another one."

Animkii said, "No, ma'am, you can't. Not anymore, not even in Canada. They don't make them. It's a shame."

Ava said, "Really, all I care about are my books. I was so afraid there wouldn't be room for them."

Animikii shrugged. "Then I'd have had to get a bigger boat, that's all. Might have slowed us up a day. How many are there?"

Ava said, "I'm not quite sure. You know, I've never counted them."

Lily said, "I did. Forty-seven."

Animkii said, "Forty-seven real books." He picked up the one he'd been fondling and fondled it some more. "That makes forty-eight souls preserved in one trip. We've never come close to doing that before." He turned to me. "Why'd you kid her about leaving them behind? Speaking of things that aren't funny."

Ava said, "Mr. Animkii, you're right about the suitcase. It is a very old and good one. Can I persuade you to take it? I'd hate to think of it just being thrown away."

Animkii said, "Just Animkii. I'm mister something else we won't go into. Animkii's my first name, it means thunder in our old Ojibwe language. Which nobody knows too much about anymore because we let the books get thrown away. That suitcase wouldn't last long in the back of my truck but if it's all right with you I know somebody who'd take care of it. You leave it to her, it'll probably be the nicest thing she'll ever have."

I figured I'd better step in before somebody said *you may now kiss the bride* and it would be time to open the champagne. I said, "That's nice, see, I knew that would all work out for the best." That wasn't as rude as what I'd wanted to say but it was rude enough to get everybody looking at me, so it did the job. "Now it turns out that Animkii has a little problem we didn't know about and we need to fix it too. I only bring it up because it has me thinking kind of squirrelly. Which I think you have a right to know."

Animkii gave me an *I hope you know what you're doing* look, but I didn't see how it mattered whether I knew what I was doing or not.

I said, "I told you about this man Boronzee? He also planned Hogarth's prison break in case I didn't mention it. And he took on this job for Lily's father. And every other job I've ever done except Ava which as you see I haven't quite finished yet. And, one last thing, he gives Animkii all his jobs and that matters because Animkii has how many people to support now?"

Animkii said, "Forty-two. Forty-two last time I counted but I don't always hear right away when it changes."

I said, "All right, forty-two then. So you do remember me talking about Boronzee, right?"

Nothing but stares now.

I said that I knew I'd mentioned but maybe not to all of them that we've got contacts now we never used to have and are taking bigger jobs than we ever used to take and so Boronzee too, Boronzee especially, is getting to be much more big time than he used to be. And what that's done, it's made him slow and careful. Which has been bothering me and which is why I probably already mentioned it once or twice. Only it turns out it's made him even more careful than I knew. It's made him so careful that now he, Boronzee, the guy who's been running this, wants Animkii to kill Lily on account of how she runs her mouth and the careful way to work is not to let her do that anymore. "Is that about right Animkii?"

He said, "It's a few more words than I used but yeah,

that's what he wants."

I said, "So Animkii's problem is–"

Animkii said, more or less, "My problem besides other people saying what my problems are is one I don't kill people for money, and two I don't kill nice people for any reason, and three, three most of all, I don't work for people who think they can tell me they want somebody dead and I'll just pass it on to my buddies without a second thought and they'll take care of it because that's the way us redskins work. That's my problem, at least the way I want to say it. Floppy's problem is that Boronzee and his boys are Floppy's whole family, but if he doesn't think it's worth mentioning I guess I'll let it drop."

Lily said, "Did you just call me a nice person?"

Animkii said, "Yeah but maybe it means something different where you come from."

Ava said, "Oh I'm so sorry for you both. It must be terrible."

Lily gave me a straight look and in a reasonable voice said, "You knew this was coming."

I said, "I did *not*. I knew something was coming. Not this."

Lily said, "You knew. You said there are only three of us now."

I looked at Animkii and said, "Well now it's back up to four."

Animkii said, "Forty-six. You take my people or you don't get me."

Lily said, "Then forty-six it is. That ought to be enough to get lots and lots of people out. Now that I'll be here to help. So who needs a Boronzee?"

I said, "You're not taking this personally? The man is trying to kill you."

Lily said, "I believe in delegating work and you're taking it personally enough for all of us."

Animkii told her, "You know, I'm beginning to think Boronzee has a point about your mouth. The problem isn't finding people who need to get out. The problem is finding people who can pay to get out. That's what you need a Boronzee for."

Lily said, "Not anymore. Not with what I have. With what Ava has I should say. Which we mean to spend on getting people out who can't pay for it themselves."

Animkii said, "No offense miss but do you have any idea how much we're talking about?"

Lily said, "No, I don't. But do *you* have any idea how much *I'm* talking about?"

Then she told him.

Animkii whistled and said, "Like Reverend Williston says, that'll put some gold in your halo."

Animkii went off for his truck and his co-worker. Millie came in and showed Lily how to wear a Chippewa whore's jacket and floppy hat. "That color, you need to put your hair up under it for sure, but you're walking perfect now."

We stole some blankets off the bed for the camper for Ava because Animkii wasn't prepared for a passenger back there. We wrapped her books up in her clothes for camouflage and Animkii loaded it all into the camper. He made a lot of trips but at least he didn't stop to read like Lily and Ava had.

Millie looked Lily over one last time and said to me, "I was going to tell you, you got lonesome while you're waiting you could come see me, but I don't think you're that crazy."

Animkii held out Ava's suitcase and said, "The lady wants you to take care of it while she's gone."

Millie said, "But isn't she—" Then her eyes got big and she grabbed it and fled.

Animkii said, "And there's people who say there's nothing you can do to embarrass a whore."

Ava said, "I want to…"

I knew what she wanted to say but I also knew I couldn't let her. I said, "Hold on to it. I'll see you up north someday." Then I figured I'd better check my Social for any last minute messages and by the time I looked up again she was walking away with the others.

The three of them were almost out the door when Animkii turned back to me. He said, "I don't know whether I have a good feeling about this or whether it's a bad feeling I just got rid of. You brought me some bad people, Floppy. I don't blame you because you didn't get to pick them but no more bad ones, okay? Now that we get our choice. Good people like this lady from now on." He had his hand on the doorknob now but something else occurred to him. It made him grin. "In one way, bad people are easier though. You don't care if you lose them on the way. Maybe I'll live to regret this new arrangement after all."

He and Lily crowded Ava into the camper and shut her in. With Ava between them and the back of the camper so close to the door of my room we hoped it looked like they'd just tossed their stuff in on their way to the cab. Lily the Chippewa whore got in one side and Animkii got in the other and they drove off. I really wanted to wave but the boys would be watching and nobody who's just got his ashes hauled by a Chippewa whore pays her or her pimp any mind afterwards. As it was, nobody'd be all that worried that they left since Millie was still right there and open for business.

I was going to have to wait there, anywhere from three days to two weeks depending on when the right kind of bad weather showed up where Animkii's people were waiting with a boat. The Media was pretty confident that by Wednesday the whole of Lake Superior would be in for it but when are they ever right? No matter what, it would be a long spell of boredom, even if I did spend a couple of hours a day building cover and selling my Bible porn. I lay down on the bed, closed my eyes and listened to the Geneva Bible read me Psalms and Proverbs. I hadn't heard the voice since I'd learned it was also Ava's and I was curious to see if that would make a difference. At first it seemed to but then I realized that was just me deciding it had to, so I undecided it. When I got up four hours later to get undressed I saw I had a bunch of coded messages on my Social from Loverbits. The first one meant *run for your life* and they didn't get any better after that.

Obadiah

All the men of thy confederacy have driven thee to ye borders: the men that were at peace with thee, have deceived thee, and prevailed against thee: they that eat thy bread, have laid a wound under thee: there is none understanding in him. –Obadiah 7, from the Geneva translation.

In all Loverbits left me four messages, an average of twenty seconds apart – just enough time between them to write the next one and make sure he got the code right.

The first message said, "Do this now, my son, deliver thyself. Psalms 6:3." What a silly mistake! It's *Proverbs* 6:3, not *Psalms* 6:3. And it's exactly that careless slip, *Psalms* for *Proverbs*, which anyone can make and everyone else will laugh at, that says *Pay attention, this is code.*

Psalms 6:3 meant *Your position is compromised: flee.*

The second message said, "Thou art snared with the words of thy mouth. Psalms 6:2." It meant *Your identity is discovered: ditch it.*

The third message said, "Deliver thyself as a roe from the hand of the hunter, and as a bird from the hand of the fowler. Psalms 6:5." It meant *Accept no contact from friends.*

The fourth message said, "Can one go upon hot coals, and his feet not be burned? Psalms 6:28." It meant *Stay away from the bus forever and ignore all future messages.*

They were sent just after seven PM, two whole hours ago.

Some moves are mechanical. I made them. I went into the bathroom, grabbed a few things, stuffed them into a small bag and stuffed the bag into my pocket. I stuffed a few pairs of socks in after them. I had just checked off the mental box that said "nobody else to warn" when I remembered Millie. I turned the lights out, walked as casually as my fear permitted to her room, picked up a nice fist-sized rock which I held in my right hand and tapped out the *I don't care what you're doing, open up now* sequence with my left. The rock was for her client if she had one but business had slowed down before the late-evening rush and she was alone.

I said, "I've been found and I have to run. They won't care about you but can you get home if Animkii can't come back for you?"

She said, "I can always get a ride. The rent's paid for two weeks. Can I stay?"

I said, "Sure" and turned to go.

She put a hand on my arm and stopped me. "Animkii left some clothes."

I was about to tell her that in that case Animkii would have to do without them when I realized what she meant. In my Bible porn seller's business suit I was a darkish white man again. Sometimes being a Chippewa is better. His jeans were a little big for me but I cinched my belt and left all the shirttails out. I checked myself out in her mirror. The floppy camo hat and the three faded flannel shirts all unbuttoned with the ratty tee shirt showing did the trick. It helped that in the mirror I couldn't see my feet. Animkii hadn't left boots and that could be a problem if anyone got close enough – but if they got that close the people I was running from would have known me anyway.

In the mirror I also saw that she'd set Ava's suitcase in front of the room's one chair, where she could look at it while she sat and waited to go back to work.

As an afterthought I gave her my Connor Alexander holocard and asked her if she could find a storm sewer for it in the morning. I said, "The best that can happen to the next person who uses it is he goes into a camp."

She said, "Animkii already told me, no stealing this trip."

I stood there a bit longer because it was a better place than most to make a big decision: in the car or on foot? *Eventually* it had to be on foot because Boronzee knew every persona I had with me and the odds were too good that he now had friends at the Interstate. But use it to get a few miles down the road?

No. In the two hours he had on me Boronzee could have dropped somebody with a scanner off on every road out of town and once they picked me up passing I'd be an hour ahead of them at best, with nowhere good to turn off. On foot then, starting now.

But the car had to be my first stop because a little case I kept under the front seat held all the pathetic little bits of me that Boronzee knew nothing about. The street was dark now and the little store was closed. The motel's sign was at the other end of the building and since it faced the other way it was no more than a dim glow. The only other light came through curtains in about half the rooms, and motel curtains are stronger than motel lamps. I should have let my eyes adjust but I walked off anyway because being outside made me good and scared again. I came up on my car, fished out the activator, stepped off the walk and onto somebody lying next to the driver's door. I jumped back – I suppose it was the first move in taking off running – and then realized that whoever I'd just stepped on hadn't moved. I stepped back onto him to make sure. I stepped off on the other side of him and knelt down for a better look. As I did so my hand passed within a foot or so of the car and the activator beeped and blinked green – what the hell? Then I realized it had just turned off the anti-tampering field. Which I had turned on when we'd left Ava in the car. Which I'd set to *serious injury.* A body lying there began to make sense.

I decided to think in simple steps. This person had tried to get into my car, and it had maybe killed him or maybe only come close. He had tried to get into my car because I'd be getting into it sooner or later. It would have been easier to come to my room but he didn't know which room I was in. Did he want to ask at the office? Anyone would, unless they had some reason to not be videoed doing it – like, for instance, if the person they're videoed asking for dies during the night or even just disappears leaving his car and his possessions. So be patient and wait for him in his car. It shouldn't be that long a wait, not once somebody sends him a message telling him to run for his life.

The activator had the usual little built-in flashlight and I put a finger over it and turned it on. Then I let a little light leak out so I could check out my visitor even though I knew by then who it had to be. Thumper's hands and face were scorched but his eyelids fluttered because he was still alive although his brain was not dealing well with the umpty-watt jolt it had taken. Next to his right hand was a shape I thought might be his Social but when I picked it up I saw that it was a supremely nasty handheld flechette launcher, the kind that can dissolve a car, the kind that clears out whole rooms in one burst. Thumper had become careful too. He had decided not to take any chances with me, and look where it had gotten him.

I stuck the weapon down the front of my pants – hell, I was wearing camo even if it was only a hat, so unlike Thumper I was lawfully entitled to carry it – and I found his Social and pocketed that. I briefly thought about dragging him into the car because it seemed like the decent thing to do for your own brother, but the temptation passed. I stood on his thighs and got the driver's door open, fished out my little case, laid the activator on the seat and walked away.

The road the motel was on led down to the foot of a short hill, where at nearly right angles it crossed a slightly wider road that was in slightly better shape. To my right this crossroad started climbing and to my left it continued down. Meanwhile the road I was on kept meandering ahead but I could only see the next thirty yards or so. It wasn't a great idea while I was this close to the motel but starting out on the wrong road was a worse idea, so I sat under a tree and asked my Social how to get downtown. The map it gave me told me to take the left branch and stay on it. That made sense since I'd driven in from the right and hadn't seen anything that looked like a downtown, so I decided to believe a Social map for once though you know where that sometimes lands you.

I started to get up and then decided I needed to do a couple of other things in case I couldn't do them later. I sent a message to Boronzee on Thumper's Social. It said, "I am half dead and lying next to Floppy's car. Somebody seems to have stolen my gun." Then I tossed his Social into the weeds. I sent a message of my own to Animkii's ancient Social and Lily's new one that read "Checked out early because it seems I'll be stuck taking the bus if I wait." I thought I'd have known if Boronzee knew how to snoop on Socials but some people can and he *was* getting up in the world. But that one couldn't tell him anything more than the one I'd just sent him on purpose.

I got up and walked over to take the left, crossing to the

far side since it seemed darker there. Halfway across I glanced to my right and saw that something seemed to be blocking the road at the top of a hill, maybe a quarter mile away. It made a big square dark hole in the dim night sky. What could do that? I could think of a couple of things and one of them was a parked bus.

I took off running down the middle of the road. About the only thing to do once you've parked your bus to wait for your assassin's return is to put on a good pair of night goggles and stare at the road. So they had seen me and it didn't matter whether they kept on seeing me – the only advantage I had left was a short head start.

After about fifty yards the road curved slightly and from then on I was out of sight from where the bus was parked. The bus hadn't started after me and I knew why. Those flechettes would go right through it and yes, I would be aiming for the front. Whoever was coming after me was coming after me on foot. Now was the time to get just a little stealthy again. I stopped running and moved onto the darker side of the road, which was darker because it was bordered by a thick mass of trees. I walked briskly. The only way to catch me from behind would be to run and that I would hear. I kept my head down most of the time to make sure I didn't step in a hole and break an ankle but every few seconds I looked up at the road ahead. This was old training I was following, old orphanage militia training that I hadn't used very much in a long time. But I'd had seven years of it which means I'll never lose it and it had my mind off everything but silence, darkness, ambushes, booby-traps, scouts, patrols, pickets, the knife I wasn't carrying and the weapon I was.

After three or four minutes of this routine I looked up once again and barely caught the shadow of a man jogging slowly toward me in the middle of the road. I moved away from the road, found a likely tree and hid. He was jogging *slowly* so he could look to the left and right, but he wouldn't see me in the trees and he had to know that. One of two things, then. He wanted me to wait till he passed so I'd walk ahead into the ambush behind him. Or he wanted to drive me back toward the bus, and that's the plan I chose on his behalf. If they had an ambush set for me they wouldn't need him showing himself at all. And they wouldn't have set an ambush in the first place, not with Thumper on the job. They'd have set a picket out on every road I could take if I went off on foot when Loverbits said run, but in that case Thumper and his gun would be following right behind me and all those pickets would have had to do to slow me down just enough was show themselves.

He wasn't quiet, not anywhere near as quiet as he needed to be. I could hear him scrape and shuffle and sniffle and sob. He was coming up even with me and he was okay with me being the only one of us who knew it. I didn't know what he had for a weapon but it had to be a lot less than what I had. When he was close enough I stepped out and faced him.

He stopped. He put his right hand in his pocket. I lifted my tee shirt and showed him the butt of Thumper's weapon. He was squinting or more likely crying – anyway, his eyes weren't right but he put a good enough sneer into his voice.

"What's in Taos, Floppy?"

"How'd you track me, Bluesbaby?"

"How's anybody track anybody? You're no different. You got chips inside your chips like all of us."

"How long?"

"What do you mean how *long?* How long you had that top-of-the-line Social of yours? How long had that *car?* How long since I been bugging things? How long you been out on the *road,* fool? What's in Taos, man?"

"What's anywhere?"

"Anywhere is one damn thing but *Taos* is special to Floppy, *Taos* is where Floppy goes when he's on his own and it's where he goes when he's supposed to be on the job somewhere else. All you had to do was tell us about Taos. But no, you don't do that. You go to Chicago and Kansas City and New Orleans and always back to Taos, which is okay, understand, it's okay because you're between jobs so why should I tell anybody? But then you're on a *job* and supposed to go to Chicago and instead you go back to *Taos* again. And when you do finally get to Chicago three days late which you have never *ever* been before you pass off some woman we don't even know as the *passenger* and you tell *Boronzee's man* that the real passenger is working for *you.* I don't know who you thought you were doing it to but you're doing it to *us*. To every one of us and to who you used to be."

"You don't know a thing about it."

"That's right. I don't. And that's all your fault and none of mine. We *asked* you about it man, me and Bits, we *asked* you in Michigan and you didn't say shit. Except it was *Boronzee* going flaky and how it was scaring *you*. And now you've probably killed Thumper for trying to clean up your mess and you definitely killed Loverbits for trying to save your ass."

"The fuck you mean I killed Loverbits."

"The fuck you think Thumper would do when Bits Socialed you? Tell him that's all right Bits, everybody gets to sell us out now that Floppy says it's okay?"

"BB. Who told Thumper that Bits Socialed me?"

He was seriously crying now. It was almost black where he stood and I could still see the water on his face.

"A fool told him. A fool who's just as big a fool as you. Same fool who thought he'd keep your travels to his self. Same fool who finally opened up about Taos when Delgado ratted you out for switching the passengers. You should have talked to us after Hogarth, Floppy, you really should have. Keep going the way I came from and don't take a turn off or you'll run into somebody else. I'll tell them I missed you. Back the way I came, and run, that's the only way you get off this road. And if I ever see you again I swear I'll kill you myself."

Then he looked away and jogged on past me. I took off running as fast as I could. After a mile I knew I could stop, that they'd be following slow and careful and in force and well spread out. But that was the calculating part of my brain and the rest of it needed to keep running for as long as Loverbits was still behind me. I ran till I saw lights ahead and I kept running till they were close. Then I got a grip and slowed to the walk of the inscrutable Chippewa, whom nothing hurries, out for his inscrutable Chippewa late evening stroll.

The first store I came to was a discount Social hardware outlet. It was doing pretty good business for after ten PM and there were quite a few of the usual kids hanging out in front. As I walked up to it I checked my regular Social for the last time. I had five new messages from Boronzee and a sixth one came in while I walked. I wondered whether they were variations on "You're a dead man you traitor" or on "It's all a mistake please come home to us" and sometimes I still wonder but not very often. I swung by the store's outside trash barrel and dumped my Social in it, muttering "Stupid fucking bitch" loud enough for at least some of the kids to hear. I made damn sure that whatever they heard they all saw a state-of-the-art Social go into the trash. I hoped they got a good quick start once they fished it out and saw what they had and realized I'd be cooling down and changing my mind any second.

The third store I came to was a Christian Warrior's Outfitters. I'd been considering something like that anyway and running right into one made up my mind. I stuffed my hat into a hip pocket, stripped off my two outer shirts, threw them in a culvert and buttoned the last one up. I walked across the parking lot and leaned up against a post outside like people do when they've held out for whole minutes and the urge to Social finally overwhelms them. I took my other Social out of my little case and started moving money. I'd had Ava's diamond cash in seven different accounts and when I'd mostly cleaned them out for Maria's bequest I left a couple of million behind in each of them, since setting up new accounts is a pain in the ass and there I was with seven perfectly good ones if I left the minimum balance in. Now that was all the money I had. I spent eight minutes of borrowed time moving the woeful contents of six accounts to the seventh. It now held fourteen million, not enough to get me *to* anywhere by a longshot but plenty to get me out of where I was if I economized. I went inside and shopped. The first thing I got was a large camo duffle and as the clerk checked the rest of my stuff out I packed it all away in it. On my way out the door I passed a rack of ten-day tattoos. I considered and passed on a genuine swas-sticker, picked out two others and went back and paid for them.

Outside two young militia kids were carrying their purchases to their car. They had that unmistakable *watch-out-world-cuz-I-got-a-pass-tonight* look all over their faces so I doubted they were headed back to camp.

I begged their pardon and mentioned that if they *happened* to be going downtown there'd be a couple of rounds of beer for whoever gave me a lift.

They regarded my shirt with justifiable suspicion and then moved on to my jeans.

I hefted the duffle, which they should have seen. "Kit's in here. I been fishing and it purely sucked. My leave's up tomorrow and there's one more thing I want to do before I head back."

The quicker of the kids said, "Brother, if you was handing out rounds of *one more thing* I think we could talk ride."

You people wouldn't understand about the bond between real fighting men. You think it's nowhere in sight but all it takes is a word or a gesture and then men who've never seen each other before are the kind of brothers who wither and pine when they have to separate once again. I threw my duffle in the back and we drove off looking for our beer and whores.

The one I thought most likely said her name was Sophia. She had some nice ink on her neck and no jail tats on her hands, but the rest of the outfit was standard uniform for the place. Most of all she had an eye for money which she proved by sizing me up for only a second before she sat down and put her hand on my shoulder.

She said, "You're a little different."

I said, "Yes I am and I'll prove it to you. The only thing I'm interested in is all night, nice and slow, and I don't have a place of my own here. You tell me how much and I say yes or no. I don't haggle because I think it's disrespectful to argue with a person over what she's worth."

She named a number, no hesitation. It left me with enough change to eat once or twice someday and what did I need with anything else?

I said, "Can we go? When I'm in a room with you and nobody else is there you get half of it and I show you the rest."

She walked us down the street and up a flight of stairs. It looked like it really was her own place. It was as rundown as you'd expect but there was a door on the bedroom where you could get away from Williston. A lot of things were scattered around that looked like they belonged to only one person. She hadn't invested in paint or rugs or anything but she had stuck up holos of every holovid star and starlet I've ever heard of. And the dishes were washed, always a sign that a trace of self-respect still lives on. I looked at those dishes and then checked out the bedroom. The bed was made, and that was enough for me.

I said, "I like your ink."

She said, "Wait till you see it all."

I said, "I can see all I need to. I like your makeup too."

She said, "Really? I don't use all that much of it."

I said, "That's what I mean. You know what works. I'm going to pay you the whole price now. I don't want any sex. What I want is your help with a makeover and then a couple hours sleep."

She was good. She didn't start swearing because she knew that starting trouble isn't how you stay out of it. She didn't ask me if anyone was going to come busting in after us because why would she want to hear my answer? She only thought it over a couple of seconds and then she said, "Sure. Why not? But let's see you move some money first." She saw, and then we did things.

The first thing we did was cut my *Connor Alexander, Mr., Employee of Jayden Delgado and Associates* chip out of my arm with the knife from Christian Warrior's Outfitters. It was so sharp I could have cut the whole arm off and not felt it, but it was no sharper than a Christian Warrior's knife ought to be. I hit flush so many times that if Bluesbaby could scan that chip at long range like I was beginning to suspect, all it would tell him was that I was at the bottom of the St Mary's river.

Then we did the fun stuff.

Before going to bed I sat by her window with the shade up and the lights off behind me. It was getting on toward two in the morning but there were still a few people on the street. Most were in groups of camo-clad warriors who looked a little the worse for wear – the better class of sinner seemed to have found beds by then. But every once in a while a solitary sober man would walk by, not quite going anywhere and not quite just hanging around. Some would be looking for things some solitary man is always looking for late at night. Some would have found theirs earlier and were walking the memory of it home. But some, I couldn't see clearly enough to know which, some were looking for their lost brother Floppy. They'd keep walking until the streets emptied out completely. Then they'd find places to hide and wait for him. Poor, poor lost brother Floppy. Where could he go once the sun came up?

Sophia pointed me to my side of the bed. She said, "Last chance to change your mind. No waking me up and I mean it."

I said, "No, you did good. If I don't get a chance later, thanks for everything."

She said, "Did you just thank a hooker? For that you get a treat." She flipped her nightgown up over her head and showed me the rest of her ink.

I said, "Wow, that *is* worth seeing. I'm impressed. My apologies for doubting you."

She pulled the nightgown back down. "I knew you'd like it," she said, "seeing how your own tastes run."

That put me to sleep with a smile on my face.

Revelations

Notwithstanding, I have a few things against thee, that thou sufferest the woman Jezebel, which calleth herself a prophetess, to teach and to deceive my servants to make them commit fornication...

And I gave her space to repent of her fornication, and she repented not.

Behold, I will cast her into a bed, and them that commit fornication with her, into great affliction...

And I will kill her children with death... –The Revelation of Saint John the Divine 2:20-23, from the Geneva translation.

The next morning at dawn, or a few minutes after dawn, or a few minutes before dawn, a curious event revealed itself on the dim and sodden streets of downtown Sault Ste Marie.

A warrior of the Lord marched out upon the pavement. His stride and his garments and his manner were martial, but his ornaments and his visage and his voice were holy.

His ornaments were holy for upon his chest he wore the Holy Cross of Jesus in brightest gold. It shone like Herod's treasure, it measured roughly the span of an elephant's foot, it hung from a great golden chain which encompassed his neck, and it swayed with his every step.

His visage was holy for on the back of his bronzed head from which not one hair grew he bore the Holy Cross of Jesus in fiery orange.

And on his bronze face he bore the Holy Cross of Jesus in shimmering blue, blue such as the Papists ascribe to Mary (may God correct their idolatry), the very blue that shines from the waters of the lakes when He suffers the sun to smile upon them.

And the upright tree of this blue cross did run from his chin to his crown, where also no hair grew. It paused not for his mouth, for his lips where it traversed them were blue. It spared not his nose but enveloped it in blue, and his nose and his cross were one, and when he smelled with his nose he smelled the holy sweat of Our Lord's torment.

And the great branch of the blue cross, the piece to which we know Our Lord's hands were bound with nails, did fall across his eyes, so that he looked out upon our sinful world from within the blue and holy cross and the invisible arms of Jesus.

His voice was holy for it declaimed all that has come down to us of the words of God Himself, as it was writ in olden time of the hands of the prophets and rendered anew for us in our modern tongue by command of His servant James when he was our earthly king.

And the men who were about in the dawn heard the words of God that issued from the warrior's mouth, and were astonished thereby, and no man accosted him.

And women still weak from the night's fornications heard them also, and were ashamed unto repentance, and no woman tempted him.

And God's words flowed ceaselessly from his lips as he strode forth. They flowed as from the mouths of the great preachers of old, men like unto Cotton Mather and Jonathan Edwards and Emancipus Healy, yea, even these of whom we yet hear honest report, that they drove Satan into hiding with the mere force of their breath.

But the warrior *was* a warrior, and his manner was martial. His gaze was ever forward, his bearing always upright, his purpose always firm.

And his garments were martial also, for they were cut of the holy camo of Jesus and his boots were the boots of the crusader. And upon his shoulder he lightly bore the burden of the warrior's office, the great sack that held his armor and provisionings. With the merest touch of one hand he bore them, and they rose and fell with the motion of a great ship at sea, and the great golden Cross of Jesus supported him as it swayed.

But this most of all: his stride was martial, for he made no movement except he *marched.* He marched like one who in the time of his youth marched many miles each day for all of seven years. He marched like one who in that time did march through seven winters, like one who marched through snow that topped his loins and was beaten when he lost the step of the march and was beaten no longer in the five last years of his marching, having in that time forsaken the froward feet of those who lose the step of the march.

He marched through the streets of old Sault Ste Marie, and his voice announced the beginning of the world and the other things that are recounted in the book called Genesis. And behind him a bare few onlookers began to follow.

He marched to the edge of Sault Ste Marie, and more listeners accompanied him, and they heard the history of Moses and all that transpired in the desert. And as he marched and they walked the words of Moses roared from his lips.

He marched out onto the old shore road and, turning to the west, he taught the wisdom of Leviticus as he went. And the people who followed heard Leviticus as though for the first time.

When the sun was high he continued westward on that road, and he and those who followed considered the genealogy of God's first people. And the people were amazed to hear the record of begetting recited entire, without fault. And some of them returned in sorrow to their daily occupations, but others took up the places they forsook.

And on that road were soldiers, who had come to each various place to perform the business of soldiers. And they were struck dumb by the words of the Lord and the eyes that burned from the cross, and they gave each other knowledge with their faces that here was one who marched with the true marching of the warrior, and in reverent silence they watched him pass.

Into each place he went were found such soldiers and all were so affected, on and on into the day.

And he stopped not to eat or drink, for in the taking of them food and drink must stop the words of God.

And the forbidden water was all one side of the road, and the deadly forest all the other. And when the sun began to fall from its height, though much of the afternoon remained ahead, a chill wind began to come out of the west, and the water turned gray as the sky, and the trees conspired in their discontent.

And his followers became stragglers and at last the stragglers turned back, saying to one another, Yea, we have passed a wondrous day, but the cares of the world beckon and the words of God must wait until the world in its mercy should permit us to hear them. And truly, such *is* the history of prophets, which impels Our Lord to great wrath.

Yet though he marched on he did not march on alone, for the soldiers he passed by sent word to the soldiers still ahead, that they should watch for him. And this they did, and as he passed them by they turned to their fellows and said with their eyes alone, Behold, friends, what our brothers did disclose to us is true. And they watched over him as he went, that he was not beset by evildoers, of which that country concealeth many.

With the waning of the afternoon the wind increased in bitterness and a cold rain began to fall. Some soldiers along his way were moved to pity and beseeched him to shelter with them, saying, It is a thing known to all true warriors, that God doth not require us to stand watch in the cold rain excepting when the battle impends. And by the merest alteration of his gaze he granted that in the ordinary instance this is so but his own battle had impended overlong, wherefore God demanded of him a redoubled watch and would send him not his relief betimes. So he marched onward and the soldiers marveled much at his faith.

Thus when evening fell he came to a narrow place in the road where soldiers camped along the troubled waters by his right hand and the forest stood tall and fierce by his left. And again the soldiers said, Come, join us, take shelter in our tents, for thou art weary with the road.

And having on that day spoken the word of God from the beginning of creation unto the hundred and thirty-ninth psalm, he shut God's voice within him at last, and spoke to them in his own voice, saying, Nay, brothers, I must not stop with you lest my thoughts stray from their contemplating of God's mercies. But grant me leave to pitch my tent there among the trees, and from this your camp watch over me while I sleep.

At which the great part of the soldiers assented, and bade him grant them leave to clear away some weeds, that his tent might stand upright and smooth upon the ground while he slept. But one young soldier, proud in his youthful valor, said to him, Nay, if thou disdaineth our shelter I shall not prepare thy bed, nor shall I watch over thee, for thou despiseth my protection.

Wherefore the warrior continued the words of the psalm wherein he had ceased his reciting, which words were these, *if I make my bed in hell, behold, thou art there.*

And among the soldiers were some that knew well these words of the Lord and also that they were fallen again as before (in David's time) in their proper place and moment. And they said to their proud companion, Behold how aptly God's words do puncture your vanity. Now therefore make obeisance to this warrior and obey his wish, or we your brethren will surely slay you. And the proud soldier fell to his knees and begged them to spare him.

And the warrior said, Rise my son and do as your brethren instruct, for they remember the seething in your heart from the days of their own youth. By their example will you learn to return your wrath to Him who has lent it, that you may pour it in the time of His choosing upon His enemies, and upon no other. And thus did Jesus snatch another soul from hell.

So the warrior pitched his tent in the lee of a great tree, which shook and bent in the increasing tempest, yet did hold him firm in its embrace throughout the long night as the God of all warriors had purposed when He commanded it to grow there in the days of our great-grandfathers' infancy.

And *fuck* did my feet hurt, and *fuck* was I thirsty. I took a long kidney-shaking whiz, dragged my little tent out of my duffle, whipped it into shape, staked it down solidly and dragged myself and the rest of my stuff inside it. I tore open my half-gallon of ale, raised it to my mouth and drained it. I exhaled a belch that blew the storm briefly back to Wisconsin, stuck the funnel in the jug and set it outside in the rain. Or I should say "set it outside" because "in the rain" was never more superfluous. I stripped off my boots and socks and camos because I would dry much faster without them, and I examined my feet to be sure I could get the boots back on in the morning. I decided that since I had four pairs of thick socks to shed I'd make it and if that didn't work I'd carry my boots. Then I ripped open four packages of jerky and lay down to munch and think.

I had done no thinking to speak of since I sat by Sophia the hooker's window the night before. I had done no thinking because when you march you don't think which is why they keep you marching, and on top of that I had been echoing Revered Healy's voice and that was a second fulltime job in case the marching hadn't been enough. So all day long I'd been free of Loverbits and Bluesbaby and Thumper and I also hadn't thought about Lily or Ava or Animkii. Now I made a promise to myself and then I made myself repeat it to be sure I'd heard – *I will think about Ava and I will think about Lily and Animkii and especially about catching up with them, and that's all I will think about because I don't have time to think about anything else.* I didn't keep it of course but I came close enough for everybody's sake but my own.

I'd figured I'd covered as many as forty miles and when I checked my coordinates my spare bugless Social told me it was almost forty-three, which is damn good for 14 hours. That meant I had only a fraction as far left to go but I wasn't terribly optimistic about the pace I'd be able to keep in the morning. My legs were fibrillating wildly and my shoulder was numb from the duffle and my back was telling me how numb it wished it could be.

After a half hour of getting warm and eating my dinner (and reflecting that good jerky is the most underrated meal I know) I stuck my face outside to try to get the measure of the storm. I pulled it back in quick and dried it in my last dry towel. I didn't want to think how wet I'd be in the morning if I had to go out to pay the rent on the ale in my belly but I was glad I'd taken that peek outside. The storm was everything we needed. I had heard the surge of the lake from across the road and over the tents of the militiamen who were guarding me. With all due respect to Emancipus Healy I had never heard anything near as lovely all day. All in all, a sense of accomplishment at this point, a sense that I had *done it*, that *we* had done it, could be fatal – but it was hard not to feel it. What I needed was a good spell of work and worry before I let Ecclesiastes carry me off.

I had to Social a message after midnight and it was a

message that had to be read. They would have got my checking-out message and they would be worrying and looking for a follow-up from me. But for now they would be busier than hell getting Ava away in her storm-tossed boat and they wouldn't be reading Socials for hours. And unless I sent my message from a Social Alias named Hey Layla Hey Chief This Is Really Floppy I couldn't be sure of them seeing it. Animkii would be looking for my old Alias and Lily's new Social would be drowning in the half-million scraps of fractured scripture every cut-rate preacher in the world dumps on newly active Aliases. I worked on an Alias they both would recognize and it took me quite a while. No matter what I came up with I would have to trust that they'd be looking for it at all, but when trust is all you have going for you it's not that hard to pretend it's a dead certainty.

A little after ten o'clock I registered The Forsaker of Unholy Books as a Social Alias of a Presence Boronzee couldn't know about. It felt more than weird to be playing on the Social while branches groaned and snapped overhead and the wind and rain tried their hardest to rip the tent away. When The Forsaker of Unholy Books was accepted I entered a message from him or her to Animkii and Lily, queued it to go out every ten minutes between one and three in the morning, and set my alarm for four-thirty. Then I lay back to listen to Ecclesiastes and hope my bladder held out.

My message said, "Thieves and Harlots, Heaven is not yet Lost! Read the Words that Jesus told the Thief! Luke 23:43."

Even if she'd never done it once before in her life, Lily would know how to find a Bible on the Social and I wouldn't have been surprised if Animkii had a real one in his truck.

Luke 23:43 reads, "And Jesus said unto him, Verily I say unto thee, Today shalt thou be with me in paradise."

The little town of Paradise, Michigan, where Animkii once picked me up – on his way as he saw it to killing his cousin's family – was sixteen and a half miles down the road.

It was a hideously gray wet chilly blustery day, the kind where you can't decide if the cloud a few feet over your head is fog trying to ascend or the whole atmosphere sitting down on you. Wet black branches covered the road and there were places where I had to break step to get over or around fallen trees. My biggest worry (since I'd sensibly decided not to worry whether Animkii would get there) was that I'd pick up a disciple or two, but I saw nobody except waterlogged soldiers who only glanced at me. My feet were barely holding up and my knees were thinking about shutting down and with nobody on the road the urge to stop marching and start shambling was getting strong.

The Upper Room Café's sign was next to the road so I saw it before I could see the place itself or its parking lot. In another five verses I could see the building and ten or so verses after that I could see the six trucks in the lot. Animkii's was one of them, backed into the space closest to the café door so he could get out of there fast. Short-cutting into the lot I stumbled into a knee-deep lake of mud. All in all I was not what you want to see walking into your dining room but I walked in anyway.

Animkii and Lily sat at a four-top near the door (of course), Animkii in a position to see the door and the room but at the moment with his face in the menu. The Chippewa whore with her eyes glued to the entrance saw me as soon as the room did. And the room saw me. The crowd was sparse but the silence that slammed down was loud enough for a Williston Revival. Then everyone slowly turned away and did that looking-everywhere-but-at-you thing that feels hotter than a stare. Everyone but Lily. It took her a second to get over the shock and then she was the happiest girl in town. Animkii's eyes raised from the menu, then his eyebrows raised, then he actually smiled, which I took as a professional compliment and not a *man am I happy to see you*.

Lily threw her hat on the table and shook out her hair. "*Armando!* Mi Amor, Darling, *Chéri!* Whatever happened to your wings and halo?"

That finished the Chippewa whore act but it was doomed anyway because Jesus warriors, half-drowned or otherwise, don't sit down to eat with Chippewa whores. I set my soggy duffle on one chair, plopped down with a loud and obscene squish onto the other, looked at the plates smeared with egg yolk and said, "I see you couldn't be bothered to wait."

Lily said, "That's okay, we're having lunch next."

Animkii said, "You walk the whole way?"

I said, "Hell no. I *marched* the whole way."

My looks killed any way to be innocent and inconspicuous and we weren't exactly out of anybody's earshot so a lot of things had to go unsaid. For example *Did Ava get off?* from me and *What the hell happened in Sault Ste Marie?* from them. The sensible thing to do was get up and drive away but my feet, legs, back and stomach had had enough of being sensible. A brave waitress who'd seen it all in her maybe thirty years at the Upper Room headed our way with a coffee pot and a couple of too-small towels.

I said, "You serious about lunch?"

Animkii said, "I am if she isn't. Launching my brother's boat was hungry work and then we had to leave before breakfast."

I said, "He went out fishing last night? Catch anything?"

He said, "Seems like it. He Socialed in this morning. Said it was a good trip in spite of it all. Some people will do anything for a few pounds of whitefish."

Whew.

The waitress ahem'd and handed me the first towel. I soaked it and she gave me the second one, poured me a cup of coffee without asking and said, "No day to be out walking."

"It's really not so bad but last night was rough."

She looked at me straight for a second. "Well, I guess you did what you had to do. Breakfast is supposed to be over but I could sneak an order in. Lunch special is meatloaf."

Lily said, "Meatloaf for me, please."

The waitress gave her a second to say she was kidding and then wrote it down. Then she looked at Animkii. "You too?"

He said, "Sure, why not?"

She turned back to me.

I said, "Can I get like a double order of meatloaf with extra potatoes on one plate?"

The waitress stacked up the breakfast dishes and said, "Anybody here asks for separate checks, they had better be smiling."

Their Williston stood in the furthest corner and was turned low. In our corner The Salvation News Network crew sat at their desks and played holos-within-holos over their heads. I said, "Any interesting news?"

Lily said, "Maybe one thing."

There were at least three tables near enough to us to listen in without trying to, but they all had their food and would be done soon enough. Animkii looked up at something behind me. I turned. A pinched-faced old man in a pressed wool shirt pulled up where he could see the most of me and the least of the riffraff I was sitting with. "Heard about you marching and spreading the word from some militia boys. We need more like you, son."

Lily said, "Isn't that just so true? Pastor Rosario here" – she nodded at Animkii – "says that sooner or later we *will* find a way to get the message to the Chippewa."

Pastor Rosario said, "We all try to do His will, sir. God bless you for your support."

The old man made a brief noise, halfway bowed and beat a retreat. I turned to see where he went. The old woman who was obviously his mate for life waited obediently with a proud glare on her face. The glare was for the other customers who watched him go in undisguised contempt and disgust. I wanted to get up and kiss them all.

The waitress brought two plates and one platter of meatloaf. We ate in the silence that sometimes descends on barnyards when the hogs are slopped.

Lily gave a small urgent nod toward Salvation News and whispered, "Here I come again." I looked over and caught a somber twenty seconds about the lack of new developments in the suspected suicide of a troubled young socialite in Orange. There were no holos and they didn't even name her. Thorkelson Industries must have been paying through the nose.

We kept watching and learned that Jesus has appeared to a woman in Nevada, promising that the foreclosure of her home will never happen. A spokesman for Williston Ministries confirms it as a genuine miracle and reports that they've already collected enough to pay off her mortgage several times.

The same spokesman advises a cautious attitude toward a sighting of the Blessed Virgin in Rhode Island as "so many of the miracles reported by Catholics turn out to be based on confused dogma and hopeful hysteria."

For the fourth year in a row a poll of churches across the country has awarded the World Championship to the Kansas City Athletics. The World Series will open in Atlanta on April the fourth but complete standings have not been announced yet as simulations of some late summer games are still incomplete.

A very old man in Charlotte says that the secret to a long life is letting Jesus come into it.

"Amid shocking rumors of organized faith-fraud, an executive named Sarah Schilling has been apprehended and hanged by a duly consecrated ad hoc citizens' court as she arrived for work in downtown Milwaukee."

I let out a low "Oh Sarah." When was I ever going to stop killing people?

Lily and Animkii looked questions at me.

"A spokesman for the Milwaukee police said no charges will be filed. I quote. 'Evidence matters and they had it. Under the law it was a legitimate act of spiritual self-defense.' Shilling's employers, Galilee Robe and Gown, agreed and said the company would not contest the Milwaukee branch of United Militias' claim for costs and damages."

Lily said, "Um…"

I shook my head.

"United Militias also said that the identity of Schilling's longtime accomplice was known and that militias across the country would not rest until he's brought to justice." That was what I'd been waiting for – the part about the longtime accomplice who (they didn't say) was waiting for his pie at the Upper Room Café.

I put my hand over my mouth and mumbled, "Boronzee bought my first righteous name from her. I never even thought to warn her but of course he'd kill her now."

Lily said, "Why?"

Animkii said, "Kill her instead of turn her in so she can't talk about Boronzee. Go after her at all because it burns one of Floppy's old names but the main thing is it's legal and profitable for anybody to shoot him on sight, plus whoever he's with by the way." He hadn't moved his lips at all which was a way of keeping it soft and also reminding us to shut up about anything that mattered.

We obeyed him and sat and waited for the room to clear out. We got our pie and ate it and ordered more and ate it too. I figured that with a good tip added the bill would about clean me out but it was getaway money and I had got away so what would I be saving it for?

Animkii seemed discontented over a pair of crossed snowshoes on the far wall. He'd glance at them, frown imperceptibly, look away, glance back, frown again. I'd have thought they were perfectly good snowshoes but then I didn't grow up wearing snowshoes. Or maybe he was thinking that nobody else in the room had ever worn them either, that they were trophies from a war we haven't seen the end of.

Our side of the room finally cleared out. We ordered another round of coffee and we began to talk low and say the things that needed to be said.

My report was pretty brief.

Animkii said that the way he saw it Boronzee wouldn't come after him and siccing someone else on him would cause more problems than it would solve. Given that whoever took the job would have to come up and fight it out on Ojibwe land.

I said that was probably right, but I was now thinking in terms of Sarah Schilling about what Boronzee would or wouldn't do.

Lily figured that we'd start getting money from Ava in a week or so and then we'd have to figure out who we'd try to bring out first. She had some idea of the two of us dressed up as nun and priest and escorting penitents away to retreats in the woods. Another thing she'd been thinking about was, did we think there was a way to find people who'd been turned down for jobs because their faith records didn't check out?

I said I thought first we ought to head somewhere and buy at least a couple of solid names for ourselves. She said oh yeah, she'd forgotten about that part. She said she'd been thinking too much about her daddy and was going to have to stop it or it would make her too stupid to be any use to us at all. She said she couldn't get over how happy Ava had been to get into the boat – happy/sad, sad at saying goodbye to everything but mostly happy, but the point, the *point* was, yes he tried to send her away because he loves her but how could he think leaving could ever make her *happy*, like Ava was?

I was trying to think of a way to get her off it when Animkii did it for me. "If you don't understand why people will do anything they have to do to save the people they love then you don't understand me."

Lily started to answer him but for once a second thought stopped her. I was pretty sure her first thought went something like *But you didn't put your people in the hole they're in in the first place.* I don't know how the second thought went but I sure was glad she'd finally had it.

Then Animkii got us all off it by asking how long it would be before my face grew back.

I said I was supposed to have eight days left but who knew if Christian Warrior's Outfitters were telling the truth?

Animkii said he was thinking of a fish camp he ought to visit anyway where we could stay as long as it took, which anyway would be at least until Ava got the money flowing. He said he hoped we liked big furry dogs and fish three times a day.

Lily said, "You know what Floppy should do while we're there? He should spend the time he's not doing the other things I have in mind for him writing out the story of his life, from way back when till now. It's the kind of thing people really need to hear more about."

Animkii and I played it like the joke we thought it was.

Lily got serious and said no, she meant it. "Look," she said. "Someday we're going to get caught, right? Maybe not for a long time but someday, and then we'll be dead, and it will be too late to tell the world what we did or why we did it. This is true, right? Someday we get caught?"

I don't know about Animkii but that was a huge relief to me. I'd been afraid that smart as she was she hadn't really gotten that part of it yet. I got a little tongue-tied. I can talk about *me* dying but...

Animkii said yes, someday it will happen.

I found my tongue and told her yes, you can't stay lucky forever. But you can't just go on thinking you're already dead. You can always get lucky one last time. I told her to look at

Ava, she should never have made it, what if she'd had a voice like Mrs. Williston? I said look at me, I should have died in Sault Ste Marie, what if my mother hadn't hung that damn sheet up and Major Joe hadn't taught me how to march all day? I told her there was no reason we couldn't all be on the last boat across the lake. No reason for it to be us but no reason for it not to be us either.

"Well anyway," she said. "Since one way or another this business is temporary, Floppy should write our last will and testament because he's the one who knows the most about it. And when he's done Animkii can get it to Ava on one of his people's trips across. And when what has to happen happens, whenever that is and however it turns out, she can put it out on that funky Canadian Social they have up there. And sooner or later somebody will sneak it back here.

"And if Daddy hasn't come to his senses and gone away by then, he and Boronzee can read it right along with everyone else. If they read fast they can finish it before the front door's kicked in."

I paid up and threw my soggy duffle in Animkii's camper and the three of us piled into the front. I was in the outside spot because Lily had earned the place next to Animkii but she took care that I noticed how she put her arm around me. Animkii took a way out of town I hadn't been before but as always we were on a little street and then a gravel road and then the truck dove into the woods. The track was pure mud and downed branches but Animkii laid on speed. Mud flew and wet branches scraped. The truck found the ruts and began to fly. It bucked and leaped but the ruts had it now and Animkii had them. Lily leaned in on me and held on tighter. Branches stopped brushing and started slapping. A devilish grin spread over me and I didn't need to see their faces to know it had them too and I didn't need them to tell me what they felt. Blessed is the seeker who finds all he needs and knows it.

ABOUT THE AUTHOR

There once was a bad boy who paid far too much attention in Sunday school and vowed to spend his life applying the lessons he learned there. Determined to keep this vow, he took to making up stories and trying with all his might to get people to believe them. Sooner or later most people caught on to what this bad boy was up to, and then he would have to move on to other places full of other people who hadn't figured him out yet. But the bad boy didn't mind doing that. He still thought making up stories was a fine hobby and he worked at it every chance he got. Finally, though, he ran out of people who would believe him even a teeny tiny bit, and then he had to move to northern Vermont, where the people are so innocent that many of them aren't aware of having ever *heard* a lie. In this paradise he passes his time, not by *lying* – perish the thought! – but by *practicing the art of fiction*. So far, nothing he's seen has cast the slightest doubt on Lenin's observation that paper will sit still for anything you care to write on it.